MAD LOVE

ALSO BY NICK SPALDING

Bricking It

Fat Chance

Buzzing Easter Bunnies

Blue Christmas Balls

Spalding's Scary Shorts

Love . . . Series

Love . . . From Both Sides

Love . . . And Sleepless Nights

Love . . . Under Different Skies

Love . . . Among the Stars

Life . . . Series

Life . . . On a High

Life . . . With No Breaks

Cornerstone Series

The Cornerstone

Wordsmith (The Cornerstone Book 2)

NICK SPALDING

BESTSELLING AUTHOR OF *FAT CHANCE*

MAD LOVE

LAKE UNION

PUBLISHING

Published by Lake Union, Seattle

www.apub.com

Amazon, the Amazon logo, and Lake Union are trademarks of Amazon.com, Inc., or its affiliates.

ISBN-13: 9781503941113
ISBN-10: 1503941116

Cover design by Lisa Horton

Printed in the United States of America

To those looking for love online.
If you're very lucky, the following will probably not
reflect what happens to you.

CHAPTERS

Article in *The Daily Torrent* online newspaper – 22 June

JESS – 25 June

News headlines – 26 June

ARTICLE IN *THE DAILY TORRENT* ONLINE NEWSPAPER

12 December

MARRIED AT FIRST CLICK!

By Sonny Duhal

Popular dating site Sociality is so sure it can create the perfect couple, it's going to marry two of its subscribers – before they've even met!

The contest is the latest brainchild of Sociality owner, Cassie McFlasterton. The thirty-seven-year-old online entrepreneur started the dating website three years ago, and in that time over two million people have signed up to take advantage of its patented *love al-*

gorithms, the designs of which are a closely guarded secret.

'We're so sure that we can match the right people,' McFlasterton explains, 'that we're going to put our money where our mouth is, and bring a hot, young couple together based just on their Sociality profiles.'

So confident is the successful business guru that she's stumping up one hell of a prize package for the lucky couple. They'll not only win £30,000, but they'll also get a glorious week-long honeymoon on the shores of Lake Garda in Italy, and a year's rental of a luxury penthouse apartment in Kensington. 'This is my commitment to the contest, and to our winning pair,' McFlasterton states excitedly. 'I can't wait to meet them and watch their brand-new relationship develop!'

Sociality will cover the new marriage on its website, Twitter and Facebook, and will launch a series of print adverts featuring the new couple during the first six months of the marriage.

If you would like to be entered in the contest, simply visit Sociality's website for full details. You'll need to be a subscriber to the site, and will have to allow your profile to be put forward once you've joined up. The subscription charge is £30 a month for a minimum of three months.

The closing date for the contest is 1 February next year, with the winners being announced just before Valentine's Day.

ADAM

Q. Describe your ideal day to us.
A. Not working. No plans. Pizza for lunch. Sleep. More sleep. Possibly more pizza.

7 February

It's not every day you wake up with a small, cross-eyed rat sat on your chest.

In fact, most people can probably go a good two or three *decades* without opening their eyes to find a member of the rodent family's least popular branch squinting at them with mild curiosity from the top of the duvet.

It's testament to how disgusting my house is that this comes as no surprise to me *whatsoever*. Frankly, I'm amazed the little sod hasn't already died of an airborne disease.

'Shoo,' I mutter, rubbing the sleep dust out of my eyes as I waft the duvet, in a half-hearted attempt to scare the bugger away.

The rat gives my nose a look of good-natured contempt, before issuing a small squeak, and jumping off the bed to return to whatever hole he scampered out from.

I heave a sigh, and throw the duvet back, not even bothering to look for where the rat has gone.

Now, you'd think that I'd be more freaked out by this rather odd and horrid turn of events first thing in the morning, but it's frankly par for the course around here.

Allow me to explain.

I live with four flatmates, all of whom are young men with a haphazard approach to cleanliness – and that's putting it mildly. They're physically in their late twenties, but mentally only about five or six. Two out of the four are in the MOD, another is an IT account manager who enjoys rugby in his spare time, and the last is an unsuccessful male escort. I'm a video games journalist, which makes me very much a beta male amongst alphas.

We rent this three-storey monstrosity in Croydon between us for a combined monthly rent that would be obscene anywhere else in England, but is actually quite reasonable this close to the city. The last time any of us saw our landlord he was hiding in the basement to avoid the local constabulary, and the last time the place was subject to a proper clean, it was after it had been slightly damaged by a wayward doodlebug.

So, as you'd imagine, if you put five partially grown men in an already dirty house with no female supervision, the place *will* become a complete cess pit about forty-two minutes after you close the front door on them.

Given that I am the least alpha of the five of us, any cleaning that does get performed around here is usually done by me. Very badly.

I would feel like Cinderella living with her ugly sisters, but there's definitely no glass slipper in my future – just more dust, green mould with hair growing on it, and a possible light case of dysentery if I don't wash the dishes in bleach.

Needless to say, I hate my life.

To get away from this sorry state of affairs I look on Rightmove every single day for somewhere else to hang my metaphorical hat, but do you know how hard it is to find a place near a station that doesn't bankrupt you in four seconds flat? It's impossible, unless, of course, you're prepared to wake up with a cross-eyed rat staring at you every now and again.

I rise to my feet with a groan, stretch my arms out above my head, and remember what day it is.

It is Monday, and is therefore *horrific*.

An entire week of work stretches out in front of me like a nightmare landscape of processed sandwiches, pointless meetings and angry emails.

This particular week promises to be even more soul-sucking than usual, thanks to the fact I have to cover the Progamer X e-sports tournament at Olympia.

The tournament will be noisy and tiring, and will force me to mingle with my least favourite group on the planet – people who work for video games companies. The gamers themselves are fine, if a little twitchy under harsh lighting, but the plethora of individuals surrounding them is quite another story. You've never experienced true pain until you've been locked in a room with a PR spokesman who is keener than the keenest mustard when it comes to convincing you how great his newest game is.

These e-sports tournaments are as much about selling games as they are about allowing basement-dwelling gamers a chance to come out into the fresh air for a few days, and that's why I look forward to attending them about as much as Jesus looked forward to a brisk walk up the hill carrying some wood.

Still, I only have myself to blame. After all, I'm the one who eagerly took the job at GamesReport.com all those years and stress headaches ago, back when I still felt like it was the coolest job in the world. *Idiot.*

Best I just accept my lot, slip on a *Call of Duty* T-shirt and get my arse into gear.

Looking out of the window at what we all laughably refer to as a garden, it appears that it's going to be a nice day weather-wise, at least. Crisp, sunny and still.

The blue morning sky is a much more attractive view than the cross-eyed rat, so my mood lifts somewhat as I climb into my clothes and make my way down the three flights of old Victorian stairs to the kitchen.

'You alright, Adam?' Calvin the male escort asks me from over his slice of toast. He's the only one in the house brave enough to endure the kitchen of nightmares this morning other than me.

'There's a rat in my bedroom,' I inform Calvin. 'It's cross-eyed.'

'You mean Gnawbones?'

My jaw drops. 'You've *named* it?'

Calvin smiles. 'Yeah. Well, Paul did anyway.'

'Gnawbones the cross-eyed rat,' I say, trying to place the concept into a world that makes any kind of sense.

'Yep. He's been feeding it cheese.'

'No wonder it's cross-eyed then. That cheddar is about ten minutes away from becoming a sentient life form itself.'

'It's only been in the fridge since Christmas.'

'Christmas *two years ago*, Calvin.'

'Fair enough,' he says a bit dismissively. Then his eyes light up. 'That games thing starts today, doesn't it?'

I groan. 'Yes.'

'What's it called again?'

'The Progamer X tournament. The "X" stands for execrable.'

'Does it?'

'No, Calvin. It stands for extreme.' The words taste like cold dead ashes as they tumble from my mouth. Sometimes I am comprehensively embarrassed by the industry I work in.

'Can you still get us in? On the guest list?' Calvin asks excitedly.

I groan again. This is the problem with working in video games. Everybody thinks it must be incredible fun *all of the time*. After all, how could it not be, when you're surrounded by Italian plumbers, busty tomb raiders and big digital explosions? I made the same mistake myself, before swiftly being disabused of the notion once I was in the actual job.

I could try to convince Calvin that after attending Progamer X for about an hour, he'll be comprehensively bored, and fed up with PR guys being keen as mustard at him, but it'd go in one ear and out the other.

'Yeah, I'll have a go,' I respond, trying hard not to scowl as I pour what I hope is still fresh milk over my cornflakes.

'Is he talking about the games show?' Paul says as he strides into the kitchen, doing up his work shirt.

'Yeah!' Calvin replies happily.

'Excellent!' Paul whacks me on the shoulder in what I'm sure he believes is a friendly fashion. Paul is, however, six three and eighteen stone of muscle, so I will be nursing a fresh bruise for the rest of the day.

'I tell you what though,' I say, spraying cornflakes everywhere, 'you twats aren't getting anything unless you start helping me clean this shithole every once in a while.'

Paul and Calvin both laugh. 'But you look lovely in those Marigolds, Adam,' Paul says.

I scowl.

Calvin is a little more pacifying. This is not surprising, as he likes video games more than Paul. 'We'll muck in, mate. No worries.'

The sincerity in his voice is, well, *sincere* . . . but I know damn well that he might be making promises today, but that doesn't mean there won't be twelve empty pizza boxes stacked up in the recycling bin tomorrow.

I try to resist the temptation to roll my eyes, and finish the rest of my cornflakes in silence.

Along with blagging free tickets for my horrendous flatmates, I have to actually watch hours of the tournament itself, and have time to fit in lunch with my mate Oliver, who I'm supposed to be meeting there. I'm really looking forward to grabbing a bite with him, as he doesn't come out much these days, but I probably won't get as much time as I'd like with him, given how busy my schedule is.

I finish my bowl of cornflakes, say farewell to my flatmates and go back upstairs to ready myself for the day ahead.

With any luck, things will go smoothly, and the day will pass by as quickly as possible . . . then I remember that it's Monday, and the last time a Monday went by smoothly and as quickly as possible, I was five years old and spent the day squishing bugs in the back garden.

And so we reach the first hurdle in Adam Holborne's day – the London Underground. And boy am I going to get a fantastic sampling of it today on my journey to Olympia.

It's usually an easy train journey to the office for me every day, given that it's only a few stops away in Whitechapel, but today I will be running the full gamut of nastiness across central London, on both train and tube.

I board the packed tube, finding myself squeezed up against one side. This provides me with the opportunity to stare at either a large black lady with a meteoric scowl on her face or two advertisements on the tube wall. I pick the latter, as the woman really does look quite, quite scary.

One advert is for the holiday company Sunsight, promising a relaxing time underneath waving palm trees. The other is for the dating website Sociality – which I created a hastily assembled profile for in a moment of boredom last year, and haven't really looked at since.

Both adverts manage to remind me that I could be having a far better time somewhere else, and with someone else, so I turn back to my angry lady friend – figuring that while she might be about to smack me in the mouth, at least she won't remind me of how much my life sucks while she's doing it. Thankfully, she gets off at the next station, retaining the scowl as she departs the tube in a rush.

The next half an hour of commuting is a kaleidoscope of thousand-yard stares, unpleasant smells and angrily rustled copies of the *Metro*, but I manage to make it through more or less unscathed, and find myself at the steps of Olympia with no damage to my physical person, or mental sanity.

As I'm queuing to get into the gigantic stadium, my phone rings. I heave a sigh when I see that it's my boss Watlow calling. Watlow is an arsehole of epic proportions. Everyone at the company hates him. This is fine, though, as he can't stand any of us either.

'Morning, boss,' I try to say as cheerfully as possible.

'Where the hell are you?' his tremulous voice responds.

'Just going in now. Got a bit held up. The District line wasn't running today, so I had to get the—'

'I don't give a *fuck*, Adam! You're supposed to be interviewing Patrice Renfart about *Farmyard Fury 3* right now! He's texting me to say where the hell are you?!'

'I don't think it's pronounced Renfart, boss,' I point out. I'm pretty sure Patrice the game designer from Montreal's surname is actually Renferd.

'Who gives a monkey swinging shit!' Watlow rages. 'Just get in there now, and do your bloody job!'

The phone goes instantly dead at the other end. Six months ago I would still have felt angry at the abuse I'd just been subjected to, but today I just shrug my shoulders and pocket the phone again. That's what half a year of Watlow, and four years of being an underpaid games journalist, will do – it beats the fight out of you completely.

Stop being such a bloody doormat, my subconscious orders me. I nod my head imperceptibly so I don't look like a lunatic to everyone else in the queue. My subconscious often chides me for my lack of self-worth, and every time it does I promise to do better next time.

I never do.

Eventually, I'm waved through the doors to Olympia with my press pass in hand. I pause briefly to speak to one of the staff, giving her Calvin and Paul's names as colleagues from my company, so they can go on the press list and get in for free whenever they turn up.

I then make my way through the entrance foyer and into the vast throng of people already filling the cavernous hall, brightly lit this morning by the cool January sun coming in through the vast glass and ironwork ceiling. Even at ten in the morning the place is packed. At one end of the hall is a giant temporary stage, where the game events are taking place. The rest of the Olympia floor space on both levels is covered in dozens of booths, stalls and stands, advertising the latest games from a whole universe of video game publishers. The Sony, Microsoft and Nintendo booths dominate the packed hall, along with EA Games, Ubisoft and Activision. The entire thing is gaudy, loud, flashy and headache inducing. Only teenagers could possibly love it.

The preliminary rounds of the *Call of Duty* competition are starting in a quarter of an hour, as are the first heats of my favourite game, *Realm of Chaos*. I'll have to miss both, though, as I need to interview the aforementioned Patrice Renfart at the *Farmyard Fury* booth, at the back of the hall. *Farmyard Fury* became a rather surprise success two years ago. A whimsical, humorous first-person shooter that acted as a nice antidote to all those grey and brown, dull as dishwater army games that have dominated the industry in recent years.

The creatively titled *Farmyard Fury 3* is out in a month, and Monde Ouvert Studios, the makers of the game, have been selling the bloody thing for all it's worth in recent weeks. Included in their extensive PR campaign is making the creator of the franchise available for a series of dull interviews.

Patrice Renferd is a talented games designer, but not a great interviewee. The last time I spoke to him, he spent most of the interview asking me whether I thought it was dog shit or mud on the sole of his loafer. I truly hope I can get something better out of him this time, otherwise Watlow will be spitting in my face when I get back to the office.

The *Farmyard Fury 3* booth is not hard to miss, given that there is a giant inflatable sheep hovering above it. Not just any sheep either. No, this is Baa Baa Bad Sheep, the star of the game. Carrying a machine gun in one hoof (which should be anatomically impossible for a sheep) and a grenade in the other, Baa Baa Bad Sheep is every inch the ridiculous caricature. Just picture Rambo crossed with Shaun the Sheep from the *Wallace and Gromit* cartoons, and you've got the right idea.

Not only is there the giant inflatable Baa Baa Bad Sheep, but there is also an ambulatory version of the game's mascot and main character, wobbling around the floor trying to bother as many people as possible.

Including *me*, it seems. As I'm crossing the floor to the booth, Baa Baa Bad Sheep spies me, and makes a beeline over to intercept me. I figure he must have seen the press pass dangling around my neck and figured I'd be a good person to target for publicity.

Baa Baa Bad Sheep stands right in front of me and blocks my path, waving his plastic machine gun in what I'm sure he thinks is a threatening manner. There's nothing more pathetic than a fully grown man dressed in several pounds of fire-retardant foam rubber and fake wool, trying his hardest to act like a warmongering sheep.

This guy seems particularly keen on holding my attention, as every time I try to step around him, he blocks my path again, much to the delight of several onlookers who have noticed what's going on and turned to watch us.

The first two times the guy does it, I smile and grit my teeth. I'm not usually a rude person straight out of the gate. It takes a good few pokes to get me worked up.

In this particular case, it's not until the stupid sheep blocks my path for the *fourth* time that my blood begins to boil.

'Look mate,' I say to a plastic sheep's face that's twisted into an expression of cartoon rage, 'I get you're only doing your job, but I've got to do mine as well, so be a sport and get out of the way, eh?'

I don't wait for a reply, but instead attempt to get past the stupid git for a fifth time. When he tries to once again block my path, I put my hands on where I presume his shoulders to be, and gently push him to one side. This takes him completely by surprise and he falls over with a spectacular crash.

I didn't push him that hard or anything, but it's probably quite difficult to manoeuvre yourself around in a heavy sheep costume like that – and once someone even gently throws off your equilibrium, it's a one-way ticket to a painful face plant.

This is precisely what Baa Baa Bad Sheep does, much to the hilarity of the onlookers. I hear the guy inside the costume shout in pain and start to swear loudly.

'Sorry mate!' I squeal. 'I didn't mean to push you over, but you wouldn't get out of the way!'

Baa Baa Bad Sheep ignores my apology and starts to get back to his feet. This is rather like watching an upended turtle in considerable distress. I'm also pretty sure that once he does achieve verticality again, I will be in for some severe ungulate abuse.

Discretion always being the better part of valour, I start to hurry away, still spouting apologies over my shoulder. Before Baa Baa Bad Sheep can catch up to me and give me hell with that plastic machine gun, I disappear into the large collection of gamers packed around the *Farmyard Fury 3* booth.

I breathe a small sigh of relief as I reach the counter, and ask the girl behind it to take me to see Patrice Renferd. There's no way Baa Baa Bad Sheep can come after me now, not when I'll be chatting to his de facto boss.

* * *

The girl takes me around the back of the massive *Farmyard Fury* stand, to a quieter area between it and the back wall of the building. Behind a large curtain is a rather pleasant quiet area, featuring several comfy-looking couches and a coffee machine. The man of the hour – slight of build, large of hipster beard – is sat on one of the couches, watching a TV set up in front of it. The TV is showing a live feed of the stage at the other end of the massive hall, where the tournament has begun.

Patrice sees me, his face withering slightly. I don't take any offence at this. Face withering is usually the sight that greets any journalist when they get noticed by your average games designer. They view us as a necessary evil, most of the time. This is okay, though, as we feel much the same way about them.

'Good morning, Patrice,' I say warmly as he rises from the couch, the withering look replaced by one of hazy concern.

''Ello, Adam. It's nice to see you again,' Patrice lies in his smooth French Canadian accent. 'Please, come and sit down 'ere. I'm just watching the start of the show.'

'Thanks very much.'

I sink into the couch.

It's about thirty-eight times more comfortable than any couch I've owned in my life. 'So, are you happy to just answer questions as I put them to you?' I say as I find the recording app on my iPhone.

'Yes, that is fine.'

He doesn't altogether look like he's fine with it, but we'll press on regardless, and hope we come out the other side unscathed.

Indeed, the interview does go quite well. It looks like someone's been giving Patrice some media coaching.

By the time ten minutes have elapsed I'm fairly sure I have enough to cobble together into a half-decent article for the website. All I have to do now is get a nice illustrative photo to go with it.

'You mind if we pop out front and get a picture of you with the booth in the background?'

Patrice blanches. 'Do we 'ave to? I'll have to speak to those people out there again.' He says this with the kind of dread usually reserved for someone about to take an involuntary part in a war crimes tribunal.

This is not uncommon amongst games developers. By and large, the last people on earth they want to interact with are the people that play their games.

'It'll be fine,' I promise him. 'Won't take more than a minute.'

Poor Patrice actually falls for my sincerity. Never trust a reporter with a story to finish – he'd lie to his own mother for a better scoop.

Patrice hesitantly follows me back through the large, protective curtain and out into the hectic Olympia floor show.

I manage to manoeuvre Patrice to a spot in front of the gigantic *Farmyard Fury 3* booth, where I can get his face in the foreground, and the fruits of his labours in the background.

We used to have a photographer who would come along to do this kind of thing, but Watlow got rid of her in his grand money-saving cull last year. Now it's down to me and a battered iPhone to get the job done.

Patrice looks like he's just about to have a close relationship with the business end of a firing squad. He cuts a rather sorry figure, it has to be said. His shoulders are slumpier than the Greek economy, his mouth is more downturned than the British car industry. You'd be hard-pressed to believe he'd made a personal fortune of over six million quid from the stupid inflatable sheep wobbling around just behind his head.

'Er, smile?' I venture.

Patrice does his best, but now he just looks like someone's force-fed him a bowl of cat vomit.

'Um, smile just a *wee* bit more?' I plead.

Okay, so now he looks like a vast invisible entity has pulled both sides of his mouth back violently into a rictus grin. It'll have to do, though, as I can see my phone battery rapidly draining as I speak.

'Right then, hold still . . .' Patrice does as he is asked, and I move my thumb to take the picture.

As I do so, a large white and black figure jumps into the shot.

Therefore, my photo does not feature a mournful games developer and a promotional stand, surrounded by a hundred gamers. Instead it features the blurred image of a giant foam rubber sheep holding a machine gun.

'Oi! What the hell are you playing at?' I demand, as Baa Baa Bad Sheep jumps up and down in front of me, obviously delighted that he has ruined my picture. 'Get out of the bloody way!'

The costumed moron stops bounding around, gives me a long, hard look, and slowly raises one hand to give me the finger. Okay, he's wearing big fake hooves, so I can't actually see it, but I know without a doubt that he's gesturing at me rudely underneath all that rubber.

'Fuck you,' I hear Baa Baa Bad Sheep say in a muffled tone from underneath the caricatured sheep's head.

Patrice steps around his mascot and gives me a look. 'What is going on, please? Can we just get this photo done so I can go back?'

'Sorry, Patrice. I don't know what this idiot is up to.'

I'm royally annoyed now. This interview is going quite well, and I want to get it wrapped up as quickly as possible, but instead I have this clown interrupting me, just because I inadvertently knocked him over. That only happened because he was behaving like a fool in the first place.

I step closer to Baa Baa Bad Sheep and attempt to address the man inside. 'Look mate, I'm sorry about earlier, but this is ridiculous. Just clear off, will you? That guy behind you is probably your boss, so it'd be a good idea if you just – *ow!*'

The little shit just poked me in the ribs with his plastic machine gun!

'What the hell did you do that for?' I screech. I am provided with no explanation, just another poke in the ribs for my troubles. 'Ow! Stop doing that!'

Now I'm forced to step away from the maniacal ungulate, for fear of getting poked a third time. You might not think a plastic machine gun is all that dangerous, but the end of that barrel is pointy and hard, let me tell you.

In desperation I look over to Patrice. 'Can you get this idiot to stop?' I plead with him.

Patrice shrugs his shoulders. 'Why would he listen to me?'

'Because you bloody invented him!' I cry in exasperation, knowing I'm going to get nowhere. Renferd doesn't strike me as the proactive type in the best of circumstances. Having him step in to prevent any further sheep-based assault to my person seems highly unlikely.

Patrice grimaces. 'Yes. But I wanted him to be a pig. They made me change it to a sheep.'

My natural curiosity temporarily overpowers my rage. 'Why did they make you do that?'

'It was the tits.'

'I beg your pardon?'

'The pig tits. They did not want the main character to have tits.'

Even Baa Baa Bad Sheep has turned to look at his creator now. You simply can't ignore a statement like that, no matter how irritated you are with the video games journalist who pushed you over.

I frown in confusion. 'Um. Why did you give the pig tits?' I ask Patrice, wishing that my iPhone was still recording. This would make a far better interview subject than how they managed to render the new game in sixty frames a second.

'Because they have them in real life!'

I try to picture your average porcine farmyard dweller wandering around the sty with a massive set of bouncing boobs.

'He means teats,' Baa Baa Bad Sheep says to me in that muffled tone I've come to know and loathe. 'It's his accent. Teats. Not tits.'

The light dawns. 'Oh,' I say, but then I'm confused again. 'Don't sheep have teats too?'

'Yes,' Patrice tells me, 'but you can cover them in wool. Look down there.' He points at Baa Baa Bad Sheep's nether regions, which are indeed very woollen, and free of teat or tit.

So now all three of us are looking down at a fake sheep's genital region. In a way, we must be approaching some kind of performance art here.

Patrice breaks the spell by looking back up at me. 'Can we get this photograph over with please?'

I shake myself out of what can only be described as an unhealthy train of thought, and try to reapply myself to the matter at hand. 'Yes, of course, Patrice.' I glower at Baa Baa Annoying Sheep. 'Can you stay out of the way, mate? I have to get this photo done.'

The sheep stares at me for an instant, and then slowly and ominously nods once, stepping back to allow me the space I need to get this stupid photo.

'Okay, Patrice, now just give me a nice smile,' I encourage, lining him up in the screen. Patrice actually manages to do this and I quickly take the photo.

Phew! The job is done. I look at the picture I've just taken with some satisfaction. Okay, I'm never going to win any awards for my photographic skill, but I do have a fairly decent image of Patrice, smiling more or less naturally, and standing in front of the *Farmyard Fury* stand. Everything is in focus, and will make a nice addition to the story when I hand it over to Watlow later.

'Can I have a look?' a muffled voice says. I turn round to see Baa Baa Bad Sheep looking down at me.

'Why?' I ask suspiciously.

He leans back a bit. 'Look, I know I've been a jerk. And I'm sorry. Maybe I could pose for a photo for you as well for your story?'

Aha! The little shit has realised that I'm someone important! That being nice to me for a change would benefit him with a little exposure on one of the country's pre-eminent video game websites!

They all come around eventually . . .

'Sure,' I say to him, and place my phone in one rubbery hoof. I'm sure that once he sees what a good job I've done of Patrice's photo, he'll be more than happy to let me—

Where's he fucking going?

Baa Baa Bad Sheep has taken to his heels – sorry, has taken to his *rear hooves*, and is legging it away as fast as his chunky, woolly legs can carry him. Ordinarily I'd be fine with this, as nothing would give me greater pleasure than to see the back of him, but the bastard is still holding my iPhone! The one I still have six months left to see out on contract, and that contains the entire interview I've just conducted with a socially anxious games programmer.

'Come back!' I holler and take off after him, dodging my way past several bystanders, who probably think this is all part of the bloody show.

You'd imagine it wouldn't take me very long to catch up with a man covered in several pounds of foam rubber, but I am exceptionally unfit, and he appears to be just the opposite. The speed and dexterity he employs as he weaves his way through the crowd is quite something to behold. The fact he is able to also wave my mobile phone at me over his head as he does this is even more amazing. I'd be impressed if I wasn't so teeth-spittingly angry.

'Give me back my bloody phone!' I roar as we steam past the *Assassin's Creed* stand, to the shock and amazement of all those gathered there.

The chase continues down the length of Olympia, and by the time we are approaching the main stage, where the preliminary *Realm of*

Chaos heats are underway, I'm running out of puff. I'm convinced that Baa Baa is making for the exit just behind the massive stage set-up, so I'm surprised to see him veer off towards the long row of PCs on the stage that are hosting the tournament. With a semi-graceful leap, he's through the crowd of spectators, up on to the stage, and sprinting between the ranks of computers.

The gap he's having to negotiate between the rows of consumed gamers is small, so it arrests his progress in a manner that allows me to catch up. It also means several innocent *Realm of Chaos* players get a smack across the back of the head with a rubber sheep's hoof as Baa Baa passes, still waving my iPhone aloft like a trophy.

I reach out one hand and make a grab for his woolly hide, screaming obscenities as I do so. I successfully grasp hold of a big handful of wool, but not before we have both reached the opposite end of the *Realm of Chaos* stage. Baa Baa Bad Sheep attempts to pull away from me with a violent jerk, but all he manages to do is lose his footing as he's trying to jump off the stage, sending him plummeting to the show floor.

Anyone thinking straight would let go of Baa Baa's woolly backside to avoid following him in his downward trajectory. Sadly, I am not thinking straight at all.

With an almighty clatter – muffled somewhat by all that wool and rubber – we both come crashing to the floor. Luckily, I land on Baa Baa, and am therefore saved a nasty head injury. Unfortunately, my testicles come into sudden and painful contact with Baa Baa Bad Sheep's plastic machine gun, so I get a groin injury instead.

'Aaaarggh!' I wail, one hand clutching my nethers as the other attempts to grab my phone away from the woollen bastard. He's having none of it, and tries to throw me off.

Bollocks to that! There's no way this arsehole is getting away from me again!

As Baa Baa twists himself around and tries to scrabble away, I lock my arms around his neck and spread my legs around his ample backside, trying to maintain enough purchase to stop him escaping.

'Oi! Paul!' I hear a familiar voice cry from beside me. 'It's Adam! Adam's over here, fucking a giant sheep!'

I look over Baa Baa Bad Sheep's head to see the rather inevitable image of my flatmate Calvin jumping up and down in delight. He is joined by my other flatmate Paul, who also looks like he's just won the lottery.

'Wahaay! Go get him, son!' Paul shouts in encouragement. 'You fuck that big old sheep!'

Both of them collapse into giggles.

'You know them?' Baa Baa shouts at me through the back of his woolly head.

'My flatmates,' I reply with a groan, knowing that I'm never going to live this down in a million years. The bastards will take the piss out of me mercilessly.

I contemplate this horror for a moment, before remembering why I'm stuck in this unfortunate situation in the first place. 'Give me back my phone, you mental bastard!' I shout at Baa Baa, smacking him on the back of the head as I do so.

'No!' he replies defiantly.

'Give it back!' I repeat, tightening my rather haphazard stranglehold. I doubt I'm doing the guy any serious harm, given that his real neck is probably nowhere near his fake sheepy one, but at least I'm not letting him get away.

'Your new boyfriend not cooperating?' Calvin asks as he and Paul get closer.

Ah, now this is interesting. Calvin and Paul are both *enormous*, and can look quite intimidating when they need to. Their presence here may work to my advantage.

'He stole my phone and won't give it back!' I moan.

Paul's eyes narrow. 'Give our little mate his phone back,' he orders Baa Baa Bad Sheep.

'No! He pushed me over,' Bad Sheep says in response.

'It was an accident!' I counter. 'You were being bloody annoying!'

'I was only doing my job!'

'Give me my phone back!' I rage, thumping him on the back of the head again.

'Give him his phone back!' Paul and Calvin both join in, also now administering blows to the back of the sheep's rubber head. Any minute now somebody is going to call the police and the RSPCA in quick succession. The only time this kind of thing usually happens is on a cold January night in the Welsh mountains – only the sheep normally puts up more of a fight.

Our assault on Baa Baa Bad Sheep is halted by the *Star Wars* theme tune. My phone, the object of this fracas, has started ringing. Paul wrestles it out of Baa Baa's hoof and hands it to me. 'You stay right there,' he tells Baa Baa, giving him another friendly slap on the head. I can see a couple of security guards waddling over to us as I take the phone and stand up. I may have some explaining to do.

The phone says that it's an unknown number calling me, so I'm tempted to leave it – but then again, it could be bloody Watlow on one of the company's lines. I'd better answer it.

'Hello?'

'Hi! Is this Adam Holborne?' an excited female voice says into my ear.

'Er, yes,' I reply. This is quite clearly not Watlow. 'Who is this?'

'My name is Cassandra McFlasterton.'

'What?'

'I said my name is Cassandra McFlasterton, and I'm calling from Sociality.'

'What? The dating website?'

'Yes, that's right.'

My face clouds. Great, not only do I have to talk my way out of an oncoming charge of assaulting a sheep in public, I now have to field some cold-caller, who no doubt wants to question me about how much I value their online service.

'Look, I don't really have time to do a survey right now, I'm afraid,' I tell the woman. 'But your website is fine, thanks. No need to ask me anything about it.'

The security guards are getting closer.

'I'm not calling about a survey,' the woman says.

'Oh? Then what's this about?' Security Guard One is helping Baa Baa Bad Sheep to his feet. The other is accosting Calvin and Paul. Everyone is looking at *me*.

'Congratulations, Adam! You're getting married!'

What did she just say?

'Sorry, what was that? You'll have to speak up. I'm in Olympia and about to get arrested for sheep abuse.'

'You've won our competition, Adam!' the woman says, gamely ignoring anything she may have just heard about a sheep. 'Your profile has been matched with a fantastic young lady, and next week you're going to marry her!'

Oh *fuck*. Oh *double* fuck with cherries on top.

'Are you alright, sir?' Security Guard Two asks me. 'Your friends here say this sheep stole your phone. Is that correct?'

'I'm getting married,' I reply in a stunned voice.

'Well, that's very nice for you, but it doesn't really answer my question.'

'I'm getting married,' I repeat, eyes glazing.

'You sly old dog!' Calvin laughs.

'Didn't even know you had a girlfriend,' Paul remarks.

'I don't,' I tell him, with some confidence.

'Then who are you marrying?' he asks, confused.

Slowly Paul, Calvin and the security guards all turn to look at Baa Baa Bad Sheep.

The rubber sheep's head shakes erratically back and forth. 'Don't look at me!' he bellows. 'He's not my type!'

In the end, I just let Baa Baa Bad Sheep go without any further action. Bringing a criminal sheep to justice for phone theft seems largely irrelevant now, given that I'm going to have a wife in less than ten days.

A *wife* in less than *ten* days.

Gorp.

I barely even remember putting my Sociality profile forward for that silly competition. It was two clicks of the mouse, performed with little to no thought whatsoever – beyond the small fantasy of living in a nice apartment and having a bit of cash in my pocket for once.

I never thought I'd be a good enough match for anyone to actually *win* the bloody thing.

But here I am. Soon to be wed.

Me. Adam Holborne.

A man who woke up this morning with a cross-eyed rat called Gnawbones on his chest, and less than three hours later was aggressively molesting a sheep called Baa Baa.

Maybe I should just call the poor girl and tell her to start running away as fast as she can . . .

JESS

Q. Describe your dream job to us.
A. Nutritional consultant to the stars!

7 February

Oh God, *no*. It's Captain Dribbles.

He hasn't come into the club for three weeks now, and we were all starting to think he'd gone away for good, but no . . . here he is again. Only ten minutes into my shift, when the place is still empty. Tonight is going to be worse than I feared.

It's not that Captain Dribbles does anything that's offensive. A lot of men come into the club who behave far *worse*, but I'm pretty sure if I took a straw poll of all the girls, they'd all agree that they'd rather deal with a guy who can't keep his hands to himself than one who deposits half the contents of his mouth on to your thigh every time you sit with him.

Not for the first time, I thank my lucky stars that I'm just a bar girl here at Sister Stocking's Gentlemen's Club, and not one of the performers. I only have to worry about wiping the *bar* down after Captain Dribbles has left, not my own body.

I cross my fingers as I watch Dribbles walk through the bar area. Will he go over to look at Tanya as she gyrates around the pole on the stage? Or will he come over here for his usual gin and tonic?

He stares over at Tanya for a moment as she takes off her sequin-clad bra.

Yeah, that's right, old man. You go look at those big bouncing boobs, and leave me alone over here behind my bar. You don't need a drink that bad, do you? Prioritise, my man!

For a moment it looks like he agrees with my silent demand and I breathe a small sigh of relief, but then he spots me, the drink Optics behind my head, and decides that the tits can wait.

Ah, hell.

'Good evening,' he says, taking off his ratty baseball cap and sitting himself down on one of the chrome stools in front of the bar. I can already see a thin line of spittle coming from one corner of his mouth.

'Hi,' I reply, trying not to grimace.

'You look lovely tonight,' he tells me.

I don't look *lovely* at all. *Lovely* would be the sleek blue dress I saw in the window of Selfridges as I walked to work this evening. The current outfit I'm wearing is as far from *lovely* as you can possibly get. I may not be one of the strippers, but that doesn't mean I'm not forced to wear an extremely tight black-and-white bartender's outfit that pushes my boobs up so much they're nearly touching my chin, and is so tight around my ass that I'm pretty sure the circulation has been cut off to my lower extremities.

What Captain Dribbles calls *lovely*, I call cruel and unusual punishment.

'Get you a drink?' I ask.

'Yes please. Gin and tonic, if you have any.'

I turn to the Optic behind me and pick up a glass. I know Captain Dribbles is looking at my butt, but there's not much I can do to stop him.

'I do love your accent. It's quite wonderful,' he tells me – not for the first time.

'Thanks.'

'Where are you from?'

'California.'

'Ah, super. Never been there myself. Do you miss it?'

Right now, more than anything, pal.

'Yeah, I guess,' I tell him, trying not to get into a proper conversation if I can help it. The more he talks, the more he dribbles.

He takes a sip of the drink I've just put in front of him. 'What was your name again, my dear?'

'Kelly,' I lie through my teeth.

'Well, it's wonderful to speak to you, Kelly,' Dribbles lets me know, sucking some of the excess fluid back in his mouth as he does so.

What an *amazing* life I've managed to carve out for myself here in the UK.

Why, I can remember sitting and staring out of my bedroom window when I was a girl, thinking that when I grow up, what I really want to do is be living six thousand miles from home, dressed like an extra from a porn movie, and serving drinks to a sixty-year-old man with a wet mouth.

Still, just think of the great anecdotes I can tell my grandchildren about the years I spent scratching out a living in *old London town*. I will of course make the whole thing sound far more like *Mary Poppins* when I retell it. There will be less dribbling pervert and more cheeky chimney sweeps, I can assure you of that.

'Can I have another?' Dribbles asks, having apparently drained his first gin in the time it took me to pour it. Once he's sat himself down at the stage, I'll have to warn the girls that he's likely to be more *productive* than usual. Rochelle's been wanting to try out her PVC catsuit for a while now. It should give her some wipe-clean protection, if nothing else.

I fix Dribbles another gin and tonic, wipe the counter in front of him, and then take myself off to the other end of the bar to serve the three nervous young guys who have just walked in.

As I hand over three bottles of Budweiser and take the cash from a shaking twenty-something hand, I breathe a deep and leaden sigh.

What the hell am I doing with myself?

I mean, *really*?

I keep reassuring my ego that we're only in this job so we can afford to get through our college course without creating a mountain of debt, but I think it's starting to ignore me in favour of looking at one-way flights to the US on Expedia.

Who knew London would be so expensive?

Ha! Who am I kidding? Of course I *knew* it would be expensive, I just chose to not think about it as I filled in the application for King's College. Just the idea – the *fantasy* – of coming to the UK and studying at such an amazing place made me forget the practicalities completely. I came down with a severe case of American Tourist syndrome, and let the whole thing go to my head. I saw cobblestones, charming older gentlemen in bowler hats bidding me good day, big shiny red London buses, and the Queen passing by my window virtually every day in her carriage, giving me an elegant wave.

It wasn't until I started looking for somewhere to rent that was less than half an hour away from the college on the Underground that I started to realise the reality of what living in this city would be like – and that I was in *trouble*. Mom and Dad have been great with the help they've given me with the rent, but even that doesn't come close to covering what I've got to pay out on the Finsbury Park shoebox I'm currently staying in.

When I saw the advertisement for the job here at Sister Stocking's, I tried my hardest not to apply for it, but gave in when I saw the hourly rate. I may have to wear my boobs up around my ears, but at least I'm getting paid danger money for the privilege.

So these days, my life consists of two things, and two things alone: study, and work. Sometimes, if I get really lucky, I can squeeze a few minutes' sleep in here and there.

I certainly have no time for a social life of any kind, beyond what I get here at the club. The drink is cheap, but I'm not likely to meet the man of my dreams any time soon, given that he sure as hell wouldn't be the type to spend his time in a moderately seedy strip club like this one.

Mom and Dad think I work at Starbucks. It's just better that way.

Don't get me wrong, it's not all bad here. There's an atmosphere to London I've never felt before – a sense of mystery about the past that gives me a secret thrill whenever I think about it. Take a turn down a side street and you could find yourself whisked back two hundred years, and surrounded by the kind of architecture you've only seen before in a Harry Potter movie.

And there's nothing quite as romantic as strolling along the South Bank with a coffee on a crisp Sunday morning – on the rare occasions the weather is sunny and warm enough to allow it, of course.

Other than Captain Dribbles and the three guys out on what's probably a low-key stag do, the club is empty. Not surprising for 8 p.m. on a Tuesday night. I take the opportunity to go sit in the storeroom behind the bar to look through some of my homework.

I've only been part of the master's course in nutrition for two months, but I already have what feels like eight years of work to get through. I thought my undergrad course back at home was hard, but I had no idea just what a steep learning curve it would be to come to the UK to continue my studies.

Take Professor Malcolm Hibbersley, for instance.

Yeah, that's his real name. I haven't made it up. You couldn't get a more British-sounding name, unless it was something like Basil TeaCupAndSaucer, or Doris DrizzlingAllDay.

Professor Hibbersley looks like a saintly old English gentleman, with salt-and-pepper hair and a pleasant expression on his face, but under that facade is an academic *monster*. Before I'd even spent two hours in his classroom, the maniac had piled me high with books, set two assignments, and given me less than a month to provide a detailed synopsis of my thesis.

Obviously I'm not the only student in his class, but Professor Hibbersley has a habit of making everything seem personally aimed at me, even when it quite clearly isn't.

I do think that being older than the other students doesn't help me, though. I'm sure he thinks that because I'm a good seven or eight years their senior, I should know more, and therefore be capable *of more*. I should point out to him that nothing could be further from the truth. It's a little hard to gain academic knowledge when you spent most of your early twenties surfing off the California coast. Unless Professor Hibbersley starts handing out assignments based on the best kind of wax to put on your surfboard, I have absolutely no advantage over the other students.

So here I sit, attempting to process a mountain of information, while trying my hardest to ignore the sound system blasting out Maroon 5, as Rochelle writhes around in front of Captain Dribbles in the sixty-pound catsuit she bought on Amazon.

The next hour goes by with me alternating between serving alcohol to men who have come to see naked breasts, and learning more about the compound structure of phytoprotectants.

I just hope and pray I never get the two things mixed up, as my thesis will end up being twenty-five thousand words on the nutritional benefit of breast milk.

The time I get to spend studying comes in smaller and smaller chunks as the night goes on and the club fills up. Thankfully, Hen joins me serving drinks by the time 11 p.m. rolls around.

Mad Love

If a twenty-nine-year-old Californian postgraduate seems out of place in a London strip club, then a twenty-one-year-old upper-class girl from Chipping Sodbury called Henrietta is from another *planet*. I've no idea how she ended up here.

'Oh gosh, getting busy then,' she says in that clipped British tone I've grown to admire and be completely jealous of.

'Yeah. Filling up,' I reply in a tired voice. Mixing drinks and study time is hard on both your feet and your brain.

Hen tips her head to one side. 'Would you like a break, sweetheart? I can cover for half an hour. Make up a bit for being late.'

I give her a look of profound gratitude. 'Thanks, Hen. I have to understand these damn phytoprotectants for the seminar tomorrow, so a few minutes away would be great.'

Hen doesn't have a clue what the hell I'm on about, but she smiles, kisses me on the cheek and gets to work, leaving me to shuffle back into the cupboard behind the bar for some more cramming.

Thirty minutes later I give up. The phytoprotectants can protect their goddamn phytos on their own for the rest of the night, because I am *done*. I'll just have to wing it tomorrow. The professor will probably eviscerate me in front of the rest of the group, but I'll take my chances. I just can't spend any more time looking at this textbook while a heavy bassline thumps its way through my brain.

I emerge from the cupboard to see that the club is really jumping now. The place is pretty much full to the rafters, and Hen looks like she could do with some help. I hurry over to her and start taking orders alongside. She gives me a grateful smile as I do so. 'Did you get any work done?' she asks.

'A little,' I reply, having to shout over the deafening music. 'Not as much as I'd like with all this going on, though! Not really going to be that well prepared for tomorrow, but there's nothing I can do about it now!'

'I'm sure you'll be fine, darling!' Hen says encouragingly.

Her words are nice, but they don't make me feel any more confident. Hen has not met Professor Hibbersley. She has not had to endure his raised eyebrow and crinkled forehead. It's the stuff of nightmares.

I try to clear my head of an angry middle-aged man wagging his finger at me, by looking around the bar to see what the clientele is like this evening. I've been doing this job long enough to know whether a crowd is going to give us any problems or not. You can usually spot the troublemakers a mile away. Thankfully, it looks like these guys are going to be okay, at least at first glance.

It's a fairly atypical selection for this kind of venue. Forty per cent young men with too much money and too little sense, forty per cent old men with the exact opposite. There are some loners who are just here for the company, regulars who treat the place like their local pub, and the odd real pervert trying not to salivate too much. Captain Dribbles is certainly enjoying himself over by the main stage. I can see the spittle glistening on his chin from here.

There are even several women in the crowd, which is not as strange as it sounds. They often come in accompanying their husbands or boyfriends, or gay girls who are keen on seeing the show as much as any man. I always prefer it when we have quite a few women in the crowd. They tend to be a good influence on all those testosterone-filled men.

Yeah, the usual crowd, then. Nothing out of the ordinary.

. . . except maybe that old guy over in the far corner that looks like Professor Hibbersley.

God, Jess, you need some sleep. You've got college on the brain and you're seeing things.

There's no way a celebrated academic like Malcolm Hibbersley would be seen dead in a seedy place like this. Especially not surrounded by three of Sister Stocking's scantily clad employees.

I peer harder.

No way. It just looks a little like him, that's all. I'm definitely seeing things.

. . . that tweed coat does look familiar, though.

'Hen? Can you mind the bar for a moment? I have to go check something out.'

'Sure, sweetheart.'

I lift the bar and make my way out through the crowd of guys vying for Hen's attention and walk slowly towards where the Hibbersley doppelgänger is sat. I make sure to keep a lot of people between him and me, just in case I am not actually seeing things. As I close the gap I spot Giselle, one of Sister Stocking's most popular girls, twerking her ass up and down in front of the old man like her life depended on it. As she does this Carla and Shayla, the dancers we refer to as 'the Twins', are cosying up to him and giggling like schoolgirls. Whoever this guy is, he obviously pays well.

Luckily, having three gorgeous strippers cavorting around is making this guy completely oblivious to my approach, and as I get within ten feet, crossing one of the dance floors as I do, the crowd of men in my way parts for a second and I'm able to get a good, close look at the man's face.

When I actually had some spare time back at home, I loved to read trashy crime thrillers. The kind of book that always has a black jacket and a red title. I've read a thousand of the damn things over the years, and know every cliché and stereotypical description there is, so when I say I am completely familiar with the concept of your blood running cold when you see something horrific, I am telling the *absolute* truth.

I've read about it happening over and over, but this is the first time I've ever *felt it*.

It's not a nice feeling. Not a nice feeling *at all*.

It is Professor Hibbersley. Those are definitely his eyebrows. That is definitely his tweed jacket.

What made me doubt my own eyes to begin with was the expression on his face. I am so used to seeing a faint look of disapproval that I got completely thrown by his current appearance. The professor looks like my Aunt Catherine's old boxer dog Conklin. Conklin always had a look of good-natured, boggle-eyed stupidity, no matter what he was doing. Whether he was sniffing his own ass or trying to screw your leg, he always looked like he'd just been injected with morphine *and* cocaine at the same time. He was the dumbest-looking dog you ever met – and here I am looking at him again, this time in human form, and surrounded by underpaid strippers.

Move, you stupid girl. If he sees you, it'll be a disaster.

A total disaster – for two reasons. Professor Hibbersley has no idea that one of his mature students is working as a bartender in a strip club. I doubt very much that if he did, it'd be met with his approval. I don't know whether it would be bad enough to get me thrown off my course for some kind of breach of college etiquette, but I have *no* intention of finding out.

Also, if the prof does see me, he'll not only know that I work here, he'll also know that *I know* he likes to come in and salivate over girls young enough to be his granddaughter.

Can you imagine what it'd be like when I walked into the classroom tomorrow?

The collective embarrassment would be so immense that all of the phytoprotectants in the universe wouldn't be enough to stop us both instantly self-destructing.

I have to get out of here, and I have to get out of here NOW.

If you like, feel free to hum the *Mission: Impossible* theme in your head while you read the next couple of paragraphs.

I crouch as low as I am able to in these ridiculously tight pants, and start to make my way, crablike, to the edge of the dance floor. Occasionally my head pops up behind someone's shoulder to see if the prof has noticed me, but every time I do he's too rapt with Giselle's butt to notice.

I *am* noticed by the men and women I'm using as a shield, though. My erratic progress towards a more concealed part of the club is watched by several curious patrons, who must be wondering why the bartender is herking and jerking around like a malfunctioning Whac-a-Mole machine.

Eventually, I reach the edge of the club. To my right is a guy at least five stone overweight, downing a Heineken and staring at Nicole's tits as she walks past. Nicole is the best endowed of all the strippers in the club, and is making sure everyone knows it tonight with a sequined bustier that must be cutting the blood off to her major organs. Figuring this is the best cover I'm going to get at short notice, I swiftly duck behind the chunky boob addict before the professor has the chance to look up and see me.

From over the big guy's shoulder I see Hibbersley laugh out loud and caress Carla's thigh without taking his eyes off Giselle's rotating ass.

This is *awful*.

'Are you having a good time tonight, guys?!!'

I nearly jump out of my skin. Our resident master of ceremonies, JC, has come on the PA for the first time this evening. That means the main show is about to start.

A loud cheer erupts throughout the club.

'That's great!' JC replies at the top of his lungs. JC does everything like that. Our DJ is two parts fashion victim, one part loud hailer. 'Your night is about to get *even better*! Coming to the main stage now is the incrrrrrrrredibly hot Nicole, who's going to rock your world like it's never been rocked before!'

This instantly starts a mass exodus over to the other side of the club. Every man gathered around me hurries over to where Nicole is striding out on to the stage, her breasts leading the way like beacons in a storm.

Sadly, the fat guy I've been hiding behind is one of her new fans, leaving me with no cover.

Michael Jackson's 'Bad' starts to blare out of the PA system, and Nicole begins to divest herself of her clothing as Mikey tells us all about just how bad he really, really is.

Unfortunately, Professor Hibbersley has taken no interest in what Nicole's doing, as he is far too happy with his own gyrating strippers to be concerned about another, no matter how large her mammary glands are. This presents a real problem, as I am now directly in his line of sight. If he so much as glances up from Giselle's wobbling rump I'm screwed.

I start to back away, trying not to draw too much attention to myself. As I am not trained in the dark arts of ninja-like concealment, all I manage to do is the exact *opposite*.

It's a little hard to ignore an uncomfortable-looking redhead in a skintight bartender's outfit, performing the worst Michael Jackson moonwalk you've seen this side of a wedding reception at one in the morning.

But I'm okay, the professor still hasn't seen me!

I'm going to get away with it!

I'm going to be fi—

'Hey, Jess!' Carla calls out to me from her place next to Hibbersley, and starts beckoning me over with her hand.

Oh *crap*.

She thinks I've come over to see if they want drinks!

What do I do now?

Continue the moonwalk, dumb-ass. Just ignore her.

I do so, edging away and trying to look in every direction except Carla's.

She frowns and waves her hand again, this time with more urgency. 'Come here!' she mouths over Michael Jackson. The prof still hasn't spotted me, as Shayla has now stood up, and is writhing around in front of him with Giselle. The prof obviously approves of this immensely as I watch him produce a large roll of cash from his pants pocket, and start to tuck the notes in both girls' G-strings. Being a professor at King's College must pay well, that's all I can say.

Maybe if I sidle up to the seats where they're sitting from the other direction, he won't notice me. Better that than Carla drawing even more attention to me with her continued wild gesticulation.

I head back towards her as swiftly as I can, my eyes fixed on what the professor is doing. I move in a wide left-swinging arc to avoid his eyeline as much as possible. Carla watches my approach with a look of confusion.

You'd be confused too, if you saw one of your work colleagues tottering towards you in three-inch heels, with a fixed look of terror on her face. Your confusion would turn to disbelief as she sat herself on the edge of the long seating area you were in, and started to slide towards you, constantly looking over your shoulder at what was going on behind you as she did.

'Are you okay, Jess?' Carla asks with no small amount of concern as I get within speaking distance.

'Yeah, fine!' I hiss. 'What do you want?'

'Er, we'd like a bottle of champagne, please.'

'Right. That it?' I reply, positioning myself as flat against the wall as possible.

'Um. Pretty much. I'll just ask Clint if he wants anything else.'

Clint? Who the hell is Clint?

. . . *oh God.* He's given himself an *alias.*

Carla taps Hibbersley on the shoulder. As she does, I try to push myself back into the seat as hard as possible, hoping that I will defy the laws of physics somehow, and phase my entire body through the back wall of the club and out into the alleyway beyond.

'You want anything else, baby?' Carla says in her best fake sexy voice. All the girls have perfected this voice to one extent or another. It tends to guarantee bigger tips.

The prof looks around. 'Just the champagne is fine, Carla!' he tells her, his eyes resting on me for an instant. My heart stops.

He doesn't recognise me! He's so caught up in Giselle and Shayla's antics that his brain hasn't put two and two together! God bless the male mind for being so one-track whenever somebody sticks a couple of nice asses in front of it!

'Okay, a bottle of champagne it is!' I say as cheerily as possible. Then I remember that I am the only girl around here with an American accent, and wince as I realise what I've just done.

If I'd kept my mouth shut, I would have gotten away with it. I'd have just been one more girl in a tight outfit, in a club full of them, but add the broad Californian accent to the equation, and even those two nice asses can't stop the professor's brain from making the connection I'd so, so wanted to avoid.

I watch the professor's body stiffen as realisation dawns. His head whips back around in my direction, and he stares at me properly for the first time.

'Miss *Madison*?' he says, in an incredulous voice.

I'm dumbstruck. What do I say?

Yes, Professor, it's me. Are you busy ogling asses? Or do you have a moment to discuss the cellular structure of a cabbage leaf?

Instead of opening my mouth, I offer the professor a wave, in the hopes it might make him feel more comfortable in what is about to become the most excruciating thing that's ever happened to him.

'Oh!' Carla cries excitedly. 'Do you two know each other?'

'Er, um, aah,' blusters the professor, a man of usually many words.

'Hello, Professor Hibbersley,' I say. 'Fancy meeting you here!'

I've been in the UK long enough to have picked up that uncanny ability the British have to underplay even the most fraught of occasions.

'Er, Miss . . . Miss Madison!' Hibbersley replies, finally able to string a short sentence together.

'Hey, Clint?' Giselle interjects, running one finger down the prof's tweed jacket arm. 'Are you going to pour the champagne over my titties when it gets here? You know how you love to do that.'

The professor goes a delightful shade of purple. I am now privy to the fact he likes to douse a stripper's breasts in Dom Pérignon, whether I wanted to be or not.

The professor slaps Giselle's hand away. 'Er . . . what on earth are you doing here, Miss Madison?' he says to me in a strangled voice.

'I work here,' I tell him, figuring that there's no point in lying now.

'Do you?' he replies in disbelief.

'She's been here a few weeks now,' Carla butts in. 'I'm amazed you two have never bumped into each other before! Clint's in here all the time!'

'Clint' now looks like Giselle is giving him a prostate exam without his prior consent.

He holds up his hands and starts to shake his head vociferously. 'I don't know what you're talking about, young lady! I've never been here before in my life!'

Oh, *damn*.

Instead of taking the honest route which I've gone for, the professor has decided to try to lie his way out of the predicament he now finds himself in.

This could get even uglier.

My academic career could be hanging by a thread here. Professor Hibbersley has the power to throw me off the course if he's feeling vindictive enough, and if I don't smooth things over here as fast as possible I might be in real trouble.

Giselle gives him a playful slap on the arm. 'What are you talking about, baby? You was only in here last week! You remember? I let you lick the cream off my nipples out in the private room 'coz you paid the extra.'

Shut up, Giselle! *Shut up!* You're only making this whole thing worse!

'That wasn't me!' Hibbersley screeches. 'You must be mistaking me for someone completely different!'

'Yes! I'm sure that's right Giselle!' I add, choosing to go along with this charade. If I can convince the professor that I believe he isn't a regular here at the club – and by extension a dyed-in-the-wool pervert – I might be able to get out of this situation intact. 'I bet this is the first time, er, Clint has ever been in here, isn't that right, Clint?'

Hibbersley's eyes bulge. 'That's right! It is!'

I stand up. 'Maybe he's just in here to do some research? For a book, or something like that?'

Actually, that's pretty good as excuses go, don't you think? A middle-aged university lecturer in a strip club to research a book sounds a lot better than a middle-aged university lecturer in a strip club to watch asses jiggling all over the place.

'A book! That's right!' the professor agrees. 'That's why I'm in here. In this . . . in this horrible place!'

Oh no. He's taking things too far now. There was no need to insult Sister Stocking's and, by extension, her workforce.

'Oi! Sod off! You loves it in here!' Giselle rages.

Needless to say, Giselle is a nom de plume. There aren't many Giselles in the world who were brought up in the East End of London, and have such a relaxed attitude to grammar. I think her real name is Britnee – spelt very deliberately with the two 'e's.

'Nonsense! I don't know what you're talking about! I am in here to research the crime thriller I've been writing in my spare time away from my busy job!'

Nice extemporising, prof. Maybe there really is a book in you. Even if it's only a guide to the best strip clubs in England.

'Perhaps I could show you out, Clint?' I offer. 'I might be able to provide you with some more information for your book before you go?'

'But he's paid for the full works,' Carla points out. 'With all three of us.'

'Keep the money!' Hibbersley says in a choked voice.

Carla, Giselle and Shayla all smile in unison. And so they should. Getting paid without having to spend fifteen minutes faking sexual arousal dressed in a piece of dental floss is always something to be happy about.

I take the professor by the arm. 'Come on, I'll escort you out of the club.' I've now taken on the role of de facto bodyguard. Or his mother, I can't quite tell which.

We leave the slightly stunned strippers and move towards the exit. Over in the corner Nicole has moved on from Michael Jackson and is now showing her undercarriage to everyone with Christina Aguilera's 'Dirty' for accompaniment.

'I really have never been in here before, Miss Madison,' Professor Hibbersley says as I propel him across the club floor.

'No, I'm sure you haven't,' I reply, trying to sound convincing.

'It's just not my kind of place,' he adds. 'Not my kind of place, at all!'

'No, I'm sure it isn't,' I half repeat, wishing he'd just shut up and let me get him out of here.

We're almost at the exit when JC walks past. He sees the professor, smiles, extends both arms out and comes in for a hug. 'Hey Clint! Good to see you again, man!' JC is six foot four and lives in the gym, so when he wants to hug you, you have little choice in the matter.

Professor Hibbersley looks horrified as our resident DJ starts to squeeze the life out of him. These two obviously have a close relationship – which boggles the mind, given that one is a twenty-six-year-old muscle-bound DJ from Brixton, and the other is a sixty-something university lecturer from somewhere expensive in Kent.

JC steps back, that gigantic smile still plastered across his lips. 'Say Clint, did you get all three girls you wanted tonight? We had the whipped cream and vibrators put in the Purple Room like you asked.'

'*Vibrators?!*' I blurt out.

What's going on here? This club is strictly *hands off*, as far as I'm aware.

JC picks up on my confusion. 'Oh, they ain't for the girls,' he tells me, with a sly smile.

Oh Jesus Christ.

'Are you getting Clint here some drinks, Jess?' JC continues. 'Only, the bar's over that way.' He points back to where Hen is being swamped by customers. I really need to get rid of this old pervert and get back to work, before my part-time job is under as much threat as my college career.

'Wow! I bet that book must be exciting!' I spit at the professor, still attempting to maintain the ridiculous cover story I've concocted to save his blushes. 'There must be a really great scene where somebody gets hit in the head with a vibrator . . . or something.'

That sounds convincing, doesn't it?

JC gives me an understandably confused look. 'What the hell are you on about, Jess? Clint here doesn't go for that kind of thing.' He pats the professor on the shoulder. 'The girls all say he's a gentleman in there, even when they strip him down to his underwear!'

It's clearly apparent now that I don't have to get Professor Hibbersley out of here just to save my place on my college course; I also have to get him out of here before he dies of a shame-related heart attack.

'Who are you, my man?!' he screeches at the DJ. 'I've never seen you before in my life!'

'Yeah, JC,' I add. 'You must be confusing this man with somebody else!'

Okay, this is getting quite, quite pathetic.

JC's massive brow wrinkles. 'What are you talking about, Jessica? This here is Clint. He's been coming here for ages. The girls all call him "the Silver Fox".'

For the briefest – the absolute *briefest* – of moments, a small, proud little smile appears on the professor's face, then he remembers the predicament he's in and it's gone again.

'No, no, no. That isn't me, young man,' he insists to the increasingly befuddled DJ. 'You must be confusing me with another devilishly handsome man in his late fifties.'

Oh, for crying out loud.

'Let's just get you out of here,' I insist, taking 'Clint' by the arm again. I start to push him towards the exit, giving JC a glare as I do so. This is completely unfair. The friendly DJ has done nothing wrong, but he's just managed to make an embarrassing situation even more fraught, so he's not in my good books right now.

Finally, we reach the front doors to the club, and I half propel my tutor out into the street beyond.

'Thank you, Miss Madison,' he tells me, straightening his tie. 'I think it might have been a bad idea to come here tonight . . . to research my book, I mean.'

'Yeah. It might have been.'

'I trust that this little adventure will stay between us?'

Hmmm. That sounds encouraging. If the old guy wants to keep his dirty little habit a secret between the two of us, it must mean he's not about to throw me off the course.

'Yeah, Professor, it can stay between us.'

'Thank you, Miss Madison. If anyone were to find out . . .' he trails off. I assume that when he says 'anyone' he means his wife. 'If anyone were to find out, they wouldn't understand that I was only in there for research purposes.'

'Yes, of course,' I reply wearily. I just want to get back inside now and help out Hen before she collapses under the weight of drinks orders.

Professor Hibbersley stands straight. 'In that case, I will bid you a good night, and will see you tomorrow.' He gives me something of a sideways look. 'I'm looking forward to seeing the work you've done. I'm sure it will be *very* good.'

I get what he's hinting at immediately. Maybe catching him covered in strippers wasn't such a bad turn of events after all.

'Thank you, Professor. Would you like me to call you a cab?'

'No, no. I think I'll walk for a little while. Some fresh air will do me good. Hopefully it will help me put this horrible evening behind me.' He looks a little haughtily at Sister Stocking's. 'I have never stepped foot in an establishment like that before,' he lies, 'and I will never enter one like it again as long as I live!'

Giselle comes tottering out into the street. She's holding a clipboard. 'Oi, Clint! You rushed off so fast I never got a chance to give you this back from last week.'

So, what do you reckon she's holding out for the professor to take? A pair of glasses, perhaps? A handkerchief? Possibly a cigarette lighter?

All of these things would be easy to explain away.

A silver flashing cock ring, though? Yeah, not so much.

The professor looks down at the wobbling rubber implement, looks up at Giselle's make-up-clad face, and turns to face me one last time. He opens his mouth as if to say something, but the only noise that comes out is a strange high-pitched squeak.

And then he's gone!

Quite literally gone as fast as his feet can carry him.

Giselle and I watch the middle-aged tweed-wearing professor run down the street like a man twenty years his junior, both of us with mouths agape. I've never seen a human being surrender what's left of their dignity quite so fast in my entire life.

* * *

The rest of the night passes with less fuss. I'm glad to say that no one who knows my parents comes into the club, nor my third-grade gym teacher, nor the guy I lost my virginity to. Each one of those would have been as sitcom-worthy as the teacher whose approval I'm desperate to gain, but given that this is what's left of my life, and *not* a sitcom, I'm pretty damn glad that the only people I see for the rest of the night are drunk men and their understanding partners.

My shift ends at 2 a.m. The taxi ride back to my apartment gets me through the front door at 2.20. Precisely eight nanoseconds later I am out of the tight bartender's gear and into a pair of sweatpants and the faded Iron Maiden T-shirt I bought ironically from Camden Market last month. I sit down on the sofa with my laptop, fully intent on a little late-night surfing before bedtime.

I certainly am not expecting to be bombarded with emails from some woman called Cassie McFlasterton telling me I've won a competition to get married.

This must be a joke. A hilarious gag to end what has been a night already full of *endless* comedy.

I read the five emails again, each one more desperate than the last to let me know I'm getting married next week, and that I need to ring this McFlasterton person as soon as possible.

I check my phone, which I have to confess I haven't looked at all day.

Nine missed calls.

If this is a joke, it's an extremely elaborate one.

I read all the emails for a second time, and look at my phone again.

Emails for a third time, phone once more.

It's when I'm reading the fifth and final email for the *fourth* time that the reality of the situation hits home.

I've won a competition to get married to a *complete* stranger, in what can only be described as the ultimate blind date.

Now, I wouldn't have created a profile on Sociality if I wasn't interested in meeting a new guy – but I didn't plan on getting married to him *at the same time.*

So why did you enter the competition, then, you dumb-ass?

I don't have an answer for that. Not a good one, anyway.

If I have a bad habit, it's throwing myself into things without thinking about them properly beforehand – and I have the scars to prove it.

With trembling fingers, I put the laptop on the coffee table, sit back in the sofa, and burst into tears.

It's probably a testament to my fragile, tired state of mind that I don't know if they're tears of happiness, misery – or sheer outright terror.

POST ON THE SOCIALITY BLOG

10 February

It's the wedding you've all been waiting for!

Yes, that's right, the day has finally arrived for our lucky competition winners to tie the knot and start their dream life together!

Everyone here at Sociality – the UK's number-one enhanced dating site – is looking forward to Valentine's Day, when our fantastic couple will say their vows at one of London's most exclusive locations – the New Horizons Hotel, located at the top of the Shard! Not only will they have unparalleled 360-degree views of the capital, they'll also wine and dine the day away on food and drink provided by the hippest French restaurant in town, Le Poulet Pretentieux.

And are the happy couple feeling nervous ahead of their big day?

'A bit, yes,' says Adam, 31, from Croydon, a member of Sociality for over a year. 'But I know the website has done a great job, and I trust that they're putting me with the right girl!'

'I wake up every morning with butterflies in my stomach,' adds Jessica, 29, from Carmel-by-the-Sea in California, a member of Sociality for the past few months. 'The wedding looks like no expense has been spared.'

And indeed it hasn't, Jessica! Sociality founder Cassie McFlasterton knows that this is a very, very special wedding, and has made sure it'll be a day nobody will forget in a hurry!

Over one hundred people have been invited to the ceremony, including specially chosen subscribers from the website, many of London's most up-and-coming young stars of stage, screen and the business world . . . and some of the couple's family and friends.

No matter who they are, though, the guests are sure to thoroughly enjoy the time they spend in the luxurious main restaurant and viewing platform – which is available for all kinds of occasions. Simply contact the hotel at the email address below for more information.

The venue has been exquisitely decorated by famed wedding choreographer Helmut Van Trinkel, in a dazzling combination of white and gold. The table centrepieces alone are enough to take anyone's breath away. Please see www.helmutlove.com for more details of the services he can provide.

And don't worry if you haven't had an invitation; you'll be able to watch the entire ceremony take place right here on the Sociality website, thanks to the live stream that will take in all the wonder and magic of a wonderful Valentine's wedding day. Just make sure your subscription is up to date, and join us right here from 11am on the big day!

ADAM

Q. Do you prefer a suit, or something casual?
A. Am I allowed to go outside in lounge pants?

14 February

A *confits de pomponce*.

What exactly is a *confits de pomponce*?

There appears to be a whole tray of the bloody things in front of me, but I have absolutely no idea what they are. Surely this is a bad sign, isn't it? That on the most important day of my life, I can't even identify the food I'm going to eat?

If I can't get a grip on something as fundamental to continued human existence, how am I supposed to navigate the difficult task of marrying a woman I've known for five days?

I say *known*, but we've only had one brief phone conversation overseen by the staff at Sociality, so I actually know nothing about my intended beyond what's on her dating profile – other than the fact that she's punching so far below her weight she must have arms like Mr. Tickle.

Jessica Madison is pretty in the way only women from an exotic place like California can be. When I first heard where she was from, I formed a mental picture of some blonde, pneumatic beach bunny, and my heart sank. My penis did the opposite, but I tried my best to ignore him, given that he is an idiot.

But Jessica appears to be something very different from the cliché that *Baywatch* tried to sell us through most of the 1990s. She is a natural redhead, rather than a bleach blonde. Her features give her something of a girl-next-door look, and she has the kind of freckles that are considered extremely cute, rather than unsightly.

Judging from the phone call we had, and the way she speaks, there's every chance she's probably at least twenty points above me on the IQ scale.

Jessica told me she joined Sociality because she didn't have time to meet a man any other way. She didn't think for one minute that she'd win this competition.

So that makes two of us, then.

Worryingly, it sounds like she takes being on the dating site a lot more seriously than I ever have. She seems like a girl genuinely looking for a proper, long-term relationship – something that I haven't given any real thought to recently. This only serves to make me even *more* nervous.

Mind you, I got the distinct impression that she's as nervous about this whole enterprise as I am – but is probably the type of person who can handle the pressure a lot better than me.

. . . look at all those 'probablys', 'seems', 'every chances' and 'distinct impressions' in those last few paragraphs, would you? I'm about to marry a woman purely based on guesswork.

How that bloody silly website put us together, I will never know. Jessica appears to be the health-conscious type with a get-up-and-go attitude and a positive outlook on the world that terrifies me slightly. Maybe Sociality's computer sees something in me that I quite clearly don't, as even with the odd embellishment, my profile doesn't appear – on the surface, at least – to be all that compatible with hers.

The people behind it are certainly not telling me how we're a match, I know that for a fact. When I asked the weird human whirlwind that is

Cassie McFlasterton about it, she simply laughed, told me it was down to 'secret algorithms', and changed the subject by asking me what colour suit I wanted to wear on the wedding day.

A wedding day that has arrived far quicker than I would have liked.

Not for the first time this week, I feel the weight of the occasion start to overwhelm me, and so I concentrate once more on the more immediate issue of finding out what a *confits de pomponce* is. This is the kind of challenge I can deal with, and if I can just find an answer, then maybe I'll be able to deal with everything else that's being thrown at me today.

Very shortly, I'm going to be dragged upstairs to the main viewing gallery, where the ceremony will take place, but for now I am being largely left to my own devices here in the reception hall below, standing by a table fairly heaving with bite-sized snacks of all shapes, sizes, smells and colours.

Easily the most wobbly of all are the *confits de pomponce*.

I don't want to eat a *confits de pomponce*, as it looks like a square of dog turd jelly, but I do want to know what goes into one. I may have little to no control over what happens to me today, but I will find out what the hell is in a *confits de pomponce*, if it's the last thing I do as a single man!

Just along the table from where I'm stood is a tall, thin gentleman with a small moustache dressed in a smart grey suit. He is peering at the treats laid out in front of him with a very critical eye. This must be someone in the know.

'Excuse me?' I say to him. He looks up at me with an expression that suggests that while the contents of a *confits de pomponce* might not be a fresh dog turd, the contents of the rented Armani suit standing in front of him most assuredly are.

'Yes? Can I 'elp you?' he replies in a clipped French accent.

'Um. Maybe. What's in a *confits de pomponce*?'

'Pardon?'

'What's in one of these?' I point to the plate of wobbly brown canapés with one uncertain finger.

'You do not *know*?'

'Um, no.'

The man gives me a suspicious look, one that suggests that if I am unable to deduce what the ingredients of a *confits de pomponce* are, then I have absolutely no business being at this wedding.

'Who are you?' he asks me.

'Me?' I say with some surprise. You would have thought that being the groom would at least make you *fairly* recognisable at your own wedding.

'Yes. Who are you 'ere with?'

'Er. Sociality, I suppose. You know . . . the website?'

The look of suspicion turns to barely veiled disgust. 'Ah. You are one of Miss McFlasterton's assistants?'

'Um, nope.'

He leans forward. 'Then *who are you*?'

'I'm . . . I'm Adam,' I squeak. 'I'm getting married today.'

You're supposed to say something like that with nervous excitement. I just sound like I'm being interviewed under caution.

The French man's demeanour changes immediately, but you can tell he's not particularly happy about it. 'Aha! You are Adam 'Olborne, yes?'

'Yes.'

'The man of ze hour!'

'I suppose.'

'It is lovely to meet you, young man!'

'Is it?'

'Of course! My name is Allard Rancourt – owner and 'ead chef of Le Poulet Pretentieux. Here, 'ave a business card.'

From his jacket pocket the man produces his card with a flourish. I take it, not really knowing what I'm going to do with it.

Is it normal to receive business cards at a wedding?

I'm going to guess probably not. But it's *also* not normal to be hiding downstairs while all the fun and games are going on above, trying to find out what goes into a *confits de pomponce*, just because the knowledge will serve as some kind of psychological crutch.

Speaking of which, I point once more at the small brown cubes of jellied something or other.

'So Mr Rancourt, what exactly is in a *confits de pomponce*?'

Rancourt's eyes light up. 'Well, it is an exquisite combination of—'

'Adam! There you are!' a voice cries out from over by the stairs.

No, no! I was about to learn the innermost secrets of the *pomponce*!

The war against my overwhelming fear was about to win its first battle!

Across the restaurant floor and dressed in a bright-red designer suit, Cassie McFlasterton is steaming towards me with a hectic look on her face, which is trying its hardest to peer out from under half an inch of thick make-up.

'There you are! Where have you been?' she hollers, in the tones of one fortunate enough to have been brought up in Chelsea since birth. 'Why on earth are you hiding down here, Adam?'

I point at the *confits de pomponce* by way of explanation. 'Do you know what goes into a *confits de pomponce*, Cassie? It's quite important for me to know . . . for some reason.'

Cassie looks down at the sweetmeat with a look of confusion. 'I have no idea, Adam. Cow balls?'

While Cassie was brought up in the well-to-do end of London, some of her language choices are definitely more East End.

'Actually,' Allard Rancourt pipes up, 'zey are a wonderful amalgamation of duck and pork, lightly seasoned with garlic and rosemary, to provide a captivating taste on ze tongue.'

'It's not jelly, then?' I respond, betraying my thoroughly working-class upbringing.

Allard's face crumples. 'No. It is not *jelly*.'

'To be fair, it does look like jelly,' Cassie says, momentarily forgetting the reason why she's so flustered.

Allard Rancourt manages to not stamp his foot, but only just. 'It is *not jelly*!' he says firmly, fixing us both with a look he'd normally reserve for walk-in customers.

Cassie pokes a *confits de pomponce*. It jiggles a bit. Just like jelly does.

She stares at it for a second, then remembers why she's come to find me, which makes me remember too.

I have to go and get *married*.

In all the *pomponce* excitement I'd forgotten for a second.

What a beautiful second that was, where all I had to worry about in the world was the contents of a light-brown wobbly pork jelly thing. It's gone now, though. Cassie McFlasterton's look of determined panic proves it.

'Come on, Adam! Everybody is waiting for you upstairs. The ceremony is due to begin in about five minutes, and you want to be in place for when your blushing bride walks down the aisle, don't you?'

Oh, by blushing bride, do you mean that American redhead whose middle name I don't even know, Cassie?

'Yes, I suppose so,' I reply, exhibiting far less enthusiasm about my impending marriage than I did about the filling of that bloody *confits de pomponce*.

Now, at this point, you may be asking yourselves a very important question. Namely: *if he's so reluctant to go through with this wedding, then why did the muppet agree to it in the first place?*

This is an extremely *good* question, and one I shall try to answer as succinctly as possible. I will also try my hardest not to sound like the most mercenary scumbag on the planet . . . and I will fail miserably.

I'm doing this for the *money*.

. . . and the penthouse flat in Kensington.

I will now allow you a few moments to tut under your breath at my deplorable cynicism.

Done?

Good.

Now if you'll allow me, I'll explain further, and hopefully bring you round to my way of thinking.

My life to this point has not exactly driven down the road I've wanted it to. In fact, I'm pretty sure I took a left about five years ago when I should have taken a right.

I don't exactly *hate* my job, as much as I hate the fact that it's nowhere near as much fun as I'd hoped it would be. Part of the reason why it's not fun is that it pays *peanuts*. Watlow has seen to that, in his ever-expanding drive to reduce costs and raise profits. I can barely afford to make ends meet these days, so I hope you'll forgive me for thinking that a large cash injection for just getting married to a complete stranger is a very tempting prospect.

I have some very definite plans for that money that'll make a big difference, so I'm more than willing to take a punt with this marriage to get my hands on it.

Also, I'm rather sick of living with a bunch of extremely messy flatmates, so yes, a penthouse in the swanky end of London would go down very nicely, thank you very much.

As I said, though, I am concerned that the soon-to-be Mrs Adam Holborne feels quite differently. There's every chance that she's actually in this for the *romance* – which could be awkward, to say the least. Oh, don't get me wrong, I'd be more than happy to meet a woman and fall in love – but right now, my priorities are definitely more prosaic, down to earth, and mainly involve getting away from large patches of mould and cross-eyed rats.

What gives me some hope, though, is that in our brief phone conversation, Jessica also seemed quite animated about the idea of moving into a Kensington flat and having some cash to spend as well. She even told me thanks to the money we're getting, she was quitting her job at the nightclub where she works to concentrate more on her university course.

So, there's at least *some* common ground there, don't you think?

. . . enough to justify going through with the wedding, certainly.

And let's not forget, Sociality put the two of us together based on the similarities in our profiles, so we must be a good match for one another by and large, even if we're coming at this thing from different angles. Hell, maybe underneath, Jessica is as cynical about it as I am, and is just keeping it to herself.

Yeah, I'm sure that's the case.

She wants that cash and flat as much as I do – I'm *sure of it*.

This all sounds well and good, until you get to the actual wedding day itself.

It may *seem* like a good idea to go through with such a hare-brained scheme for financial gain, but the prospects of views over Hyde Park and a bank balance in the black both get utterly lost in the terror of being dragged to the top of a skyscraper to get hitched to a complete stranger.

'Try to smile, Adam,' Cassie insists as she propels me up the grand staircase. 'This is supposed to be the happiest day of your life.'

'Is it?' I reply in disbelief. 'Nobody told me that.'

Cassie rolls her eyes and tightens her grip on my elbow. 'Stop it. This is going to be *fun*! You and Jess are a perfect match, trust me. This may seem all a little ostentatious, but just go with the flow, try to enjoy yourself, and keep thinking about that honeymoon.'

This is *extremely* good advice.

Cassie McFlasterton is a very persuasive person – that's the first thing you learn when you meet her. She knows just what to say at just the right time. Dangling the carrot of a week in Italy was a well-calculated move.

I try to fix the images of a big pile of cash, a luxury flat, and a *quattro stagioni* with extra olives in my head as we reach the top of the staircase and take in the scene beyond.

Imagine a big glass box three hundred metres in the air, decorated to within an inch of its life with gaudy crap, and crammed full of gormless-looking people dressed in expensive outfits.

At the head of the seated mass of a hundred guests is a white plastic arch festooned with flowers, beneath which stands a young man in a vicar's suit. He's jiggling from one foot to the other.

Poor bloke must be as nervous as I am.

That doesn't bode well. If a man of God thinks this could go badly, then what hope does a godless heathen like me have?

The seated guests are split along traditional lines. What members of my family could be rustled up at such short notice are sat on the left-hand side, and the few relatives that could be flown over from California for Jessica's benefit are sat on the right. Given that Cassie and her team only had a week to arrange the wedding, it's a miracle I've got seven of my family here, and that Jessica has four.

I have banned my hideous flatmates from proceedings, on the grounds that they would have done all they could to embarrass me in front of my new bride in some way. She really doesn't need to know that her future husband enjoys molesting fully grown men dressed as farmyard animals, for instance.

The rest of the audience consists of people I've never met, which is rather disconcerting, to say the least. I'm sure it's very nice for Sociality shareholders to be invited to a nice wedding in the sky, but it doesn't help me much. Nor does the prospect of tying the knot in front of several carefully chosen members of the website's two million subscribers. Not least because with a slight change of computer algorithm, I could be marrying one of them today, instead of a redheaded American woman.

Cassie also reliably informed me earlier that there were several reality TV stars in the audience as well. As I have an intellect larger than a shaved chimp's, I have never watched any of the shows these people have been in, and so could not pick them out of a line-up if you held a gun to my head.

I can only assume that the few heavily tanned people dotted around the audience must be the 'stars' in question. There's one particular woman sat near the back whose fake breasts are trying their hardest to escape from the bright-green sequined dress she's almost wearing. The vapid expression on her face indicates that she is no stranger to a public phone vote.

Beyond the audience of people I either deeply care about or have never met are the press. They are the main source of my nerves about today's proceedings. It's one thing to get married to a complete stranger in a lavish wedding that wouldn't look out of place on a particularly expensive episode of *Hollyoaks*, it's another to do so in front of the bloody *media*. I'm a journalist myself, so have an intimate knowledge of what a bunch of wankers they are. I'm about to go through one of the most important events in a person's life, and all of it will be watched by a group of individuals who are *desperate* for something awful to happen – preferably to either the bride or the groom.

I'm one of those people with a tendency to become a self-fulfilling prophecy at the drop of a bloody hat. If people are waiting for me to screw up, then there's every chance I will do it for them, in *spectacular* fashion.

I spot several video cameras dotted around the big glass box, and remember that this whole thing is also being streamed across the Internet.

You know . . . that thing accessible to *millions* of people, across our *entire* planet? Where videos of people embarrassing themselves at weddings can become viral sensations on YouTube in a matter of days?

Urgh.

'Adam?' I hear Cassie say from about a thousand miles away. 'You've stopped moving, Adam. Come on, we're nearly there.'

No. I'll just stay here, thanks. If I concentrate really hard, I think I can fuse my feet into the soft cream carpet, and live out the rest of my life as a very realistic statue at the top of the Shard. They can charge people to come over and give me a slap, if they like.

Cassie McFlasterton is surprisingly strong for a five-foot-four-inch woman in her mid-thirties. Every fibre of my being wants to stay rooted to the spot, but every fibre of hers wants me down that bloody aisle and waiting on my marks. She obviously gets more fibre in her diet than I do, because I find myself dragged once more inexorably towards my very public executio – sorry, *marriage*.

As we get to the head of the aisle, I have time to give my mother a look of sheer terror. Mum apparently misinterprets this expression for one of happy excitement, as she waves at me enthusiastically, and blows me a kiss.

My father smirks.

Nothing else. Just a small smirk that seems to say *Hah! Now you get it, don't you, son?*

Yes, Dad. Now I do get it . . . and thanks for the bloody warning.

My exposure to the concept of marriage, like most single people, comes from my parents' relationship. They've always seemed quite happy together, as far as I could tell.

I grew up with a vague sense that one day marriage might happen to me, but never really gave it that much thought – until now.

They both seemed equally happy when I told them I was getting married. Mum even called it *quite romantic*. Dad immediately asked me what I was getting out of it, so I guess my father knows me better than my mother.

Hence the smirk. He knows I am completely unprepared for what I'm about to do.

I return the smirk with a dark look that he instantly understands.

My father rarely laughs.

I'd like to say it's a lovely thing to see, but I'd be lying.

'And here we are then,' Cassie remarks with some relief, as she parks me in front of the floral arch.

There's no best man waiting for me here. In the short time available to choose one, I just couldn't think of a friend who I was close enough to. My best mate, Max, moved to Australia two years ago, and I certainly don't want someone like Calvin or Paul handing the wedding ring over. Thankfully, and rather predictably, the mighty Miss McFlasterton has stepped into the breach, and will act as my best woman. I would have objected, but it was either her or my old man, and I just couldn't stand to see that smirk too up close as I wave my single life goodbye.

'Good morning, Julian,' Cassie says to the twitchy priest. 'Lovely day for it.'

Julian the priest's eyes bulge. 'Hmmmm? What now?' he replies, sniffing loudly.

Cassie's eyes narrow. 'I said, it's a lovely day for the wedding.'

Julian scratches at his neck. 'Yeah, yeah, yeah. Lovely day, isn't it? Isn't it?' He throws his arms open. 'I mean, just look at the light in here! Isn't it fabulous? It's really fabulous!' He fixes me with a stare I'd usually expect from next door's slightly insane cat. 'God's work, you know! The sun is in the heavens! Glorious! Glorious!'

It appears what I'd taken to be nerves was actually boundless enthusiasm. This Julian seems *very* keen.

'Are you feeling alright, Julian?' Cassie asks him in a worried tone.

'I'm fine, Cassandra! Just full of the joys of this very special occasion!' Julian the priest sniffs loudly again as he says this, setting off alarm bells in my head.

The last time I was around somebody in this kind of mood was at the GamesReport Christmas party. Watlow had invited several PR execs from a variety of video game publishers, one of whom was a six-foot-seven hipster called Pedro, who disappeared off to the toilets every half an hour or so, to return a few minutes later about 100 per cent more animated than when he went in. A couple of times he even came back with a light dusting of powder under one nostril, giving the game away completely.

But the same thing could not apply to our good friend Julian here, could it? A man of God such as he would not indulge in recreational drug abuse, surely?

I pull Cassie over, as Julian suddenly finds himself fascinated with the texture of his jacket.

'Er, is he alright?' I ask.

'Yes, yes, he's fine. I think. Why do you ask?'

'Well, to be honest, he looks and sounds like he's as high as a kite.'

Cassie offers me a blank expression. 'Does he?'

'Yes. I've worked around pretentious people in London long enough to recognise the symptoms.'

Being one of those pretentious people herself, Cassie is well aware of what I'm getting at. I'm sure she's no stranger to *those kinds of parties*, held in *those kinds of apartments*, featuring *those kinds of people*.

'But, but he's a man of God,' she replies in a horrified voice, looking over her shoulder at Julian, who is now wiping his nose with one sleeve of his immaculate shiny black priest jacket, while the other hand is twitching down by his side, holding a rather threadbare-looking Bible.

My eyes narrow. 'And where exactly did you find this guy?'

'He came highly recommended.'

'Who by?'

'One of my best friends – Jacquelina Ravensbrooke.'

This is the single most London socialite name I've ever had the misfortune to hear. I very much doubt Jacquelina Ravensbrooke knows anyone who doesn't have a cocaine dealer on her speed dial – up to and including her parents. I say as much to Cassie.

'Oh God,' she moans, realisation dawning. 'What the hell do we do?'

'Well, unless you have a spare vicar in the audience, we'll either have to put up with Jim Morrison's religious cousin over here . . . or call the whole thing off.'

Cassie provides me with a smile that barely touches her eyes. 'I'm sure he'll be fine, Adam,' she says in a feverish tone of voice. 'All he has to do is read a few passages, and pronounce you man and wife.'

'Yes, you might be right,' I say, not believing a word of it.

But it's too bloody late to do anything about it now, isn't it?

The audience is assembled, the groom is in his place, the press have their cameras and notebooks on standby. It's time to get this show on the road – drug-addled priest or no drug-addled priest.

Cassie looks at her hideous diamond watch. 'Right, it's just about to hit eleven thirty. That's when it starts.'

I know she's talking about the wedding, but to me it sounds like she's predicting the onset of a major battle.

I look up at the rather ostentatious clock set deep into one of the granite pillars holding up all this heavy plate glass, and see the minute hand move slowly round to the number six. The instant it does, the wedding march begins.

And not a subtle version of it either. No string quartet for this wedding, *oh no*.

Instead of a classically arranged rendition of the famous theme, we get one done on electric guitar. It's catastrophically awful in every respect. Tonally out of place, barely in tune, and turned up so loud I have to consciously stop myself from wincing.

This is what happens when you let someone like Cassie plan your wedding. She may be able to run her own online dating business with remarkable success, but planning a wedding is a different thing entirely. It's a project that requires a degree of subtlety, and an empathy for the occasion; something best left to the type of person who doesn't believe her jewellery should be visible from outer space.

I stare at Cassie and see a look of delight cross her face. It's like the taste centres of her brain were malformed at birth, and nobody thought to recommend treatment.

From the selfsame staircase that Cassie just dragged me up appear the heads of two girls of about ten years old in stylish, light-blue dresses. These are Jessica's bridesmaids. Neither of whom she had met until today. From what I understand, both were hired from one of the more salubrious modelling agencies in town. As such, they both look very pretty, but then that's kind of what you'd expect when you're paying a hefty sum for their presence, isn't it?

The two girls elegantly reach the top of the stairs and start sauntering down the aisle as if it were a catwalk – which I'm sure somebody told them to pretend it is.

Behind them I see an old man's head appear over the last tread of the staircase. I've never met this man before, but I make the logical assumption that this is Charlie, Jessica's father – flown all the way out here from California to give his baby daughter away to some idiot who gets into fights with ballistic sheep. He must be so *proud*.

And then my heart starts to trip the light fantastic, as my soon-to-be wife has appeared in my field of vision for the first time.

Now, if you're going to look at a woman for the first time ever, you can't get much better than seeing her in a wedding dress that cost several thousand pounds, and the kind of make-up job that requires a team of experts to pull off.

Jessica Madison is *stunning*.

She also looks like someone's holding a gun to her head.

Her shimmering red hair is being held up in a feat of cranial engineering that must be beyond the wit of normal man to understand. There's even a rather large tiara parked up there, in apparent defiance of the laws of physics. The thin wedding veil falls gracefully over her shoulders, framing her head and neck wonderfully, and the strapless dress itself is a masterpiece of understated beauty.

I can only assume that Cassie had nothing to do with choosing it, otherwise I'd probably be watching Jessica being consumed by a giant glittering marshmallow right about now.

As it is, she looks every inch the beautiful bride.

. . . aside from the fact that she still looks like someone's about to pull the trigger.

'Doesn't she look *amazing*?' Cassie says breathlessly from my side.

'Yes, yes she does.'

She also looks like a *complete stranger*.

Still, I've got at least another thirty seconds or so to familiarise myself with her face as she walks slowly down the aisle, one arm laced in her father's.

If Jessica looks like she's about to go in front of the firing squad, her father looks like he's already been there, but they all missed. There's a look of worried disbelief on his face that paints a rather concerning picture.

Neither he nor Madison looks like they are particularly enjoying themselves, it has to be said.

In an attempt to make them feel better, I offer a little wave and a smile. I try to make the gesture light and breezy, but given that I'm as terrified as Jessica is, I probably look more like the Joker just before he pulls out his favourite flick knife and goes for an eyeball.

Jessica looks at me and gulps.

Yep, that's what you want from the woman who's about to take your name – a nervous gulp. Nothing says a happy future together like trying to hold down a load of terrified vomit.

The hideous guitar-based wedding march reaches a crescendo as Jessica and her father arrive at the archway. The two accompanying underage catwalk models strike pretentious poses for a moment, before sauntering off to one side, their cheekbones leading the way like the prows of a ship.

I again try to offer Jessica a cheery smile as she gets close to me. Now the Joker has moved on from the flick knife and has got out the blowtorch.

'Hello,' my soon-to-be wife says to me in a quivering voice. 'How's it going?'

'Um. Fine, thanks,' I reply, trying to think of something constructive to say. 'I found out what a *confits de pomponce* was just a minute ago.'

Jessica's brow wrinkles.

'It's wobbly brown pork,' I finish, unnecessarily.

The wedding march mercifully ends, leaving the big glass room to fall silent, apart from my jackhammering heart.

You'd expect a 'dearly beloved' right about now from good old Julian, wouldn't you? And you'd probably get it, from a priest who wasn't high on cocaine.

'Howdy, folks!' he screams, in what can only be described as the worst American accent in history.

This is met with some titters from the less easily shocked in the crowd, but mostly with stunned silence from everyone else.

'I said *howdy, folks!*'

Oh good Lord, he's not taking no for an answer here, is he?

Obviously our good friend Julian knows that the bride is of colonial extraction and wants to make her feel at home.

This time there's a few desultory 'howdys' from the assembled onlookers. It's the best response he's going to get at short notice.

'How nice it is to see you all in this lovely, panoramic place!' Julian continues, this time thankfully in his own accent. 'It truly is wonderful to be this high up!'

I have to stifle a laugh. Cassie elbows me in the ribs.

'Are we all having a good time!?' Julian shouts, as if he's about to embark on an opening number at the O2, rather than officiate the marriage of two people caught in the crossfire.

Julian receives acknowledgement only from the members of the audience who have managed to find themselves a drink at this time in the morning.

'We're gathered here today for something very special!' Julian continues, sniffing as he does so. 'Yes indeed, it's very, *very* special! The most special thing of all. More special than anything else I can think of. And you're all special people for being here with us, at this special time. And just look at this lovely venue! It's almost as if we could reach out and touch the Lord himself.' There are actual tears forming at the corners of Julian's eyes. 'It just all feels so . . . so . . .'

I'm not 100 per cent sure, but I'm willing to take a guess that the next word out of his mouth is going to be *special*.

'. . . wonderful,' he finishes, throwing his arms open wide.

Bastard.

I look over at Jessica, who is still stood in front of the priest with her father. Both of them are staring at the mad bugger with exactly the same look of blank incomprehension. Obviously they don't get many coke fiends hanging around the streets of their Californian hometown.

'Bring them together,' Cassie hisses at Julian.

'Hmmmm?' he replies.

'Bring them together in front of you and get on with it!' she continues, her eyes bulging in barely concealed rage. Cassie is not one for having things go *off book*, that much is certain.

'Oh right. Yes,' Julian says, getting a proper look at the woman's face for the first time. I doubt he'd describe it as *special*.

'If the bride and groom would stand before me, I'll get this show on the road.'

Not the conventional way of ordering the happy couple into position I'm sure, but at least he's getting to the point.

Jessica and I shuffle over to stand in front of Julian. Jessica's father retreats with a grateful look on his face.

'Children!' Julian nearly screams. 'You are children of God, are you not?'

He seems to be addressing this to Jessica and me. I'm agnostic, but at this point I feel it's probably better not to push the issue.

'Yes?' I reply uncertainly. Jessica does the same, slightly more sure of herself.

'Good stuff!' Julian gives us a thumbs up. 'As children of God you have come here today to do something very special.'

Oh God, here we go again.

'The most special thing two people can do together . . . at least in public, eh?' Julian waggles his eyebrows.

This is *cringeworthy*.

Most people just get very talkative on cocaine. This idiot seems to think he's a stand-up comedian.

'You have come together today in the presence of God, to give yourselves to one another, as no other two people can give themselves to anybody else in this way.'

That made *no* sense, right? I'm not going mad here, am I?

'You will love, cherish and adore each other, as no two people can love, cherish and adore themselves in the presence of God, man or both.'

What?

'It's that love that will hold you together, in the place, and in other places, where you are yourselves together, with God, and alone, and with others. But those others will not cherish each of you, as you cherish each other's love yourselves.'

I think he's still speaking English, but I could be wrong.

'You must trust in God yourselves, as you trust in each other's trust. For love from each other is as much as love from God himself, to yourselves, and others.'

This is going *wonderfully*, don't you think?

'And now, you must vocalise your love and trust to one another yourselves, to all those gathered here, and God as well, himself.'

Julian gives us both an expectant look.

'What?' I ask. 'Are we supposed to say something?'

Jessica leans towards me. 'Does this make any sense to you?'

I know she means Julian's sermon, but she could just as easily be talking about this entire wedding.

'Not a word of it.'

Jessica looks a little relieved. 'Thank God for that, I thought I was losing it.'

'Well? Can you?' Julian asks us both.

'Can we what?' Jessica replies.

'Give yourselves to love, and to each other, by saying to those assembled that you cherish and love yourselves, one another . . . and God.'

'Er . . . yes?' Jessica hazards. She sees me looking at her with a dumb expression on my face, and nods once.

'Yes!' I repeat.

Julian leans in. 'Yes, what?'

'Yes, *sir?*'

The coked-up priest shakes his head. 'No. No. Say that you will love and cherish one another under God.'

This throws up the unpleasant image of being pinned to the floor by an angry deity.

'We will love . . . and . . . cherish each other . . . under God.' Jessica and I both fumble our way through it somehow.

'Louder!' Julian barks.

'We will love and cherish each other under God!'

'Louder! Louder! So that all here may witness, and so that God himself will be forced to sit up and take notice!' Julian exultantly throws his arms skyward.

'WE WILL LOVE AND CHERISH EACH OTHER UNDER GOD,' I scream at the top of my lungs. Jessica tries her hardest as well, but I get the feeling she's worried about dislodging that tiara.

'Oh God! Oh merciful God! These truly are your children!' Julian trumpets to the heavens. He then looks down and fixes Jessica's father, Charlie, with a bloodshot stare. 'Who gives this woman away this day?'

'I do,' Charlie tells him, leaning slightly away from the maniacal holy man's steely gaze.

'Excellent!' Julian says, shaking one triumphant fist. 'And who has the rings?'

'I've got the bloody rings,' Cassie says half under her breath, fishing the things out from her clutch bag and thrusting them at me. You can tell she wants this whole thing over and done with as quickly as possible, before Julian bursts a blood vessel.

'Amazing!' Julian cries. He points a finger at me. 'Face your bride!'

I do as I'm told. This is all moving so fast now I can barely keep up, but at least it's going to be over and done with as swiftly as possible.

Julian's finger stabs at Jessica. 'Face your groom!' he orders.

This gives me the first real chance I've had to get a proper, close-up look at my very soon-to-be wife.

The tiara's a bit skew-whiff, and she hasn't really lost that look of someone who's got a gun barrel to her head, but other than that, this is an *exceptionally* pretty woman I'm about to marry.

Julian has started another rant about how we should cherish something or other in the face of God, but I choose to ignore him in favour of concentrating for the first time on the whole point of this ridiculous ceremony.

'How do you feel?' I ask Jessica quietly. We're standing close together enough for her to hear me even over Julian's nonsensical ramblings.

'Like I've been hit over the head with something hard and unpleasant,' she replies, but with a slight smile.

'Look,' I continue, 'just do what I'm doing . . . picture yourself drinking an espresso on the balcony of our lovely new apartment in a couple of days . . . when all of this has gone away.'

The smile widens. 'Okay. That sounds good.' Her brow wrinkles. 'Mainly because it sounds *normal*.'

I smile too. 'It does, doesn't it?'

Her face crumples a bit. 'This wasn't how I wanted my wedding day to be, you know.'

'Nor mine.' I swallow hard. 'Not that I've ever thought about it much, to be honest with you. But, if it's any consolation, you look absolutely beautiful in that dress. And once this is all over and done with – and is a distant memory – the pictures will still look fabulous.'

Her smile returns.

Hard to believe, I know, but even in such an awkward, bizarre setting, I am just about managing to come across as *charming*. It's a moment I will cherish. Myself, under God and in other places.

Sadly, I am brought back into the room by the simple expedient of having a twitchy priest smack me on top of the head with a Bible.

'Ow! What did you do that for?' I complain.

'I said you must now hold out the ring, Alan!'

I shake my head in disbelief. 'My name is *Adam*.'

'Hold up the ring!' Julian demands. 'You!' he says, addressing Jessica. 'Please hold out your hand!'

Jessica does so.

Here we go then. The moment of truth.

'Do you, Alan—'

'Adam.'

'Do you, *Adam*, take this woman . . .'

There's a pregnant pause.

'Jessica,' Jessica hisses under her breath.

Julian looks flummoxed. 'Is it? I thought it was Eileen?'

'No, definitely *Jessica.*'

Julian shrugs. 'Oh well, whatever you say.' He composes himself. 'Do you, Alan—'

'Adam!!'

'Do you, *Adam*, take this woman, Jessica, to be your wife?'

I take a deep breath. 'I do.'

'Goody goody gumdrops,' Julian says with a broad grin. 'And do you Eile – sorry, *Jessica*, take Al—'

'Adam!'

'Al . . . Adam, to be your husband?'

'I do,' Jessica tells him – which is lovely, although there's every chance she's just agreed to be married to a man called Aladdin.

'Goody goody *goody* gumdrops!' Julian exclaims, and then talks over our heads. 'It gives me the greatest of pleasure, in the sight of being under God, with all of ourselves here gathered, in love and much cherishment . . .'

That's not even a fucking *word.*

'. . . to now pronounce these two wonderful people husband and wife!'

The crowd erupts into spontaneous applause. Less because we're now married, and more because it means this farce is over at last.

I've never been starved of oxygen before, but I'm pretty sure I know what it feels like right at this moment.

I'm married.

I'm fucking *married.*

Julian whacks me on the shoulder with the Bible. 'I said, *you may now kiss the bride.*'

Kiss?

Bride?

Oh crap.

The last time I felt this unsure about kissing a girl, I was seven, she was six, and we'd just eaten an entire bag of Jelly Babies between us.

Jessica fixes me with an intent look. 'Espresso on the balcony, remember?' she says quietly.

It's exactly the right thing to say.

I lean forward, as does she, and I plant a short but gentle kiss on her lips. It's brief, it's perfunctory, but it gets the job done.

Who ever said romance is dead, eh?

Skip forward forty-eight hours, and welcome to the balcony of my dreams.

It's large, airy, does indeed overlook Hyde Park, and even on a cool February morning like this one, it's lovely and warm up here, thanks to the perfect suntrap created by the bi-fold patio doors and white granite paving stones.

There are no cross-eyed rats or patches of hairy mould.

The past two days have been chock-a-block with Cassie McFlasterton–arranged publicity opportunities, so this is the first chance Jessica and I have really had to just hang out with one another. I've not had time to ask her how she's feeling about the whole thing, but I'll assume from the content expression on her face that she's feeling much the same way I am – relieved, and looking forward to reaping the full benefits of this glorious new pad.

I pick up my espresso cup and take a long, slow sniff of the glorious black liquid contained within.

Across from me, my new wife, Jessica, does the same thing.

'You were absolutely right, Adam,' she says, looking particularly radiant in her new soft, fluffy white dressing gown. 'This does make it all worth it.'

I close my eyes. 'Yeah,' I agree. 'Even what happened at the reception with the *confits de pomponce*.'

Jessica looks momentarily aghast. 'I'm sure they managed to clean it all up okay.'

'Yes . . . I'm sure they did.' I take another deep whiff of the coffee. Nothing is going to break my good mood this morning.

Nothing. *At. All.*

No, on this day, Adam Holborne is at peace.

He does not know what this marriage will bring. He does not even know what this *day* will bring. But he does know that *right now* he is about to take a sip of coffee made in a machine that he couldn't otherwise afford on a month's salary – and that is *a very good thing indeed.*

The crisp sun bathes my face in its warmth as I bring the cup to my lips. This will be wonderful, this will be exquisite, this will be—

Slurrrrrrrp.

What the hell's that?!

My eyes flick open. They fully expect to see that a walrus has inexplicably appeared on the balcony in front of us.

Slurrrrrrrp.

It's Jessica.

My new wife, Jessica.

She drinks coffee like a regurgitating hippo.

Jessica catches my eye. 'Everything alright, Adam?'

It's nothing, really.

Just a silly little thing that I'm sure I'll get used to.

Not a problem *at all*.

Slurrrrrrrp.

. . . oh God.

JESS

Q. What's your ideal holiday destination?
A. Anywhere beautiful, warm & not too crowded!

24 February

The spoonful of ice cream pauses in front of my mouth. 'He's right behind me, isn't he?'

Adam looks over my shoulder. 'Yep.'

'With that damn camera.'

'Yep.'

'And any second now, just as I'm putting this ice cream in my mouth, he's going to take a picture, isn't he?'

'Probably.'

'And that picture of me stuffing my face with chocolate ice cream will be up on the website in a matter of hours, won't it?'

'That's been par for the course on this honeymoon so far.'

I drop the spoon back into the bowl. 'This isn't a honeymoon, Adam. It's an extended photoshoot,' I say to my husband with disgust.

Husband! I have a husband! Aargh!

I turn around to give Derek a long, hard stare. 'Derek? Can you come here, please?'

'Sure, Jessica. What's the problem?'

'Well, I hate to say it, Derek, but you're the problem.'

He scratches his ample belly and gives me a confused look. 'Why's that?'

'Look, I know Cassie said capture us in a natural setting as much as possible, but do you have to do it every second of the day? Can't we have a little privacy, *please*?' I gesture down at my bowl of melting Italian gelato. 'I really want to enjoy this, but I can't if I know you're looming over my shoulder all the time.'

Derek contrives to look hurt.

'I'm only doing my job, Jessica,' he says.

'Yeah, I know you are, Derek. But you've been doing your job really, *really* well now for three days straight, and it's starting to make my teeth itch.'

Derek nods a couple of times. 'So, you'd probably like me to go away for a while, then?'

I give him a conciliatory smile. 'That would be *wonderful*, Derek.'

'I'll have to come back in an hour, though. Cassie wants lots of shots of you taking the boat tour around the lake.'

I sigh. Of course she does. 'That's fine, Derek. We'll see you down at the jetty at two o'clock.'

This seems to be good enough. 'Fair play. I'll leave you both in peace.'

And with that, Derek and his intrusive camera walk out of sight. My blood pressure lowers slightly with every step he takes.

'Well done,' Adam says. 'You handled that much better than I would have.'

'Yep,' I agree. 'I didn't swear at him, if that's what you mean.'

Adam looks at me reproachfully. 'The guy was trying to take a picture of me changing into my swimming trunks.'

'I know. What was it you called him again?'

'A nosy pillock.'

'You called him a nosy fish?'

'That's a pollack.'

'Whatever.'

Some British idioms really have passed me by.

As have the last few days, in a whirlwind of camera flashes, life-changing events, and semi-awkward conversations with the man I agreed to marry what feels like five minutes ago.

The wedding night itself was probably the most awkward of all those chats. Everything was fine while we were in the company of other people, but once Adam had carried me over the threshold of our fabulous new apartment (with Derek the cameraman, Cassie McFlasterton and several journalists watching our every move) and shut the door behind us, the atmosphere understandably *changed*.

This is usually the time when a newly married couple make straight for the bedroom, leaving a trail of clothes across the floor as they go, but Adam and I instead spent twenty minutes exploring our new home, making polite comments to each other about how nice the tiles were in the bathroom, and how well the curtains in the lounge matched the sofa. It was like a late-night episode of *Location, Location, Location*. We even stood in the open-plan kitchen for five minutes guessing how much the apartment was worth, before Adam *shook my hand*, and made off for the spare bedroom as fast as his newly married legs could carry him. It was more like he was concluding a pleasant business transaction than saying goodnight to his new wife.

I found this extraordinarily *frustrating*. Okay, I wasn't expecting any bedroom antics – we had only known each other a few hours – but it would have been nice just to sit and chat for a while on the incredibly comfortable couch. We need to get to know each other, and that's not going to happen if Adam hides in his bedroom out of some misplaced bashfulness.

Mind you, it's not like I tried to coax him out, so maybe he's not the only one feeling a little reticent to get this marriage underway properly.

This pattern repeated itself over the next week.

We are two people thrust into a situation usually reserved for couples who know each other intimately. This leaves us tentatively trying to negotiate each other without causing offence or embarrassment.

Throw Derek and his long lens into the equation and you can probably guess my general state of mind, right about now.

Still, I can't complain too much. Lake Garda is easily the most beautiful place I've ever visited – staged honeymoon or not.

Okay, it's not exactly warm here, as it's only the end of February.

To be honest, there's a small voice inside me that thinks it would have been more appropriate for Cassie to send us somewhere tropical and far away for our honeymoon. I guess after spending what must have been tens of thousands on the wedding itself, she was probably trying to save a little cash by sending us somewhere closer to home in the off season.

We've been lucky, though, as the weather looks like it's going to be clear and sunny the entire time we're here.

The small town where we're staying is called Sirmione.

It sits at the end of a long, thin promontory that juts out into the lake at its south end. The farther along the slim stretch of land you go, the older and more quaint the buildings become. By the time you reach the centre of Sirmione's old town itself, you would feel transported back about three hundred years – were it not for the hardy off-season tourists, expensive restaurants and gelato bars.

I am completely enraptured by all these old cobbled streets and terracotta-tiled buildings.

There's even a *castle* here. I think I took about seven thousand pictures of the castle, every one of which I will show to my family the next time I go home – and they'll love every second of it too.

Adam's British, so spent most of the time wandering around the castle complaining it wasn't as cool as the ones he's had sat on his doorstep all his life, but I tried to ignore him as best I could. To me it was a thing of wonder.

Tomorrow we're supposed to be walking up to see the ruins of a Roman fort that's 1,500 years old. I'm not sure my brain will be able to cope.

Even the hotel we're staying in was up and running before my hometown of Carmel was founded. Called the Hotel Internazionale, it's perched right at the back of town with amazing views over the lake, and an infinity pool I may try to smuggle back home in my suitcase. It's absolutely the *perfect* romantic retreat, with a honeymoon suite so opulent I can well believe that Brad and Angelina once stayed here – which is what the bellboy told me the other day.

It's therefore a huge shame that I feel about as romantic as the star of your average porn movie.

Not Adam's fault in the least, you understand. He's a good guy, from what I can tell by the week I've spent with him, but he could quite frankly be George Clooney's younger, more emotionally available cousin and I'd still be struggling to feel anything other than anxious all the time.

Perhaps it's Derek and his camera, perhaps it's the whole weird, contrived situation I find myself in, but I'm just not able to relax and go with the flow.

Adam doesn't seem to be having the same kind of trouble, but then he's a man, and men are simple creatures. I think he relaxed into the honeymoon the second he took a bite out of his first pizza. He was *definitely* relaxed the moment he finished his first Italian beer.

Me, though?

Yeah, not so much. I tried to down half a bottle of limoncello yesterday afternoon, but it just gave me a headache, and I had to go lie down in a dark room for an hour before dinner. I don't quite know what else I was expecting. The sugar content of that stuff would be enough to send a whole schoolyard of ten-year-olds off into an apocalyptic frenzy.

Cassie keeps telling me to enjoy myself, but as she's the one mainly responsible for my agitated state, her advice is falling on deaf ears.

Yes, that's right. Cassie McFlasterton is here too.

Now can you understand why I'm on edge?

If there's one thing I've come to understand about the head of Sociality, it's that she is a control freak of such magnitude, I'm amazed she hasn't tried to overthrow the British government. This became apparent in the short run-up to the wedding, and is only being reinforced by her presence here in Italy – organising our days and nights to maximise marketing potential for her website.

She *lurks*.

There I'll be, attempting to enjoy the heated infinity pool and mojito I've just been served, when out of the corner of my eye I'll notice her, sitting in what I'm sure she considers to be an unobtrusive manner, down by the bar at one of the patio tables. Wearing a big floppy hat and massive sunglasses, she'll be bent over her iPad, no doubt planning what other exciting and prescribed entertainment she can get Derek to photograph Adam and me doing next. It's very, *very* disconcerting.

In fact, if I look past Adam's shoulder right now, I can see her, sat at another one of the dining tables that line the broad expanse of the hotel's main veranda, that damn iPad in her hand again. She looks angry, which makes me more than a little worried.

I say as much to Adam, who cranes his head around.

'Oh, for crying out loud,' he says in an exasperated tone. 'Why did she even bother marrying the two of us? She should have just hired a couple of actors and faked the whole bloody thing.'

Which is a very astute observation, I think you'll agree.

Adam is *smart*. Smarter than he gives himself credit for. This is one of the things I've decided I like about him most. He has a way with words that I admire, and a turn of phrase I can't help but be impressed by.

I've watched too many Richard Curtis romantic comedies, that's my problem.

He's also quite handsome, especially when he smiles. In the past, I've always gone for the classic blond Californian look – very much a case of style over substance. To find myself with a dark-haired Brit whose smile is as intelligent as it is warm makes a rather refreshing change. I can be sure of a decent conversation with Adam, something that I've struggled with in the past with some of my boyfriends – most of whom would probably panic if they had an original thought.

I'm less enamoured with other aspects of Adam's personality, though. He's a born cynic, which can get tiring. He swears a little *too* much for a girl brought up in a Christian household, and has a few OCD tendencies that are going to take some getting used to.

Okay, I don't *instantly* put my dirty dishes into the dishwasher when I'm done with them, and I have no problem leaving the TV on even when I'm not actually watching it.

If we're going to be man and wife for any length of time, these are the kind of things both of us are going to have to get used to, I guess.

Besides, Sociality put us together, didn't they? Out of all those subscribers it was *us* their algorithms chose to be the most compatible couple, thanks to our respective profiles.

Okay, I filled mine in one evening last October, fuelled by a combination of cheap prosecco and the bleary-eyed optimism alcohol always imbues me with, but we'll just try our best to ignore that fact . . . because would you *just look at that view?*

Adam told me that he filled out his profile in about five minutes while he was sat on the toilet, but we'll try to ignore that as well . . . because *just how good does this chocolate gelato taste?*

Okay, I know. I'm deflecting. You don't need to beat me over the head with it.

. . . but I agreed to go through with the wedding, didn't I? I just have to accept that the situation is probably less than perfect, and play the hand I'm dealt.

I'm prepared to do this, because at heart I am an eternal *optimist*. This is why I always vote Democrat, and keep going back to see movies starring Ben Stiller. They've got to get better at some point, haven't they?

I genuinely jumped into this surreal agreement hoping that something real might blossom from it. It's a risky move, but then I was the only girl brave enough to have a go on Tyler Woodrow's rope swing back home, about seven thousand years ago – the one across the rockiest part of the river that had earned itself the nickname 'Bonebreaker'.

Okay, I did manage to fall in the water, and only narrowly avoid severe head trauma while doing so – but I was the only girl brave enough to have a go. It earned me Tyler's respect, and a kiss on my cold, wet cheek for my troubles.

I've never been risk-averse when it comes to romance, even when there's clear and present danger lurking just underneath the water.

There are a lot of other positives to this marriage as well, don't get me wrong. I have a much larger, nicer place to live, and I've been able to quit work at Sister Stocking's, so I can concentrate on making Professor Hibbersley proud of my understanding of phytoprotectants. Whatever this marriage throws at me, it's got to be better than wiping up another pool of oral effluence created by Captain Dribbles.

Okay, there's not a lot of romance going on right now between Adam and me, but hopefully it will grow organically as time goes by.

It just needs to be cultivated properly.

Like a nice red rose bush.

Or a fungus.

'What bullshit do you think she's cooking up for us now?' Adam asks me, taking a bite of millionaire cheesecake. The only time you ever eat rich gelato and cheesecake at lunchtime is when you're on holiday. This is some kind of rule that can never be broken, for fear of civilisation descending into chaos.

'It can't be any worse than the guided tour of the olive oil factory,' I reply.

We did that the first day we were here. No sooner had I dropped my suitcase on my bed (a single, in case you were wondering. You should have seen the look on the concierge's face when Adam told him we wanted the enormous double divan bed in the honeymoon suite split into two) than we were whisked off to our first photo opportunity – touring the antiquated olive oil factory with Derek in tow, snapping gleefully away as we tried to look impressed by the three-hundred-year-old wooden olive press. I tried to show as much willingness as I could, even telling the ancient tour guide that olives are a great source of nutrition. He looked at me suspiciously for a moment, before walking away in an Italian huff. I still have no idea why.

The pictures of that trip were up on the Sociality blog within the hour. I look like I'm deeply distressed at all the suffering those poor olives must endure on their way to the bottle, and Adam couldn't look more bored if he was looking at a wet painting of a three-hundred-year-old wooden olive press, waiting for it to dry.

'What about the "spontaneous" stroll through the cypress garden she made us do yesterday?' Adam reminds me.

I make a face. 'Oh yeah, that was *wonderful*. What with Derek climbing every tree in sight to get a better angle, and those poor locals that Cassie shouted at when they walked into the shot.'

'At some point before we leave,' Adam continues, pulling absently on one earlobe, 'I entirely expect pictures of me taking my morning shit to be posted on the Internet. Derek will probably want you in there with me, cleaning your teeth, just to show everyone how close we've become in only a few days of blissful marriage.'

I rub my eyes. 'I would laugh, but I'm afraid you might actually be on to something,' I say, looking past him again to see that Cassie is now banging one fist on the table and shaking her head. The tour of the oldest pizza factory in Italy must be proving harder to organise than she expected.

'I hope nothing's gone wrong with the speedboat ride this afternoon,' Adam says. 'I'm actually quite looking forward to that.'

I glance at my watch. 'It's only an hour away. If that were a problem, she'd probably be throwing the iPad in the lake and punching the nearest waiter.'

Adam laughs and looks at the time on his phone. 'What do you fancy doing while we wait for it?'

My eyes light up. 'Can we go back down to the castle?'

'*Again?*'

'Yeah!' I'm far too excited about a pile of old bricks, I know this for a fact, but the American tourist in me is never far from the surface at the moment.

Adam rolls his eyes, but then smiles warmly. 'You know, when we get home, I'm going to show you some *proper* castles, with *proper* battlements, and *proper* drawbridges.'

A hugely pleasant image enters my mind. In it, Adam is leading me by the hand across a drawbridge leading to a magnificent old English castle. There's a moat surrounding it, and a hazy mist hangs in the air. Somewhere, there's probably a unicorn, and somebody playing something pretty on a mandolin.

For some reason all of this seems unaccountably *sexy*.

I think I have a real problem.

This is the first time I've felt that kind of thing around Adam. It's an interesting, and quite welcome, development. Maybe those algorithms got it more right than I gave them credit for.

Adam burps loudly behind one closed hand, rather ruining my train of thought. 'Shall we make a move, then? That waiter over there is looking anxious for us to be on our way.'

'Okay,' I agree. 'I think I could do with a walk after all that gelato.'

And what a walk it is! From the Hotel Internazionale you can stroll down into the medieval town of Sirmione in less than ten minutes, walking past antiquated villas and their gardens full of cypress trees and olive groves. There's even a delightful church that wouldn't seem out of place in one of the less hectic chapters of a Dan Brown novel. I could cheerfully fill up an entire computer hard drive with all the photos I could take, documenting every single building, garden and view of Lake Garda in this town.

'I bet they don't get good broadband up here,' Adam remarks, squinting at a telephone pole.

I'm coming to learn that this is something of a character flaw for my new husband. He does have a habit of being rather unimaginative, and quite negative. Where I see stunning vistas, he sees inadequate communications technology.

I have no idea how he even *noticed* the telephone pole, given that it's stood next to a large archway leading to an Italian garden so exquisite I want to have it tattooed on my body somewhere inconspicuous.

I'm going to put this difference in perspective down to the fact that he's British and I'm American. If I've learned one thing from being around the Brits, it's that they're deeply unimpressed with pretty much *everything*, whereas my fellow Americans are far more positive about the world around them. I know which I prefer to be.

Even Adam can't complain about the weather, though. While it's still cold enough to need a sweater and pants, the sun is still out, and the sky is an eye-watering shade of blue, with scarcely a cloud to interrupt it.

The fact that it's the off season means the streets are quiet – which suits me just fine. Having lived in London for a while now, I cherish each and every moment of peace I can find. Living in a penthouse flat goes a long way towards having a quieter life in the capital, but even from there you can hear the traffic and general hubbub of the city all the time.

This place, on the other hand, is so blissfully quiet, it's like being wrapped in a duvet that smells of olives and pancetta.

Walking down to the jetty where our speedboat is moored takes us back to the castle, and the sure and secure knowledge that my iPhone's hard drive will need emptying again this evening.

'Come on, Jess,' Adam says in a flat tone of voice, as I'm framing a rusty portcullis on the phone's screen. 'We've got a boat to catch.'

Adam is a guy who likes to be on time, which is a pretty admirable trait, providing he's not trying to do it when you're attempting to take the perfect picture of a thirteenth-century castle doorway.

'The castle isn't going anywhere, you know,' he adds. I roll my eyes and take the picture.

Adam needs to chill out a little. I've noticed he does have a tendency to be a little anal about the world. He's a clock watcher. And a watch watcher. And a phone watcher. Not a minute seems to go by without him checking what the time is. He's like Doctor Who without the blue box and sonic vibrator.

We're in a beautiful place, with our entire lives mapped out for us by a maniac in a light-blue Chanel suit – we might as well just sit back and enjoy the ride. Figuratively and literally, given that we're about to jump on a speedboat for a tour of the lake.

I hope it's a big speedboat, as it looks like we're going to be accompanied by both Derek *and* Cassie.

Fantastic.

I know we were supposed to be meeting Derek here, but I had no idea Miss McFlasterton was also coming along for the ride. And how the hell did she get down here so *fast*? Do they provide London socialite entrepreneurs with some sort of special forces training I wasn't aware of?

'Ah! There you both are!' she crows as we near the entrance to a long private jetty that juts out into the lake. It's one of about seven or eight on this side of the promontory, the largest of which is the one reserved for the public ferry that moves between all the major towns on Lake Garda. 'We thought we'd have to go without you!'

She means it as a joke, but there's an edge to her voice that tells me Adam's not the only one who likes punctuality.

'Er, you're coming too then?' Adam says to her.

Cassie actually looks taken aback. 'Why, of course I am, Adam. We have to make sure you have a great time, don't we? And Derek here always needs a little direction.'

Derek looks like the only direction he wants to go in is as far away from Cassie as possible.

'Let me introduce you to our captain today,' Cassie continues, moving aside to reveal a catalogue model, who must be moonlighting as a sailor between photoshoots. 'This is Niccolo. He owns the boat we're going to be taking out on the water.'

Niccolo is beautiful, and boy does he know it. The hair is perfect, the beard is trimmed to within an inch of its life, the nautically themed navy-blue jacket has buttons on it so shiny you could quite easily mistake him for a small passing nebula. The white trousers are very tight.

Yes, *that* tight.

The loafers are brand new, and the socks are completely absent.

'Ciao!' Niccolo says, and nods his head briefly towards the both of us.

I'm waiting for him to grab one of my hands and kiss it. That would be entirely in keeping with the image this guy is portraying. I'm disappointed, however, when he simply gives us a curt smile and turns to unlock the gate leading on to the jetty.

I do notice that Niccolo is conspicuously avoiding eye contact with Cassie as we walk down the jetty towards his boat. Maybe his usual Italian good humour has been tempered by five minutes in the company of our highly strung marital benefactor. With any luck, getting out on the water will relax the guy a little, and I'll get my kiss on the hand eventually. I would ask Adam to do it, but he's wearing an Arsenal hooded top and a pair of battered old Nikes, so it just wouldn't be the same thing.

Niccolo arrives at one of four boats moored at the end of the jetty. This one is a long, sleek black number that wouldn't look out of place in a two-part *Miami Vice* special. It'd be the boat driven by the villain – a Colombian drugs dealer brought to inevitable justice by Tubbs and Crockett just before the final advertisement break.

Picked out in golden writing down the side of the boat is the legend *Amante dei Laghi*. My Italian is extremely poor, so I translate this in my head as 'Whore of the Lakes'. I have a feeling this isn't *entirely* accurate. Either that, or Niccolo has some rather large issues with women.

Our captain jumps into the boat like someone who has been jumping into speedboats all of his life, which he very probably has. Derek doesn't appear to suffer any issues with getting in either, even with that ample belly.

Cassie is a different matter. I doubt she has much of a chance to mess about on the water back at home, unless someone suggests an evening cruise down the Thames, so it comes as no surprise when she has difficulty getting into the *Whore of the Lakes*. The Louis Vuitton high heels are the main culprit, but I doubt the tight pants, floppy hat and enormous sunglasses are helping matters. If you wanted to deliberately choose an outfit less practical for a turn in a speedboat, you'd be hard-pressed to do better than Cassie's ensemble.

I have to offer a silent prayer of thanks that I decided to wear a pair of Levi's and my black striped Banana Republic sweater. Okay, the cute pumps might not be the ideal footwear for the occasion, but at least they're comfortable, and I won't risk life and limb while I'm clambering off the jetty and into the gently rocking speedboat.

To prove this, I leap in with no problems whatsoever. I catch a look of disgust from Cassie as I do so. I don't care. Banana Republic beats Louis Vuitton hands down, as far as I'm concerned.

Adam does not immediately follow. 'That thing's rocking about quite a lot, isn't it?' he says. His face has gone a little pale.

Niccolo laughs abruptly. 'It's fine! The water today is very, very calm.'

Adam squints out over the lake. 'It doesn't look that calm.'

I can't see what he's talking about. Okay, it's not a millpond out there, but what waves there are, are small and inoffensive.

I give Adam a confused look. 'You like boats, don't you?' I ask him, shielding the sun from my eyes with one hand as I stare up at him.

'Do I?'

'Yes. Your profile says that you love to go jet-skiing. It's more or less the same thing.'

Adam instantly looks guilty. 'Yeah. Jet-skiing. That's right. I love it.'

I have to smirk. 'Really? Can you tell your face that? Because it looks terrified.'

He holds up a slightly quivering hand. 'No. No. I'm fine.'

'Well, come on then,' I encourage. 'You were looking forward to this, remember? It'll be fun.'

He gives me a worried look, stares back briefly at the lake, then clenches his jaw.

'Yeah. I'm sure you're right,' he says and steps over the side of the boat.

Well, that's nice to know. He actually trusts my judgement. Not bad, considering he's only known me a week.

Niccolo hands out four yellow life jackets. You can imagine the look on Cassie's face as she weighs up how badly it's going to clash with her blue suit.

'Everybody ready?' Niccolo asks, once we've all donned our protective gear.

'Yes!' I say enthusiastically. Now I'm on board the sleek black boat, I can feel my heart rate rising in excitement. The only boat I've ever spent much time on before is my father's old fishing boat that he likes to putter around Carmel Bay in during the summer months. It has a top speed of one very frayed knot, and is only exciting when the engine starts to make that strange grinding noise again.

'I'm ready,' Adam adds, sounding less enthusiastic.

Derek just provides a hearty thumbs up between swapping lenses on his camera, and Cassie is too busy trying her level best to look stylish and elegant in one of the rear seats to respond to Niccolo at all.

'Fantastico!' Niccolo exclaims. It looks like I was right. He seems a lot happier now we're in the boat – with Cassie at the other end. 'We start by circling tha town, and then-a we make our way further out.'

I'm expecting the boat to roar off at top speed, but Niccolo obviously knows that a majority of his clients are in this for the opportunity to pose at the locals, rather than go hell for leather across the water. Instead of roaring away, the speedboat gently picks up speed as it clears the jetty and starts to circle past the huge public dock to our right. It's all very civilised. And rather boring.

I turn to Adam, who still looks scared. I immediately make an accurate deduction. 'You don't like going out on the water at all, do you?' I whisper to him.

'Yes I do!' he says, face very stiff.

I smile and fix him with an amused stare. 'Adam . . .'

He maintains the stiff face for a moment, before throwing his hands up. 'Oh alright! You've got me. I hate water. I went jet-skiing once for five minutes and it was all I could do not to throw up the second I left the shore.'

'But your profile said—'

'Um. A little white lie . . . to make me sound more adventurous?'

The look of remorse on his face is something to behold.

I rest a hand on his arm. 'Don't worry about it. I totally understand. You know I said I loved hiking?'

'Yeah?'

'Complete lie. I don't mind a walk in a sunny park, but the idea of fifteen miles of trekking across open countryside makes me nauseous.'

Adam looks visibly relieved. 'Thank God for that. I don't want you thinking I'm full of shit.'

'As long as you didn't lie about anything important, I think we'll be fine,' I reply with a laugh.

'No. Nothing like that. I promise.'

'Good. Do you want to go back?'

Adam looks around at the calm water. 'No. I think I'm fine, thanks. It is quite pleasant out here, once you relax a bit.'

Pleasant, but as I've already stated, rather *boring*, given how slow the speedboat is going.

My mood lifts considerably when we pass the pier and its enormous ferries, and get our first good look at Sirmione from the water.

Oh good Lord, it's even better from a distance.

'You like-a da town?' Niccolo asks, rather redundantly, given how my jaw has dropped and my eyes have gone a little glassy.

'Yes. It's beautiful,' I reply, cursing myself for filling up my phone memory taking so many pictures of the castle from land. How was I to know it'd look even more magnificent from the water?

'Here, use mine,' Adam says, handing out his Samsung.

What a thoughtful gesture. Those algorithms are proving their worth once more, it appears.

I look briefly over at Cassie, who has evidently been studying the both of us, given the smug look on her face.

I smile at my husband, take the phone, and raise it to start snapping away at the castle again – but then stop myself, as I've had a far better idea. 'Adam? Shall we take a selfie?'

He makes a face.

'Go on,' I persist, 'it'll be a nice one, considering how good the background is.'

He rolls his eyes but shifts himself along so he's sitting closer to me. 'Okay then, snap away,' he says.

I hold the phone up, and frame us both in the shot with the castle in the background. 'Say cheese,' I tell him, and just at the last second before I hit the button, I turn and plant a quick kiss on his cheek.

There's a look of surprise in his eyes as I move away, but it's a look of *pleasant* surprise, which is a good thing.

Again Cassie contrives to look smug.

I'm very much looking forward to being somewhere *alone* with Adam, so that every single small act of new-found affection isn't automatically accompanied by the self-satisfied expression on the face of an unwanted third party.

'Derek, get off your arse and take a few professional shots of our happy couple,' Cassie demands from her temporary throne at the back of the speedboat. 'Make sure you get lots of pictures with the Hotel Internazionale in the background. That was part of our deal.'

Aaah.

So there's the reason why we're staying at that particular hotel. Cassie has obviously made some sort of 'you scratch my back, I'll advertise yours on my website' arrangement with them. And there was me thinking she was only worried about our comfort during this trip.

Cassie points a finger at Derek. 'Remember! Always get the happy couple in every shot! That's why we're here after all.'

Derek duly moves forward and bids Adam and me to sit together on the side of the speedboat. We do so, and attempt to look happy about it – with mixed results.

The next forty minutes or so are exclusively about feeling embarrassed and awkward in the confines of a wide-angle lens. Cassie wants a lot of material to work with, and *boy* is she going to get it.

We have our picture taken with the hotel about two thousand times, before we move on to the whole of Sirmione itself, then just the castle, then just the rocky beach at the rear, then even more of the hotel to get a different angle of it. After that, Niccolo is ordered to take the speedboat out into deeper water, so Derek can capture Lake Garda in all its scenic glory.

Snap. Snap. Snap. Snap. Snap.

After nearly three-quarters of an hour, I feel like my lips are about to fall off.

Eventually, my patience runs out. 'Enough!' I cry, hands held out. 'I need to take a break. If I smile any more at that damn camera, it'll probably steal my soul.'

'Agreed,' Adam puffs from my side. 'I have severe face ache.'

I give Cassie a pleading look. 'Can we call it a day, and have some fun?'

Cassie's brow wrinkles. The concept of 'fun' is not one familiar to her, it seems. As far as she's concerned, we're not here to have fun, we're here to work. You can tell she wants to say that to me, judging from the look in her eyes. Thankfully for our continued cordial relationship, she manages to rein it in.

'Okay, Jess. That should be enough for today. Derek?'

Derek nods in rapid agreement. He must be as sick of taking pictures as we are of having them taken.

'Great!' I exclaim, and turn to Niccolo, who looks so bored it's a wonder he hasn't fallen asleep at the wheel. It's probably only the tightness of his bright-white trousers that is keeping him awake. 'Niccolo, can we see what this thing can do?' I say, patting the side of the sleek black speedboat.

He smiles broadly. 'Of course! It would be a pleasure!'

Adam goes a bit white.

Cassie goes a bit red.

Derek picks his nose. I am too disgusted to figure out what colour his face is.

'Er, is that a good idea, Jessica?' Adam asks in a tremulous voice.

'Yeah! It'll be great. Exciting!' I reply.

'Er, I'm not sure I'm ready for that kind of thing either,' Cassie says, echoing Adam's reluctance.

Oh, good grief. What's wrong with these people? We're on a speed-boat with what I can only assume is several paddocks' worth of horse-power under the hood; the weather is crisp and clear, and the water is calm. Why wouldn't you want to go *faster*?

'It'd make a great photo, Cassie,' I point out. 'Just think of how great a shot of me and Adam at the front of the boat would look on the website as we're rocketing across the lake.'

'Rocketing?' Adam pipes up in a worried voice.

I wave a hand. 'Figure of speech.'

This has the desired effect. 'Okay, Jessica,' Cassie says, 'just let me get my seat belt on.'

I make two excited fists and wave them in front of my chest. 'Yay!' I exclaim, sitting in the seat nearest to Niccolo. 'Join me, Adam,' I say. 'We need to be sat together so Derek can get the best action shot.'

This earns me a rather dark look, but I ignore it, as I'm about to go full throttle. 'Go, Niccolo, go!' I demand, once Adam has strapped himself in.

The suave Italian captain doesn't need telling twice. No sooner are the words out of my lips, than the boat is gaining speed rapidly. So much so that I feel pushed back into the plush leather seat I'm safely strapped into.

'Woo hoo!' I cry, punching the air, as the speedboat starts to thrash along, sending plumes of water up on either side. I now sound and look like a redneck at a NASCAR race, but I don't care. So far this 'honey-moon' has been one long prescribed exercise in promoting Sociality, and not much of a thrill for me. This ride is changing all of that.

I turn my head to see Derek gamely trying to get photos, and Cassie gamely trying to hold on to her floppy hat. I laugh, and turn back, just as Niccolo makes a hard turn to the right, sending up a massive plume of spray.

'Wahaay!' I exclaim. This is *amazing*! I'm actually having fun now! This is what a honeymoon should be abo—

BANG!

What the hell?!

BANG! BANG! BANG!

What's going on?!

BANG! BANG! FLURRRMMMMMPPPPPHHHHH.

Oh God! I think there's something wrong with the engine.

SKREEEEEEEEEEEEEEEEEEEL.

The sound of heavily tortured metal reverberates across the lake.

'Oh fucking shit!' Niccolo exclaims, proving that his command of the English language doesn't stop at the swear words.

He immediately throttles the speedboat down – not that he really needed to, as the engine is quite clearly destroyed, and the boat is coming to a stop no matter what he does with the controls.

As we slow, great plumes of black smoke are starting to issue from the prow, making us all cough violently.

'Do something, Niccolo!' Cassie demands in a panicked voice.

Niccolo jumps over the small windshield and throws open a hatch on the front of the speedboat, sending even more black smoke into the air. He clambers back almost immediately, getting away from the thick, acrid smoke as fast as he can.

He looks at us. 'I have-a the good news, and I have-a the bad news.'

'What do you mean?' Adam asks, his voice nearly as panicked as Cassie's.

'The good news is that the smoke will bring out the *guardia costiera* . . . the, er, how you say . . . *coast guard*.'

'And the bad news?' Adam asks, eyes narrowing.

Niccolo shrugs. 'It looks like something large 'as gone through the side of the boat.'

'Meaning?'

We all know what he means, but it's probably important to get that fucker right out in the open for everyone to hear – apologies for my language.

'There is a hole in-a the boat. We are sinking.' Niccolo smiles and gives us a thumbs up. 'But only slowly! It is a little 'ole.'

'A little hole!' Cassie roars, and looks over the side. I follow suit. Sure enough, I can see bubbles on the surface near the boat's prow, indicating that air is getting out somewhere, and water is most definitely getting in.

'Damn,' I say in a quiet voice.

I wanted a bit of excitement today, but this is maybe taking things a little *too* far.

Things are getting even more exciting fifteen minutes later, when there's still no sign of the *guardia costiera*, and the speedboat has taken on a very noticeable list to one side.

Cassie is now apoplectic. 'Haven't you got a bloody radio!?' she demands of poor Niccolo, whose trousers are now ruined thanks to some clambering around trying to see exactly where the little 'ole actually is.

'No. I have-a never needed one,' he replies. 'I never go far from tha shore, and this boat is very reliable.'

'Very reliable!?' Cassie screeches.

Snap.

Cassie stabs a finger at where the little 'ole is more or less situated under the water. 'It doesn't look very *reliable* to me!'

Snap.

'I am-a sorry,' he says, running a hand through what is now very unkempt hair. 'This has-a never 'appened to me before.'

I know he's talking about his speedboat, but the trousers are still very tight, so my mind is inadvertently dragged elsewhere.

Snap.

'Well . . . do something, man!' Cassie insists. 'We're going to bloody drown!'

Snap.

She may be exaggerating more than a little, but the situation *is* beginning to look dire. I can now quite easily dip a finger in the waters of Lake Garda from where I'm sat. Give it another ten minutes and the water will be in here with us.

I look at my husband.

Adam has vacated the boat, though, and has left a lifelike dummy sat in his place. You can tell it's a dummy by the pale skin, extremely glassy eyes and complete lack of movement.

Snap.

'Have you got any flares?' Cassie demands of the Italian.

Niccolo contrives to look very confused. 'I am-a sorry? I do not know what you mean?'

Snap.

'Flares, man! Bloody flares!' Cassie hisses, waving her arms about.

Snap.

Niccolo still looks confused. 'I do not have any, I am afraid. They went out of fashion here a long time ago.' He points to his skinny trousers. 'This is what we all wear-a these days.'

Snap.

For a second, Cassie looks dumbfounded. Then the rage is upon her. 'Not those kinds of flares, you bloody idiot!! *Distress* flares!!'

Snap.

'Derek!' Cassie screams. 'If you don't stop taking fucking pictures of this fucking catastrophe, I'm going to shove that fucking camera up your fucking arse!'

Italy is a very Catholic country, so I'm sure at least three saints just died.

'But it's dramatic!' Derek wails.

Cassie stands up, consumed by towering rage, which makes the ailing boat rock alarmingly. 'Give me that bloody thing!' she demands, reaching out to grab Derek's pride and joy from his sweaty grip.

'Here! No!' he protests, pulling it away from her.

Cassie, panicked and supremely angry, loses her grip on the camera . . . and then loses her balance in the boat.

Over she goes, in a confusion of Chanel, Louis Vuitton and bright-yellow life jacket.

SPLASH!

'Oh dear,' Derek remarks.

I jump out of my seat as Niccolo also makes his way towards where his employer is now thrashing around in the lake as if a school of piranhas were snapping at her heels.

'Don't-a panic!' Niccolo tells her. 'Everything will be fine!'

'Don't tell me not to panic!' Cassie screeches. 'Just get me out of this bloody water!'

We both hold out a hand to her.

She wisely takes Niccolo's, given that mine is shaking a little too much from all the barely concealed laughter.

I know, it's cruel, but this woman is responsible for quite a lot of recent stress in this girl's life, so I think I'm allowed to laugh just a little bit at her misfortune.

Misfortune that continues when Niccolo loses his grip on her arm, sending her plunging back into the depths with a loud squawk.

'Oops-a! I am-a sorry Miss Mackerflasterton!'

'Aaarggh!' Cassie wails. 'My Louis Vuittons! I've lost one of them! Oh God! Oh God! Get me out of here! Get me out of this water NOW!'

Snap.

I look round.

Derek is leaning over and taking pictures.

It's too much.

I have to retreat back to where Adam is sat before I start laughing out loud at Cassie's misfortune.

From the safety of my seat, I see two things occur: Cassie eventually being manhandled back into the boat, soaking wet and crying, and Derek continuing to take pictures.

And here's the kicker – he remembers his orders.

Get the happy couple in every shot, Cassie McFlasterton told him, and Derek is one to follow instructions *to the letter.*

'Excuse me,' he says, sidling around to where Adam and I are sat, and getting himself into a good position. 'Now smile for the camera, you two,' he tells us.

I oblige. Adam is still struck dumb with terror, so can only manage a horrified look at the camera.

Derek momentarily looks over his lens. 'Oh look, here comes the coast guard,' he says, twiddling his focus ring. 'This'll be really good.'

Snap.

The photo that goes on Sociality is one of Adam and me sat on the side of the still-functioning speedboat, with the Hotel Internazionale in the background, looking resplendent in the crisp February sun. Beneath it is a link to the hotel's website, and an encouragement to book a holiday there as soon as is humanly possible.

The photo I begged Derek for an hour to give me is much better, though.

In the foreground are the Holbornes. One is grinning like a lunatic, the other looks like the hounds of hell are after him.

But it's behind them the picture *really* starts to shine.

Cassie's big floppy beige hat has not survived well in the waters of Lake Garda, and has drooped completely over her head. It looks a bit like a dead squid. This gives the impression that Captain Niccolo has caught himself a particularly interesting human–sea creature hybrid from the deep – one that likes to dress almost exclusively in Chanel.

Behind *them* is the coast guard, who, a few minutes after the picture is taken, will be towing the stricken vessel and its occupants successfully back to dry land.

I'm going to get the picture framed when I get home, in the safe and secure knowledge that it is, without a doubt, the most *unique* honeymoon photo ever taken.

ADAM

Q. If you had a million pounds, what would you do?
A. Start worrying about burglars.

6 March

'Will you venture forth into the Citadel of Carakor?'

Hmmmm.

It's a difficult decision, and no mistake.

'What do you reckon, Oli?' I say into my headset.

'Not sure,' comes the response back through my headphones. The line is nice and clear this afternoon, the server must not be very busy. 'Are we levelled up enough for this? Maybe we should go back to the Silver Shores and grind for a bit longer?'

'Really?' I reply with a groan. 'We spent three hours there last week. I'm getting bored with killing Water Trolls over and over again.'

'Will you venture forth into the Citadel of Carakor?' the vagabond sorcerer Rapscallion repeats.

'Oh, come on, Oli, let's just go for it,' I insist. 'What's the worst that can happen? We just die and respawn back at Holliton.'

'With a twenty-minute trek to get back here, because we haven't unlocked any fast-travel points yet,' he replies with evident disgust.

'I didn't say it wasn't risky.'

I hear Oli sigh at the other end of the line. 'Alright, alright. Let's go,' he agrees, though he definitely doesn't sound happy about it.

I quickly bring up my inventory to check that I've got the Blood Sword equipped. I might need it if we come up against any Death Heads or Lycans.

Having done that, I move to follow Oli's barbarian lord as he walks up the steep, rocky path to the citadel's entrance.

Now, there's every chance this conversation would sound like utter bollocks to a large majority of the population. Those that don't own a PlayStation 4 and a copy of *Realm of Chaos*, that is.

But I make no apologies for my addiction to this particular online role-playing game. It comes with the territory of working as a games journalist. Most games I just play for review, but every once in a while one comes along that really gets its teeth into me, and in the past year that's been *Realm of Chaos*.

I met Oli playing the game quite a while ago now, and we became fast online friends when we defeated the Moon Slayer together. It was a great time.

Since then we have gone on to defeat many, many strong and dangerous opponents. None have stood in our way, as we have explored the vast realm of Heranor together, building our fortunes and making our characters so powerful that other players stand aside as we walk through the streets of the towns and villages that dot the digital landscape.

I say 'we', but of course mean our online characters. Oli's is the barbarian Asgod, and I am the warrior monk Londo. We are a team who *no one* has been able to defeat.

No quest is too difficult, no objective is too remote, no monster is too powerful. Heranor is ours to conquer, and none will stop us!

* * *

'You go in first,' Oli tells me, pausing by the citadel's cavernous entrance.

'What? You're the big, strong barbarian. Why don't you go first?'

'This was your idea.'

Damn. Oli's logic is unassailable.

'Alright, alright. Just watch my back for Death Heads,' I grunt.

I push the stick forward on the joypad slowly, and Londo moves into the darkness.

There could be anything in here. Death Heads, Dark Trolls, Nuclear Spiders – even the Pyromancer Borinbor, one of the most feared non-player characters in this part of the Heranorian continent.

But I am prepared.

Prepared for monsters . . .

Prepared for traps . . .

Prepared for *anything*!

'*ALL THE SINGLE LADIES! ALL THE SINGLE LADIES!*'

Jesus Christ!

While I am prepared for evil Pyromancers and floating skulls with laser eyeballs, I am *not* prepared in the *slightest* for bloody Beyoncé at full volume.

'Er, Jess?' I shout over the cacophony.

'Jessica!' I repeat, even louder. Competing with Beyoncé telling us all about how he really should have put a ring on it is no easy task. 'Jessica!! Can you turn that down a bit?!' I more or less scream. 'I'm just about to enter the Citadel of Makaror!'

'Carakor,' Oli corrects, now barely audible thanks to the assault of R & B emanating from behind me.

Jessica has once again decided to turn the dining room section of our open-plan living space into her own personal gym. The chrome-and-black table and chairs have been pushed to the edge of the room, the brightly coloured orange mat has gone down, the Lycra shorts have gone on, and the awful music has been turned up as high as the iPod dock will allow.

'Jessica! For Christ's sakes, turn it down!'

My wife stops doing lunges, fixes me with a dark stare, and leans across to turn the volume down on her iPhone. 'Sorry, I thought you were playing your game.'

'I *am* playing my game. Something I can't do if Beyoncé is destroying my eardrums with her caterwauling!'

'You've been playing it for *four hours*,' Jessica says, standing up and folding her arms. 'I can't just hang around in my bedroom all day, you know.'

'Isn't there a gym nearby?' I ask.

'Yes, but this is *my* apartment too, Adam, remember?' There's an edge to her voice that is ever so slightly scary. I'm used to Americans sounding bright and friendly, so when they suddenly *stop* being bright and friendly it's quite alarming.

Jess isn't happy, that much is certain. But then again, neither am I right now.

Jessica and I have lived together now for a few weeks. This has been long enough for me to discover that my wife is loud. Very, *very* loud.

I know, I know, it sounds like a cliché – an American who's noisy – but in this case it's bloody *true*.

My first indication that Jessica Madison – sorry, Jessica *Holborne* – likes the world to know she exists in no uncertain terms was a mere day after we got back from Italy. I was quite content to have a lovely lie-in, given all the travelling we'd done the day before, but those plans were put to the sword when I was rudely awakened at seven thirty by a combination of coffee machine and the MTV chart show.

It is clinically impossible to sleep through a combination of a milk frother and Justin Bieber.

I came out of my bedroom with a look of slack-jawed exhaustion on my face, and shuffled out into the living area. 'What are you doing?' I asked my new wife incredulously. 'It's half seven on a *Sunday*.'

Jessica looked up at me from over the espresso machine. 'Oh, I'm sorry, was I being too loud?'

Yes, Jessica. You *were*. And you have been *too loud* every bloody day since.

I had rather hoped that moving out of that cramped room in Croydon, and into this expansive penthouse, would lead to a quieter, less stressful life. If for no other reason than I would no longer have to worry about flesh-eating bacteria and inquisitive rats.

The change has not come without its own set of problems, though.

The TV is always *up loud*.

iTunes is always *up loud*.

Jessica bangs cupboard doors shut, slams coffee cups down, scrapes her fork across the plate, has the extractor fan on full blast when she's cooking bacon, chews the same bacon loudly once she's fried it to within an inch of its life.

She can't even study quietly. You'd think learning all about the nutritional value of mushrooms would keep the volume level down, but she even manages to make that a cacophony of competing noises, thanks to all the gum chewing, pen tapping, humming and hard iPad poking that goes on.

I actually find myself looking forward to going to work, as it's quieter there, even with the occasional tirade from Watlow when somebody uses all the printer ink.

She even manages to have a bath loudly. I fully expect to walk in after she's done to find water splashed up every wall and every wall tile smashed, but there's no evidence of such violence, even though I can hear her when she's in there from outside on the bloody terrace.

Speaking of the patio, that's where I got the first indication that Jessica enjoys a workout at home every day.

I was quite contentedly watching an old episode of *Doctor Who*, when Matt Smith was rudely interrupted by Demi Lovato banging on about how cool she was for the summer. I don't care about her general state of well-being during *any* of the four seasons, so was quite annoyed to have her drown out the Doctor's speech on how evil the Daleks are.

I craned my head around to see Jess out there in the sunshine, clad in a tight Lycra gym outfit, warming up with a few stretches.

. . . which brings me on to the *second* problem I'm having in this new relationship, and the living arrangements that come with it.

Jessica may be loud, but she more than makes up for this by being unbearably *sexy*.

I didn't quite know *how* sexy until we'd spent a week under the same roof, in an environment where she could feel fully relaxed.

And boy, when it comes to her body, Jess is *extremely* relaxed.

She'll quite happily wander around in next to nothing, provided the heating is right up – which it invariably is, seeing as she comes from California, and this is the UK in March.

The girl is not body-conscious in the *slightest*, and this is incredibly traumatic for me. The Lycra outfit she works out in consists of a black sports bra, small black shorts and a pair of Adidas trainers.

Hurrrngh.

I assume this is all because of her laid-back American upbringing. She tells me Carmel-by-the-Sea is quite a bohemian place, devoted to the arts, recreation, and a healthy, liberal attitude towards the human body.

I, however, am English, and am therefore naturally embarrassed by my own body, as well as the bodies of every other human being I come into contact with, unless they are hidden under several layers of man-made fibre.

You can imagine what Jessica's approach to clothing at home is doing to my libido. I am in a near-constant state of sexual arousal, with the capacity to do nothing about it, other than masturbate under the covers at 3 a.m. like an overexcited sixteen-year-old.

This is an absolutely *ridiculous* statement, when you remember that I am her bloody *husband*. I should have no problem instigating a sexual encounter.

Sadly, I've only known her a month, and we were thrown together in the most unromantic of circumstances when you get right down to it. Initiating sex in this odd situation is nigh on impossible. Also, sex would probably be a bad idea anyway. It complicates things faster than the plot of a Christopher Nolan movie. My dark knight rising does me no good whatsoever.

This puts me in a position that is as unique as it is awful – and one I was not prepared for *at all*. In all the excitement of the wedding, moving into the lovely new flat, and the hectic honeymoon, I've barely had any time to think about what it would actually mean to be *married* to this woman. To live with her day to day. To get to know her away from Derek's camera, and Cassie McFlasterton's constant interference.

It turns out it either gives me a headache or an erection, depending on what she's doing at the time.

Therefore, I am not finding the first few weeks of married life relaxing in the slightest – hence my escape into the much safer environment that *Realm of Chaos* provides. Okay, I might get eaten by a Nuclear Spider if I don't tread carefully, but at least I won't feel comprehensively awkward about the whole experience, as the spider happily eats my digital brain.

This truly is a sad state of affairs.

I would rather live a life online with barbarians and Nuclear Spiders, where I know where I stand, than attempt to live a proper life *offline* with a loud and unbearably attractive American, who permanently keeps me off balance, whether she means to or not.

Of course, it's a little hard to play *Realm of Chaos* when Beyoncé keeps interrupting with her flamboyant screeching – which brings us back to the present, and Jessica's folded arms.

'Can't you just come off that thing for a while?' she says, brow furrowed.

'Can't you do that outside?' I counter.

Jessica's lips become thin white lines. 'It's raining, Adam. And blowing a damn hurricane out there.'

'Er, Adam?' Oli says. 'A Nuclear Spider has just eaten your head.'

I look back at the screen. My poor warrior monk Londo is currently being masticated from the neck down by a large, hairy, glowing spider. This means a one-way ticket all the way back to the hub town of Holliton, and the disgrace of respawning around a bunch of newbs.

'Fuck,' I mutter with a sharp exhalation of breath. 'Now look what's happened!' I say in dismay to my wife.

Jessica looks at the screen. 'Did you die?'

'Yes! Yes, I died!'

'Does it matter?'

I open my mouth to issue a firm response, framed around the concept that it matters a *great deal*, as I will now have to retread my steps to meet up with Oli again – *and* I'll have to haggle with Peaknuckle the dwarven weapons dealer to get a new Blood Sword, as I hadn't had a chance to save it in my travelling inventory, which is bloody annoying because it'll affect my XP progression on a weekend when it's double points for—

Yeah. None of that would go down very well, would it?

'No,' I say sullenly. 'It doesn't matter.' I roll my eyes. 'Oli?'

'Yep?'

'I'm going to call it a day. I'll message you when I'm back on next.'

'Oh, okay.'

I rub my eyes. I really hate to disappoint Oli, but it's probably best I turn my attention to Jessica right now. I may have only been married for a few weeks, but I've been in enough relationships before this one to know that it'd be a very good idea to choose her over online gaming for the next few hours.

'Er, do you mind if I tackle the citadel on my own, then?' Oli asks.

I want to say yes. The idea of him getting all that lovely loot without me doesn't appeal at all, but then he might not have any more luck with the Nuclear Spiders and Death Heads than me.

'No, no, that's fine. Good luck with it.'

'Cool. See you later then.'

'Yep.'

I exit the game on the PS4 gamepad and stand up. When I turn to look at Jessica she is still standing with her arms folded.

'You know, a girl could get the impression that her man would rather spend time with his friend on a computer game than with her,' she says, brow furrowed.

'That's not true,' I counter.

'Isn't it? You've certainly spent more time with Oli since we got back from Italy than you have with me.'

Oh dear. She's noticed. I was rather hoping that wouldn't be the case.

'It's not that I don't want to hang out with you Jess, it's just that . . .'

Just what? Just that I'm either annoyed or horny when I'm around you? Just that it's easier to keep my distance? Just that I entered into this marriage for a place to live, rather than a relationship, and have no idea what I'm doing?

'You know him better than you know me, right?' Jessica finishes for me.

'Yeah. I guess that might be it.'

She shrugs her shoulders. 'I get it. This is still weird for you. Hell, it's still weird for me too, but if we're going to get along, then we should try to do more stuff together, don't you think? Get to know each other better that way?'

'How do you mean?'

Jessica cocks her head slightly. 'Why don't you join me?'

'Sorry, what?'

She briefly looks to the ceiling. 'Why don't you work out with me?'

I'm flabbergasted. 'You . . . you want me to do *exercise with you*?'

Has the woman gone stark staring *mad*?

'Yeah! Sure! I think you'd really like it. Much better than just sitting on that couch all day.'

This doesn't compute. This doesn't make any sense whatsoever. Doesn't this woman know me at all?

Of course she doesn't know you, *you idiot. That's the whole problem.*

'Um. I don't really like exercise, Jessica. I actually think I'm allergic to it. I once went for a jog and it gave me a rash on my bum.'

She looks confused. 'But your Sociality profile said you *liked* exercise. It said you liked to keep fit.'

Oh no. This again.

First it was the jet-skiing, and now exercise. I was wilfully creative on my Sociality profile, and now I fear that lack of sincerity may be coming back to haunt me.

But who the hell tells the truth on those bloody things anyway? What was I supposed to write? I don't do exercise because it gives me a big red baboon arse?

I scratch my chin. 'Yeah. That may have . . . may have not been *entirely* honest.'

Jessica looks exasperated. 'You mean you lied about that *too*?'

'I might've.'

She slaps her thigh with frustration. 'Oh come on, Adam. I don't want this kind of thing to keep cropping up, you know.'

'You were fine with the jet-skiing!' I protest.

'Yes. I was. But we were in Italy and it was *sunny*.' She puts her hands on her hips. 'What else have you lied about? You're not already married, are you? Or got kids you haven't told me about?'

'No! I told you it was only little things I'd fibbed about.'

She fixes me with a stare. 'Little things can become big things *very quickly* if you're not careful.'

Oh dear. Jessica is not happy. Not happy *at all*.

I'd better do something constructive here, before my annoyed wife gets on the phone to Cassie and lets her know that I am a really big fibber, and that the marriage is therefore null and void.

This thing can't fall apart already. I haven't had a chance to use the spa bath or the icemaker yet, and the prize money still hasn't reached my bank account.

'I guess I could try some stretches . . . or something,' I say hesitantly.

'Really?'

'Yeah, can't do any harm, can it?'

This earns me a smile. 'Great!'

'But please . . . no Beyoncé.'

Jess claps her hands together. 'No problem. How about something a little more mellow?'

'Now you're talking.'

'I could show you some yoga, if you like.'

Never, EVER, agree to do yoga. If there's one fundamental law of the universe I can impart to you, it's that you never, EVER agree to do yoga – for reasons which are about to become readily apparent.

Jessica plays with her iPhone for a moment, and the room is filled with an ambient piece of techno music that includes panpipes, a waterfall and what sounds like a woman sighing heavily. She's probably just been told she has to do yoga.

Still, it's not loud and obnoxious, which suits me just fine.

'We'll start with a few simple moves,' Jess tells me. 'They should be really good for you, after all that time sat down.'

'Okay.'

'I'll show you them first, and then you have a go.'

'Fair enough.' I stand back a little to give her some room.

'This is called the downward dog,' Jess informs me, before lying down on the ground.

She then lifts her backside into the air, forming an upside-down V with her entire body.

Oh *dear.*

This isn't good. I really shouldn't be standing where I'm standing.

Don't stare at her arse, don't stare at her arse, don't *stare at her* arse*!*

'See?' Jessica says, the blood running to her face. 'Easy. Why don't you give it a go? . . . Adam? . . . *Adam?* . . . Adam, are you looking at my butt?'

'What?! No! No! Sorry!'

She laughs. 'I don't mind, you know. We are married after all.'

Yes, we are, love. But one-half of this very brief marriage is British and brought up in a provincial household, so all of this is brand new and exquisitely uncomfortable territory.

I quickly drop to the ground. 'It's like this, is it?' I say, attempting to replicate Jessica's perfectly held pose – and cover my own discomfort.

My version is less downward dog, more manky mongrel.

'Not bad,' Jess tells me. 'You just have to work on your form. Try this one as well.'

She moves into a new pose, one that doesn't feature her Lycra-clad bottom presented to me for appraisal. Instead, my wife simply stands straight and puts both hands above her head as if she's about to take a dive off a non-existent diving board. 'This is the mountain pose.'

'I can definitely do that one,' I say with conviction, and do so.

Her hands then part and she tucks her left foot up into her thigh, and balances her entire weight on the right. 'Try this one, then. This is the tree.'

The tree is trickier, and I wobble around a little before achieving some stability, but all in all, I do a pretty good job of it. It seems I'm getting the hang of this.

Jess then proceeds to do another dozen or so yoga poses, all of which I can follow without too much trouble. And what do you know, it *does* feel quite good. The stiffness I didn't even know I had starts to trickle away, and by the time we've been at it for about twenty minutes I'm feeling pretty good about myself. Who'd have thought being firmly pulled out of my comfort zone like this would actually be of some benefit?

'See? It's fun, isn't it?' Jessica says.

She's right, it *is* fun. I cheerfully admit I'm the kind of guy who isn't keen on trying new things if I can possibly get away with it, but Jessica has done the impossible – got me off my arse and doing something new that I'm *actually enjoying*.

Not only that, it's the first thing we've done together as a couple that hasn't been arranged for us by Cassie McFlasterton.

'Well, you seem to have the hang of it, Adam. Want to try some more difficult poses?'

'Yeah, why not,' I say.

Jess then performs a slow lunge, bending with her left leg until her body is only a foot or so off the floor. Her right leg extends out straight behind her. This looks bad enough, but she then twists her torso, snakes one arm around her left calf and holds her other arm out towards the ceiling.

'This is called the revolved side,' she tells me. It looks more like the double hernia with a side order of ligament damage to me.

But I've done alright so far, haven't I? So why not give it a go?

Cretin.

I just about manage to get my legs into something approximating a lunge. I can only tuck my left arm around my knee, and get my right arm up just above my shoulder, but it could be worse.

'Now hold this for thirty seconds,' Jess says.

Thirty seconds? I can already feel my legs trembling like mad.

'Breathe deep, and relax,' she suggests. 'Close your eyes if that helps.'

This sounds like the type of thing a kindly executioner would say to his latest client, before finishing the job.

But I do hold the pose for five seconds . . . for ten . . . for fifteen. I might just be able to do this!

Prrrrrrrrrp.

That, friends and neighbours, is the sound of an escaping fart.

Anyone who has done yoga will know that this is quite a common occurrence. It's a little hard to contort your body in all those weird and interesting ways without compressing the digestive tract and forcing the expulsion of air from whatever orifice it is closest to.

And how embarrassing for poor old Adam is this, eh?

When he was doing so well?

Getting some much-needed exercise, and bonding with his new wife at the same time?

What a colossal shame to have his body let him down at such an inopportune moment!

. . .

Hah!

Well, that's where you're wrong!

The fart does not emanate from my backside, but from *Jessica's*!

The humiliation will not be mine, but hers!

'Excuse me!' Jess exclaims, and laughs.

Hang on . . . *laughs?*

That's not right. That's not how humiliation works. She should be cringing in horror, not *laughing*. She just farted in front of me. It's an awful thing to happen to her. Why is she *laughing*?

'This is a good position if you've ever got trapped wind,' she informs me. 'Try it if you ever have a problem.'

Oh, great. Not only is she comprehensively *not* embarrassed by her flatulence, she's moved on to giving me *health tips*.

What kind of lunatic have I married?

Unfortunately, all this wind-based excitement has made me forget that I am still contorted like a pretzel, and that the thirty-second time limit has long since passed.

I feel a disturbing twinge from my lower back.

'Okay, I think I'm done with that one,' I tell her, extricating myself from the odd yoga pose, before the slight twinge becomes anything worse.

Jessica does much the same. 'You did really well, Adam. Great work!'

'If you say so. It didn't go anywhere near as badly as I thought it would.'

She smiles. 'Thank you for trying. It meant a lot to me.'

And now I'm starting to blush. This is partly due to the fact that I don't know how to take a compliment, and partly because I've just realised the intervening space between Jessica and me is barely a foot wide. We are well and truly within each other's comfort zones.

'Um. Ah. Er,' I say.

Oh, fucking *spectacular*. I've turned into Hugh bloody Grant.

Every other man in the UK would be soundly kicking me in the balls right now for letting the side well and truly down.

Jessica's smile turns knowing, and not a little amused.

Then her eyes widen. 'Do you want to worship the fishes in reverse?'

'Do I want to what with the what now?'

She laughs. 'It's a couple's yoga pose. One of the simpler ones. It's called something completely unpronounceable in Sanskrit.'

'Oh, right.' This is quite a clever move on Jessica's part. We've obviously reached a rather uncomfortable segue here, and she's trying to smooth things along. 'How do you do that one then?' I enquire in a shaky voice.

'Easy.' She moves around to stand at my side. 'All you have to do is stand next to me, the other way around, and then twist your body so it's parallel with mine holding your arms out as you do it.'

Jessica demonstrates her side of the pose. It doesn't look too complicated.

I stand next to her and mirror her manoeuvre. Now we are virtually touching noses . . . and other body parts. If I stopped holding my arms out to the sides, I could easily wrap them around her body.

I've suddenly gone a bit light-headed.

'See? Easy,' Jessica says, looking right into my eyes with a smile. We're so close I can feel her breath on my cheeks.

'Seems it.'

'I read that this is a pose the yoga gurus say you should do before making love.'

'Do they?'

'Yes, they do.'

'Jessica?'

'Yes, Adam?'

'Are you making this shit up?'

'Yes, Adam. I absolutely am.'

And now we're kissing.

Not just kissing, but *fondling* as well.

Marvellous.

I feel myself pushed back against the nearest wall, where there is a lot more kissing, but the fondling rapidly gives way to all-out *grabbing*.

It's quite amazing how much sexual tension can build up in a relationship involving two people who got married the first time they saw each other, and have spent the last few weeks sizing each other up.

I would ask other people if the same thing had ever happened to them, but I'm sure we are the only couple on the planet who have ever been through this surreal process, so it's a moot point.

Anyway, back to the matter at hand. My T-shirt is now off. Jessica will want to be careful when she pulls my jeans down, for fear of having an eye poked out.

'Take me in the bedroom, husband,' Jess whispers hoarsely in my ear.

Well, this *is* an important moment, and no mistake. I've been given the all-clear to proceed with some much-needed sexual congress. Something I should be *delighted* about. And indeed, a large part of me is. Or rather, a medium-sized part – I know my own limitations.

Unfortunately, there's another part of my brain that is telling me to move away from the attractive young woman and take a cold shower. This is the practical part of me that only agreed to this marriage on the basis of *financial gain*. It never expected to find itself pushed up against a wall, with an erection you could hang a towel off.

The two opposing sides of my brain fight with each other for a moment, as Jessica's breath warms my ear.

Then when my wife's hand snakes down to my crotch, the practical side of my brain realises that the battle is lost, waves a metaphorical white flag, and bunks off work for the rest of the day, leaving me and my libido to it.

'Okay, let's go,' I whisper back to Jess, squeezing her bottom playfully.

Then, I do something very foolish indeed. Instead of merely leading my wife by the hand, I decide to pick her up and carry her to the bedroom.

'It's more fun to do this without Derek and his camera shoved in our faces,' I tell her with a smile.

'Do what?'

Jessica lets out a cry of surprise as I lift her off her feet in one deft move. 'This!'

She giggles. 'I've never actually been swept off my feet before.'

'I aim to please!' I say with a charming smile.

The charming smile falters, however, when I realise that despite the fact that Jessica is five foot five and of slim build, she is also *quite bloody heavy.*

All those workouts and yoga sessions have clearly paid off. Jessica's body feels firm and supple under my grip, and, as I've already stated . . . pretty damn heavy.

You know what doesn't like holding up an unexpectedly heavy human being after half an hour of yoga?

The average untrained, unexercised human back. Mine, in this case.

That twinge from earlier suddenly becomes a lancing pain.

'Aaaarggh!' I yowl, and instantly drop my wife like a sack of spuds.

She falls on to her feet with a cat-like grace, I collapse in a painful heap with a walrus-like lack of it.

'Adam! Are you okay?' Jessica exclaims, crouching next to where I've ended up on the floor, writhing round in agony. All thoughts of consummating this marriage have departed in a nanosecond. Now all I care about is the few square inches of my body just above my arse.

'My back,' I whine, partly in pain . . . and partly in self-pity. We were *so close.*

'Is it bad?'

I give her a look. 'Jessica, can you see the tears in my eyes?'

'Yeah . . . Oh. Pretty bad then.'

'Yes.'

'You want me to help you to the couch?'

'What? The place I should never have let you talk me into leaving in the first place?'

Okay, that's hideously childish, but if I hadn't agreed to take part in her bloody yoga sessions I wouldn't be looking at days, if not weeks, of ibuprofen and minimal movement.

Jessica sits back on her heels. 'Don't be such an asshole, Adam,' she says, quite correctly in these particular circumstances. 'I'm only trying to help.'

'Sorry,' I tell her, wincing as another wave of pain hits.

'This is like what happened to my brother when he was playing football.'

'He was carrying one of his teammates off to have sex and his back gave out?'

Jessica shakes her head. 'No, he was tackling the quarterback before he had time to throw the ball to the wide receiver. He hurt his back doing it.' She looks thoughtful. 'I watched the college physio do something that seemed to make it a lot better, really fast.'

'Five painkillers and a double Jack Daniel's and Coke?'

'Not quite. Can you roll over?'

I hold out a hand. 'Um. You think this is a good idea? Should we just get me to the couch and call a doctor?'

'Trust me, Adam. I'm not going to do anything bad. I don't want to hurt you even more.'

I look up into her face and know I have to make a decision. Either I put my trust in her and let her do whatever this physio did to fix her brother, or I don't trust her, argue against her suggestion, and potentially ruin whatever progress we may have made here today.

Marriage.

I had no idea there would be so many difficult choices I'd have to make.

I can see you laughing there, you know. *Stop it.*

'Alright, just go easy,' I tell her, and roll over.

I feel her straddling my thighs, and her warm hands on my lower back. This feels unaccountably nice.

It doesn't do much for the back pain, though.

'Okay, just take a deep breath in,' she instructs. I do as I'm told. 'Now breathe out slowly.'

As I do, Jessica starts to press downwards and outwards with her hands. At first, this feels awful, but as her hands slide to either side of my spine I feel an instant relief.

'Wow, that's doing something,' I tell her.

'Good. Let's try it again.'

I breathe a load of air in again, and let it out slowly as she again presses down. This feels even better the second time around.

By the time I've taken in and let out another four deep breaths, the pain has lessened considerably. So much so that my thoughts again turn to the bedroom, and I feel my penis twitch from his cramped position underneath my pelvis.

Another couple of these and I might be good to go again!

I breathe in super deep this time, wanting to get the full effect of Jessica's treatment, and let it out as slowly as possible as she presses down harder on my back.

Ffffsssssblblblblblblbblblprtrtrtrgurtrufnasutututut.

Like some kind of evil creature composed of pure vapour rising from the bowels of hell itself, a loud, unescapable, unpreventable fart escapes from betwixt my buttocks.

Right into Jessica's face.

She gags and jumps off to the side. 'Oh my God!' my wife cries, holding a hand in front of her face.

'I'm so sorry!' I wail, attempting to turn to look at her. This does two things. Firstly, it brings me into the invisible cloud of my own fart gas. This is so noxious it makes my eyes water.

I hadn't even eaten anything that day that would cause such a hideous smell!

Two Weetabix and a chicken-and-mushroom Pot Noodle should not produce the kind of aroma usually associated with an abattoir that's about to go out of business!

Secondly, the movement wakes up my back again, and I'm immediately crippled by a fresh bolt of pain that travels through my entire body.

Jessica looks down at me, horrified. 'Have you . . . have you . . . *followed through?*'

'Oh God no!'

'What's wrong then? Do you have some kind of bowel problem? Should we call someone?'

Like who? An *exorcist*?

'I don't know, I'm not sure. I get a touch of IBS every now and again, but . . . but . . .' I flounder, trying to think of something constructive to say that might mitigate this awful turn of events. 'You farted too!' I blurt out, pointing my finger at her.

This is comprehensively *not* a constructive thing to say.

'Not quite like that,' Jessica replies, edging further away from the fallout zone, just in case there's another air strike incoming. 'I'm sorry, Adam, I don't mean to embarrass you but, that was just . . . just . . .'

It appears that while Jessica can laugh off a ladylike fart during yoga, she is not quite so able to laugh off the kind of flatulence that could skin a grizzly bear at twenty paces.

'Your system must be very imbalanced,' Jessica notes thoughtfully. 'Maybe your alkalinity is too high. Have you been eating a lot of alkaline foods recently?'

'I have no idea.'

'That might be it. I might make you a nutritious smoothie. Possibly with wheatgrass and a little cardamom. Do you think that would help?'

'With my back, or the farting? Because I'm pretty sure I need painkillers for the first one.'

'Drugs aren't always the answer, Adam,' Jessica says pointedly. 'You'll often find that natural solutions are the best.'

'Really? Have you got a root in the cupboard I can suck that'll stop this bastard hurting, then?'

'It doesn't work like that.'

'Oh. Do I have to stick it up my ar – aaarrgghh!'

My back protests once more about my twisted posture, and I'm forced to lie back flat on the carpet to ease the throbbing pain.

Being eaten by Nuclear Spiders in the catacombs of Carakor would be a breeze compared to this.

A few moments pass.

I spend them looking at the ceiling and wishing I was dead. Jessica spends them trying to breathe in clean air, and no doubt thinking of how she's going to apologise to Cassie for having to leave me due to my extreme bottom problems.

'I think it would be best,' I begin, swallowing hard, 'if you could help me up to the couch, and maybe go buy me some Nurofen? If that's not too much trouble, of course?'

Oh, don't try the charming Hugh Grant bullshit now, mate.

Not even he could smooth over farting right into a girl's mouth, no matter how many times he stumbled over his words and spoke politely.

'No, no. That's fine,' Jessica replies. I watch her take a deep breath before shuffling back over to me. This isn't all that unexpected, but it still makes me want to curl up and die.

My wife now feels the need to hold her breath when she comes near me. I fear any sex we could possibly have would either be over very, very quickly, or result in asphyxia.

Slowly, with every movement a symphony of agony, Jessica helps me over to the couch.

I lie down carefully, and breathe a sigh of relief as the comfortable sofa takes my full weight.

'You stay there,' Jessica tells me. 'I'll go get you some painkillers.'

And probably some clothes pegs for her nose while she's at it.

'Okay,' I say in a forlorn voice.

As Jessica grabs her coat, pulls on her shoes and shuts the front door behind her, I hear the notification alert go off on my PS4, and look round to see what's happened.

The notification comes from *Realm of Chaos*, and it informs me that Oli has conquered the Citadel of Carakor, killing all the denizens contained within with his flaming axe, and has earned himself three thousand gold coins in the process.

Hah! That's nothing, mate, I think disconsolately to myself. *I can destroy a burgeoning relationship, guarantee a sex-free life* and *wreck a hugely expensive promotional campaign with just my arsehole.*

My back takes four days to heal. In that time Jessica and I don't exchange much more than a few sentences. She's at university a lot, and I take pains to avoid her when she's around the flat.

What exactly do you say to a woman after you've dropped a massive one in her face?

This period without conversation gives me time to pause and reflect about my life up to this point. I don't come up with anything particularly profound, motivating or life-changing, but I do come to one very definite conclusion:

I am never doing fucking yoga again for as long as I live.

JESS

Q. An intimate dinner date? Or big party?
A. Depends on my mood & who the date is with!

26 March

'So, let me get this straight.'

Oh God, here comes the *face* again.

The *Adamface*.

The expression he pulls when he disapproves of something.

This is a face I've seen altogether too much in the past month of my life, and one I now want to punch every time I do see it. My father always taught me that violence solves nothing, but he never had to contend with *Adamface*.

Today's Adamface is a pretty extreme one. The brow is more furrowed, the mouth is more twisted, the nose is more wrinkled.

Who'd have thought telling someone they were going to be having a party would be such a bad thing?

'So you're saying we're having a party for all the people in the building?' Adamface says.

'Yeah! I thought it would be great. Get to know a few people, have some *fun* . . .'

* * *

Fun hasn't exactly been a part of the Holborne household recently, what with the bad back and everything.

I still feel guilty as hell that the yoga did Adam such a huge amount of damage.

Okay, he did fart in my face, so my guilt is a *little* tempered, but I still feel pretty bad. I persuaded him to work out with me despite his reservations, when all he really wanted to do was play his game . . . and look where it got us.

The yoga started out as a great icebreaker, but ended up putting a wall up between us thicker than the fart that ruined the whole thing.

If Adam was awkward around me before, it's a *thousand* times worse now. I'm sure he's convinced himself that I'm disgusted by him and wouldn't want to have sex with him if he were the last man on earth. It's very difficult for me to deal with. I'm used to brash, confident men, who have no self-assurance problems. Okay, they might also tend to be colossal *assholes* because of it, but at least I know where I stand with them. Adam is very different. He's smarter, kinder and more self-effacing than any man I've been with before, but also lacks some of the confidence I've been used to – including when it comes to his body image.

If my father taught me violence is never the answer, then my mother taught me to never be ashamed of my body – even when it lets me down. Adam's let him down twice thanks to me and my yoga, but that doesn't make him *disgusting*.

If anything, seeing him lying on that couch looking small and vulnerable brought out the mothering instinct in me, and it actually made him *more* attractive – once I'd managed to forget just how bad that fart truly was.

But what I think doesn't seem to matter. He's convinced himself that we're never going to move into the same bedroom together, and there's not much I seem to be able to do to change that, short of slipping him Rohypnol.

I'm not *quite* that criminally minded, however, so I figured I'd settle for the next best thing: booze.

And what better way to get the booze flowing than an impromptu party to get to know the neighbours? We can have some fun, meet some new people, and then throw them out of the apartment early enough to do something about breaking that wall back down again.

Good plan, eh?

Except there's Adamface, and everything it implies.

Adam is not what you'd call the *spontaneous* type.

'*Fun*? With a bunch of people we've never met?' Adam moans, leaning against the kitchen island with his arms crossed.

'Yes. What's wrong with that?'

He gives me an exasperated look. 'The thing is, you're American, and as such are open and welcoming by your nature. Correct?'

'Um. I guess so. We try to be as friendly as we possibly can.'

'Right. Whereas I am British, and we, generally speaking, can't stand one another. Especially strangers.'

I shake my head. 'That's not true, Adam. Come on.'

'No, no, no. It *is*. We do a good job of *pretending* we're happy to meet complete strangers in a so-called *relaxed and happy environment*, but in reality we find the experience to be largely traumatic, and best avoided under normal circumstances.'

My eyes narrow. 'You sure you're not just talking about yourself here, pal?'

'Nope. It's a part of the great British psyche. We'd much rather hang around with people we've known for years, simply because we don't have to be on our best behaviour, or be polite. Put us in a social situation with friends and family and we're golden, but stick us in a room with twenty or so strange faces and the blood pressure skyrockets.'

'That's a very cynical world view.'

'It's a very cynical country.' He raises a finger. 'And on another note, the people who live in this apartment block are likely to be quite, quite *awful*.'

Oh, this is getting ridiculous now.

'What the hell makes you say that?' I ask. 'Have you even *met* any of them?'

'Nope, but you do know where we are, don't you?'

'London.'

'*Ah ah* . . . not just London. *West* London. The posh bit. And this entire block of luxury flats is converted from an old hotel called the Cardington.'

'So what?'

Adam gives me a condescending look that makes my blood simmer. 'Jessica, do you know what kind of people live in luxury flats in a converted building called the Cardington, that has excellent views over Hyde Park and a twenty-four-hour concierge service?'

'What?'

'*Cunts*, Jessica.'

I *hate* that word. Hate it, hate it, hate it!

'Gold-plated cunts, in actual fact,' Adam continues, 'whose levels of cuntosity stretch higher and further than any other kind of cun—'

'Enough!' I snap. Beside me is the cutlery drawer. I open it and produce the first thing I can get my hands on. 'If you say that word again, I'm going to shove this right up your ass!'

'You're going to stick a pizza wheel up my bottom if I say cu – if I say that word again?'

'Yes!'

Okay, this may seem a little excessive, but I really do *hate* that word.

Adam looks a combination of suitably apologetic and mildly terrified. 'I won't say it again, I promise.'

'Good.' I poke the pizza wheel in his direction. 'And the party?'

'What about it?'

'We're going to have it, Adam. You may be right, those people might be awful, but I'm going to do something that's probably never occurred to you to try . . .'

'What's that?'

'Not make my mind up until I've actually *met them*.'

Adam sniffs. 'Sounds risky to me.'

I wave the pizza wheel again. It's a lot more threatening than you'd give it credit for at first glance. 'It's happening, Adam. I posted invites through their letter boxes last week, and talked to a few of them in the hallway. Everyone can make it, other than the Iranian couple on the ground floor and Jurgen the surgeon on floor three.'

'Wow. You seem to know a lot about our neighbours already,' Adam says with surprise.

I make a face. 'That's generally because I don't rush past them as quickly as I can, giving a cursory head nod and a half-whispered *good morning* as I do so.'

Adam shrugs expansively. 'But that's how we say *hello* in this country!'

'Yeah, well, you'll have twenty people tonight to say hello to the American way.'

'Tonight? The party's *tonight*?'

'Yep.'

'And you're springing this on me *now*? Why didn't you give me any warning?'

I put my hands on my hips. 'What? And give you the chance to wriggle out of it like you did last week when I wanted you to come to the club where I used to work to meet my friend Hen?'

'I was *busy*.'

'Playing *Realm of Chaos. Again*.'

'Yes.'

'Instead of meeting my friend at a strip club.'

'Yes.'

'A *strip club*, Adam. Your wife offered you the opportunity to spend time with her in a strip club, and you turned it down in favour of a computer game.'

Adam looks at the floor. 'It's a *video* game. And I'd say most wives would be happy their husbands didn't want to ogle naked women all night.'

Damn it, he's got a point there.

I choose not to admit it. 'Regardless, husband dearest, this party is happening *tonight*, and you're going to be there.' I think for a moment. 'Would you like to invite your video game friend Oli along too?'

Adam shakes his head. 'No. He wouldn't enjoy it.'

'Why not?'

'Just trust me, he wouldn't.'

I choose not to pursue this. If Adam wants to keep his damn friends separate, then there's not much I can do to change that.

'Alright, Adam. No problem. Anyway, who knows? You might meet somebody new who isn't a gold-plated word I'm never going to use.'

'Oh, alright. *Fine.*'

'Great!' I put the pizza wheel back in the drawer. I feel its work here is done. 'I'm going to Oxford Street to see if I can buy myself a dress. I suggest you come along. You could do with a smart shirt.'

Adam looks at me suspiciously. 'How do you know I don't have a smart shirt? You haven't seen my entire wardrobe.'

I laugh. 'Adam, I know we've only been married a few weeks, but I already know you well enough to know that you don't own *any* shirts. You go to work in a Superman T-shirt half the time.'

'Fair point. I'll race you to Primark.'

'Oh no.' I wag my finger. 'We've got thirty grand to play with. We're going *designer*.'

Adamface makes a triumphant return at this point, but I have a strategy to head it off at the pass. 'I don't mind if you want to go into Forbidden Planet as well to get some comics.'

'Great!'

* * *

I'm actually very proud of how that entire conversation went.

It's important to me to get to know this man properly, so I know whether I made the right decision or not in going ahead with the wedding. I'm pleased to say I'm getting a pretty good handle on what makes him tick already.

It's not just conversations I need to have with the guy, though. I need to know whether we're physically compatible as well. I may sound like some kind of horny teenager when I say that, but it's important for a girl to know if her man is a good fit in the bedroom – figuratively and literally. I didn't have the luxury of several months to get to know Adam before our wedding – and I sure as hell don't want to spend the *next* several months in some kind of sham marriage with a guy who's totally unsuitable for me.

Hence tonight's party, and my attempts to loosen Adam up.

Oh God, I sound like one of the jocks at college, don't I? An impromptu party to *loosen somebody up*? Next thing you know, I'll be chugging a beer bong and waving my ass out of a second-storey window.

By some miracle, Adam manages to find himself a nice dark-blue shirt, and I pick up a purple strapless dress that actually seems to complement my red hair. If nothing else, the Holbornes will look great tonight.

As will the terrace that runs down the entire left-hand side of our penthouse apartment. I spent a constructive hour stringing a series of cool blue-and-white fairy lights around the railings, and have also wheeled out the drinks trolley that Adam discovered in a kitchen cupboard this afternoon, while he was searching for matches to light the two gas patio heaters.

This apartment really is the gift that keeps on giving. I'm going to have a good search top to bottom next week to see if there's a secret cupboard full of iPads and Pandora bracelets somewhere.

'You want a drink before people start arriving?' I ask Adam as he comes out of his bedroom and up on to the terrace, buttoning up the bottom of the shirt as he does so.

It makes me cringe to still say that he's coming out of *his* bedroom, rather than coming out of *our* bedroom, but that's what this whole evening is about. The closest we've got so far as a couple was that yoga session, and that was ended abruptly by an unwanted bodily function. I'm just hoping a social function like this might get things back on track again.

The double Jack Daniel's and Coke I've poured for him should be a good start to my master plan.

'Is that wise?' he asks.

'Yeah! Of course! It'll loosen – I mean, it'll calm your nerves before everyone gets here.'

He looks dubious. 'I'm not really that much of a drinker, Jessica.'

'Oh, go on,' I cajole. 'It'll be *fine*.'

Adam still looks reluctant, but you can tell from the look in his eyes that he's given up the fight. He plucks the drink out of my hand and takes a sip. 'Got the trolley nicely stacked, then,' he notes.

I nod happily.

The thing is *overflowing* with alcohol. Thank God there's an off-licence less than two streets away.

Adam looks around at the decorations. 'Not bad, not bad. I think I saw something like this in a movie once. Probably some bad romantic comedy starring Hugh Grant.'

It was an episode of *Friends* actually, but I'm keeping that to myself so I don't sound too hideously 1990s.

The doorbell goes. Adam looks at his watch. 'Bit early,' he states.

'You go see who it is, Adam. I'll wait here and turn the heaters up.' It's March, so there's still a chill in the air. We don't want our guests who choose to come out here to feel cold, so I figure turning the heaters up full blast will do the trick.

Also, it's an excuse to make Adam do the meet-and-greet. I know I'm good with people, but he evidently needs the practice.

For the briefest of moments I have the image of my mother when I was twelve years old, ordering my father to go speak to his brother's wife after Thanksgiving dinner. *And do it nicely, Charles. She didn't really mean what she said about your boat.'* The tone I just used on Adam to tell him to go open the front door was exactly the same.

I take a long, deep gulp of the glass of red wine I poured for myself before Adam emerged.

I am not my mother, I am not my mother, I repeat silently to myself.

Of course, the minute you start saying that to yourself is the instant you have in fact *become your mother*, but I don't have time to worry about it now, as Adam has appeared again, with an orange person beside him.

Aah . . .

I was hoping a few more of the neighbours would be here before introducing Adam to Hugo Wentworth. Meeting him first probably isn't the best way to convince my husband that not all of our neighbours are rich idiots.

Adam's lips are pursed together, and his eyes are flinty as he approaches me. 'Oh look, Jessica, our first guest has arrived. His name is *Hugo*, apparently.'

By the expression on his face, that's not the only four-letter name he'd give our neighbour from the floor below.

'Hello, Jessica!' Hugo says. 'I was just saying to Adam here how fabulous it was to meet you the other day, and how much I've been looking forward to being in your company again.' Hugo smoothly moves past Adam, invades my personal space, squeezes one of my arms in a relatively uncomfortable manner, and plants a kiss on my cheek that goes on for a second too long.

'Hello, Hugo,' I reply. 'It's nice to see you again.'

Hugo Wentworth is in his mid-forties, but dresses like he's still twenty-three – white skinny jeans, loose pink Burberry shirt and a black Superdry beanie.

Yes, that's right, I said *beanie*. A forty-four-year-old man, who spends far too long under the tanning machine, wears a beanie.

And Gucci flip-flops, apparently. In March.

Jeez . . . where's Cassie McFlasterton when you need her? These two would make the perfect couple.

'Sorry for getting here a little early,' Hugo continues, flicking his fringe out of his face. 'I'm full of energy after my herbal shower, and avocado-and-chia-seed power shake. Just couldn't hang around the old apartment any longer.'

The Adamface this comment creates is so enormously Adamface that I'm starting to worry for Hugo's personal safety.

I'm personally quite impressed by Hugo's approach to nutrition, but I wisely keep this to myself, as Adam might well explode if I start chatting to the guy about the detoxifying attributes of chia seed.

'Adam? Why don't you go make sure the music is playing on the iPod dock? I'll pour Hugo a drink.'

'Okay, will do,' my husband replies, sounding like he's being strangled. I hope some other people arrive very soon. If Adam has to spend much more time alone with Hugo here, the amount of energy his Adamface will consume might lead to some kind of coronary episode.

Luckily, the doorbell goes again just as Adam is selecting random shuffle on the iPod, and Hugo is telling me about how much the blue fairy lights remind him of his Maserati's headlamps.

This time Adam lets in Aiden and Melody, who live in the apartment next to Hugo on the floor below. I breathe a sigh of relief.

These two are pretty down to earth. Adam should have a better time with them.

Indeed, he has a smile on his face as he brings them over. 'Aiden and Melody are here, Jessica. Aiden says he likes my articles on GamesReport!'

This is *excellent* news. Adam will have at least one person here who he shares something in common with. As long as the two of them don't bust out *Realm of Chaos* at any point, I'll be very happy.

Also, Melody is Canadian, so we have a lot in common with each other, coming from 'across the pond' as we both do.

Saying that an American and a Canadian have *a lot in common* gives you some idea of how truly alien the United Kingdom can be sometimes.

Over the course of the next half an hour, the rest of our guests arrive, and the apartment is abuzz with conversation.

It's an eclectic bunch we've got here, I'm not going to lie. There's Antoine and St John, for starters. A couple of gay architects who live on floor two, they are apparently trying their level best to bring the cravat back into fashion, with mixed results.

Sally and Peter both work for the same insurance company in the city, and are therefore quite relaxingly dull.

Then there's Beedle.

Beedle is what you'd call *distinctive*. She's an artist who lives next to Antoine and St John. A terrible artist by all accounts. She showed me some of her work when I dropped off the invite the other day. I can only assume that Beedle is independently wealthy, as she sure as hell hasn't made her money selling her artwork, which largely seems to consist of people with missing limbs having complicated sex – sometimes with each other, and sometimes with a variety of farmyard implements. It's quite disturbing.

Beedle favours a kaftan and a headscarf, which is only right and proper.

Last on the guest list is Lachlan, a very polite young Scottish guy whose father owns half of Dumfries. Lachlan has come to London to seek his fortune as an actor – or rather he's come to seek *another* fortune, as there's already an extremely large one waiting for him back in Scotland when he fails to make it past the auditions for a Weetabix advert.

However you want to look at it, this is a group of people that don't make for a boring evening – except Sally and Peter, I guess, but even they can talk about their last holiday in the Seychelles if they really want to.

I'm curious to know how Adam will interact with all of them as the evening goes on. He bellyached all day about not wanting to mix with people like this, but actions often speak louder than words, and I'm keen to see how prejudiced Adam actually is.

I realise that what I'm doing here this evening is actually conducting one giant social experiment, and find that I'm not bothered by this at all. If the career as a nutritionist goes to the wall, I could have one as a poorly paid psychologist instead.

With this speculative thought in mind, I pour myself another glass of wine and go over to where Sally and Peter are chatting to Beedle about how much she can insure *Armless Lovers in a Rapeseed Field* for.

Two hours pass.

These people are *assholes*.

Sally and Peter were extremely condescending to me when I asked about additional cover for the apartment, Antoine told me that my complexion didn't go well with my purple dress, Lachlan won't shut up about how good the trout fishing is on the River Esk at this time of year, Beedle wants to put one of her appalling paintings above our fake mantelpiece, and Hugo Wentworth keeps touching me on the arm. He also stroked his index finger down it the last time. It left a wet mark.

I look at my watch. It's ten o'clock.

Can I throw them all out now?

What's the etiquette when your living room is full of assholes?

Set off the fire sprinklers?

You'd think I'd get some support from my husband, given everything he said about our neighbours before the party, but my plan to get him inebriated enough to relax him into some late-night sex has gone a little *too* well.

He's *shit-faced*, and appears to be having a whale of a time.

I see Adam out on the terrace, and go out to join him. Maybe I can take him to one side and get him to help me come up with a plan to get rid of the asshole convention as quickly as possible. This means getting him away from Hugo Wentworth, who inexplicably has become Adam's new best friend.

'No! I swear I'm telling you the truth, my boy!' Hugo is saying to him, arms held wide, and fringe now plastered to his forehead with excited perspiration. 'It was eight feet long and moved so fast it was almost gone before I got the chance to get a good look!'

'Wow!' Adam replies, wide-eyed and aghast. He has that unique, hectic look on his face that only the well and truly over-the-limit can accomplish. He sees me come over. 'Jeshica! Hugo saw a shark! He was surfin' in Hawaii, and saw a bloody shark!'

I am less impressed than my husband with this revelation, as I'm still fairly sober, and was brought up with the Pacific Ocean lapping at my ankles.

'That's cool,' I tell him. 'Seen a few myself surfing back home.'

Adam points a wobbly finger at me. 'Oh! Oh! Thas right! You come from California!'

'Yes I do.' I suppose I should be pleased he can remember that much, given the state he's in.

'Surfin' sounds grrrreat,' Adam exclaims, in a wistful voice. 'I always wanted to go surfin'. Tried it once down in Cornwall. A seagull shit on me and I caught the flu.'

Hugo claps Adam on the back. 'You should try it as soon as you can! There's nothing like you and the wave . . . it's *poetry*.'

I roll my eyes. Hugo sounds like every guy I bought weed off when I was a teenager.

'My mate Davo tried to teach me when we was down in Cornwall,' Adam continues. 'He showed me how to lie on the board and paddle out.' He gives me an unfocused grin. 'I can show you, if you like?'

Visions of my new husband spreadeagle on the floor, thrashing his arms around like a madman, fill my head. 'Um. No. That's okay, Adam. Can I get you anything? A glass of water, perhaps?'

'No, no.' He waves me off. 'I'm good.' He then notices the drinks trolley sat by the bi-fold doors and points at it. 'Hey look! That'll do!'

'That'll do for what?' I ask.

'I can show you how to surf!'

'I *know* how to surf, Adam! My brother taught me when I was seven years old.'

He completely ignores me and goes over to the now largely empty drinks trolley. Adam pushes a few remaining cans of lager off its shiny surface and lies down on it haphazardly. 'Hugo! Gis a push!' he demands.

Hugo laughs and immediately goes over. 'Now, hold on tight there, Adam! I can deadlift twice my own weight, you know!'

'Pfft!' Adam exclaims, waving one drunk hand. 'Push me as hard as you can.' He looks up. 'Out of the way everyone! I'm going surfin'!'

'Stop! Adam, this isn't a good idea,' I insist, but he's too drunk to listen to anything resembling good advice.

'Push me, Hugo! Push me!' he repeats, eyes bulging.

Wentworth doesn't need telling twice. With a loud grunt he gives the drinks trolley an almighty heave, sending it and Adam hurtling across the terrace. The guests scatter, and the trolley narrowly misses knocking over one of the two huge patio heaters.

Adam then careens headlong for the railings surrounding the terrace – the only thing between him and a very grisly death five storeys below.

'Adam!' I shout and run after him.

Everyone at the party watches as Adam, laughing his head off as he pretends to do the front crawl, flies head-first into the railing with an enormous *GLOING* noise.

And boy, oh boy, *head-first* is absolutely the most important word in that last sentence, because Adam's head neatly slides right between two of the railing's wrought-iron bars. He couldn't have done it with more accuracy if he'd been stone-cold sober and had spent four hours working out the calculations on a flip board.

A line of the blue fairy lights I've strung up for the party inexplicably wraps itself around his forehead as well, compounding the problem.

'Aaaarggh!' my husband screams and tries to pull his head back. Sadly, while it's easy for a head and ears to slide *forward* between two metal bars, it's extremely difficult for them to slide back out again.

He's stuck fast.

'Adam! Are you okay?' I ask, reaching him, having to make a wide berth around his flailing arms and legs to save myself from injury as I do so.

'Pull me out! Pull me out!' he wails.

'I'll get you free!' Hugo Wentworth bellows, and grabs both of Adam's legs.

Before I have the chance to object on the grounds of sanity, Hugo yanks Adam's legs backwards with all of his orange might.

'Yeeeaaaarrgghh!' screams Adam. 'Stop! Stop!'

'Stop it, Hugo!' Melody orders, pulling the orange maniac away. 'You'll rip his ears off.'

I lean over the railing to see if I can make eye contact with my stricken husband. I've never seen a birth happen live in front of me, but if I ever do, I'm sure the baby's crowning head will look pretty similar to the vision of Adam's red, blotchy cranium poking from between the bars.

What's even more disconcerting is that he still has the bright blue fairy lights wrapped around his forehead, which roughly resemble a brightly lit crown, so he's no normal baby – he's the sweet Little Baby Jesus . . . Las Vegas edition.

'Get me out, Jessica! Please!' he entreats me.

Oh my. This is *horrible*.

I think my mothering instincts are about to kick in again.

I look up to see that all of our party guests are now surrounding Adam with a mixture of curiosity, horror and concealed amusement on their faces.

Beedle is making framing gestures with her hands, suggesting that very soon she will be embarking on a new, exciting project – *Headless Drunkard Inserted into Skyline*.

Lachlan has produced his smartphone and is clicking away with a smile on his face. The pictures will no doubt give his friends a good laugh while they're waiting for the next poor trout to swim along and get caught on their hooks – the little Scottish shitheads.

'Alright, everybody just give Adam a little room please!' I say, affecting what I hope is the voice of authority.

'How are we going to get him out?' Aiden asks.

'No more pulling!' comes the muffled, pained reply from over the railing.

'Butter!' Antoine pipes up. 'My leettle sister got caught in the fence at our villa in Andalusia. Luckily, my grandmother had a *lot* of butter. She used to churn it herself.'

I shrug my shoulders. 'Worth a try. You guys stay here and keep him calm while I go get it.'

I'm only gone thirty seconds, but when I get back, the crowd has closed tight around poor Adam. 'What's the view like?' Lachlan asks him.

'Oh, it's fucking *marvellous*!' Adam replies, voice pebble-dashed with sarcasm. 'The angle I'm getting of the pavement below is *remarkable*. Maybe I'll just stay here for an hour or so to really *soak it in*!'

'Move out of the way, people,' I demand. 'I have butter.'

This will hopefully be the weirdest sentence I'll ever say.

I lean back over the balustrade, stick of Lurpak in hand. 'Adam, I'm going to have to smear you in butter. It should help free you.'

'Really?'

'Yes, it's the only way.'

Except . . . have you ever tried to smear Lurpak straight from a cold fridge? It's not easy.

I start to rub the cold, hard butter along the side of Adam's head.

'Ow! Ow! Ow! What are you doing?'

'It's cold! I'm trying to warm it up!'

'By scraping it up and down my face like that? You're giving me friction burns!'

'I'm sorry, but it's not spreading!'

Hugo Wentworth leans over the other side. 'You'll need to warm that up a lot more before it'll start spreading, you know,' he tells me, stating the blindingly obvious. 'Why don't you pop the end in his mouth? That should do the trick.'

'What?' Adam snaps.

'You think I should stick it in his *mouth*?' I reply with disbelief.

Adam's face goes even redder. 'I'm not having a load of butter shoved in my gob! I'm not a suckling pig, you lunatic!'

'Yes, Hugo,' I agree. 'It's a very bad idea.'

Hugo shrugs. 'Well, it's either his mouth or one of ours.' He looks down at Adam. 'Whose mouth bacteria would you prefer spread all over your face?'

Which is, I hate to say it, a good point.

'What about the patio heater?' Aiden suggests. 'That'll melt it.'

Hugo shakes his head. 'It'll be too hot. The butter will melt too fast.' He gestures towards Adam's mouth. 'Go on, just pop it in for a few seconds. It'll do the trick, I promise.'

I look down at Adam and his fairy-light crown. 'What do you think?'

He looks like he's about to burst into tears. 'Okay. But make it quick. There are a load of cabbies down there looking up at us.'

Sure enough, I look past Adam's head to see a gathering of four or five taxi drivers all looking up and taking pictures. Best we get this over with as soon as possible.

'Open wide then,' I tell him. 'Here comes the butter.'

This comment results in ultimate Adamface, only made worse by the bright blue glow provided by the fairy lights.

I place the Lurpak lightly in Adam's mouth. Now I feel like I'm force-feeding the neon Little Baby Jesus a stick of butter, and my guilt levels skyrocket. Sunday school never prepared me for this kind of thing.

'Hmfn lngf dn stfm lfnm?' Adam asks.

I have no idea what he's saying, but it's probably not good. I doubt there are many people in the world that would have anything good to say in such circumstances, other than your average right-wing politician.

'Okay, I'm going to remove the butter now,' I tell Adam after a good twenty seconds.

As I pull it out, he retches. 'I'm never eating toast again as long as I live,' he moans.

But, miraculously, the warmth of Adam's mouth has done the trick. The butter has melted enough for me to get to work.

In no time at all, Adam's head is covered. I've been very liberal with the smearing, as I don't want it to hurt him when we try to pull him out.

I'll have to throw those fairy lights away, though, which is a shame as they were from John Lewis.

'Excellent!' Hugo crows as I step back. 'That should do it!' He grabs Adam's leg again. Hugo is going about this with way too much enthusiasm for my liking. 'Shall we?' he exclaims happily.

I take Adam's other leg and call over the balustrade to him. 'Okay, Adam?' No reply. 'Adam? Can you hear me? ADAM?!'

'What? *What?* My ears are full of fucking butter!' he shouts back.

'We're going to pull you out slowly!' I shout back.

'What!?'

'I said, WE'RE GOING TO – oh, never mind.' I look up at Hugo. 'Take it nice and easy.'

And with that, we start to pull Adam backwards.

At first there's no movement. He still seems stuck fast.

We're going to have to call the fire service out at this rate. Can you imagine the humiliation?

I start to put more effort in, trying not to panic as I do so. Hugo also starts to pull harder.

'Oww,' Adam moans.

A little harder.

'Owwwww,' Adam moans louder.

Harder still.

'OWW.'

Harder.

'Fuck! Fuck! Fuck! OWWW!'

'Oh bugger this,' Hugo says, and once more puts all his strength into it.

'FUCK! AAARGH! FUCK!' Adam screams.

Schlurrrp!

Adam's head comes free with an audible squelch. Such is the force that Hugo used, it makes the drinks trolley rocket backwards. One of Adam's feet slams painfully into Lachlan's testicles – in an amazing case of instant karma, if ever I saw one.

The trolley then leans drunkenly to one side as the wheels on the left give way, sending poor butter-covered Adam to the patio floor in a squalling, red-faced heap.

I go over, pushing past Lachlan, who is now bent double and has gone quite red-faced himself.

The next thing I say is possibly the dumbest question anyone has ever asked another human being. 'Are you okay, Adam?'

At first there is no answer. My husband merely sits up, rubbing at his reddened ear with one hand. He then looks up at everyone gathered around him and appears to reach a very definite conclusion.

'Get out,' he says in a level voice. 'All of you, please *get out*.'

Sally baulks. 'Well, that's a bit rude,' she says, earning a nod of agreement from Peter.

Adam stares at her. 'I am drunk, covered in butter, and my ears are ringing like a bastard, so I think you'll forgive me if I sound just a *tad* rude.' He takes a deep breath. 'Now, pretty please, if you'd be so very, very kind, all of you – leave me alone!'

I suppose this is as good a way to finish a party as any other.

I would object to the level of rudeness on display, but these people are still assholes by and large, so I'll forgive Adam his trespasses on this occasion.

While he stumbles into the bathroom to clean himself up, I wish our guests a good night at the door.

'Good party!' Hugo Wentworth tells me as he sidles out last. 'We'll have to do it again sometime.'

'Er . . . yeah. Sounds like a plan,' I say, closing the door immediately in his face.

I walk back into the living room and down the corridor to the bathroom. Adam is nowhere in sight, but the sink is covered in watery butter, indicating that he has definitely been here.

With a sigh, I open his bedroom door. Sure enough, there he is – fully clothed, face down on the bed, with the remnants of the Lurpak still clogging one ear.

'How are you feeling?' I ask him in a quiet voice.

'Fantastic,' comes the muffled response. Adam rolls over to look at me bleary-eyed. 'This would have been only the second-worst night of my life, after what happened at the school disco with Penny Braintree, but the stick of butter in the mouth puts it right at number one.'

'I'm sorry,' I say with a sigh. 'This wasn't how this evening was supposed to go.'

Adam rubs his eyes. 'Oh? And how was it supposed to go, Jessica?'

I squirm a little. 'You know . . . I hoped we'd have some fun . . . have a few drinks . . . see where things went?'

He seems genuinely surprised. 'Oh. I see.'

My brow creases. 'Do you?'

It's Adam's turn to sigh. 'Yes. Yes I do, Jessica.' He sticks one finger in his ear and scoops out some butter. 'But as plans go, it didn't really pay off, did it? Unless you get a kick out of smearing your men in warm butter, I suppose.'

'Of course not.'

He looks to the ceiling. 'Well, look. I'm tired, I have a headache, and I'm pretty sure when I'm sober tomorrow I'll feel incredibly embarrassed and unable to ever leave this apartment again, so if you don't mind I'm going to try and get some sleep now.'

'Oh, okay. I really am sorry, Adam.'

'Yeah. Okay. Thanks.'

Damn it.

I close the door on my upset husband with a sigh, walk back through into the kitchen, and pour myself another large and badly judged glass of red wine.

Tomorrow I'll try to explain myself a little better to Adam. All I wanted to do was bring us closer together again, I hope he can understand that. Okay, I pushed things too much, which I have a nasty habit of doing sometimes when things aren't going my way, but I can't help but feel a little impatient at the moment.

I want this marriage to work. I want something *real* to happen between Adam and me, and I'm deathly afraid that unless I'm the one to instigate it, it'll never happen. Maybe if I can talk through all of this with him, it'll mend some fences.

I think my heart was in the right place, even if my brain quite clearly wasn't.

I'm also going to pop down to the Tesco Express across the street first thing tomorrow morning, because if there's one thing I know for definite, it's that we are completely out of butter.

ARTICLE IN *THE DAILY TORRENT* ONLINE NEWSPAPER

1 April

IS SOCIALITY'S BIG GAMBLE PAYING OFF?

By Sonny Duhal

It's been seven weeks since Sociality married off two complete strangers. How is the marriage going? And was the stunt wedding worth all the hassle?

Cassie McFlasterton looks positive when I ask her those questions, but there's something in her eyes that tells me she's feeling the pressure. After all, the entrepreneur has gambled a lot on the success of this campaign. If it doesn't run smoothly, then it's a gamble she may well end up losing.

'It's all going wonderfully!' she assures me, offering one of her ultra-confident smiles. 'The happy couple are doing incredibly well!'

'What about the sinking speedboat?' I counter. 'And I hear reports on the grapevine of a party gone wrong, involving an accident with some butter?' Neither of these has been mentioned on the website, or in the lavish adverts, but it doesn't take much detective work to find out that not all is going according to McFlasterton's plans.

The ultra-confident smile cracks, proving my point. 'Oh, those are nothing!' McFlasterton tries to reassure me. 'Just a few teething problems. Trust me, the Holbornes are doing well – and falling for each other quite nicely!'

I move on to ask her how the wedding has impacted the dating site. Has Sociality seen a positive reaction from new and old subscribers alike? 'Yes!' she replies enthusiastically. 'Everyone's talking about Adam and Jess on social media, and our subscriptions have seen a 10 per cent increase in the last month.'

This is a good sign for the company, given how much money they need to recoup from the campaign's total costs.

Costs which are only set to increase with McFlasterton's plan to fly the couple out to California for a week to spend time with Jessica's family. This will be the second trip the Holbornes will be making together, and will no doubt provide the Sociality marketing machine with even more material to use in their extensive promotion.

All this forces me to ask two questions: Is this really a marriage? Or just one big publicity stunt? Do those Sociality algorithms actually work? Or are they just a big con job, when you get right down to it? Can you really put two complete strangers together, based just on a profile on a website?

I, for one, would love the chance to speak to Adam and Jessica, to see how they would reply to those questions, but so far my requests have been denied by the owner of that ultra-confident smile.

ADAM

Q. Do you love the sun? Or are you a winter snuggler?
A. The sun, thanks. In small doses, though. I'm not a lizard.

9 April

'Would you like the Continental breakfast, or the full English, sir?'

'Do either of them come with butter?'

The flight attendant blinks at me a couple of times. I doubt many people are that concerned with the butter content of their in-flight meal. 'The Continental breakfast does, sir,' she reliably informs me.

'I'll have the full English then,' I decide.

I have resolutely gone off butter. Once a food product has caused you public humiliation and hearing difficulties, it's a little hard to maintain a healthy relationship with it.

Speaking of finding it hard to maintain a healthy relationship, I think I've made a big mistake when it comes to the one I'm currently in.

I didn't really know what kind of woman I wanted to marry, but I'm fairly sure I wouldn't have stipulated that she'd be the type to ply me with alcohol until I nearly killed myself with a drinks trolley, just to see whether I'm any good in bed or not.

I confess I still haven't been able to work the logic out in Jessica's plan, but then again, from talking to her about the whole debacle the next day, neither has she.

Okay, I kind of get what she was trying to do.

I cheerfully confess to being royally confused about this entire marriage so far, and have been more wishy-washy than Widow Twankey's eldest son, so Jess trying to force the issue is understandable. She seems to have a clear idea of what she wants from this relationship, even if I don't. I know she wants love and romance – whereas I don't know if I want sex, romance or just the opportunity to keep a West London postcode.

This all seemed a lot more straightforward before I said 'I do', but since then my life has become a jumble of very perplexing emotions.

Is this marriage something I want to make an effort with any more?

Or should I just call it quits and move on with my mercifully butter-free life?

There's those living arrangements to take into consideration, of course. If I do walk away from this thing, I am homeless. Calvin and those other nobs have already replaced me in the house over in Croydon, so I'd have to move back in with my parents – and suffer a two-hour commute every morning from the coast. You can imagine how keen I am to avoid that.

Then there's my cut of the thirty grand, which I've spent hardly any of yet. There are important things I need that money for, and I'm sure Cassie (who I can currently hear behind me, complaining about the quality of her airplane coffee) would whip the cash out of my bank account before you can say boo to a goose, if I decided I wanted out.

All of this means that I'm going to continue to live under the same roof as a woman who would have got me killed, if the railings around the patio had been a foot lower. Even though I wasn't shuffled off this mortal coil by a sixty-foot plunge, the events of the other night have made it impossible for me to leave the apartment without cringing every time I see one of our hysterically Londonite neighbours.

Jessica has also made me despise butter, which is a real pain in the arse, as I enjoy a good crumpet.

But then, she did look dynamite in that purple dress, and the look of remorse in her eyes when she got a proper chance to apologise to me was quite adorable.

I'm sure I'm not the first man in history to be attracted to a woman who's nearly killed him – though I am quite sure I'm the first to need Lurpak syringed out of his ears afterwards.

All in all, I am well and truly stuck between a rock and a redhead, to ruin a well-known phrase.

I turn to look at the object of my confusion, who is happily munching a croissant and watching an old episode of *The Simpsons* on the small TV screen in front of her.

Jessica's going home, so you can't really blame her for looking pleased about it.

The several hours we've spent on the plane together have been the most time we've been in each other's company since the party. We've lived more or less separate lives since that night, and haven't really spoken much.

I'm sure she's had a lot of the same thoughts running around her head as have been running around mine . . . except the thing about the butter. She must be questioning the decision to get married as much as I am. I'm racked with confusion over how I feel about the whole thing, and that can't be easy for her to deal with, considering she seems a lot more certain about what she wants from this relationship. The party was her first attempt to understand what the hell I'm about – and given how much of a failure it was, I'm not entirely sure whether she'll stick around for a second.

We are in an exquisitely awkward limbo at the moment. Jess seems to know what she wants from this relationship, whereas I comprehensively do not. We should have sat down at the beginning of this thing and made our feelings about what we wanted from the marriage clear from the outset, but we didn't, and now we're stuck in the marital mud without a spade to dig ourselves out.

I'm avoiding any such conversation, at least until I've got my own head straight, which makes me careful at best . . . and a coward at worst.

Needless to say, the atmosphere in the apartment has been what you could call *tense*.

When Cassie came round last week and told us this trip was happening, it broke the tension quite nicely – for Jessica anyway. There's nothing like being told you're getting a free trip home to brighten your mood considerably.

I wasn't so sure, of course. When you're having severe doubts about the future of your advertising-campaign marriage, the last thing you really want to do is jet off to meet the in-laws.

But then Cassie told me she'd already arranged seven days' annual leave for me from GamesReport, so I had my mind made up for me. Who the hell says no to a week off work? Not me.

Especially as Watlow has now raised his levels of petty nastiness beyond that of your average pantomime villain. He's started charging us for our coffee, including the sugar packets. If we flush the toilet more than once, we're issued with a reprimand for wasting water. I'm now so scared to take a crap at work that I've become somewhat constipated. I would ask Jess to whip me up one of her smoothies, but I don't particularly want to expose her to any more of my bowel problems right about now.

Also, not going to work means I get to avoid seeing those Sociality posters on the tube. They never used to bother me that much, but now they've got *my bloody face on them*, the ride into work every day has become an exercise in *exquisite* embarrassment.

Given all of that, the seven days away from my hideous commute, and Watlow's reign of terror, are something of a godsend. I'm very glad to have the time off, and will put up with whatever plans Cassie has in store.

This is what Cassie McFlasterton is very good at – manoeuvring you into agreeing to whatever she wants you to do, by the simple expedient of dangling a big fat carrot in front of your face.

If she'd been the one trying to manipulate me into the bedroom, I'd have been hog-tied and covered in baby oil before I could call in backup.

This image puts me off my anaemic-looking full English breakfast, so I push it away and look out of the window at the very pretty Californian countryside as it slides by beneath us. We'll be landing in San Francisco in about forty-five minutes, and my first visit to America will begin.

Hopefully it will be a pleasant one that won't make things even worse between Jessica and me. In fact, who knows? Maybe a dose of Californian spring sunshine will be just the thing we need to get back on an even keel.

I will be avoiding butter as much as is humanly possible, though. This will probably prove difficult, as most of America is covered in the stuff.

We're met at the airport by two swish rental cars, driven by a couple of talkative and friendly chauffeurs of Mexican extraction. Cassie and her new photographer, Alex, get into one car (Derek was quietly 'let go' after the speedboat incident) and Jessica and I climb into the other.

The car is *enormous*. Ridiculously so.

If I had wifi and a bucket, I could live in it for an extended period of time.

Jessica is nearly vibrating in her seat with excitement as we pull away from the terminal.

'It'll take a couple of hours to get home at this time of day,' she tells me. 'The 17 will be busy, but it shouldn't be too bad once we're past Santa Cruz.'

I don't really understand much of that, having never been here before, but it's interesting to hear Jessica talk about the place with such familiarity. If nothing else, this week is going to give me a good idea of how she feels living in my neck of the woods – far from home, and in a place that's both familiar and unfamiliar at the same time.

I settle back into the voluminous seat and close my eyes. Jessica may be too excited to sit still, but the jet lag is starting to really hit me now, so I have no problem with it.

As I slowly doze off, I find myself looking forward to meeting her family for the first time, and being shown around the home that she quite clearly loves. If nothing else, it's better than being sat in the office, getting excoriated by Watlow for not updating the GamesReport website fast enough.

As soon as I get a good look at Carmel-by-the-Sea, I can tell why Jessica was so excited to be back here. It's *gorgeous*.

From the highway leading to it that snakes its way along the edge of a rugged and beautiful coastline, to the chocolate-box town itself, Carmel is the kind of place you wish you'd been brought up in – and then never left.

Given the European influence in Monterey County as a whole, I'm distinctly reminded of a town in one of the warmer southern countries, like Spain or Italy, rather than a small town in the USA. This place would give any rustic European village a run for its money in the quaint, picturesque stakes.

Okay, it is an extremely affluent town in one of the prettiest parts of the USA, so I don't know why I was expecting anything else, but I sure as hell won't be making any complaints about my home away from home for the next seven days.

As we're driving past a stunning beach of white sand and windswept cypress trees, I turn to Jessica. 'So, you were born and brought up in this place?'

'Yeah.'

'And you left it *why?*'

She gives me a rueful smile. 'Every time I come back, I ask myself the same question.'

The car wends its way along the coastline for another five or so minutes before turning left up into what looks like a residential area, and then back out on to the highway.

'Hang on, why did we go through the town like that?' I ask Jessica. 'We could have just stayed on the main road, right?'

Jessica smiles again. 'I asked the driver to take us the scenic route so you could see the place a bit better. I thought you might like it.'

This is a very thoughtful thing to do. 'Thanks, Jessica. It is a lovely place.'

'I'm glad you think so. Sometime this week we can take a walk along the beach if you like.' She looks down at her seat for a moment. 'I'm sorry about the party, Adam,' she says in a quiet voice.

'I know. Don't worry about it,' I reply with a smile.

I'm hoping that will bring this particular marital crisis to an end. I could continue to hold a grudge, but it's a little hard to stay angry with someone when they seem this contrite – especially when you yourself are at least partly responsible for your own downfall. I am at my worst when I drink too much. It was my idea to try surfing a drinks trolley after all, even if the thought only entered my head thanks to all the booze Jess had been plying me with.

Regardless, trying to stay mad at yourself or someone else is a little difficult when you're in a town ripped straight from one of the better

Disney cartoons. My zip-a-dee is definitely doo-dahing right now, which has lifted my mood magnificently.

We turn off the highway once more on to what I'd call a dual carriageway, but what the locals probably refer to as a small residential street, before a final turn on to a single-lane road that winds up a steep hill into the countryside.

'Nearly there!' Jessica exclaims, her excitement levels rising. 'Mom and Dad are waiting for us . . . and Doofus too.'

'Doofus? Are you talking about your brother?'

Jessica looks shocked and whacks me playfully on the arm. 'No! David's in New York with his girlfriend! Doofus is our dog's name.'

'You named your dog *Doofus*?'

'David's idea. He was thirteen years old when we got him. It seemed an appropriate name.'

I do a little mental arithmetic. 'So that makes the dog, what, fourteen years old?'

'About that!'

Jessica points out of the window. 'I fell off my bike right there when I was seven.' She rolls up her sleeve and shows me a tiny scar on her elbow. 'That's where I got this.'

I have a feeling most of the next few days are going to consist of conversations like this . . . which I have no problem with at all, to be honest.

The car turns into a large, expansive driveway, at the end of which sits a huge single-storey property, designed with the look and feel of a Spanish hacienda. The walls are a pleasant cream colour, which contrasts with the dark-red terracotta-style roof tiles.

The house has two distinct wings that form a courtyard, with a tall central tower that dominates the rest of the property. At the end of the left wing is a large double garage, its door ajar. I catch a glimpse of what looks like an old white car sat behind it.

Tall cypress trees are dotted around the front garden, providing the whole place with a pleasant, earthy smell. Back home, a house like this would set you back a cool couple of million quid, quite easily. Here in Carmel it's probably affordable to anyone with a decent wage packet.

I'm forced to wonder again why Jessica would ever have wanted to leave.

'Mom and Dad fell in love with it the moment they saw it,' Jessica says, seeing the expression on my face. 'They backpacked around Europe before I was born and got to love the style.' She points to the large fountain that sits in the centre of the courtyard. 'I used to flick quarters into the fountain every day, wishing for something that I'm sure was very important to me at the time.'

The car drives around the fountain that probably still contains most of Jessica's childhood spare change, and pulls up underneath the central tower. The arched main doorway opens, and I see Charlie and Monica for the first time since the wedding day as they walk out, a large and slow St Bernard dog in tow.

'Mom! Dad!' Jessica exclaims happily, and jumps out of the car.

By the time I've climbed out of the other side, she is already in mid-hug with both parental units and the large, shaggy old dog.

By all accounts, it's the perfect family reunion.

'Quick! Get a picture of that!' I hear Cassie McFlasterton screech from the other side of the courtyard. They must have taken the more direct route and got here before us.

I sigh and rub my eyes, watching as Alex starts snapping away, capturing the happy family scene. It seems deeply wrong to intrude on such a special moment.

Then the inevitable happens.

'Adam! Get in the picture too!' Cassie orders. 'This will look great on the blog this evening!'

Well, of course it will. How can we possibly do anything nice any more without it going on that bloody website?

I go over and join Jessica with her parents, posing for a few semi-awkward shots, as Jessica asks how her brother is doing, and the dog butts me gently in the testicles.

Once Alex is apparently satisfied, we are allowed to go into the house, which looks even bigger on the inside than it does on the outside. The Old World–hacienda style is continued throughout the interior, only with all those modern American touches you'd expect, like extremely large electronic appliances and even larger soft furnishings.

'We've had rooms made up for you all,' Monica says. 'Jess, you and Adam are in your old bedroom. Miss McFlasterton, you'll be in the guest bedroom and your photographer can have David's old room. We're sure you'll all be comfortable.'

'Thank you Mrs Madison, I'm sure we will.' Cassie's voice drips with sincerity. You can tell there's been a lot of schmoozing going on recently between Jessica's parents and the instigator of this whole silly affair. Monica's eye twitches a little as Cassie talks to her. Cassie must go through life thinking everyone she speaks to has some kind of eye disease.

'You guys go get settled in,' Charlie says, 'and I'll make us all coffee.' He looks down at the St Bernard, who is gently dribbling all over the hardwood floor. 'Come on, Doofy,' he says to the big silly dog, who gives me a rather vacant stare before ambling off behind his owner.

Monica leads us into the right wing of the house, stopping at two rooms to let Cassie and Alex get settled in, before walking to the far end to show Jess and me into her bedroom.

'This is bigger than the house I grew up in,' I note with amazement, once Monica has left us alone. The bedroom is *gigantic*. The bed is *huge*. The long couch on the other side of the room is equally colossal. The en-suite is large enough to bathe a fully grown elephant.

'They redecorated it when I moved out,' Jessica says, putting her flight bag on the bed. 'It used to be a lot . . . *pinker*.'

'Couch looks comfy,' I say, plonking down my own rather tattered suitcase on to it. 'I think I'll sleep okay.'

Jessica makes a face. 'Really, Adam? We can sleep in the same bed, you know.'

'What? In your *parent's* house?'

'We're married!'

'Yes, well . . . *technically*.'

Ooof. You can tell that didn't go down well by the look on her face.

'Whatever,' she sniffs. 'Just promise me you'll pretend that it's more than just *technically* while we're here, won't you? Convincing my parents this whole idea was worth it was hard enough in the first place. If they see we're not high on the romance of it all, it'll really upset them.'

I put my hands up. 'Yeah, yeah. No problem. I know it's important we show a united front, especially to Cassie.'

Jessica makes a face. 'I'm not worried about her. Frankly her opinion doesn't matter to me one bit.'

'Well, her opinion might not matter, but if she sees that things between us aren't all sunny and light, we could lose our apartment – *and* end up looking like idiots to an awful lot of people.' I unzip my bag and start pulling clothes out. 'Don't worry about it. I'll be on my best behaviour. Your parents won't suspect a thing.'

And so begins several days of pretend marital bliss.

To prove this apparent bliss, Jessica and I hold hands a lot – as that's the done thing, isn't it?

Her hand is usually quite clammy, and mine is *always* sweaty, but we still do it as much as possible.

We don't kiss, unless ordered to by Cassie so she can get it in a photograph, and we sure as hell don't engage in any other displays of affection, especially when nobody else is around.

Our conversation is a *little* stilted, but I think we still sound convincing enough to not arouse anyone's suspicions. After all, we are a couple that's only been together for two months. The slight awkwardness is easily explained away by that.

If you put the stress of keeping up appearances to one side, my visit to the California coast is very pleasant. Jessica and her parents (with Cassie and Alex in tow like a pair of badly trained CIA agents) show me some of the shops and restaurants in town, each more charming than the last. We also spend time walking around the rolling hills and the dramatic coastline, in what amounts to more exercise than I've had in many years.

Jessica does indeed take me for that walk along the beautiful crescent-shaped beach that the town hugs like an old friend.

As we're strolling along she points across the bay to the green headland that curves out into the sea. 'That's Pebble Beach golf course,' she tells me.

'Really? Cool. My dad would be dead jealous. He says his handicap is thirteen, but my mum says his handicap is actually golf.'

Jessica chuckles. A wicked smile crosses her face. 'My boyfriend Tyler and I once snuck on to the green at hole ten during the night . . . and enjoyed ourselves in the bunker until we saw a security guard in his buggy.'

I go wide-eyed, partly in amusement, partly in amazement that she'd confide such a secret. I figure if she's in a confessional mode, then I can be too. 'The nearest I can get to that is when Carly Morris and I got pissed on White Lightning and tried to have sex in the churchyard. It was all going okay until she realised we were on someone's grave. She ended up kneeing me in the testicles as she scrambled away in horror.'

Jess looks suitably horrified by this. I feel a sharp twinge of memory pain in my nether regions, and try to ignore it.

Jess smiles again. 'So, come on . . . how many girlfriends have you had then?'

Aah.

This conversation.

I'm amazed it hasn't cropped up already.

Is there a more exquisitely awkward conversation to have with a woman? I struggle to think of one.

The question is, do I tell Jessica the truth? Or lie through my teeth to sound more experienced? I remember the look on her face when we talked about how I'd fibbed about exercise on my Sociality profile, and decide that being honest is the only way to go here.

I expel a loud breath and look down at the sand. 'Just two.'

'Really?' She sounds quite shocked. Not surprising. I am over thirty.

'Yeah. I've never been good at this whole dating lark.' Now my face is flaming red with embarrassment.

'Were they good relationships?' Jess asks.

'Well, one girl kicked me in the testicles on top of a decomposing body, and the other cheated on me with her tutor at university, so all things considered . . . *not particularly.*'

Jessica's hand flies to her mouth. 'Oh no! I'm so sorry!'

'So was I, both times,' I reply ruefully, but with a grin on my face.

'Why only two?' Jess asks. 'After all, you're a good-looking, intelligent guy, Adam.'

'Thanks, that's nice of you to say. I've had other prospects, but I think after those two disasters, I've tended to steer clear of any commitment. Played it safe.'

'Until I came along.'

'Ah . . . yeah. I guess so.'

This probably isn't the time to mention that I only originally got into this marriage for the lifestyle change. 'How about you?' I ask, changing the subject. 'How many boyfriends have you had?'

'Seven,' she says with a definite tone. Then she looks to the sky. 'Eight, if you count Noah Freemont – though that only lasted two weekends over spring break.' She looks unsure for a moment. 'Maybe nine, actually. There was this exchange student from Croatia called Emil, who could speak five languages and knew his way around a bra strap. But that was only for a few weeks too, so . . .'

'And were *they* good relationships? The actual seven proper ones, I mean?' I ask her, wanting to move on from Emil and his Croat expertise with underwear as swiftly as possible.

Jessica scratches her nose. 'Yeah. Pretty much. A couple of unpleasant break-ups, but all in all I had a pretty good time with them all. No regrets.'

My face darkens. 'Okay, there's no need to look smug about it,' I say, giving her a playful push away with one arm.

Jess shrugs. 'I guess I've just been lucky,' she replies, trying to sound a little contrite, given how much better her previous love life has apparently been compared to mine.

I'm just teasing her about it, but I also can't pretend I'm not feeling quite inadequate now, having had this brief conversation with her. Whatever way you cut it, she's had a lot more relationship experience than I have, and can compare me to a series of other men – all of whom appear to have been winners at life.

Fabulous.

'Have you ever actually played golf there?' I say, looking back at Pebble Beach.

Jessica can see my discomfort, and wisely moves away from the topic of ex-partners before I curl up into a ball and die. 'Nope. The closest I've got is playing crazy golf up in Monterey.'

'Once, when I was nine, I ate so many choc ices on a crazy-golf course that I threw up in the windmill,' I tell her.

'Really?'

'Yeah. People's balls were coming out of it covered in sick for a good week afterwards, apparently.'

This sends Jessica off into a gale of laughter that is so infectious I find myself joining in almost immediately. I think it's partially in relief that we've moved on from discussing our love lives.

By day four of my US vacation I'm feeling well fed, well exercised and at relative peace with the world.

My mood is ruined, however, when I come out of the shower on the morning of day five to find my wife nowhere in sight. I get dressed and pad quietly down the corridor towards the hub of the house.

Have you ever noticed that whenever you stay in somebody else's home, you always tend to tread more carefully?

I reach the end of the wide corridor that leads back on to the entrance hall, and hear voices. I stop in my tracks to have a listen. This is extremely rude, but I do have some nosy parker tendencies that I find hard to resist, every now and again.

The voices belong to Jessica and her mother, and they're drifting downstairs to me from somewhere above my head. They must both be on the first-floor landing that leads to the master bedroom suite and Charlie's home office. Jessica's father is down in town getting Doofus his biannual arthritis shots, and Cassie and Alex are in San Francisco for the day on business, so the house is quiet, except for the low tones of two female voices.

I can't quite hear what they're saying, so I creep out into the hallway, and park myself at the bottom of the large hardwood staircase, where I can hear the topic of the conversation.

Oh, great. It's *me*.

'What do you mean? I thought you guys were happy?' Monica whispers.

'I know. We're trying to make it look like that, Mom, but it's not really going all that well. This week has been okay, but things just aren't going anywhere.'

Oh, *fantastic.*

After all that talk of not letting on so we don't upset her parents, Jessica has let the cat out of the bag *herself!*

'What's the problem, sweetheart?' The voice of a concerned mother is always a comfort, unless *you're* the source of the concern, of course.

'I just don't think we're that compatible.'

'But you said that was the whole point of that website thing? That it put you two together because you were a perfect match?'

Jessica tuts. 'Yeah, well, it turns out Adam didn't exactly pay that much attention to filling out his profile, so a lot of the information wasn't that accurate.'

I now wait for Jessica to admit that she was drunk when she filled out *her* Sociality profile, and also told a few half-truths of her own, just so it doesn't sound like I'm the only arsehole here.

. . . I'm in for a bloody long wait, unfortunately.

'What kind of stuff wasn't accurate?' Monica continues.

'Oh, I don't know. It's just . . . just that he sounded like he had a lot more . . . *get up and go* in his profile.'

'So not quite the man you were expecting?'

'No. He's a little immature, to be honest.'

My blood instantly boils to three hundred degrees.

'Oh, don't get me wrong, Adam is a good guy, Mom,' Jessica continues. 'He's intelligent, funny, well spoken . . . but he's just missing that . . . that *spark*, I guess? He's not the kind of man I imagined he'd be.'

'How so?'

'Well, he likes playing computer games a lot,' Jessica says, trying to keep the distaste out of her mouth, 'and when it comes to, you know, the physical stuff . . .'

'He's not living up to expectations?' her mother finishes for her.

'Well, he has *tried*, and we did kinda get somewhere, but then things got tricky, and it all kinda . . . went away again.' She sighs. 'I just wish he was . . . a little *different*. A little more . . . *in charge*.'

'Like a real man, you mean?' Monica suggests. Jessica does not reply.

She's hedging around the issue, but I'm intelligent, funny and well-spoken enough to know that she thinks I'm a fucking *wuss*. An immature man-child, who would get sand kicked in his face – if he ever actually worked up enough courage to go to the beach in his swimming trunks.

She obviously thought she'd be marrying a big strapping man who would sweep her off her feet – but what she got was a tiny Tinker Bell fairy-winged creature, who couldn't keep a woman satisfied if he had a thousand years and a long run-up.

I should *never* have admitted I'd only had two relationships in my life. That obviously just added fuel to her fire.

I am *incensed*.

I am *enraged*.

What I'm not, is admitting to myself that I *did* lie quite a bit on my profile, and that Jessica can't be entirely blamed for her point of view. Also, I haven't exactly been Captain Romance over the course of this marriage, for all the reasons I've already outlined, so it's not surprising she's frustrated.

Having said that, Jessica could have actually talked to *me* about these problems, instead of keeping her mouth firmly shut until her mother pops up, asking awkward questions.

I am *furious*.

I can't stand to listen to any more of this character assassination, so I quietly back away in the direction I came from. Once I'm out of ear-shot, I stamp back towards the bedroom, and close the door behind me.

For the next five minutes I enact a pantomime of silent rage in Jessica's bedroom.

How *dare* she say that about me to her mother?

Missing a fucking *spark*, am I?

And they are not *computer* games! They are bloody VIDEO GAMES! It's a *video* games console! Why is that so hard for people to understand?

I punch my pillow three times in quick succession. This makes bright flashing lights appear in my field of vision, so I have to sit down on the couch for a little while until I get my breath back.

As I sit there feeling my blood pressure slowly slide back to normal, I begin to feel epically sorry for myself. Here I am, trapped in a predicament that I willingly walked headlong into for a better quality of life. Little did I think it would result in having my manhood questioned six thousand miles away in a Spanish-style hacienda.

What's really worrying here is how *hurt* I feel by Jessica's words. Why is it getting to me quite as much as it is? Okay, no man likes to have his credentials as a man put through the wringer, but if I'm really only in this for that aforementioned better quality of life, then why am I so upset? Why do I care what she thinks of me so much?

Skip forward a few hours, and it's mid-afternoon. I have calmed down enough to be civil to my wife. I do not let on that I eavesdropped on her little confessional.

My mind has been racing, trying to come up with a convincing way I can change her opinion of me, but nothing immediately presents itself until I wander out into the front courtyard with a cup of coffee for Charlie, who is tinkering around in his garage.

As I approach, I see the object of his attentions – an old white muscle car with two great big blue stripes running down the centre of its bodywork. It's the kind of car Steve McQueen would have definitely been seen dead in.

The car is a monstrous-looking thing, with thick, wide sports tyres, jet-black leather seats and a big bulgy bit in the middle of the bonnet, suggesting that the engine is trying to force its way out.

Charlie is busily polishing the bulge, whistling happily as he does so.

'Wow,' I say, quite genuinely awed, as I plonk his coffee down on an old sawhorse just by the garage door.

'Hey, Adam,' Jessica's father replies when he sees me. 'I trust that *wow* is for the car and not the mess this garage is in?' Charlie and I haven't really had many conversations beyond bland small talk, so actually having something concrete to chat about might prove interesting.

'It's amazing,' I tell him. 'What kind of car is it?'

Charlie stands up straight and places one hand on the car's roof. 'This is a 1966 Shelby Mustang, Adam. Three hundred brake horse-power from an iron block V8 engine.'

I don't watch *Top Gear*, so have no idea what any of that means, but it *sounds* damned impressive. 'Cool. I bet it's fun to drive.'

'Oh my, yes. The best fun you can have with three hundred horse-power, anyway!' Charlie has one of those laughs that are quite infectious, so as he starts to chuckle, I automatically join in.

'What are you two laughing about?'

Oh look! It's the woman who thinks I am a big wet drip.

My good humour is instantly quashed.

'Adam was just asking about the car, honey,' Charlie tells his daughter. 'I was telling him how much fun she is to drive.'

Jessica rolls her eyes theatrically. 'Dad, that car is noisy, messy and breaks down every five minutes.'

'Ah! But when it goes, she's a beauty!' Charlie counters. He looks at me again. 'Say, Adam? Why don't you take her out for a spin? Take Jess here with you.'

I'm flummoxed. This is quite clearly the man's pride and joy. Why on earth would he want to let me have a go in it?

Charlie provides his daughter with a knowing expression. 'You never know . . . it might be good for you kids to spend some time away from us. Give Adam here a chance to show off his driving skills in a big, powerful car . . .' he trails off, leaving Jessica and me in silence.

Then something clicks into place.

Wonderful.

I see what's happened here.

Monica has obviously told her husband all about my perceived shortcomings, and he's trying to do something to bolster my pathetic levels of masculinity, using his prized muscle car as leverage.

I would be grateful for the gesture if I wasn't so bloody embarrassed.

Jessica shakes her head. 'I don't think that's such a good idea, Dad. I know how much you adore that car, and—'

'I'd love to, Charlie!' I interrupt. 'Thanks for the offer!'

I wouldn't love to in the *slightest*.

Living and commuting around London means I haven't sat behind the wheel in a good two years. The last car I owned was a Vauxhall Astra that farted down the road on its last legs for six whole months, before the exhaust fell off and it went to the scrapyard on the back of a low-loader. It was a pup.

Driving this monstrous thing in front of me will be rather like trying to wrestle an angry Dobermann.

But what the hell else am I supposed to do?

Look at that expression on Jessica's face, would you?

It screams her lack of confidence in me.

'Are you sure that's a good idea, Adam?' she asks me, her voice deep-fried in doubt.

'Why wouldn't it be?' I reply haughtily. 'It's just a car. Don't you think I can handle something as easy as driving a car?'

She crosses her arms. 'A three-hundred-horsepower muscle car, in a country you've never been to before, where we drive on the other side of the road?'

I also cross my arms. 'Yeah? So what?'

I can see a light of suspicion dawning in Jessica's eyes. She knows there's a definite subtext to all of this, but doesn't know what it is . . . *yet.*

'I'm sure he'll be fine, honey!' Charlie says confidently. 'This old thing is a pussycat, as long as you treat her right.'

I gesture towards Jessica's father with an open hand. 'See? Your dad says it's okay, so we're *doing it.*'

Jessica looks taken aback with my demanding tone.

Yeah? Well, get used to it, woman! This is me taking control! You want a real man? You're going to get *one!*

Charlie fishes around in his jeans pocket and produces a set of glimmering car keys. 'Here you go. Just take it easy to begin with. She'll come to you, don't worry.' He throws the keys at me, which I singularly fail to catch in a smooth manner.

When I've picked them up off the dusty garage floor, I make a quick beeline over to the car, trying to look enthusiastic. Charlie opens the driver's-side door for me, with more than a little effort. It takes a fairly hefty pull on the door handle for it to open. 'She gets real sticky sometimes, so don't be shy with her if she's being stubborn.'

I'm about to get into the car, when movement from the back seat makes me jump out of my skin.

'Oh, don't mind old Doofy,' Charlie tells me. 'He loves the back seat.'

Doofus looks up at me and cocks his massive head to one side, as if to say *You? He's letting you drive this thing?*

'Er, is he coming with us?' I ask, pointing at Doofus.

'Yeah. You won't get the old bastard out of there in a hurry!'

'Dad!' Jessica seems genuinely shocked by her father's use of a swear word.

Charlie's face instantly colours. 'Sorry, sweetheart. Don't tell your mother.'

Jessica gives her father a reproachful look as she opens the passenger-side door and climbs into the car. I sit myself down, trying to ignore the heavy doggie aroma wafting towards me from behind my head.

Charlie leans into the open window. 'There's your ignition. The car's a stick shift, and one you don't need to be gentle with. The accelerator is hard too, so really put your back into it.'

I laugh nervously. 'Okay.'

Am I about to drive a car, or an industrial digger?

'Here's the parking brake,' Charlie says, pointing at a lever under the dashboard. 'Make sure you pull it when you're parked.'

'Yep. No worries,' I say, as I slide the key into the ignition and turn it.

'Give it some on the gas, Adam. That'll fire her up properly,' Charlie suggests.

I do so, and the world erupts in a cacophony of growling, rumbling, hate-filled noise.

'Bloody hell!' I exclaim.

Charlie laughs. 'She's a beast, alright!'

Doofus barks in alarm from the back seat, adding to the clamour. I've managed to turn a peaceful afternoon in the Carmel hills into a heavy-metal concert next door to Battersea Dogs Home.

Jessica remains quiet, sat in the passenger seat with her arms still crossed. You can almost hear the cogs going round in her head. Well, you can't actually, given that the Mustang is fired up, and ready to rock-and-roll.

'Okay, Adam, now just stick her in first gear,' Charlie instructs, 'and gently pull out of the garage.'

It dawns on me for the first time that I now have to actually drive this monster.

Licking my lips, I carefully put the clutch in with one shaking leg, and wrestle the gear stick into first gear with my right hand. Having done this, I breathe in deeply, and slowly start to let out the clutch.

The Mustang rolls forward.

'Have a good time!' Charlie hollers after us. 'Bring her back in one piece!'

Jessica moans quietly. 'He likes to joke that this car is his second wife,' she says in a low voice. 'You'd better know what you're doing, Adam.'

I give her a look that I hope speaks volumes, then turn Charlie's second wife on to the driveway and negotiate my way down to the road.

'Which way should we go?' I ask Jessica when we get there.

'Take it up into the hills. The roads will be quieter up there. Turn left.' Her responses are clipped and short. You can tell she doesn't want to be here.

I follow her directions, and find myself on a winding road that cuts its way through the hills outside Carmel, past a series of large, expensive houses.

The Mustang is bloody hard to drive, I'm not going to lie.

The clutch is heavy, the accelerator is even heavier, and the brake makes me sweat with effort every time I have to use it. The steering has no power, so I have to wrench the wheel for all I'm worth. It's just as well we're more or less sticking to the one road.

Other than all of that, though, I'm actually not having too bad a time with it. So far, so smooth. Even Doofus has relaxed into the back seat again.

Jessica is *not* relaxed, however. She is sat bolt upright and tight-lipped, staring out of the windscreen deep in thought.

Feeling confident, I decide to open the taps a little. My wife wants a man who can handle a car like this, and I'm going to prove that I am just that kind of man.

I accelerate, and the car speeds up to forty . . . then forty-five . . . then fifty.

It's when I push the Mustang past this point that Jessica finally opens her mouth. 'Take it easy, Adam. The limit is fifty along here.'

'Pffft. It's fine. You said it yourself. The roads are quiet.'

I press my foot down harder and the V8 engine roars.

We hit sixty.

We also hit a part of the road that starts to twist and turn as we leave the sprawling houses behind us and climb further into the hills. I'm really having to concentrate to make sure I keep the car on the asphalt now.

'Adam! Slow down! If you wreck my Dad's car, he'll kill you!'

'Oh what? Don't you think I'm man enough to handle *sixty miles an hour*? How about seventy?' I push down even harder on the pedal. The car responds magnificently, and thunders along even faster. Now I can hear the tyres squealing in protest as we continue to round ever-tighter corners.

Yes, my behaviour is very juvenile and probably quite dangerous, but I feel like a wounded animal right now – and they tend to lash out when confronted.

At seventy, and as we hit another tight bend, Jessica's temper gives way completely. 'Adam! Pull this car over *right now*!'

'Why?'

'Because you're scaring me, and I fucking *said so*, that's why!'

I slam on the brakes, and turn into a gravel lay-by at the side of the road. A great plume of dust is sent up into the still afternoon air as I bring the Mustang to a halt. No sooner is it stationary than Jessica is out of the car.

I also jump out, slamming the door shut and waving the dust out of my eyes as I do so.

As it clears, I can see Jessica stood on the other side of the bonnet, staring at me with her hands on her hips. 'What the hell is the matter with you, Adam? You're acting like an asshole!'

'Am I?'

'Yes, you are!'

I point angrily at my chest. 'I'm not the one who's an asshole here, Jessica!'

She looks shocked. 'What the hell have *I* done?'

I point the finger back at her over the bonnet. 'I heard you! I heard what you said to your bloody mother about me!'

Ha! That did the trick!

Jessica looks mortified. 'I . . . I . . . er . . .' she stumbles.

'No! You don't have to say anything!' I spit. 'I know what you really think of me! I know you think I'm a stupid little boy, who couldn't satisfy a woman in a million years!'

Jessica looks aghast. 'I never said any of that!'

No, she didn't – but through the prism of my wounded ego, that's how I've chosen to interpret her words, for better or worse.

. . . *worse.* Definitely worse.

'Yes you did!' I retort.

'No I didn't, Adam!' Jessica stabs a finger at me. 'But, come on! We haven't exactly been a pair of happy newly-weds, have we? In fact, we might as well be a couple of strangers in that apartment!'

'And whose fault is that?!' I spit.

Jessica's eyes widen. 'Yours!'

I affect a look of aghast innocence. 'How is any of it *my* fault?'

'Oh, I don't know, *Adam.* How about your complete and total lack of interest in having an actual *relationship* with me?!'

'What do you mean?'

'I mean that all you seem to care about is the bloody apartment and the money Cassie's given us! It's like you only married me for what you could personally get out of it!'

Oh Christ.

I didn't realise she thought that.

I thought I'd kept my original intentions to myself, but it appears I'd severely underestimated Jessica's natural women's intuition.

'That's . . . that's not true!' I splutter.

Of *course* it's true.

'Isn't it? You mean you didn't marry me to escape a cross-eyed rat and a dose of scabies?'

'No! Of course not!'

Yes! Of course!

'Then *why*, Adam? Why did you agree to marry me?'

I look to the heavens for inspiration. 'Because . . . because . . .'

Screw you, heavens.

Jessica has me bang to rights. I'm like a worm on a hook.

'Well?' she snaps, hands on hips.

My shoulders slump. I simply don't have a decent response. How can I be honest and tell her that she knows the truth? It *was* all about the flat and the money!

And then how do I tell her that my feelings started to change once we were in the flat together? How could she ever begin to believe *that*?

'I thought this would be easy,' I eventually say, rather pathetically.

'*Easy?!*' Jessica slaps the car bonnet. 'Relationships are never *easy*, Adam. Not when you're actually invested in them! But then I guess you just wanted a nice bed to sleep in, rather than a woman to have by your side in one, didn't you?'

This has all gone wrong. Jessica is quite clearly to blame here. Why can't she see that? Why am *I* having to defend myself?

Time to steer this ship back around to where it should be pointing – at a giant fucking iceberg.

'Well, I'm certainly not the kind of man you'd want to sleep next to anyway, am I, *Jessica?!*' I spit back at her, my voice reaching new levels of hysterical rage.

Doofus, who may be old and slow but is still a faithful dog, doesn't like the tone of my voice and sticks his head out of the window to bark at me. Such is his bulk that the entire car rocks back and forth on its suspension as he does this.

'Calm down, Adam,' Jessica says. 'Doofy's getting angry!'

I sneer at the dog. 'Oh, what's he going to do? Drown me in saliva?'

Doofus has obviously decided he isn't going to take a chunk out of my neck as his head is already moving back away from me. He knows when he's met his match! 'See? He's backing off already,' I say to Jessica smugly.

Her eyes have gone painfully wide. 'The car!' she yells. 'The car's rolling backwards!'

Oh fuck me, she's right! The stupid St Bernard isn't moving, it's the ruddy Mustang! The old dog's movement must have unsettled it on the sloping gravel.

And I forgot to put the parking brake on!

Ohshitohshitohshitohshitohshitohshitohshit!

'Stop it!' Jessica screams.

I leap forward, fumbling with the door handle. As the Mustang picks up speed and heads towards a large, deep ditch at the side of the gravel lay-by, I gain purchase on the door handle and pull.

Nothing happens! The bloody door won't open!

The Mustang continues to rumble towards the ditch, now less than twenty feet away.

'Get in the car!' Jessica demands at the top of her lungs.

'Woof!' Doofus agrees, sensing that he's about to have his doggie day ruined by being involved in a minor car accident.

'Sticky!' I scream in panic, remembering what Charlie told me in the garage.

Twelve feet to the ditch.

'What?' Jessica exclaims.

'Sticky!' I point at the door. 'Sticky, sticky, sticky!'

'What?!' Jessica repeats.

There are tears of frustration in my eyes now.

Eight feet.

'She's being stubborn! I can't be shy!' I continue to bellow nonsensically, my brain going over Charlie's exact advice about the car door in sheer panic.

Five feet.

The door is not budging. 'Why is she so fucking *sticky*?!' I squeal. 'I'm a man, Jessica,' I then wail at my wife in terror, 'but what am I supposed to do when she's being so *sticky*???!'

Zero feet.

The Mustang reaches the ditch, and the back end drops into it with a crash, crushing the rear bumper and bending the exhaust pipes as soon as they come into heavy contact with the rock-hard gravel underneath.

Horrid, horrid silence descends.

'Woof,' Doofus barks quietly at us from the back seat, letting us know he's alright.

'Adam?' Jessica says, looking up from the crashed car to my stricken face.

'Yes, Jessica?'

'My father has an old Remington shotgun in the same garage he keeps this car in. If you start running now, you'll probably reach the Mexican border in about three weeks.'

I'm *fairly* sure she's joking. Then again, if this Mustang really is Charlie's second wife, I've just smashed her rear end in.

'Canada is closer, isn't it?' I reply to my wife, as I watch the front wheel spin slowly round uselessly in mid-air.

I can be glad of *two* things.

One, that the plane is due to fly me away from Charlie and his shotgun the following day, and that, two, the house he owns is large enough for me to successfully hide in for the twenty-four hours preceding the flight.

It gives me no pleasure to report that I have to thank Cassandra McFlasterton for my continued good health. She managed to calm the situation down magnificently, promising to pay for the repairs to Charlie's car out of her own pocket. I'm still not quite sure whether the tears in Charlie's eyes were of gratitude or grief at how badly the car's chrome fender was buckled.

So now I owe Cassie one.

Oh joy.

Jessica, needless to say, ignores the living shit out of me for the rest of my time in California, choosing instead to spend all her time with her parents. Doofus still occasionally waddles down the corridor to where I'm holed up in the bedroom to say hello, before watering my left knee with spittle and wandering off again.

It is a supremely testing twenty-four-hour period, as I'm sure you can imagine. One that I am *immensely* glad is over once we go back through security at the airport.

On the plane home, Jessica and I sit in seats with Cassie and Alex strategically placed between us, because nobody needs to hear us chundering on at each other at thirty-five thousand feet.

I can safely say that my relationship with Mrs Holborne has reached a new low – one covered in warm butter, and requiring *nine thousand dollars'* worth of repairs.

I now know she thinks I'm utterly incapable as a man, and she's pissed with me because I scared the crap out of her with some very stupid driving, and ended up nearly destroying her father's pride and joy, and she quite clearly believes my reasons for marrying her were entirely selfish – which they weren't. Not really.

Quite how we're going to fix it is beyond me.

Hopefully it's not beyond Cassie McFlasterton, otherwise I'm going to be on Rightmove looking for a new shoebox to live in very soon, and Sociality will be haemorrhaging subscribers quicker than you can say *fast-tracked annulment.*

JESS

Q. You're in the kitchen. What's your ideal meal to whip up?

A. I love baking. Give me the chance to bake a nutritious,
delicious cake and I'm happy!

30 April

Being called into Cassandra McFlasterton's office is rather like being summoned to see the principal. Both have a certain amount of power to make your life a misery, and both will happily do so unless you promise to stay married to Adam Holborne, or promise to stop pulling Patty Farantino's hair during math class.

'So, how are you both?' Cassie asks from behind her ludicrously large white plastic desk. You'd think this kind of vacuum-formed furniture would have died out in the 80s, but here it is, featuring a brand-new iMac on its glossy surface, along with a framed picture of Cassie with Donald Trump.

'Fine,' Adam states.

'Fine,' I parrot, in equally bland tones.

Cassie's eyebrow shoots up. 'Fine? You're both *fine*? No problems at all?'

'No,' Adam says.

'No,' I parrot once more.

'So that whole wrecking the priceless sports car thing . . . you've put that behind you, have you?'

'Absolutely,' I tell her.

'Absolutely,' Adam parrots.

'And being humiliated at a party with a stick of butter . . . also done and dusted, am I correct?'

'Yes,' Adam says.

'Yes,' I parrot.

There are more parrots in here than in the Amazon basin.

Cassie leans back in her vacuum-formed white chair. 'Bullshit.'

We both choose to remain silent.

'Neither of you have anything to say, then? Neither of you have anything you want to say *to me*?' Cassie sits forward again, and pins us both to our vacuum-formed chairs with a piercing gaze. 'Neither of you have *any* problems, and absolutely do *not* feel the need to be honest with me . . . the person who put you together in the first place, and could be considered responsible for any grievances that you might—'

'It's not working!' I blurt out.

'Jessica!' Adam hisses. 'We agreed to not say anything!'

I grip the vacuum-formed arms of my vacuum-formed chair, desperate to tell the truth about my vacuum-formed marriage. 'I know! But I was brought up to be honest! I can't stand all this *deception*!'

Adam throws his hands up in disgust. 'Oh well, go on then. Ruin the whole thing. I'll just be sat here quietly downloading the Rightmove app.'

Cassie's mood softens, sensing a light touch is needed. 'What's the matter, Jessica? Tell me all about it.'

So I proceed to do so, with the occasional unneeded interruption from Adam.

It isn't a pretty twenty minutes, and results in tears at the corner of my eyes, a terrible case of Adamface, and a look of deep concern showing through all the make-up on Cassie's.

She remains quiet for a few moments, deep in thought. Then she looks at us both with a look of steely determination.

'This doesn't change anything,' she tells us, in no uncertain terms.

'What?' Adam says.

'Are you kidding?' I add.

'No. This isn't a problem. No one outside this office needs to know you two can't stand each other.'

Adam and I begin to protest, but Cassie cuts us off with a raised hand. 'Figure of speech. Let's just say you might be having *teething problems* with your relationship and leave it at that, shall we?'

'Okay.'

'Alright.'

'Anyway . . . no one needs to know that you two are anything other than madly in love.'

'Pfft. Mad's about right,' mutters Adam.

I bite my lip. 'Are you suggesting we just carry on and pretend nothing's wrong?' I ask Cassie.

'Yes, Jessica, that's precisely what I'm suggesting.'

'Why?'

'*Why?*' Cassie looks at me in disbelief. '*Why?* Because less than three months ago you two got married in front of an online audience of millions, in a wedding ceremony I'm still paying for. Because since you two *got married*, subscriptions to Sociality have gone up 12 per cent. Because this company is still in debt to a Russian business consortium to the tune of two and a half million pounds. Because, and believe me, this is the most important one . . . because if we turn around now and say that the whole thing has been a disaster, then all *three of us* are more fucked than the only cow in a field of horny bulls!'

Cassie is now stood up and leaning over her desk. Her usually perfect hair has become somewhat dishevelled during her rant, and I think I can see a slight crack appearing in her foundation at the temples.

Adam snorts. 'Fine with me. If I get to keep using that coffee machine, I'm happy.'

I remain silent.

Both of them fix me with a stare.

'I don't know if I can do that,' I mumble. 'I mean, it's not right, is it? All those people will be thinking that we're getting along fine, when we're really not. It's dishonest.' I look up at Cassie. 'It's not a real relationship.'

She gives me a withering look. 'Love, I've been married *three* times. It's not a real relationship if you're not spending at least half of it pretending to get along fine for the benefit of other people.'

Adam reaches out and clasps me gently on the shoulder. 'It'll be okay, Jess,' he promises me in a smooth voice.

Damn it.

I don't like doing dishonest things, but what the hell else am I supposed to do, other than go along with this stupid plan? Okay, it's quite clear that I've married a deceitful idiot who had his head turned by a thousand square feet of prime London real estate, rather than by me, but there's no simple way for me to get out of this thing without doing severe damage to my future prospects.

If we blow the whistle now, all three of us are probably screwed. Our reputations will be ruined. I won't be able to show my face at King's College again – even though I am Professor Hibbersley's star pupil these days – and I very much doubt they'd take me back at Sister Stocking's Gentlemen's Club. Bartenders aren't exactly hard to recruit in London, what with the countless Australian backpackers milling around.

I put my head in my hands for a moment, struggling with the morality of this decision. Then a vision of the disappointed looks on my parents' faces swims into view and my mind is made up.

'Okay,' I sigh. 'I'll stick with it . . . for the time being.'

Both Cassie and Adam smile broadly.

I return Adam's grin with a steely look of my own. 'But this doesn't mean we're square, buster,' I warn him.

He baulks at this, but wisely chooses to remain silent.

'Excellent!' Cassie exults, slumping back into her chair with obvious relief. 'I'm sure you'll both manage *magnificently.*' She then pulls a folder over from a pile next to her iMac. 'Now then, how do you both feel about a spot of cookery?'

'Cookery?' Adam and I both exclaim in horrified unison.

It turns out that Cassie's latest promotional stunt is inspired by both of our Sociality profiles. We both indicated that we enjoy cooking, so what better way to demonstrate just how perfect we are for each other than a staged cookery lesson with none other than Allard Rancourt, at his exclusive restaurant in Soho?

Never mind that I only like to occasionally bake a cake when I'm either drunk or hormonal – or that Adam only put that he liked cooking because his buddy Calvin told him to do it. *'Birds like a bloke who can cook,'* Adam was apparently told. *'It's a guaranteed way of getting a shag!'*

'But you're studying nutrition, this is perfect for you,' Cassie said when I pointed out this issue.

'Nutrition isn't bakery, Cassie,' I replied with a groan. 'It's the study of how the human body uses the energy provided by food. It's *science.*'

'Well, you can science yourself up a nice soufflé, can't you,' she told me in no uncertain terms, ending the discussion before it really got a chance to get started.

The whole enterprise will be filmed, photographed and streamed on the Internet, of course. Both dating site and restaurant will benefit greatly from the exposure, I have no doubt.

So, it's on with the stupid aprons and fixed smiles – and let's all pretend that Adam and Jessica are lovebirds so enamoured with each other that they *love* the idea of learning how to cook something small, French and pretentious together.

'We're not making *confits de pomponce*, are we?' Adam asks, as we're ushered through into the gleaming steel kitchen at Le Poulet Pretentieux.

'Pffft!' Allard Rancourt says via his nasal cavity. 'Of course not! Zat is far too complicated for you to try.'

'Oh good.' Adam looks visibly relieved.

'Good morning, everybody!' Rancourt says expansively, as he greets the dozen or so people squeezed into the back of the kitchen. These include Alex the photographer, two guys controlling a video camera, Cassie and one of her myriad personal assistants, and the now obligatory lucky subscribers to Sociality – hand-picked to come and marvel at how exquisitely in love Adam and I are, as we stuff sausage rolls and look adoringly into each other's eyes. Most of them look a little uncomfortable to be here, but one – a small woman with mousey hair and round spectacles – is grinning from ear to ear. At least someone is pleased to be in this kitchen.

'We're ready to start whenever you are, Allard,' Cassie tells the tall French chef, indicating the camera to her left.

'*Oui, oui!* Zat is good.' Allard gestures to Adam and me. 'Stand either side of me, 'Olbornes. When ze camera rolls we will start. All you 'ave to do is follow my lead, and remember what we talked about in ze briefing session yesterday.'

I shuffle into position behind the massive steel kitchen worktop, recalling the information we were given twenty-four hours earlier.

The cookery demonstration will be kept simple. Rancourt will reveal what we are going to be cooking. He will then take us through it step by step, before allowing us to each have a go at the recipe ourselves.

The chef will then decide which one of us has done the best job, and award the winner appropriately. The footage will then be edited into a brisk half an hour that will be uploaded to the Sociality website and YouTube.

Easy, quick and simple.

I just hope Rancourt doesn't want us to make something out of pastry.

I *hate* pastry.

It's a load of flaky bullshit that tastes like cardboard covered in olive oil, and gets down my top whenever I take a bite. The amount of times I've had to fish bits of pastry out of my cleavage doesn't bear thinking about.

Also, I've watched enough *Great British Bake Off* to know it's a real ass to make.

So, as long as it's not pastry, we'll be *fine*.

'Very well, we are ready to start,' Rancourt tells Cassie and her cameramen. 'You may now begin.'

Rancourt composes himself, draws in a deep breath, and addresses the camera. ''Ello, everyone at 'ome watching. Welcome to my restaurant Le Poulet Pretentieux, and a very special cooking session, wiz some very special guests! Say 'ello to Adam and Jessica 'Olborne, winners of the Sociality wedding of ze year competition!'

Adam nods at the camera.

'Hello,' I squeak.

'Today, we are going to put zeir cookery skills to ze test, to see if they love it as much as zey love each other!'

Groan.

'And we 'ave picked a French classic for zem to try . . . *la pâte feuilletée!*'

What the hell is that?

'Ozerwise known in English as flaky pastry!'

Oh, for crying out loud.

'I will show zem both 'ow to make the lightest, sweetest flaky pastry of all, and 'ow to fill it wiz gorgeous sweetmeats. Zen we will 'ave a special French-themed competition, to see who is ze best 'Olborne chef!'

From the look on Adam's face, and mine for that matter, the best Holborne chef will be the one who doesn't burn this kitchen down and give everyone food poisoning at the same time.

As long as I pay close and careful attention to what Allard Rancourt says, though, I might make it through this thing alive.

I'm not eating any of the pastry at the end of it, though. I want that made *absolutely* clear.

Thankfully, Rancourt's promise to keep the recipe simple is honoured. The flaky pastry doesn't appear to be all that difficult to make at all.

He takes Adam and me through the process, and despite the thick French accent, I am able to keep up with his instructions quite well. It's just a question of mixing the flour, butter, salt and water together properly, in the right amounts, then rolling the mixture well, and chilling the pastry dough for thirty minutes afterwards. Nice and straightforward.

Things get a *little* more complicated when Rancourt starts to introduce ingredients that go into the flaky pastry to make a proper dessert. I'm okay with flour, butter and water, but now he's talking about things like sugar, glazed fruit, cream and cinnamon, which is throwing me off my stride completely.

What's also ruining my concentration somewhat is the constant sound of a still camera shutter, and the whir and whine of a video camera. Quite how actors and actresses get anything done is beyond me.

Occasionally I glance over at Adam to see how he's doing, and for the most part he looks like he's picking things up as well as I am. He seems to be following Allard's instructions closely, and has even asked a few sensible questions that I wish I'd come out with first.

As this is a competition between us though, I'm rather hoping he hasn't followed the instructions *too* closely, as I'd like to win. With any luck he'll have as many problems opening the door to the oven as he did opening the door to my poor father's cherished Mustang, the big dumbo.

Now, now Jessica! We agreed not to think like that. It won't help keep up the pretence of a happy marriage in public if all you're doing is carrying around that kind of resentment. It's bound to show itself sooner or later. Just take a deep breath, count to ten again, and try to pay attention to what the spindly French chef in front of you is doing with that icing sugar.

Rancourt tells us how to make the perfect filling for a further ten minutes, before retrieving the pastry from the fridge, rolling and shaping it into a neat, tight latticework, and sticking it in the oven to cook for a brisk fifteen minutes.

'Zo, that is in ze oven and cooking nicely,' he tells us. 'It will be a little while, so let us relax and drink wine!'

Rancourt claps his hands together in the manner of a Roman emperor, and from a side door a small, skinny waiter appears carrying a bottle of white wine and three glasses.

This puts a smile on my face.

It's only two o'clock in the afternoon, but it's an afternoon where I'm compelled to perform like a baking monkey in front of a camera, so I have no issues with downing a glass of white to keep me on an even keel.

I also have no issues when the waiter refills my glass, as Rancourt returns to the oven to produce his masterpiece. 'Now, it must cool for anozer fifteen minutes.'

Fine with me, Ranky. This wine is going down very easily.

'Okay! Time to put everyzing together!' the chef eventually announces, and he proceeds to do just that, creating a very attractive iced pastry cake with a cream filling that I could quite happily devour right here and now.

'And zere we 'ave it! *Bon appétit!*

'It looks lovely, Allard,' I tell him truthfully.

'Yep. Like the cream horns you get in the baker's,' Adam adds, earning him the darkest of dark French looks.

'And now, 'Olbornes . . . it is your turn!' Rancourt exclaims with a flourish.

I swallow the last of my wine in one swift gulp. This is where the fun begins.

'You 'ave followed everyzing I have done today, and can now make ze wonderful pastry. As an extra challenge . . .'

Do we *need* an extra challenge?

'. . . you will 'ave to make a pastry that reflects French culture! Eizer in its shape, style or flavour!'

Really? As if this wasn't going to be hard enough.

'You 'ave an hour and a 'alf to finish your creations . . . starting now!'

Allard Rancourt is no Mel and Sue, but the challenge is much the same as you'd find on your average episode of *Bake Off*, only the amateur bakers on that show are exactly that – amateur *bakers*. Adam and I are only here because we both suck at filling out dating profiles.

But here we go anyway. Pass the flour, and retire to a safe distance.

As I start to make the dough, following Rancourt's example as best as I can, I rack my brains trying to think of something that represents French culture.

A beret? A string of onions? A surrendering soldier?

No! I've got it! The perfect thing!

I'm going to make my pastry look like the Eiffel Tower! All I need to do is cut the shape of the tower out in the pastry before it goes in the oven. That should be easy enough. Then for the filling, I'll use icing sugar and cream so it looks like snow. It'll be *amazing*. Allard Rancourt will love it, and so will everyone watching at home.

Satisfied that I have a potential competition winner on my hands, I get to work on the dough with renewed effort. Occasionally I look up to see Adam in a frenzy of action too. We lock eyes briefly, and I can see that the competitive spirit has overtaken him as well. There's a determination in his eyes that matches mine.

Game on, buddy. *Game on.*

My pastry dough goes in the fridge before Adam's, giving me the first small victory of the day. Then it's on to my filling. The cream is easy enough to whip up, but I have more difficulty with making the frosting I'm going to use on my wintry Eiffel Tower. The icing sugar and water just won't mix to the right consistency, so I'm left with a lumpy mixture that's going to be very difficult to squeeze out of the piping bag. Looking at the time, though, I won't have the chance to make up another batch, so I'll just have to do the best I can.

Once again, I look up over at Adam, to see that he is screwing around with a lot of glazed fruit. What the hell is he making over there?

It doesn't matter! There's no way it will be better than the Eiffel Tower in winter!

'Everything okay?' he says to me, noticing that I'm looking at him.

'Yeah,' I reply with a cagey expression on my face. 'I'm doing just fine, Adam. Just *fine.*'

He looks bewildered by this. 'Okay. Cool,' he remarks, before returning to his food.

Yeah, you just keep playing with your glazed fruit, pal. It's going to do you no good once I reveal my glorious tower . . .

The thirty minutes are up, so I go to retrieve my pastry dough. It looks paler and less fluffy than Rancourt's, but it'll do the job. So far, so good.

Now comes the hard part.

With my tongue poked out of my mouth in intense concentration I go about the task of rolling the pastry dough out, and shaping it into what approximates the outline of the Eiffel Tower. This is far from simple, as I can't let the pastry be too thin. So much so that I have to sacrifice much of the delicate lattice framework I was intending to use, and go for a simpler shape, with only a few lines of pastry lattice running up the inside of the tower.

Still, when I'm done, I think I've made a pretty good job of it, all in all. It definitely looks Eiffel Tower-like. The top has a bulging bit to represent the observation deck. The tower itself curves downwards like its real-world counterpart, and I've done a pretty good job of the archway at the bottom, even if the dough gets a bit thick on either side of it.

I give myself a little self-satisfied nod, and pick up the baking tray. As I pop the pastry tower in the oven, I notice that Adam has caught up with me. From the brief glimpse I get of his pastry I can see that he's gone for a much easier design that looks vaguely bowl shaped.

Ha! This one is in the bag!

Twenty minutes later, the pastry comes out of the oven, and it's looking good – for the most part. It's gone a perfect shade of brown, and has cooked just right, rising into a crisp, flaky, horizontal sculpture that I'm sure even Allard Rancourt will approve of. Okay, so the thick pieces of dough at the bottom have now bulged out quite a lot, rather ruining the base of the tower, but I'm not going to let that affect my triumphant mood. Overall the bake has been a great success.

I'm even more confident when I hear Adam swear under his breath. I look over to see him leant over his pastry, which looks a lot paler and less golden brown than mine.

Excellent!

I cover the pastry Eiffel Tower with an opaque cake cover while it cools. The last thing I want is for Adam to get a good look at it before it's ready for the big reveal.

Piping out the white frosting is as difficult as I was afraid it might be. Instead of a nice even line of icing, I get lumps and bumps throughout, forcing me to just awkwardly cover the top of the tower, and leave it at that. Less is more, that's what they say, isn't it?

'Finished!' I cry exultantly, noting that I'm done a good ten minutes before the time limit is up. The cake cover goes back over for the final time. I want Allard Rancourt to be the first to see my creation when he judges them both.

Five minutes later, a tired and dejected Adam also tells everyone he's done. The man has defeat written all over his face.

'Bon travail, mes amis!' Allard Rancourt exclaims as he rejoins us at the kitchen work bench. 'I 'ave been watching you from ze back, and can see zat you 'ave put your 'earts and souls into it.' He addresses the camera again. 'But now, it is time to see who 'as won our special challenge!'

Me, Allard. It's totally, totally *me*.

'Adam, let's see your pastry first, eh?' Rancourt says.

'It didn't quite go the way I wanted it to,' Adam replies, revealing what looks like a battered pastry bowl full of random bits of glazed fruit and sickly green icing.

Rancourt looks nonplussed. 'What is it, Adam?'

Adam is downcast. 'It's meant to be a fruit salad.'

A fruit salad? How in hell is that *French*?

'The pastry didn't cook right,' he continues in an apologetic tone. 'It's got a soggy bottom.'

Allard Rancourt lays a comforting hand on Adam's shoulder. 'Ah yes. That is ze danger we all face when baking, Adam. You are new to zis, though, do not let it trouble you. Shall we see 'ow she tastes?'

'Okay.'

Rancourt pulls out a fork and proceeds to cut a big chunk out of Adam's failed fruit salad pastry bowl, popping it in his mouth with relish.

'A little undercooked,' he states between chews. 'But ze flavour is delicate, and ze fruit is wonderfully tangy. Well done, Adam! Well done!'

What bull hockey is this? Adam's stupid bowl is quite clearly not French, not properly cooked and not inventive in the slightest!

Allard Rancourt is an idiot! A giant French, pretentious idiot!

. . . look, white wine makes me aggressive and competitive, okay? Just be glad it's not Jim Beam, otherwise we'd all be in real trouble.

'And now, we come to your creation, Jessica,' Rancourt announces, moving to my side of the bench. 'What do you 'ave for us?'

'Well, Allard, I have something that I think you're really going to *love*.' My voice drips with the smugness of inevitable victory.

'Will I?' the chef replies with curiosity.

'Yeah! When I think of France, this is the first thing that springs into my head.'

'*Fantastique!* Zen reveal your creation to the world!'

'Alright!'

I whip off the cake cover and stand back, ready to receive the praise and adulation of everyone in the room.

'Er . . .' Allard says, peering at the Eiffel Tower closely. I see the guy controlling the video camera pick it up off the tripod and come in for a much closer look at my pastry tower.

Allard Rancourt is silent for a moment, inspecting what he sees before him.

Wow. He's struck dumb. I must have done a very good job of this!

He turns and looks at me. 'And zis is what you think of when you think of my 'omeland?'

'Yeah!'

Oh God . . . there are actual *tears* in his eyes now!

Adam comes over and stands next to Rancourt. He too inspects the Eiffel Tower. His reaction is totally unexpected though. He bursts into laughter.

Screw you, Adam! *Screw you!* I slaved over that thing! You didn't hear me laughing at your squidgy bowl, did you?

'It's a cock and balls,' Adam whispers in a disbelieving voice. 'She's made a giant pastry cock and balls.'

'What?' I exclaim in disgust. 'What the hell are you saying?'

Allard gives me a forlorn look. 'Why would you think zis of us, Jessica? Zat my country is like a big *pénis* and *testicules?*'

What are they both talking about?

'It's the Eiffel Tower!' I snap at them. 'Look at it!'

'We are, Jess. We really, really are,' Adam replies, shoulders shaking with mirth.

I point at the bottom. 'Look, there's the archway. Okay, the two bits on either side are too large and rose too high, but other than that it's *fine!* And there's the tower, rising up to the round observation deck at the top that I've covered in white frost—'

Oh God, it's a giant cock and balls.

Adam points at my delicately worked lattice. 'Look Allard, she's even got the veins in it.' He claps the chef on the shoulder in a friendly manner. 'And what about that spunky icing, eh?'

My face instantly flames red.

The video camera zooms right in on my pastry cock and balls, close enough to pick out every gruesome detail.

In the background I can see the carefully picked Sociality subscribers collapsing in merriment. Cassie looks like someone's inserting a bowling ball into her somewhere obvious.

'It's supposed to be the Eiffel Tower,' I tell everyone. 'Not a penis . . . It's definitely not meant to be a penis.'

But it IS a penis. A big, flaky, semen-covered penis that I have spent the last hour and a half lovingly crafting with my hands.

There's every chance this might be my subconscious telling me I need to get laid.

'I wonder what it tastes like?' Adam ventures, obviously delighting in my discomfort.

'Er . . . I suppose I should 'ave a try,' Rancourt replies. 'Maybe Jessica's *Tour Eiffel* can be saved by the flavour?'

It's a cock and balls, Allard. But thank you for the support.

The chef picks up his fork, and pauses over my pastry concoction, evidently trying to decide where he should take a mouthful from. Does he go for the shaft, tip or balls?

Oh God, this is *excruciating*.

In the end, Rancourt decides to go the whole hog, and takes a chunk out of the helmet, bringing along with it a healthy dose of my ejaculate icing.

As he brings the forkful up to his mouth, it looks like he's about to eat rancid dog food. This goes to show that the first bite truly is with the eyes. The pastry I've made could be the most delicate and light ever created on God's green earth, but it would still look like a throbbing erect member, and would therefore be about as appetising as a four-day-old *confits de pomponce*.

Can you imagine poor Mary Berry laying eyes on this thing in the baking tent? Even she would have a hard time praising the pastry's crispness if she had a large flour-based phallus staring her right in the eye.

Paul Hollywood would probably love it, though.

To be fair, Allard Rancourt makes a game effort at enjoying his mouthful of cock. 'Ze taste is good,' he says. 'The pastry is light and airy.' His expression changes for the worse. 'But zere are definite, er, *lumpy bits* in the icing.'

'I had that problem once,' Adam chimes in. 'Had to go to the doctors for some pills.'

It's a blatant lie, but it has the desired effect. Allard Rancourt visibly heaves, and turns away from us to spit the masticated remains of my penis pastry into the nearest sink.

You utter bastard, Adam.

Look at him – grinning like the Cheshire Cat and no doubt loving every second of my baking disgrace. He's so, so smug right now it makes me want to smack him with the nearest kitchen implement.

Where can I get my hands on a pizza wheel?

'Oh, ha ha. Very *funny*,' I say to him, folding my arms.

'It *is*, isn't it?' he replies, as Rancourt turns back to the both of us, wiping his mouth with a napkin.

'Well, I zink I have made my decision,' the chef says. 'I must award Adam ze winner of today's competition!'

Well there's a *huge* surprise. It's almost as if baking a giant set of genitals wasn't a good idea. Who'd have thought?

Adam looks suitably proud of himself, going so far as bowing at the camera, as the small crowd behind it claps his success.

This is unbearable. I have to do something.

'Well done, Adam,' I tell him in a light, breezy voice. 'You really did do a good job.'

'Thank you, Jessica,' he responds, that smug grin still plastered on his face.

'I was a bit worried about you there for a while . . .'

'Oh? And why was that?'

'Oh, I just saw you holding some butter earlier, and thought you might try to stick your head in the nearest plug hole. We all know how you like to do that kind of thing.'

The smug smile instantly disappears.

Perfect.

'Thanks for your *concern*,' Adam replies through gritted teeth. 'I'm amazed you had time to look at me, judging by how much hard work you were putting in making your big fat pastry cock, Jessica. It's a good job we weren't told to make doughnuts, otherwise poor Allard here would have been eating your freshly baked arsehole.'

'I zink it is time to wrap today's competition up!' Rancourt interjects, sensing that things are going downhill rapidly.

I am *far* from done, however.

There are many more insults I could probably fling Adam's way. I could comment on how much he loves to play kiddies' computer games, or that when he farts, birds die in the trees a hundred yards away. I could even tell everyone that Adam is *so* dumb, he can't even open a car door. Or how about the worst of his crimes? That he only married me to get his hands on a spa bath and a twenty-four-hour concierge service? I could let everyone know that I'm stuck in a marriage with someone who apparently only saw me as a *meal ticket*, and not a wife?

None of these seem quite appropriate enough to the situation.

What I really need here is something more *proactive* to demonstrate my displeasure.

Not taking my eyes off my stupid husband for even a split second, I scoop up one of the large Eiffel Tower testicles, and throw it at his head.

My pastry is *so* light and *so* fluffy that it explodes magnificently all over him.

There are audible gasps from the audience. The guy with the camera doesn't know where to point the thing. Allard Rancourt starts to step away in the manner of someone who has just stumbled across a sleeping lion.

'Bloody hell!' Adam barks in angry disbelief.

'Oh, I'm sorry, husband dearest, did I get a little pastry on you?' I ask, fists clenching involuntarily.

I receive a nine-hundred-megawatt blast of Adamface in return. Then, his eyes narrow. 'Oh, that's fine, wife *dearest*,' Adam replies, and grabs a handful of creamy glazed fruit from his soggy bowl. 'Would you like some fruit salad?'

'Not really, I don't like—'

SPLAT.

That's going to take ages to get out of my hair.

Still, Adam's going to have enough problems washing off this entire *BAG OF FLOUR, YOU SONOFABITCH!!*

I lunge forward and upend the entire bag over his head. He tries to back away, but I pursue him across the kitchen, not letting up with my flour-based assault for one moment.

'My kitchen! My kitchen!' Allard Rancourt screeches in dismay.

'Stop it, you two! The camera is still rolling!' Cassie exclaims, finally shocked into action by the impromptu food fight taking place between her favourite married couple.

Adam manages to clear the flour from his eyes long enough to spy a bag of icing sugar, and retaliates with it, pouring it back over my head, and creating a culinary dust storm that causes us both to start coughing loudly.

'You broke – *COUGH* – my daddy's – *COUGH* – car – *COUGH*!' I scream.

'You – *COUGH* – nearly broke – *COUGH* – my back – *COUGH*,' Adam retorts at similar volume.

My hands scrabble around on the kitchen top and find purchase on the perfect thing to put this fight to an end – a steel bowl full of my lumpy semen icing.

'Try not to get any of this in your fucking ears!' I yell, and upend the bowl over Adam's head.

'Oh my God!' he wails and backs off, pulling the bowl off his head and feverishly trying to wipe the icing from his face as fast as he can.

Then the fire alarm goes off.

It's obviously decided that a giant cloud of flour and icing sugar is close enough to billowing smoke to warrant putting itself to good use.

'Everybody out! We must evacuate!' Allard Rancourt orders, his voice barely audible over the high-pitched alarm's shriek.

Not that anyone needs telling twice. The sound is so painfully deafening that we're all headed for the exit before the words are out of his mouth.

Then the sprinklers come on, and the day takes a proper turn for the worse.

You see, the thing about icing sugar and flour is that when you mix them with water, they tend to get very slippery, *very* quickly. And let's remember that Adam and I are covered in both.

His legs go out from under him mere seconds after the water starts cascading out of the sprinklers. I'm right behind him headed for the exit, so as he goes down, I follow right along behind him, landing on his back. The combination of my forward momentum, the lubrication provided by the sugar, flour and water, and the polished kitchen tiles beneath sends us both sliding gracefully out of the large exit doors, taking out Allard Rancourt, Alex the cameraman, and two Sociality subscribers in quick succession as we go.

Luckily, friction reasserts itself before we go too much further, and we come to a rest with me still on top of Adam, in the middle of a crowd of confused, sugar-covered people.

'Can you get off me, please?' he entreats painfully from below.

I do so, rolling off his back and on to the kitchen tiles, panting heavily and still coughing from the icing sugar caught in my throat.

Cassie stands over us both, surveying the damage for a moment, speechless.

Then she finds her voice again.

I kind of wish she hadn't.

'You fucking idiots!' she screams.

At precisely the same moment, the alarm comes to an abrupt halt, saving our eardrums from further abuse.

Everyone, including all of us still on the floor, is left in abject silence for a few moments.

Allard Rancourt eventually breaks it when he says, 'Cassandra? I zink it would be best if we do not use zis video to promote my restaurant.'

She stares at him in disbelief. 'You *think* so? What exactly is it about two fully grown adults chucking ingredients at each other like two pissed-up chimps that you think won't promote your restaurant very well?'

'Zey do not represent ze clientele well *at all*.' Allard points at me and Adam. 'This is a place for people with class. Not like zem.'

How rude! He's saying Adam and I aren't *classy*!

'Now hang on a minute!' I protest.

'What you saying, mate?' Adam adds, in the same angry tone of voice.

We both get up off the floor – two sugar- and flour-covered monstrosities – ready to give Rancourt combined pieces of our minds.

Not large pieces, though. I think we've clearly demonstrated that neither of us have that much to go around.

'Excuse me?' a small voice interrupts.

We all look round at the small woman with mousey hair and spectacles.

'I was just wondering . . . could we get the recipe for the cock and balls before we leave? It'll go down a scream at Claire's hen do next week.'

A day later, and we're back in Cassandra McFlasterton's office.

The atmosphere is considerably *thicker* than the last time we were here.

'I think it would be best,' she says to us, nursing a cup of tea in what look like hands that are trying their level best not to tremble, 'if we just put yesterday behind us and pretend it never happened. What do you both think?'

Adam and I nod several times.

'And we should all be thankful that I didn't invite any of the press along.'

We nod again. This seems the best course of action for the time being.

'And that the guests I invited were easily paid off with two years' free subscription, and some T-shirts.'

Nod, nod, nod.

'Allard isn't taking my calls any more. That's a shame, isn't it?'

Nod, nod, nod.

'I guess we should hope that's the only fallout from your cookery session, shouldn't we?'

Nod, nod, nod.

'And you're both going to be on your best behaviours from now on, aren't you?'

Nod, nod, nod.

'Aren't you?'

'Yes, Cassie!' I blurt.

'Yes, Cassie!' Adam repeats.

And we mean it too. We absolutely, 100 per cent mean it.

From now on the Holbornes will behave, and act, like mature, rational adults.

Absolutely.

Without a doubt.

Hmmmm.

LIVE BLOG IN *THE DAILY TORRENT* ONLINE NEWSPAPER

12 May

MEET THE HOLBORNES – A LIVE Q&A SESSION

With Sonny Duhal

6.55pm

Hi, everyone, and welcome to the live blog I'm running during this special Q&A, featuring the Sociality couple, Adam and Jessica Holborne. The session is due to begin here at a packed Neon Joe's nightclub in about five minutes – giving me just enough time to set the scene a bit. It's a small nightclub, so cramming in all these members of the press and Sociality subscribers hasn't been easy. The temperature in here must be eighty degrees! Let's hope it's all worth it. This is the first time in three months we've been given proper access to the couple, so let's hope they have something worthwhile to tell us.

7.07pm

No sign of the happy couple yet . . .

7.13pm

Okay, here they come. Better late than never!

7.14pm

Neither of them look too relaxed. In fact, Adam keeps looking nervously offstage as if someone is watching him like
a hawk.

7.19pm

Jessica is more natural onstage than Adam. She's very comfortable speaking into the tie mic. Her accent is very Californian,
but every now and again I detect a few British inflections. Not
surprising given how long she's been living here.

7.22pm

Okay, first question. And it's an easy one. A woman with
mousey brown hair and glasses just asked them what they
most enjoy about being married. The answers are as scripted
as the question, I believe. Adam says it's waking up with someone by your side every morning. Jessica tells us she loves
having a companion to share life's ups and downs with.

7.30pm

Second question, this one also from a very obvious plant in the audience. This man asks the couple if they think Sociality's algorithms are as good as they say they are. Of course, both of them agree wholeheartedly. Jessica does a better job of making the rehearsed lines sound more natural . . . but only just.

7.39pm

It's occurred to me what this event closely resembles – a particularly bad episode of *Blind Date*. The whole thing reeks of a put-up job, and I've been following this campaign long enough to know who's behind it. Cassie McFlasterton really needs someone to help her with her scripts, as Adam and Jessica are currently sounding like a pair of romance robots, answering bland questions in a bland manner. Any minute now I expect one of them to malfunction and need rebooting.

7.50pm

Now it's time for carefully selected questions from the media. Thank God. Let's hope we get more juicy stuff now!

8.03pm

Nope! It sounds like Cassie has made sure that the media are on her side tonight as well. Okay, the guy from BBC Online asked about what happened at that party a few weeks ago, but he got another pre-scripted response, brushing it aside as a funny anecdote. While he was answering, though, I saw

Adam's eye start to twitch in one corner, a dead giveaway that he's struggling to feed us this bullshit as much as we're struggling to accept it. Now I know why McFlasterton only let me in to *watch* tonight, rather than let me ask a question of my own!

8.08pm

A question from that weird woman at *The Guardian* who covers the tech pages. She's actually asking Adam and Jessica how much they'd recommend Sociality to their friends. Not *if* they'd recommend it, but *how much*. Telling.

8.15pm

Great. Back to the canned questions from Sociality subscribers. This is excruciating. The question this time is what kind of grand gesture would the couple make to the world to show how much they love each other. I could quite honesty throw up.

Jessica replies that she'd be happy to stand in the middle of Leicester Square on a busy day and kiss her husband in front of everyone. This gets a few half-hearted chuckles from the crowd. Lame.

Then Adam adds something I'm convinced isn't in the script. 'Completely naked,' he says with a big grin. Jessica looks suitably horrified at the suggestion. It's quite clear that Adam has gone off book here. 'And we'd have a one-man band right behind us,' he continues. I can hear some rustling from backstage. 'He'd be playing a really good song.' Adam appears to think for a moment. '"The Lion Sleeps Tonight" by Tight Fit. I love that one.'

Oh look! Here comes Cassie McFlasterton on to the stage to tell us there will be an impromptu short intermission for refreshments. She ushers Jessica and Adam off the stage in a hurry. This was clearly not a planned break in the Q&A!

8.17pm

Oh my God! Their microphones are still on! No one's turned them off! We can all clearly hear Cassie chastising Adam for saying something he wasn't meant to. Now Jessica is piping up as well, calling him an idiot! Doesn't sound like a loving wife to me!

'We're never going to actually bloody *do it*,' Adam tells them both, the hiss and pop of static accompanying his words, 'so what's wrong with having a little fun?'

I have to say, Adam, I agree! That's the first honest thing I've heard come from either of their mouths all evening. Everyone out front is starting to look at each other. Laughter is starting to ripple around the room as people realise what's going on. Cassie tells Adam that he must not say anything else that they haven't already rehearsed! This is just too perfect!

Finally, someone seems to tell the owner of Sociality that she can be heard by everyone in the nightclub, as there is the sound of what I think is a gerbil being squeezed to death, before sudden and unequivocal silence.

8.25pm

The couple retake the stage. Cassie's with them. She says they are both tired, and there will only be time for one more question this evening. Nobody's mentioning what we all just heard from backstage.

Screw it, if this thing is going to end like this, then I'm going to take my chances – and grab the mic to steal the last question for myself!

8.45pm

The Q&A is over, and I'm sat back in my car. One of the night-club bouncers is still watching me from the club's fire exit, but he's already done his job throwing me out of the place, so I don't think I have to worry about him too much.

I got to ask my question, even though I made a mortal enemy in the guy from HuffPo when I stole the microphone right out of his hand.

'Do either of you have anything to say about the problems you've both been having with the marriage?' I said quickly into the stolen mic. Neither of them responded, which I wasn't surprised about at all. 'Either of you care to comment properly about your disastrous party? Or what happened at the filming in Allard Rancourt's restaurant?'

Both Jessica and Adam look terrified. I feel a little bad as they seem like a nice pair, but there's something going on with this whole set-up I don't like, and it's my job as a reporter to get to the bottom of it.

'Is this marriage real?' I press. 'Or are you both living a lie to sell Cassie McFlasterton's website for her?' There's no answer again, but I see Adam nod involuntarily, and look at Jessica, who gives him a stern look in return. I *knew* it!

McFlasterton is back onstage once more, waving her hands. 'That's the last question for tonight, everyone!' she snaps at us. 'I hope you'll all thank Jessica and Adam for their time tonight.' She fixes me with a stare of purest hate. 'Have a safe journey home.'

It's at this point that the bouncer appears behind me and kindly asks me to leave the premises, so I don't get to see or hear any of the aftermath from my interruption.

Everyone must realise that all is not well in the Holborne household, though.

And it'll only get worse. Surely the cracks that are definitely showing in this sham marriage will just get wider and wider?

I'll be keeping a close eye on proceedings – though I very much doubt I'll be invited back for an interview with Cassandra McFlasterton any time soon!

ADAM

Q. Have you ever achieved something you're really proud of?
*A. Well, I won my school's ping-pong tournament when I was twelve,
so probably that.*

4 June

Cassie's getting desperate now – and with desperation come bad decisions. This is why I'm dressed in a pair of white shorts, and have a sweatband tightly wrapped around my head.

Okay, so the whole '"Lion Sleeps Tonight", one-man band' gag was probably a step too far, but after no less than *three days* of being rehearsed, trained and brainwashed before our big public question-and-answer session, I was ready to gouge my brains out. I've never been one for doing as I'm told for too long, and going off script like that was my way of letting everybody else know that as well.

Besides, I don't think it really did much harm. Not nearly as much as the sound guy not doing his job, and that Indian bloke grabbing the microphone and asking all the questions I'd certainly want answers to if I was a punter looking in on this mess from the outside.

I knew sticking us both onstage like that would be a comprehensively bad idea, and I was proved well and truly *right*. Cassie is one of those people who can't just leave well enough alone, though. She has to do something dramatic and spectacular whenever a problem raises its ugly head.

It didn't work with the cookery lesson, it didn't work with the Q&A, and it sure as hell isn't going to work slinging Jessica and me out on to a court at *Wimbledon* for a bloody tennis match.

If I'd known how much trouble I was going to get into filling out that bloody dating profile, I would have played *Candy Crush* while I was sat on the crapper instead.

Jesus Christ, I was only on the toilet that long because I'd had a meat feast pizza the night before and it was like trying to pass a house brick. If I'd eaten salad instead, then there's every chance I wouldn't be standing in the middle of Court 12 dressed like an arsehole and about to play the world's worst game of tennis against a woman who irritates me more than the haemorrhoids the pizza caused.

I only said I liked ping-pong when I was *twelve*, for crying out loud! How the hell does that translate into playing tennis at Wimbledon?

If I'd written that I liked to do doughnuts in a car park, would I currently be hurtling down the Hangar Straight at Silverstone in a Formula One car with my backside on fire?

I'm blaming Jessica for this, because it's something I'm having less and less trouble doing these days. *She's* the one who likes tennis, and *she's* the one who talked me into going along with yet another one of Cassie McFlasterton's bullshit publicity stunts by making me feel guilty about what happened at the Q&A.

Naked kissing in Leicester Square to 'The Lion Sleeps Tonight'? It's *funny* for Christ's sakes!

I wasn't the one who screwed up that night! Why isn't Geoff the sound man out here dressed like Björn Borg's fatter cousin, instead of me?

'Heads or tails?' the dapper umpire asks me from over the net.

'Heads,' I mutter, watching as he flips the coin into the air.

This is a *proper* Wimbledon umpire, not some goon dragged in off the street and thrown into a well-ironed green jacket – and this is one of the proper courts they use for the championships, which are starting in only a few weeks.

When Cassie first proposed this outing, I thought we'd be stuck on a practice court for the day, but *no*, here we are, standing somewhere that will soon see the number-seven seed crash out to the plucky young lad from Estonia in a shocking straight-sets defeat.

How Cassie wrangled this one, I'll never know.

Bollocks. I know exactly how she wrangled it. The same way she wrangled me into these awful white shorts and silly headband.

Cassie McFlasterton is a *bully* – there's no two ways about it.

She'll either coerce you with a carrot, or beat you about the head with a very large stick. I have no doubt there's some poor official from the All England Lawn Tennis Club somewhere who's nursing heavy and severe bruising to his cranium right now.

Jessica, of course, looks as cute as a button. How could she not? A physically fit, pretty redhead from California is only ever going to look *cute as a fucking button* in a bright-white tennis top and skirt, topped off with fluffy wristbands and knee-high sports socks. Everyone will think she's adorable.

Only I know she's pure evil, summoned from the depths of hell to make Adam Holborne's life a misery.

Now that we've abandoned any pretence of being a married couple in private, things have gone downhill faster than an Olympic skier with explosive bowels.

We argue about everything. Quite literally *everything*.

You wouldn't think it possible for two grown adults to spend an hour shouting at each other over who got cheese crumbs in the pesto jar, but fuck me, it is.

I've now stolen the television and put it in my bedroom, just so I don't have to endure her constant whining about how much time I spend on the PlayStation. I mean, it's not like it's my *bloody job* or anything, is it? And anyway, besides that, the time I get to spend hanging out online with Oli in *Realm of Chaos* is very important to me, as it is to him. We're nerds, and proud of it.

Jessica has taken to calling Oli my other wife, which is only about 23 per cent as funny as she thinks it is. In actual fact, poor old Oli has become my marriage guidance counsellor over the past few weeks. When we're not engaged in mortal combat with the lizard warriors of the Mergo Plains, I'm moaning to him about how bad my relationship with Jessica has become. The poor guy must be sick of the sound of my whiny little voice as I regale him with how angry I am about her constantly leaving the heating on all day.

Still, it's not all bad. I've started picturing my wife's face on the aforementioned lizard warriors, and have been ploughing my way angrily through them like a dose of salts.

I have a Magic Staff of Lightning to deal with the creatures of the Mergo Plains. If only I had a Magic Staff of Wife Silencing to deal with the creature of the Kensington Apartments.

Sadly I don't, so Jess constantly moans about how much time I'm online with Oli.

Do you hear me complaining when she destroys the kitchen virtually every day, making experimental smoothies for her nutrition course?

. . . well, yes you *do*, but the blender is noisy enough to drive you round the bend after it's been on for just a few seconds. Imagine what kind of damage it's done to my brain after *three sodding hours*.

Not only that, but I'm forever tripping over folders of Jessica's work, which she likes to leave lying around the place haphazardly. If I'm escaping the atmosphere in the flat by playing *Realm of Chaos*, then she's burying herself in her studies for much the same reason.

It's definitely been what you might call a trying time – made even worse by the increased press coverage we're getting since the Q&A. This guy Sonny Duhal seems obsessed with getting to the bottom of what's going on with this marriage. I swear I've seen him loitering around outside the flat a couple of times, trying to look inconspicuous – and failing miserably. A day doesn't seem to go by without him posting something new to that tacky – but inexplicably popular – online newspaper he works for. I've gone so far as to set up alerts on my iPhone, just so I know when he's picking at the scab again. Forewarned is forearmed, and all that.

Mr Duhal is not here today, and neither are any of Fleet Street's finest. Cassie appears to have learned a valuable lesson – don't invite the press when your two shining stars are always on the edge of an argument. It can only end in tears.

The press might not be here, but the Sociality subscribers are out in force once more. There's more of them at this debacle than at any other of the theatrical performances we've had to endure so far. There's a good three rows of the buggers taking up the seating area close to the umpire's chair. Behind them are Cassie's production crew again. I notice that she's had a change of heart and hired Derek back. He looks to be taking photos of me, while his younger counterpart Alex is down at Jessica's end of the court. The video crew are all present and correct. I can see the camera pointed at me right this moment, no doubt getting a close-up of my scabby knees.

It's a shame the June weather isn't cooperating.

It looks decidedly grey up there, and the wind is whipping around my knees uncomfortably. Let's hope we get on with this game soon, just so I can warm myself up a bit with some out-of-breath exercise.

'Heads it is,' the umpire tells us both. 'Mr Holborne to serve first.'

I groan inwardly, remembering how bad my serving was this morning in the warm-up session for this afternoon's match.

Even Lily, the All England Club's happy-go-lucky tennis coach, couldn't do much to improve my game in the two hours she had available to her. No matter how many times she told me to throw the ball straighter and keep my left leg forward, I always reverted to my default serving motion of chucking the ball out about three metres in front of me, and running after it with the tennis racket held aloft like I'm trying to catch the world's most recalcitrant butterfly.

Jessica's serve is much better than mine, needless to say. She actually likes the game, and played it quite a lot when she was back home in California. She even came third in her high school competition one year.

I think about the only advantage I might have over her is the fact I can thwack the ball a bit harder, thanks to the muscles my male genetics have given me. This isn't going to count for much, though, if I can't actually hit the ball back over the net.

Lily had to go off for a lie-down after the training session was over. I can see her now, sat down at the front of the hundred-strong crowd. She looks like she's about to watch a public execution.

'Good luck,' Jessica says to me with a tight smile.

'Yeah, and you,' I reply darkly.

Both of us are still smarting over this morning's 'discussion' about who was supposed to take the clothes out of the washer-dryer. I'm *1,000* per cent positive she told me she was going to do it, but she's *2,000* per cent sure she told me to do it.

Neither of us did it.

Consequently, her favourite blouse came out wrinkled, and the material doesn't like to be ironed, so it was obviously *the worst thing to ever happen in human fucking history.*

'Can I get a picture of you two shaking hands before the match?' I hear Derek shout from behind me. I turn to see the portly little photographer jogging over, an enthusiastic grin on his face.

'Do we have to?' Jessica asks with a grimace.

'It'll be a good picture!' Derek reassures us.

I give my wife a look that suggests it's best if we just get it over and done with. She looks skyward but nods curtly and sticks out her hand over the net. I take it and pump it up and down once, looking at Derek's camera as I do.

Jessica can't wait to pull her hand away.

'How about a little kiss as well?' Derek cajoles.

It sounds to me like Cassie hasn't bothered to fill Derek here in on what's been going on between the Holbornes recently, otherwise he'd know not to ask that question.

'No, Derek,' Jessica tells him.

'Oh, go on. Just a little one for the—'

'*No*, Derek!' Jessica repeats.

'I wouldn't push it,' I warn him. 'She nearly stabbed me with a pair of scissors over a wrinkled shirt . . . and I'm married to her.'

Derek baulks at this. Jessica looks daggers at me. 'Let's get on with this,' she says to the umpire, and strides off towards the service line on her side of the court.

'What's going on?' Derek asks me. 'The last time I saw you two, you were having a great time with one another.'

'What can I say, Del Boy, married life just doesn't seem to be agreeing with us any more.'

He chuckles. 'Married life doesn't agree with anyone after long enough, chief. It's like spicy food – great going in, awful coming out. You ask my ex-wife . . . *wives*.'

Where were all these wise little aphorisms about marriage the day before I agreed to get hitched? I could have done with the bloody warning.

'Just go get some photos of me serving like a twat, Derek,' I suggest with a sigh. 'That should keep the punters happy.'

And with that I trudge off to the back of the court, trying my best to not look like I'm going to the gallows.

'Welcome to Wimbledon, ladies and gentlemen,' says the umpire, after he's sat himself in his high chair. 'Today it will be Adam Holborne versus Mrs Jessica Holborne.'

Even from here I can see Jessica's rather disgusted expression.

'The match will be a single set,' the umpire continues. 'It will be Adam Holborne to serve.'

I turn to get a ball from the amused-looking teenager acting as one of the three ballboys we've got for this event. I saw him watching me practise my serve this morning, and he now no doubt thinks he's in for a real treat.

With a nervous gulp, I bounce the tennis ball on the hard grass surface a couple of times, chuck the thing in the air, and take a wild swing at it with the racket. All I manage to strike is my own body, as the racket completely misses the ball and I hit myself on the shin.

'Ow, for fuck's sake!' I holler, using language that doesn't usually echo around these illustrious grounds. Unless John McEnroe's in the over-fifties competition.

Titters of laughter ripple through the crowd. Even Jessica is smiling.

Oh *good*. I'm so glad to see that her mood has *improved*.

Setting myself, I throw the ball in the air again, and this time I don't take my eye off it. The racket comes into contact with the ball in a most satisfactory manner.

It then comes into contact with the net, which is far less satisfactory.

'Fault. Second serve,' the umpire intones.

This time when I serve, I hit the ball like a limp-wristed clown and it barely makes it over the net. Still, Jessica isn't expecting my impromptu drop shot and I win the point.

The crowd applauds, and suddenly I feel a little more confident.

This results in the next two points going straight to my wife as I serve the ball into the net twice, once at the umpire's chair, and once into the crowd.

Come on, you blithering idiot. You can't let her win this.

Oh, I think you'll find that I fucking *can*, Mr Subconscious. Quite bloody easily as it turns out.

I only manage to serve one ball into Jessica's side of the court, which she pops straight back over the net with ease, seeing as there's about as much pace on my shot as on a sloth with arthritic knees.

She wins the game convincingly. The audience politely clap. They can see who the underdog is here, and in true British tradition, they're supporting him. It probably helps that Jessica is foreign. There's nothing like a bit of friendly competition between nations to spark off some patriotic support.

This is borne out when Jessica also launches both of her first two serves into the net. I smile and pump my fist when the crowd cheers her failure.

There are no cheers for the next serve, though, as it goes whistling cleanly past my head for an ace.

'Fifteen all,' the umpire says, in the tones of one bored by life.

More groans come with Jessica's next ace. You can see her getting visibly annoyed by the lack of support, which gives me some comfort as I'm fecklessly thrashing at the air while the tennis ball inevitably flies past me once more.

Very soon, Jessica is up two games and a break of serve. This could be over very quickly.

Now I'm not trembling with pre-match nerves, my first serve of the next game is ever so slightly more competent. Competent enough to fox Jessica and win the point, anyway.

To the delightful and encouraging cheers of the crowd I manage to stumble my way to forty–thirty, and the chance to win the game. There's no way I'm going to win the match, but if I can just get a game off my wife, I will feel some small sense of victory here today.

Concentrate, Holborne. *Concentrate.*

Up goes the ball. Back goes the arm. Forward comes the racket, hitting the bright-green fluffy ball as hard as I possibly can.

Let's call it beginner's luck. Let's call it divine providence. Let's call it a random confluence of elementary physics.

Call it whatever you want, but this serve is absolutely fucking *majestic*.

Andy Murray would be proud of it. That Serbian Novak bloke would be equally as proud, but I have no idea how to spell his surname, so he doesn't get a proper mention.

The ball flies from my racket, skims over the net, hits the grass just before the line, bounces back into the air . . . and smacks Jessica Holborne right between the eyes.

An audible gasp erupts from the crowd. It's like they've all developed acute emphysema at exactly the same moment.

'Ow! You bastard!' Jessica screams, holding a hand up to her forehead.

'Sorry!' I call down the court to her.

I'm not really.

Hee hee hee hee.

'Game Holborne,' the umpire says. 'Mrs Holborne leads by two games to one.'

The crowd cheers again, only it's a little muted, as nobody likes to see an opponent getting hurt. Even John McEnroe in the over-fifties competition.

The red welt on Jessica's face looks quite tender. She is otherwise unharmed, though, so I feel free to do a tiny victory dance.

Jessica looks at me in such a way that I suddenly feel a strange but distinct kinship with my ancestors from a couple of centuries ago, during the American Revolution. That was the last time such an epic battle between Britain and the USA took place.

I would have just given them all the tea they wanted and buggered off home if they'd looked at me like that.

My adversary – and let's not forget, *wife* – chucks the tennis ball into the air, wildly thrashes at it with the racket, and sends the ball hurtling towards me so fast I have no time to get out of the way. There's no attempt on her part to get it into the court, as the ball sails a good two feet over the net before dipping slightly, skimming off the grass past the service line, and rocketing back up into my stomach.

'Jesus!' I cry in a choked voice, the wind knocked out of me.

Now the crowd sound like their emphysema has got a lot worse. I can see a few hands held over mouths. I deliberately do *not* try to seek out Cassie McFlasterton's face. I've seen her look of horrified disbelief too many times over the past few months, and most certainly do not need to see it again.

Winded, I sit down hard on the grass and try to catch my breath.

'Fault! Second serve,' the umpire informs the crowd.

'Sorry!' Jessica calls over. Usually when someone apologises for causing you physical harm, they don't do it with a smile on their face. I fear Jessica's expression of regret may not be as sincere as it could be.

Rubbing my stomach where the ball hit me, I get back to my feet and take my place at the service line again. I stand a couple of feet further back, though.

Jessica serves again – another high-speed whopper.

This time I am happy to report that the ball does not hit me in the stomach.

My testicles are not quite so lucky.

'Yeeaaargh!' I shriek, my body convulsing.

'Sorry!' Jessica once again shouts at me. The smile is even wider.

'Fault! Love–fifteen,' the umpire reports. Even he sounds amused now. The usual, unflappable demeanour of the Wimbledon umpire has been cracked by a shot to the balls. Who'd have thought it?

Clutching my wounded genitals I move cautiously over to the other side of the court, readying myself for the next serve coming my way. Now Jessica has hit me in the testicles, I'm assuming she'll return to thrashing me at tennis, safe in the knowledge that her revenge for me smacking her in the face is comple—

'Yeeaaargh!'

Nope. Straight to the balls again.

This time with more accuracy and power. It looks like my wife has well and truly got her eye in.

'Fault! Second serve,' the umpire tells us.

For the second time in as many minutes I'm down on to the grass, both hands cupped protectively over my groin.

'Sorry!'

'Oh, sod off!' I spit back at her. She has the sheer bloody audacity to *laugh*.

Is this it? Is Jessica just going to aim for my balls for the rest of this match?

I do a little pained calculation in my head, and realise that gives her at least another twenty-five attempts to ruin my chances of ever having children.

Of course, I would also win the match by default.

I just don't know if I have the testicular fortitude to cope with such groin abuse, though, not even for the chance of a sweet and unexpected victory.

I look up to see the crowd leaning forward as one. All of them are studying me intently, waiting to see if I get up off the ground, or stay here until Serena Williams comes along and kicks me out.

All I want to do is shuffle off back to the dressing room and find a nice big bag of ice, but I can't let this match finish this way, can I? With the pride of Britain vanquished by the colonial interloper, thanks to a couple of shots to the balls?

Wincing a little, I struggle to my feet again.

A few people actually clap as I do this.

I look at them all and provide a weak thumbs up, trying to ignore the throbbing coming from my lower regions. I get a few cheers in response, along with a 'Go get her!' from a lady in the audience with mousey brown hair and spectacles.

Okay, it's not the end of *Rocky* or anything, but the applause and encouragement from the bipartisan audience is quite rousing nonetheless.

Right then, Jessica, let's see what you're really made of.

I stand straight, fix my wife with a steely gaze, and raise one hand, giving her a beckoning gesture as I do so.

Bring it on.

Jessica rolls her shoulders, spins the racket in her hand and demands another tennis ball from the nearest ballboy.

This serve comes at me harder and faster than any other, but this time I'm ready. My racket covers my groin just as the ball flies towards it, and the small green round missile bounces harmlessly off it.

The crowd greets this with a roar.

I nod enthusiastically a couple of times, and pump my fist at them.

'Fault! Love–thirty,' says our friendly umpire, looking more invested in this match now that he knows there's a genuine bit of needle to it.

Jessica tries the same trick with the next serve, but my racket is ready once again to deflect her testicle-bound shot.

For the sake of variety, the next ball comes straight at my head, but I duck out of the way like Neo from *The Matrix*, resulting in another fault, and giving me a shot at winning the game.

My evil wife obviously realises this, as the next serve is actually one designed to win a point, rather than damage me physically. This brings her back to fifteen–forty, and the next serve is also a doozy, making the score thirty–forty.

Her head is back in the game now. I think my chances of turning this thing around are slipping through my fingers fast.

Unless I stoop to some truly underhand tactics . . .

As Jessica throws the ball up to send another service rocketing past me, in order to bring the scores level, I cough loudly.

'Hrrgh – *Mustang* – hrrgh,' I croak, loud enough for it to carry right across the court.

That does the trick.

Jessica is completely put off, and the tennis ball flies far over my head to the left.

'Game Holborne!' the umpire announces, much to the crowd's delight.

'Sorry!' I shout at Jessica, making sure she sees how broad the smile on my face is.

'Asshole!' she responds, quite understandably.

Still, that's levelled the match nicely, hasn't it? Two games apiece and everything to play for. That'll teach her to aim for my meat and two veg!

It's my service game again, and I'm determined to not let my momentum dribble away.

The first serve I deliver is an actual, honest-to-goodness ace! Okay, it's also a complete bloody fluke, but I'm having it! The crowd cheers again. They're eating this up now.

Time to really put the boot in!

I aim the next serve at Jessica. This is the first time I've done this, and a small voice deep, deep within the furthest recesses of my brain tries to call me a heartless bastard, but it gets drowned out by the pain centres of my brain communicating to me how much my bollocks still hurt.

The tennis ball shoots like a lightning bolt towards Jessica.

. . . oh, alright. It's nothing like a lightning bolt. Let's not pretend I've suddenly become proficient at tennis, here. I'm riding on adrenaline-fuelled luck at the moment, and we all know it.

The tennis ball flies at about the speed of a dog fart towards Jessica.

It would be very easy for her to hit it, or just jump out of the way to avoid getting hit. But I am dealing with a very smart woman here, when you get right down to it. One certainly smart enough to know that this stopped being a tennis match some time ago, and is now purely a popularity contest.

Jessica allows the tennis ball to hit her in the chest.

She theatrically clutches one hand to her boob, and lets out an anguished cry. Anyone would think I'd just shot her with an air rifle, not hit her with a badly paced tennis ball.

The crowd gasp.

Jessica drops to her knees . . . and starts to cry.

Yes, she actually starts to bloody *cry*.

Not heaving great sobs or anything, but certainly enough for the audience to see and sympathise with.

'Are you alright, Mrs Holborne?' the umpire says.

'I . . . I think so,' she replies, struggling for breath.

I see about a hundred sets of eyes slowly turn to look at me. All of them are expressing the same unspoken judgement.

How could you? How could you hurt the poor woman like that? She's your wife, *you bastard!*

In an instant, Jessica has turned the crowd completely against me. It's no longer a match between the dominant American superstar and the plucky young Brit, it's now all about the spousal abuse.

I am comprehensively *fucked*.

Jessica should have gone into amateur dramatics instead of nutrition, as she's giving a bravura performance down at the other end of the court. With a look of pained betrayal on her face, she rises to her feet unsteadily.

A few of the more easily manipulated members of the crowd cheer this. *'Go get him!'* I hear the mousey woman in the spectacles say, swapping sides quicker than the Italians in the Second World War.

Where's the loyalty of your fellow compatriots when you most need it, eh? Gone up in smoke the second they realise you're no longer the underdog, but have resolutely become the bad guy. It's a heel turn of epic proportions.

I have to hand it to Jessica, she's read the crowd *magnificently*, and manipulated them thoroughly with one simple but extremely effective bit of acting.

I now feel a confusing mixture of emotions as I watch her play the crowd like a fiddle.

On the one hand I still want to crush her beneath my heel – but on the other, I want to rip all of her clothes off and have sex with her right now on this tennis court.

For some reason, there's something undeniably sexy about someone turning to the dark side.

I am quite clearly in need of counselling.

. . . and tennis lessons.

'I'm really sorry!' I call down the court, trying to sound as contrite as possible. This gets a couple of honest-to-goodness boos from the audience. This tennis match has apparently turned into a pantomime while I wasn't looking.

'That's okay, Adam,' Jessica calls back in a wavering tone. 'I'm sure you didn't mean it.' She wipes one tear away from her eye as she says this.

Oh, for pity's sake.

So, what the hell am I supposed to do now? Throw the match? Still try to win?

Either way I lose.

I either get beaten by a woman at tennis, or end up looking like a colossal misogynist. It's a no-win situation.

Best to just take things one serve at a time, I think. See how it all pans out.

In other words, I've pretty much given up trying to retain any control over this tennis match, and am metaphorically burying my head in the sand, hoping nobody shoots me up the backside with a well-aimed tennis ball.

Needless to say, this does not do wonders for my tennis skills, and Jessica wins the game.

As she celebrates the final point with her new-found fans, I can see her looking over at me slyly every so often, making sure that I know she manipulated this whole change of mood with her over-the-top theatrics. It's one thing to defeat your enemy, but it's another to know that they realise how clever you were whilst doing it.

As I watch her high-five Lily the tennis coach, that confusing welter of emotions rises to the surface again. Part of me would like nothing more than to never see Jessica *Madison* again. She is a constant annoyance, a thorn in my side, and someone who knows how to rub me up the wrong way with no trouble whatsoever.

She has been the direct cause of some of the most humiliating experiences of my recent life, and I can't shake the notion that things would be a lot quieter and less stressful if she weren't around any more.

And yet.

And *yet* . . .

Here I am looking at her jumping around like a madwoman in her cute little tennis outfit, having quite neatly turned a whole crowd of people against me, and I can't help but feel an intense admiration for her.

'Oh for fuck's sake,' I say under my breath and rub my eyes.

What the hell is wrong with me?

'Sixth game, Mrs Holborne to serve,' the umpire says over the speaker system, reminding me that I still have the rest of this damn tennis match to see out.

I take my place on the baseline and await whatever it is Jessica is going to fire at me this time.

Oh good, she's decided she wants to wrap this one up, and has gone back to firing aces past my head, instead of aiming for my testicles.

The rest of the set flies by with me hardly winning a point, and before you know it, we're at match point.

When the serve comes my way, I make my best effort to hit it back, and for only about the fifth time in this entire match, I do get the ball back across the net. Okay, I've launched it skyward so high that they can probably reach out and grab it from the International Space Station, but at least it's going in roughly the right direction.

Jessica readies herself below the ball as it reaches the fullest extent of its arc, and starts to fall earthwards again. I have time to look to my left, and see the crowd lean forward in anticipation of the glorious smash that she's no doubt about to deliver.

The concentration on my wife's face is absolute. She wants to end this thing with a dramatic flourish as much as the crowd wants her to.

The ball falls closer, Jessica's racket goes back, and as the tennis ball reaches the right height she gives it an almighty wallop that sends the small green projectile back over the net at thunderous speed.

It's a smash worthy of Steffi Graf in her prime – or at least it would have been had Jessica not lost her grip on the racket as well, sending it also flying across the net closely following the ball.

Oh, would you look at that? Both of them are flying *at me*.

We've already established that a tennis ball is detrimental to the testicular region – can you imagine what damage a tennis *racket* might do?

You'll have to imagine it, because I'm sure as hell not going to stand here and let it actually *happen*.

In the past few months I've spent an inordinate amount of time falling over, so have got very good at it. Whether it be on to a man dressed as a sheep, or off a drinks trolley while covered in butter, I have learned how to take a massive bump and survive more or less intact. Little did I know that this was all perfect training to ensure that I can get out of the way of a ballistic tennis racket before it embeds itself in my forehead.

I go to ground and watch as both ball and racket fly over my head. When the ball hits the scoreboard at the back of the court, it does no damage. When the racket hits it, I know that ducking as quickly as I did may have actually saved my life, as the damage the thing does to the no doubt very expensive piece of finest Wimbledon technology is horrific.

As sparks fly and bits of screen crack and fall off the scoreboard, Jessica gives the umpire a horrified look. 'Sorry!' she exclaims, this time completely genuinely.

'Game, set, match, Mrs Holborne,' the umpire states, looking with dismay at the sparking, sizzling scoreboard. It looks like the repair bill might be coming out of his wages.

The crowd, who didn't expect fireworks at the end of the match, but are supremely glad to get them, rise to their feet in honour of Jessica's victory. When they do, my wife forgets that she's just accidentally vandalised thousands of pounds' worth of equipment, and goes over to accept their applause with a bow and a bit of manic fist pumping. She also throws her fluffy wristbands into the crowd. This is just a tad over the top, but she is American after all, so it is probably to be expected.

That confusion of emotions is still with me as I watch her do this.

On the one hand I'm angry at being comprehensively beaten by a woman I'm at near-constant loggerheads with – on the other I'm taking a great deal of pleasure in seeing her bounce around happily like that.

Why?

Why do I feel like this?

Have I got some sort of bizarre multiple-personality disorder? Am I a secret masochist? Or have I developed Stockholm syndrome?

Ever since this bloody marriage began, I haven't been able to think straight. I just can't make my mind up about Jessica, no matter how hard I try.

I don't know if the marriage is a complete sham, or if there's more to it than just a flat and a pile of cash.

If it is just about those things, then are they really *worth* all this grief?

Or is there something about Jess that I can't pull myself away from, no matter how bad things seem to be on the surface?

She's an infuriating human being, has humiliated me on more than one occasion, and quite clearly isn't the right woman for me – and yet . . . and yet . . . I think *I'd feel bad if she weren't around.*

Is that why I've struggled to be honest with her this entire time?

Because I just haven't been honest with *myself?*

What the hell is wrong with me?

Questions, questions, questions!

Aaaarggh!

I'm scratching my head about the meaning of all this as Cassie comes on to court with her two photographers and Lily the tennis coach.

'Come to the net, you two!' Cassie commands. 'Let's get a nice picture of you, the umpire and the ballboys for the website.'

Ah yes, the ever-present website. What would my life be like if I didn't have to pose for a photo every five minutes?

A *pleasure*, that's what.

Derek and Alex start to argue over the best way to arrange us all for the picture. I'm guessing Derek will win the argument, as he has about fifteen years and fifty pounds on the other man.

Jessica and I stand together on either side of the net again, as the others are corralled into position.

'Well done,' I tell her.

'Thanks,' she replies, her tone a little short. As she speaks, she rubs the fading red mark on her forehead.

'My balls are fine by the way,' I point out. If she's going to make a thing of her injuries, then so am I.

'Good.'

'Everybody smile,' Derek instructs, taking several pictures in quick succession.

'Kiss her!' somebody shouts from up in the crowd.

Ah, hell. This isn't good.

Both Jessica and I start to shake our heads and make protesting noises, but that just makes even more members of the crowd scream for the same thing. Let's not forget that these are all single people from Sociality, and they're probably not getting much romance in their lives at the moment. They want this tennis match to be capped off with a nice flamboyant romantic gesture, and they're not taking no for an answer.

'Go on! Give them what they want!' Derek roars. Cassie keeps her mouth shut in a tight line, studying us both. She knows what's going on between us, and can probably appreciate just how awkward this is for the two of us. There's a pleading look in her eyes as well, though.

I look at Jessica, who clenches her fists a couple of times at her side. 'Come on then, let's get it over with,' I say.

It truly is a *beautiful* moment.

Jessica leans forward, and I do the same, issuing my wife with a kiss on her tight, pursed lips. There's an audible sigh of disappointment from the audience as I pull away.

I stay where I am for a moment, studying her stony expression . . . and then something positively *dreadful* happens.

I don't know whether it's my confused emotional state, or just my libido at work, but the results are the same either way.

I lean back in towards Jessica, wrap one arm around her waist over the net, and kiss her again, this time with a passion that's bordering on the aggressive.

For a moment she resists, going as stiff as a board. Then, she's coming back at me with equal passion, in what I'm sure will result in us both having bruised lips for the rest of the day.

The crowd cheers. This is more like it!

Then sanity reasserts itself, and I yank myself away from Jessica like she's suddenly had an electric current passed through her.

For her part, my wife looks a combination of sexually aroused and spitting angry. Her eyes are wide, her mouth is agape, her hair is a red, wavy mess.

'You son of a bitch!' she exclaims, and throws a punch at my face.

Yes, that's right. In the heat of the moment, my loving wife has decided that the best way to respond to my spur-of-the-moment kiss is to smack me in the mouth.

It's not a hard punch, or a particularly accurate one – it glances off my mouth rather than hitting me square on it. However, I am tired, sweaty and a little light-headed from all this unwanted exercise, so the effects of the punch are multiplied beyond all recognition.

'Oh, cobblers,' I enunciate clearly as my hand goes to what I know is going to be a marvellously bloody lip. I bring my finger away, and sure enough, it's covered in claret.

I think at this point, all things considered, it might be best if I have a little lie-down. Just to recharge my batteries a bit, you understand.

The soft Wimbledon grass comes up to meet my face in a loving embrace that I am deeply grateful to experience. From quite far away I hear the crowd gasp the loudest they have all day.

Boy, they've got their money's worth, haven't they? A little conflict, a little romance, a little violence . . . what more could anyone ask for?

How about a wife who doesn't punch you in the face when you give her a kiss?

Yeah . . . that'd be *nice*, wouldn't it?

JESS

Q. Are you the private type? Or do you let it all hang out?
A. I try not to let it all hang out because I don't want to get arrested.

15 June

'I wanted boneless!'

'They didn't have any *boneless*!'

'Liar! They *always* have boneless! They *advertise* the *fact* they have boneless! They *always have boneless*!'

'Well not today, Jessica! Today, our local branch of Kentucky Fried Chicken didn't have any boneless boxes available for me to purchase, so you've got boned!'

'Oh yeah! That's the truth, isn't it? I definitely got *boned*! Completely fucking *boned*!'

Hello, and welcome to an argument.

You join us near the start of this particular disagreement – about the KFC takeaway we were due to eat this evening.

I really shouldn't be eating fried chicken – I am a nutrition student after all, but there comes a time in life when things are so bad that you just need to stuff your face with the worst food imaginable. If I were a smoker, I'd be on a pack and a half a day.

We won't be eating the KFC now anyway, thanks to the argument. It will just get cold on the side while we rage at one another for the next hour.

'Are you *seriously* trying to convince me that our KFC couldn't sell you a goddamned boneless box?'

'Yes! Yes I am!'

'So, it's not that you just *forgot* what I asked for, and bought me the same thing you wanted?'

'No . . . no, that's not true at all!'

'Ha! Yes it is, you asshole! You know that's the truth! I know when you're lying, and you're lying through your teeth right now!'

'Oh for crying out loud, it's a box of bloody fried chicken! Who cares whether it's got bones in it or not?'

'I. DON'T. LIKE. BONES!'

'AND. I. DON'T. LIKE. FUSSY. BITCHES!'

Not nice, is it?

It shouldn't be possible for a simple thing like fried chicken to create such a nuclear argument, but there you have it.

To tell the truth, if it wasn't about chicken, it would just be about something else. Adam and I have raised arguing to the level of an art form recently. We should go on the road with it. The audience members could pick any innocuous object they like, and we could have an apocalyptic argument about it there and then in front of them.

We'd make a fortune on the carny circuit back home.

Roll up, roll up! Come see the Calamitous Couple in action! They'll amaze! They'll shock! They'll make you glad you're single! Just ten cents a show!

'Maybe if you hadn't been playing that damn game with Oli again, you might have paid attention to what I asked you to get!'

'Oh, here we go again! You're like a broken fucking record! *Stop playing the PlayStation, Adam, get off* Realm of Chaos, *Adam. You're an adult not a kid, Adam.*'

'You ARE an adult, Adam!'

'It's my *job*!'

'No! No it isn't! Your job is across town! You go to work, you do your job, then come home and you *do something else*. That's how normal people are. You don't just do the same thing at home as well, *all of the time*!'

'Well, there's not much else to do around here, is there?! I can't just spend my entire evening getting shouted at by you!'

'Maybe if you actually *listened to me*, you wouldn't!'

I hate to think what the neighbours are saying about us.

This was probably a quiet, well-mannered apartment block full of people quietly going about their pretentious West London lives in relative peace. Then the Holbornes moved in, and the place turned into a trailer park.

We're the white-trash couple who won the lottery and moved in next door, as far as they're concerned.

Beedle gives me the evil eye every time I walk past her, Lachlan cups his testicles, and even Hugo – a man who will strike up a conversation just so he can hear the sound of his own voice – has taken to rushing past me in the corridor without more than a brief hello.

Anyway, back to the fun and games . . .

'I do listen to you, Jessica! It's a little hard not to when you're banging and crashing around the place at all hours of the day! Can you do *anything* quietly?!'

'No, Adam! I like to do *everything* loudly! Especially sex! But you wouldn't know about that, would you?'

'Oh, that's fucking *low*, even for you!'

'*Is it!?* Is it!? I wandered around this place for the first two months we lived here in my fucking *underwear*, and you didn't try *anything*!'

'What?! I just thought that was the way all you Californians behaved!'

'Why?'

'Well, you know . . . it's always sunny and hot, so you don't have to wear much.'

'I come from *Carmel*, Adam! Near San Francisco. You know? That city in America where it's always foggy and sixty-two degrees?'

'No! I don't know. My geographic knowledge of your stupid bloody country doesn't stretch that far!'

'No, it doesn't, does it?! But you know your way around the realm of fucking Herbivore though, don't you?'

'It's Heranor!'

'I don't care, you cocksucker!'

Oooh. Listen to that language.

It takes a lot to get this girl using phrases like 'cocksucker'. In fact, the last time I said it I was twenty-three, and had just discovered that my boyfriend Harrison had been seeing Lorrie Petersen behind my back for a good three months.

I called him a cocksucker – and more besides – as I raged at him outside our local Chipotle at 10.30 p.m. in the empty car park. I managed to rip a muscle in my arm when I threw my burrito at his head.

My father always said I was like a malfunctioning firework. It takes an age for my fuse to burn down, but when it does I explode all over the place – and injure anyone standing too close.

Today, I'm exploding at Adam Holborne . . . and it *feels good*.

'I don't care about how nutritious your bloody smoothies are, Jessica, but I still have to drink the bloody things, don't I?!'

'You said you liked them!'

'*Liked them?!* You put bananas and cauliflower in the same drink! What kind of lunatic does something like that?! I couldn't get off the toilet for the rest of the bloody day!'

'It's part of my thesis, you bastard!'

'And what's your thesis about?! How fast can you give a man the explosive *shits*??'

'Ah, it's all coming out now, isn't it?!'

'Yes, Jessica! Quite bloody literally!'

It's not like I expected any of this to happen.

When we first got married I wanted to make the best of it. Okay, I was swayed by having money in the bank and this apartment, but I certainly wouldn't have gone through with a marriage to a complete stranger if I didn't want to give it a genuine shot.

Being single, nearly thirty and six thousand miles from home is *not fun*. I was hoping this guy was the right one for me, and me the right one for him – just like the computer assured us.

Obviously Adam's approach to the whole thing was a lot more cynical than I first thought. Quite cold and calculating, to be honest. He was all about the money and the apartment as we headed into the day of the wedding.

Something tells me that started to change once we'd moved in together, but it was too little too late by then. If only he'd been more honest with me from the get-go. If only he hadn't been such a *coward*.

Looking back on this whole mess, I think the only mistake I made was believing a computer could decide who was the perfect match for me.

Those things are great for getting people together in the first place, but it's quite clear they don't know *jack shit* about keeping people together past that first meeting.

So now I'm just gritting my teeth and trying to hold on until the year in this apartment is up – and then I will gratefully get out of Dodge. Mind you, things have now descended into open warfare around here, so I'm not even sure I'll be able to do that.

'I wish I'd never met you!'

'Oh, *do you*, Jessica?! I couldn't quite tell. I thought maybe you liked to knock out every man who tries to kiss you!'

'You took me by surprise, you idiot!'

'Yes, well, having to be carried off the court on a stretcher came as something of a surprise to me too!'

'I said I was sorry!'

'Yes, and it was so *heartfelt*, wasn't it?'

'I thought so!'

'You did it by *text*! From the cab on the way home!'

'It was better than nothing!'

'Oh my God, you're *so* fucking sympathetic!'

'Yes, I am. Just like you were when I made my little mistake at the restaurant!'

'It was a massive cock and balls, Jessica! What was I supposed to do?!'

'Not laugh at me!'

'I wasn't laughing at you! I was laughing at – Okay, I *was* laughing at you, but come on! You even covered it in spunk!'

As follows with an argument of this nature, you eventually start bringing up everything the other person has done wrong that you still haven't forgiven them for. Usually, couples have years of material to work with, but poor old Adam and I have only known each other for a few short months, so that's why we keep going back over the same old boring mistakes and screw-ups.

Of course, neither party will back down once you get to this stage. This isn't the time for apology or reparation, this is the time for accusation and recrimination.

Neither of which do anybody any good *whatsoever*, so the argument generally just degenerates into name-calling.

'Jesus Christ, Adam, you're such an asshole!'

'Well thank you very much, you Yank *bitch*!'

'Oh yeah! That's *great*. Why not get into a little racism, huh?!'

'*Racism?* You're the whitest person I've ever met!'

'Yeah, well you're the biggest twat I ever met!'

This is a mistake. I'm on solid ground with American slang, but now I'm trying to work a little British swearing into the mix, and that never goes well for me. Okay, so the word 'twat' does get used in the States, but only when insulting fellow women. The British are far more equal opportunities about their use of that particular swear word, though. 'Twat' is a universal term here, as is that other four-letter epithet beginning with 'c' that you will never hear coming out of my mouth, no matter how angry I am.

'What did you call me?'

'A twat! I called you a twat!'

'What the hell is a twot?'

'A twat!'

'A twot?'

'Twat! You are a twat!'

'Do you mean *twat*? Are you trying to say *twat*?'

'That is what I'm saying! Twat!'

'No, you're saying *twot*, Jessica. You mean *tw-a-t*, but for some reason your sand-filled Californian brain isn't processing it right, and you keep saying *twot*.'

'Oh God! Twat! Twat! Twat! Twat! Twat!'

'Why are you doing an impression of a steam locomotive now? Are you going to stick with that, or move on to a combine harvester any minute?'

God *damn* it. This is where Adam – and probably the rest of his countryfolk – always have an edge over us Americans.

They do arguing better than *anyone*.

Everyone else on this planet can scream, shout and rage, but only the British can throw a little well-timed humour in there to throw the other person off their stride completely.

'Oh you can just go to hell, Adam Holborne!'

'No worries, Jessica. I have to wake up to you working out to Beyoncé every morning, so in a very special sense, I'm already *fucking there*!'

'Oh, that's it! That's fucking it! I'm going to—'

My rant is interrupted by my phone. Unfortunately, my ringtone at the moment is 'All The Single Ladies' by Beyoncé. What a tremendously bad piece of timing.

'Hah! You see what I mean?' Adam bellows triumphantly.

I ignore him and grab the phone off the coffee table. I'll get rid of whoever this is as quickly as I can, and then get back to destroying my stupid husband. This time I'm going to bring up the party again. Maybe I'll go out to the kitchen and throw some butter at him. I'll try not to tear my bicep while I'm doing it, though.

Oh, it's Mom on the phone.

We're not due to talk for a couple of days.

I take a deep breath to compose myself and answer. 'Hi, Mom. What's up?'

'Hey sweetheart. Can . . . can we talk?'

Instantly, I know something is *very* wrong. My mom's voice is thin, cracked and worried. She's definitely been crying.

'Mom? What's going on? Is it David? Is David okay? Has something happened to him?'

I try not to fall for any of those bad big-city clichés you hear about New York, but right now all I'm picturing is my poor brother being mugged somewhere close to Times Square by someone high on heroin and carrying a handgun.

'David's fine, sweetheart. It's . . . it's your dad.'

My legs collapse from under me. If the couch hadn't been beside me, I'd be on the floor.

He's dead. My daddy is *dead*. I know it. Any second now my mother is about to destroy my world.

'Is he okay?' I say, voice trembling.

'What's going on?' Adam says in a low, urgent voice. I ignore him. This is family, and that has nothing to do with him.

'Your dad . . . your dad had a heart attack, honey,' Mom says quietly.

'Is he? Is he . . .' I can't say it. I can't get the words out of my mouth. They just won't come.

'No. But he's in a very bad way, Jessica.'

Mom never uses my full name. It's exclusively set aside for when I'm in trouble, or when somebody else is.

'How bad?'

'We're up in Monterey at the community hospital, but they're going to transfer him to San Francisco soon.'

It's really bad, then. If they're taking him up to the city, they must need a lot of special equipment.

'Is he awake?'

'No honey.' Mom's voice cracks again. 'He's unconscious. They're not sure . . . they're not . . .' Mom starts to cry and my heart breaks into a million pieces.

'I'm getting a flight out,' I tell her. 'I'll get online and book it now. The first one I can find.'

'Okay sweetheart.'

'I'll call you back once it's done, and I'll be with you as soon as I can.'

'Okay, Jess. I love you.'

'I love you too, Mom.' Now I'm crying.

I have to get off this phone and do something practical. The last thing my mother needs is to hear me bawling my eyes out right now. I have to be strong.

I end the call and pull the phone away from my ear.

My hand won't stop shaking.

My hand *won't stop shaking*.

'Jessica? What is it? What's wrong with your dad?' Adam asks with concern.

I wipe away tears with the back of my hand. 'He's had a heart attack. He's in hospital.'

'Oh God.'

My hand *won't stop shaking*.

'I have to get online and book a flight out there,' I tell him.

'Alright, alright. Yeah. Of course you do. We'll look together. We should be able to get a couple of seats last minute, with any luck.'

What?

'You don't have to come, Adam,' I tell him flatly.

'I want to come! I want to help you.'

Oh God. Am I about to say this?

Yes I am, and I *don't care*.

'I don't *want you* to come, Adam.'

He looks shocked. I don't blame him.

'Why not?'

'Because . . . because this is about my *family*, and you're not part of it. I need to be focused on my dad, not worrying about what you'll say or do.' I give him a withering look. 'I need to be around people I know love me, Adam.'

Adam looks deeply shocked. He sits away from me and looks down at his feet.

In other circumstances I'd feel bad, but right now I need to *concentrate*.

Grabbing my iPad from the arm of the couch, I take myself off into my bedroom to look for flights. As I close the door behind me, I see that Adam still hasn't moved an inch from his place on the couch.

* * *

There are no flights tonight! None that will get me into San Francisco tomorrow morning anyway. The best and quickest option is taking off at 9 a.m. from Heathrow.

For a few moments I punch the pillow in uncontained rage and frustration, but after I've calmed back down again, I book the flight, as it's the only option I have.

I call Mom to tell her I'll get to them at about 2 p.m. her time. She sounds disappointed that I won't be there earlier, but there's nothing I can do about it. David is flying in from New York and should be home by early evening, though, so at least he can be there to comfort her. The idea of my mother without her kids at such a horrific time turns my stomach. I wish I'd never come to this damned country. What the hell was I *thinking*?

I hear a knock at the door as I'm packing my flight bag.

Adam.

I guess I'd better talk to him, now I've calmed down a little.

I know I was horrible to him earlier, but I still feel the same way. Nothing has changed.

The fight has gone out of me now, though. I just want to focus on my father.

'Hi,' I say as I open the door.

'Everything okay?' He grimaces. 'What a stupid thing to say. Of course everything isn't okay.'

I try to offer him a weak smile, and fail.

'Have you got a flight booked?'

'Yeah. Not until tomorrow morning, though. I'll try to get some sleep here and leave about 6 a.m. for the airport. The cab's booked.'

'Sounds like you've got everything under control.'

'More or less.'

Adam shuffles in the doorway for a moment. 'I wish you'd let me come with you. I really want to.'

I hold up a hand. 'Adam. I know you mean well, but it's not a good idea.'

'But I'm your *husband*.'

'No you're not,' I reply, with a heavy heart. 'This isn't a real marriage, and it's never *going to be*. It's time we just accepted that. We have nothing in common, that much is obvious.'

'But I care about you,' he tells me insistently.

I throw the jeans I'm holding into my flight bag angrily. 'Do you? Do you *really*? You seem to care a lot more about a plastic box hooked up to the TV than you do me. Best you just stay here and play that while I go see my father before he . . . before he . . .'

Crying again, and being grossly unfair to Adam as well, probably. Again, I don't really care. It's not like anything I'm saying isn't true. He does care about that stupid games console more than he cares about me.

There's anger in his eyes now. 'That's not fair, Jessica.'

I wave my hand. 'Okay, whatever. It's not fair. I'm not fair.' I point to my flight bag. 'I have to pack, Adam.'

'No. You can do that later. I want you to do something for me first.'

My hands go to my hips. I can feel the rage starting to bubble away again. Is he really trying to start an argument *now*? 'What, Adam? What could you possibly want me to do? When I have a bag to pack so I can get on a plane and fly six thousand miles to see my dying father?'

'Don't say that, Jess. He could be okay. You don't know he's dying.'

'You don't know he isn't!'

Adam takes a deep breath. 'Look. I don't want to get into another argument with you now. I just want you to do something with me. And after we've done it, if you want, I won't insist on coming out to America with you. What's more, I'll get on the phone to Cassie tomorrow, tell her that the marriage is over, and be moved out by the time you get back.'

That sounds fair enough, actually. 'What do you want me to do?'

'Get in a cab with me and come to Bexleyheath.'

'What? Why?'

'Because there's somebody I want you to meet.'

'Who?'

Adam shakes his head. 'It's best you see for yourself. It might . . . it might help you think a bit differently of me.'

I put my head in my hands. 'This is crazy, Adam. I don't have time for this.'

'*Please*, Jessica. It won't take long. I'll even help you pack when we get back, if you want me to.'

This is the last thing I need. Adam's feelings have clearly been hurt, and he wants me to go along with this trip to no doubt make himself feel better, but I don't need the aggravation. What could he possibly show me that would change anything? I don't want him to come home with me, and I don't want to be married to him any more either.

And there it is . . .

If I do go to Bexleyheath on whatever wild goose chase this is, he's promised to end this stupid marriage when we get back. It's an offer I'm more than happy to accept.

'Okay, Adam. But I can't be too long.'

'No, no. That's fine.'

Adam pulls his phone out of his pocket and calls a cab. He then goes off to his bedroom and appears to make another call. I'm assuming this has something to do with where we're going. I would be more curious about his plans if I wasn't so worried about my poor father.

Less than ten minutes later we're in the taxi and making our way out of West London.

Adam's foot is jiggling up and down nervously. 'You alright?' I ask him, despite myself.

'Yeah. It's just . . . I've never done anything like this before. It's kind of a private thing. Something nobody else really needs to know about.'

I huff. 'Not even your wife?'

He makes a face. 'You're my wife, Jessica, but you're also someone I've only known a few months. This thing is . . . is important to me.'

I shake my head. 'So why are we doing this *now*? On tonight, of all nights?'

'Because of your dad, and because of the way things are between us. Because of the way you see me now.'

'Meaning?'

He holds up a hand. 'Please. Let's just get there. If I try to explain, I won't get it across right.'

Great. On the most stressful night of my life, Adam decides to become Captain Cryptic. I'll just have to hold my tongue and see what he's got in store for me. As long as I'm back by 9 p.m. so I can pack, I guess I can put up with it.

The taxi arrives in Bexleyheath about thirty minutes later. The ride over here was mercifully brief thanks to the lack of congestion on the roads at this time of day. The low summer sun is bathing everything in a warm amber glow as we turn into what looks like an average, everyday suburban street.

'Okay, we're here,' Adam says, leaning forward to pay the cabbie.

'And where is here?' I ask, looking out of the window at the rather nondescript row of terraced houses.

I have to say I was expecting something a little more dramatic, given the way Adam's been talking. For all his cagey language I was envisioning a night-time plunge into an underground bunker, complete with guard post and men with machine guns.

'A house,' Adam says, climbing out of the cab. 'A friend's house.'

So this is it? He's brought me all the way here . . . for what?

Then my blood runs cold. It's going to be someone who's recently lost a loved one, isn't it? Adam thinks that the best way for me to cope with the impending death of my father is to sit down with someone who's had something similar happen to them.

I can't do it. I just *can't do it.*

He means well, and I wouldn't want to offend them, but if he's about to introduce me to someone pale and sad I don't think I can stand it.

Oh God, Adam! Why are you putting me in this *position?*

I get out of the cab, dread clamped around my heart.

'Come on, he's expecting us,' Adam tells me.

So it's a *he.* I rack my brains trying to think if Adam has told me about any friends who have lost relatives lately, to prepare myself a little for this unwanted meeting. Nothing springs to mind, though. But then, I haven't exactly been paying much attention to what Adam's been saying recently, have I? That's the hallmark of a failing marriage, right there.

I follow Adam up a short garden path to the large front door of one of the Victorian terraced houses that line the street. He rings the doorbell with one slightly shaking finger.

He knows I don't want to go through with this as much as I do.

The door is opened, not by a bereaved male friend, but by a pleasant-looking middle-aged woman.

'Good evening, Adam,' she says and looks at me. 'And this is Jessica?'

'Yes, Mary. Jessica, this is Mary.'

'Hi,' I say to her, trying and failing to raise a smile.

Mary gives me a knowing look. It's the kind my mother uses from time to time.

I can feel my lip trembling and have to clench my teeth together.

'He's in his room. The one downstairs,' Mary tells Adam.

In turn, my husband looks downcast. 'Oh . . . maybe this wasn't such a good idea.'

Mary puts an arm on Adam's shoulder. 'No, no. It's fine. He's okay this evening. More of a precaution than anything after the appointment last week.'

'Okay, good.' Adam turns to me. 'Shall we?'

'Alright . . .' I respond. What's going on here?

Mary and Adam lead me down a long corridor, past a comfortable-looking living room and a compact kitchen. As we go, I notice handrails running along the corridor at regular intervals.

I'm starting to get the feeling I've read this situation a little wrong.

'Did the new bank transfer come through okay?' I hear Adam ask Mary.

'Yes. Thank you so much, Adam. It makes all the difference not having to worry about those cheques any more.'

'No problem.'

Mary takes us into a large room that was obviously once a second reception room, but has been converted into a bedroom. The bed itself is long and low, and by the looks of things is one designed for someone with medical needs. It has an electric motor clamped to the side for raising and lowering the top half.

Other than that, and the wheelchair sat by the bed, this looks more or less like the room of any normal teenage boy – one who really likes his video games, judging from the posters tacked up on the walls.

A door on the other side of the room opens, and out of what is apparently an en-suite bathroom comes a young boy of about sixteen, wearing a *Realm of Chaos* T-shirt and blue jeans, making his way slowly towards us on a pair of crutches. I can see that his legs are distorted and out of shape. He's obviously suffering from some kind of illness that forces him to use these crutches to get around.

When the boy sees Adam, his face lights up. 'Hello, shithead,' he says with a grin.

'Language, Oliver,' Mary says, disapprovingly.

Oliver laughs and sticks his tongue out at her.

Mary also chuckles. I have a feeling this is par for the course for these two.

'How's it going, nobhead?' Adam replies.

'Well, I was having a good night until you showed up,' Oliver replies. He has some difficulty speaking, and his words are a bit slurred, but he still knows how to put my husband in his place without much trouble. He then looks at me. 'Hi, Jessica,' he says, taking one hand off a crutch to wave at me. 'You're prettier than this twat told me you were.'

Oliver has no trouble pronouncing the word 'twat' properly either.

'Shut up and sit down, Oli,' Adam tells the boy. 'You're still not 100 per cent after last week.'

Oli laughs and points at his legs. 'I'm pretty sure I'm never going to be 100 per cent, you berk.'

I snort with laughter, which seems to please Oli no end. He then does as he's asked, though, plonking himself down on the bed and throwing the crutches into the wheelchair.

'I'll make you all a nice cup of tea,' Mary says and leaves us.

Oli points with a tremoring hand at a couch parked on the other side of his bed. 'Sit down, guys,' he says. 'How was it getting over here?'

'Fine,' Adam remarks as he sits himself down on the couch. I follow suit, looking at Oli's *Realm of Chaos* T-shirt. My brain is starting to make some fairly obvious connections.

I have to confess I'm a bit stunned.

In my head, Oli was basically another version of Adam. Just an annoying friend who took up way too much of my husband's time . . . time that he should have been spending with *me*. I've built up a lot of resentment towards him over the past few months – but now I'm starting to realise that I may have grabbed hold of the wrong end of the stick – and been mentally hitting Adam over the head with it for no good reason.

Oli looks at me. 'He's shit with the . . . the introductions, isn't he?' he says. 'I'm Oli.'

'He *is* shit, isn't he?' I reply, which makes Oli giggle. 'It's lovely to meet you, Oli.' I then give Adam a withering look. 'It's a shame we haven't met before now.'

'I agree,' Oli says, looking at Adam. 'Maybe it's because he knows I love redheads, and didn't want me to steal you away from him.'

'Oi!' Adam protests.

I lean forward. 'You might be right there, Oli,' I tell him. 'You're far more handsome than he is.'

'Oi!' Adam repeats.

Oli laughs out loud and picks up a PlayStation controller. 'Adam says you've never played *Realm of Chaos*?'

'No. He's never let me.'

Adam crosses his arms. 'Pfft. Like you've ever wanted to play it.'

My forehead creases with frustration. 'Did you ever *ask*?'

Adam has no response to this – which shouldn't come as a surprise to anyone.

Oli laughs. 'You're so crap with women, Adam!' he says, and then picks up a second controller from his bedside cabinet. 'Here, Jessica. I'll show you how to play it.'

I take the controller. 'Okay. You'll have to take it slowly, though. About the only thing I know is that Adam gets killed by something called a Nuclear Spider a lot.'

'Yeah! He's well shit at fighting them!'

'Oi!' Adam says for a third and final time, before sitting back in the sofa with a grumpy expression on his face. It's quite, quite lovely to have such a good new ally in my ongoing war with Adam Holborne. It'll guarantee me victory every single time.

For the next hour Oli takes me through the finer points of how to play *Realm of Chaos*. His enthusiasm and love for the game shines through with every word he says, and I start to get a little invested in the strange world of Heranor myself as we play.

So much so that it even takes my mind off what's happening with my father for a moment. The ever-present spectre of his heart attack never goes away, but at least the time I spend trying to walk around the digital village of Holliton makes it feel less overwhelming – even for just a little while.

Before I know it, it's 10 p.m. I've just killed a sewer rat with my brand-new elven sword, and Oli is yawning his head off.

'Time for bed, young man,' Mary says, coming into the room to clean away our mugs.

Oli grimaces. 'But I was just about to show Jessica the thieves' guild, Mary!'

'Well, you can do that another day.'

'I'll set her up with an account,' Adam says, then realises he probably shouldn't have made a promise he won't be able to keep. As far as he's concerned, I'm not going to be around to play *Realm of Chaos* any time soon.

'Sure,' I say to Oli, not wanting to upset him by contradicting Adam. 'I'll meet you online and you can show me then.'

Oli gives me a thumbs up. 'Great!'

Adam looks a little surprised, but stays silent.

'Say goodbye to Adam and Jessica now,' Mary instructs, earning her another poked out tongue.

'Right then . . . night, tossface,' Adam says to Oli, before coming round the bed to give the boy a hug.

I go over as well. 'Good night, Oli, it was lovely to meet you,' I say.

Oli then gives me a hug of such intensity that I can feel the tears starting to well up in my eyes. He feels so thin and brittle under my arms, but there's a power and a strength in that hug that takes my breath away.

'I'll see you in the thieves' guild!' he says happily, before yawning again.

We leave him, and Mary shows Adam and me back out on to the doorstep. 'The cab should be here soon,' she says. 'The man told me ten minutes.'

'Great,' Adam replies. 'It's a nice evening, so we'll stand outside. Thanks for having us tonight, Mary, it means a lot.'

Mary smiles. 'A pleasure. He always loves it when you come around.' She then looks at me. 'Even more so now, I think. He's really taken to you, Jessica.'

I smile. 'Good. I like him too.'

Adam and I walk back out into the street as Mary closes the front door behind us. Adam leans against the garden wall, and looks up at the starry sky above our heads.

'So that's why you're always on that game,' I say, standing directly in front of him.

Adam contrives to look sheepish. 'Yeah.'

I think hard how to phrase my next question. 'What illness does Oli have?'

Adam looks down. 'Muscular dystrophy.'

'Oh God.'

'It's . . . it's still fairly early. But, but it'll get worse. *Much* worse.' Adam looks skyward again. Anything to avoid my gaze. This is obviously hard for him to talk about. 'Eventually it'll start affecting his hands. He won't be able to . . . won't be able . . .'

'To hold the controller any more,' I finish for him, my heart breaking.

Now Adam *can* look me in the eyes. 'But not yet, though! He still has time!' he says, voice mixed with sadness and anger. 'And we still haven't found the Lost Temple of Tethis yet. We've *got* to do that.'

'How did you meet him? In real life, I mean?'

'At a games tournament a couple of years ago. He was entered in the *Realm of Chaos* PvP championships, and I was covering it for work.'

'Does he have family?' I continue. 'Mary isn't his mother, is she?'

Adam shakes his head. 'Foster carer. His parents are both gone. He doesn't have anyone.'

I cautiously take Adam's hand. 'He has *you*.'

Now there are tears in his eyes. 'Yeah. I guess. I can't do that much, though. Couldn't before we won that stupid competition, anyway. Now at least I can help Mary with the money. Help her take care of him.'

'You've been giving her some of your share of the thirty thousand?'

'Yeah. Is that alright?'

Oh Christ.

'Of course it's alright, Adam!' I pause. 'That's the real reason you entered the competition in the first place, isn't it?'

Adam shrugs. 'And the flat. Don't forget the flat.'

My eyes narrow. 'Are you telling me you'd have gone along with this marriage just for a nice place to live?'

Adam rubs his eyes. 'I guess not, no.'

'No. I didn't think so.'

'Why didn't you *tell me*, Adam? Why didn't you say anything about this?'

Adam tries to wipe the tears away with his hand. 'Not right, though, is it? Didn't want to . . . didn't want to use him just to make myself look better, did I? Not doing it for that. He's my friend. Like my little brother. Not his fault this happened to him. It's his business, you know? I . . . I . . .'

I put my arms around him as he starts to cry properly. 'Oh, you stupid bastard,' I whisper into his ear and hold him tight.

I think of my father, probably lying in a bed much like Oli's, and immediately join Adam in his tears.

What a pair we make. Standing together on a quiet suburban street, both in floods of tears over just how unfair this idiotic, nasty little world can be sometimes.

This is the most connected to Adam I think I've ever felt.

When we both calm down a little, I pull away and regard my husband with tear-stained eyes.

'Adam?'

'Yeah?'

'I think I'd like it if you did come home with me.'

'Really?'

'Yes.' I hold my arms out. 'If this visit was to show me what the man I married is really like underneath all that bullshit and cynicism, then mission accomplished.'

Adam nods, sniffing back the snot in his nose as he does so. 'I wasn't trying to keep the marriage going or anything,' he tells me. 'I know we've probably gone too far for that, but I just wanted to show you that I do care . . . even if I might not show it sometimes. I have problems with that kind of thing.'

I laugh quietly. 'Of course you do. You're *British*, Adam. You don't have that much choice in the matter.'

This makes him smile. 'No, I guess I don't.' He takes my hand in his. 'I guess I just didn't want you to think I was such a bad guy before you left . . . you know?'

My hand squeezes over his. Behind us I hear the taxi arrive. 'You are very far from being a bad guy, Adam Holborne,' I tell him, and give him another hug.

This changes things.

I'm not sure what, or how much, but my perceptions of this strange man I've married have shifted inexorably, thanks to one visit to see a sick but extremely brave kid.

I'm not sure Adam and I have any kind of future together. I just don't think we're compatible on that score, but at least I know the real measure of the man now.

. . . and not a moment too soon.

To be honest, my emotions are in such turmoil at the moment that I couldn't tell you if I had any strong feelings for him, even if you held a gun to my head.

There's only one man I can think about right now, and he's six thousand miles away, in danger, and needs his daughter by his side.

ADAM

Q. In a crisis, do you take control, or let others take the lead?
A. I'm not sure. Happily, I've managed to avoid them so far. Must be lucky I guess.

16 June

Convincing Jessica to let me come with her to the States was one thing – actually proving to be any use whatsoever during the trip is completely another.

Neither of us slept well last night. She was understandably too upset to sleep, and I was having trouble making head or tail of my own emotions.

It was an even bigger deal for me to introduce her to Oli than I thought it would be. It's not that I try to keep my relationship with him a secret, it's just that I'm fiercely protective of him, and this leads me to be irrationally untrusting. I never had any real brothers or sisters, but Oli makes a great surrogate.

I know it's not common for a man to keep a close relationship from his own wife – unless of course that relationship is with another woman. But then, I return to the fact that I've only known Jessica for four months.

I have mates that I have known for a lot longer who don't know about my friendship with Oli.

I ended up lying awake all night pondering why I felt it had been the right time to introduce the two of them. Was it out of some purely selfish desire for Jessica to think I was a nice bloke? Or did I genuinely feel that her meeting Oli would be good for everyone concerned? It certainly seemed to take her mind off what had happened to her father, and Oli had been wanting to meet her for weeks, so on that front, it was something of a success.

Jessica seemed a little too good at *Realm of Chaos* to be a complete beginner, though. The way she killed that sewer rat, taking no damage, was masterful. I swear she must have been watching me play when I wasn't looking.

And what does all of this mean when it comes to my feelings for Jessica?

Okay, so I'm obviously still attracted to her – the punch in the mouth at Wimbledon proved that – but is there more to it than just a desire to get into her sports bra? I suppose there must be, as I felt comfortable with letting her meet Oli – but then again, was that just me trying to inflate my own ego by showing her my compassionate side?

Or am I genuinely just reacting to seeing Jessica so vulnerable and upset about her father? I obviously want to be there for her, otherwise I wouldn't have volunteered to come along – or let her meet Oli.

Is this just about me? Or is it about *her*?

Aaargh!

Is it any wonder that I got about three hours' sleep, and therefore feel like death warmed up as we go through customs the next morning, on our way to an unpleasant eleven hours in the air?

If *I* feel like death warmed up, Jessica looks like someone with the spectre of death perched on her shoulder, which is more than fair enough, because it actually *is*. I can't imagine how bad the stress and the worry must be, but I try my best to lighten her load by taking care of all that tedious admin that comes with flying internationally.

The flight itself is pretty smooth.

I watch a couple of movies and try to sleep a little, but all my wife seems able to do is stare straight ahead and sip countless cups of water.

It's strange being around Jess when she's quiet. When you're dealing with a dreadful shock like the one she's suffered, the human brain does have the tendency to switch to some kind of default mode.

Jessica spends most of the flight like that, only occasionally coming up for air when they bring food around, or when I manage to engage her in a little listless conversation.

Getting to San Francisco can't come quick enough.

We're met by Jessica's mother, Monica, and her brother, David, at arrivals. Jessica immediately throws her arms around her mother the second she sees her, and David joins in, wrapping his arms around them both.

The lad has no trouble doing this, as he's *gigantic*. Jessica had told me that David was once the champion on his school's wrestling team, so I knew he was the athletic type, but I had no idea he was this *huge* – dwarfing his mother and sister by a good seven or eight inches.

We've never met before, and I would have liked the circumstances to be more pleasurable, but I'll have to make the best of it. I have no idea what I'm going to talk to the bloke about, though. We're about as far from each other on the man spectrum as it's possible to be. He can bench-press half the eastern seaboard, and is an important executive from New York. Quite what he'll make of this weedy video games journalist from the unfashionable end of London is anyone's guess.

I give the Madisons some space to reacquaint with one another. I don't do group hugs at the best of times, and hardly think this is the time to start.

Eventually, they break off and turn towards me.

'Hello, Adam,' Jessica's mother says in a clipped tone.

'So . . . you're Adam then,' David says, looking me up and down.

I've had less frosty receptions, it has to be said. Not surprising, however.

I fear that before this latest emergency occurred, Jessica may have told her family less than flattering things about me. I'm sure most of my trespasses were probably recounted to them over Skype in graphic detail.

In the rush to support Jessica through this trying time, and mend a few fences with her, I've completely forgotten about what her family's opinion of me might be, based on what's been going on between the two of us in recent weeks.

This could be trickier than I was expecting . . .

I'm not the only one to pick up on the veiled hostility. 'Adam's been fantastic, Mom,' Jessica says. 'He's been really supportive.'

Monica's face softens a little. David's does not.

I think it'll take a little more than a couple of platitudes from his little sister to convince this behemoth that I am anything other than a worthless git – who thinks it's funny to humiliate his beloved sister in front of a live kitchen audience, and who screams at her for being a fussy bitch for not liking bones in her chicken.

'I'll get the car,' David intones, and strides off towards the entrance.

Jessica gives me a weak smile, but then turns her attention back to her mother.

This is fine. She has more important things on her mind now than how her husband and brother are going to get along.

I follow the two Madison women out into a clammy, foggy San Francisco day, and immediately wish I'd packed a thicker jacket. When you hear *California*, you think sun and heat, but when you think of California, you also think of the *southern end*. It may be the middle of summer here in the Bay Area, but from the sky above, you'd be forgiven for thinking it was a bank holiday Monday in Dunfermline.

David packs our bags in the trunk of his car, and is soon pulling out of the airport and on to the freeway, headed for the city.

Charlie Madison is apparently being taken care of at the University of California, San Francisco. When Jessica told me this, I had immediate visions of the poor old bugger being poked and prodded by a bunch of students still hung-over from the night before, but she assured me that the heart and vascular centre at the university is one of the best in the world. Luckily for Charlie, he is white and middle class in modern America, so he gets the best healthcare his money can provide. If he's going to survive the damage done to his heart, it sounds like he's in the best possible place.

'It was caused by something called a coronary artery spasm,' David tells us from the driver's seat when Jessica asks for more information. 'A severe one, so the doctor said.'

'One minute he was out in the garage repairing the Mustang,' Monica says from next to her son, 'the next he was coming back into the kitchen, telling me he had tremendous pain down his left-hand side.' She takes a deep, shuddering breath. 'If the paramedics hadn't gotten to the house as fast as they did, he might have . . . might have . . .'

'Don't say it, Mom,' David interrupts. 'It didn't happen. He's going to be *fine*.'

Hmmmm.

I wonder – is it possible for me to survive, if I jump out of a Honda sedan travelling at sixty-five miles an hour? Would it just result in a few broken bones? Or would it kill me outright?

Charlie was working on the Mustang *I crashed* when he had his heart attack.

I broke Charlie's car, and it also appears I quite literally broke his heart as well.

I try to make myself very small in the seat.

Maybe it would have been a good idea for me to stay at home after all.

When we get to the hospital . . . university . . . whatever, the three Madisons stride towards the entrance, keen to get in and see the head of the family as swiftly as possible.

I, however, hang back.

Jessica notices I'm not with them, and looks back at me. 'Adam?'

'Um. I think I'll just wait here. Maybe that's best.'

How can I go in there? How can I go and see the poor man I probably had a hand in nearly killing? David and Monica already resent me because of Jess; how are they likely to feel if I'm standing by Charlie's bedside, when I'm the one *who put him there*?

Jessica sees the look of distress on my face. 'Guys,' she says to her mother and brother, 'you go in ahead. We'll catch up in a second. Floor six, right?'

'That's it,' David replies and looks at me with a stony expression. 'Is he alright?'

'Yeah. We'll be in in a minute,' Jessica repeats, walking back towards me. 'What is it? What's the matter?' she says, as her family disappear from view.

I tell Jessica about the realisation I've just had.

This earns me a punch on the shoulder.

'Ow! What's that for?'

'You are an idiot sometimes, Adam,' she says ruefully.

'What's that supposed to mean?'

Jessica folds her arms and huffs. 'My father has been eating crap for the past three decades. Mom and I have scolded him for *years* over how much red meat and cheese he eats. Trust me, Adam. You didn't have anything to do with putting him in this building. I love him with all my heart and soul, but even I know this is his own damn fault – nobody else's.'

'Oh. Okay.'

She holds out her hand to me. 'Come on. I want to see my dad.'

Jessica's hand is warm and very pleasant to hold. 'You know, I think this is the first time we've ever held hands – when we're not in front of a camera, anyway,' I tell her in a slightly amazed voice as we cross the car park.

Her eyes widen a little. 'You're right,' she agrees, and gives me a small smile. 'It feels nice.'

That's the last smile I see on Jessica's face for the next few days. Her father is not in a good way *at all*.

He was transferred here for something called an *angioplasty*, which is a serious bit of surgery performed on those who have suffered a serious heart attack like the one Charlie had.

The surgery went okay, but that didn't mean he was out of the woods. The heart attack and surgery severely weakened his entire body, and for a man in his late sixties with a less than exemplary level of fitness, that meant the possibility of further surgery – or even death – was not off the cards.

I saw Jessica go through hell in those three days, and could do absolutely bugger all to help her.

Nothing makes you feel so exquisitely useless as when somebody close to you is seriously ill. I feel it about Oli and that bastard disease he's been cursed with every time I see him, and I feel it about Jessica's father during that cold and foggy seventy-two-hour period in San Francisco.

And then, on a day when the sun finally decides to show itself, so does Charlie Madison.

He woke up at six thirty in the morning asking for a drink.

Less than an hour later his hospital room is full of some very happy and tearful people – me included. I'd only met the old bugger twice before this, but he was polite to me both times, and didn't even try to murder me in my bed after I'd wrecked his favourite car.

Charlie Madison is one of the world's few remaining good guys – and also not one prone to violence when his son-in-law does something characteristically idiotic.

The same, however, cannot be said for his son.

Later that day, as everyone is happily getting used to the fact that the patriarch of the Madison family is not going to die any time soon, I elect to take a little walk in the rather idyllic park area at the centre of the hospital complex. The sun is shining, and I'm in desperate need of some vitamin D after being cooped up under hospital lighting for the past three days.

This also gives me a little time to myself. Now the emergency has passed, and I've done my bit to support my wife and her family, I figure I'm allowed a brief bit of *me time* sat on a bench and watching the world go by.

Okay, as this is a hospital, the world is largely full of sick people, but we'll gloss over that fact, as those birds in that tree are making a lovely noise, and this cup of coffee I've just bought from the café isn't half as bad as it could be.

I close my eyes and take a long slow sniff. I do love the smell of coffee, especially when I'm allowed to enjoy it in peace and qui—

'Adam.'

I open my eyes. David Madison is standing there, nearly blocking out all of the sunlight.

'Hi, David,' I say jovially. I think I can get away with jovial now. Charlie is sitting up and cracking jokes six floors above my head, so I don't think the tone is out of place.

'What are you doing?'

'Um. Just thought I'd take five minutes for a cup of coffee. You guys all seem to be doing well up there, and, you know, I'm not really part of the family yet.'

David looms over me like a man trained in hard-core looming from an early age. 'No, you're not.' He folds his arms. 'And you're never going to be.'

Oh dear.

Now his father's not going to die, David has turned his attention to other family matters.

'You . . . you don't like me much, do you, David?'

'No.'

'Because of the way you think I've treated your sister?'

'Yes.'

There are ways I can diffuse this situation before it gets out of hand. The next words that come out of my mouth are not one of them. 'It was as much her fault as it was mine, you know.'

'*What* did you say?'

'*I said* . . . it was as much Jessica's fault as it was mine. It takes two to tango.'

Yes, I am an idiot for taking this kind of tone with an angry man who outweighs me by two stone, and outheights me by four inches. But then I've been my own worst enemy so many times in my life that I could really do with going to court and getting a restraining order against myself.

David looks proper mad now. His cheeks are starting to flush nearly as red as his gingham shirt. 'Are you saying you didn't deliberately hit Jess with a tennis ball? And you didn't wreck Dad's car on purpose?

And you didn't make fun of Jess's cooking, humiliating her just to make yourself look better?'

'What?'

Wow. Jessica isn't worried about putting her own spin on a story, is she? Even I think I sound quite awful, having that little lot relayed back to me – even if none of it is actually true.

'Now just a minute,' I protest. 'You're only getting her side of the story. She's done horrible stuff to me too!'

David doesn't reply, but he unfolds his arms and clenches his fist.

Oh heck.

And yet I *still* feel the need to defend myself. I must have a death wish.

'She . . . she punched me in the mouth on a tennis court!' I rise to my feet, sliding to one side of David's massive frame. 'And she nearly broke my back doing yoga!' I step away from the maddened Madison as his face darkens considerably. I need to shut the hell up right now before he twists me into a pretzel. 'And . . . and she got me drunk just so she could have sex with me!' David's eyes go wide. 'She covered me in fucking butter!'

Yeah, that should do it. Nothing like having a weedy British man reveal what sexual habits your little sister likes to indulge in to really get your blood boiling.

David pushes up his shirt sleeves.

I have apparently stepped into a Popeye cartoon.

'You little son of a bitch,' David spits. 'I'm going to kick your ass all over this hospital.'

. . . and I'm running.

Full pelt running away from this gigantic maniac, who is now intent on choke-slamming me into a San Francisco sidewalk.

'Come back!' he yells, taking after me with long, loping strides.

My getaway would be more successful if I could see an obvious exit from this circular patch of greenery I just wanted to enjoy my cup of coffee in. Sadly, in my blind panic, I can't see an obvious way out, so I just run around the perimeter, gibbering like an idiot as I am hunted down by Hulk Hogan's illegitimate offspring.

Also, the park is empty today, thanks to the fact that San Franciscans are quite the healthy bunch by and large, so I have no one to come to my aid.

As I run gamely around a small beech tree and start another circuit of the park, I know that David must be closing the gap. He is an athletic man with manly thighs, whereas I am a video gamer with legs like those of a particularly underfed chicken.

David inevitably catches up with me by the simple expedient of cutting across the grass while I stick to the path, thus chopping off the rest of the distance between us almost instantly.

'*Mrrrghhkkle!*' I exclaim in a literally strangled voice as David grabs hold of my jacket collar, arresting my flight in a split second.

And now the punching will begin. Hard and unforgiving punching. Still, the orthodontics centre is only a short walk away. I'm sure they'll be able to fit me in with no problems.

Colour me surprised when David does not start removing my teeth with his fist. Instead, he spins me round, and picks me up in a bear hug.

Maybe he's had a change of heart! Maybe in our little jaunt around the hospital park he's decided that good old Adam isn't such a bad chap at all, and just wants to give me a big brotherly hug.

Nope.

He's squeezing the life out of me, that's what he's doing.

'Hurrrnnnnn,' I strain, as David applies vice-like pressure to my midriff. As the breath is forced out of my lungs, I have a horrible flashback to Jessica trying to relieve my yoga back pain. Given that David is exerting a great deal more pressure on me than Jessica did, there's every chance I won't just fart on him, but will follow through all over his gingham shirt too.

What a horrible way to die, covered in poo in San Franciscoo.

. . . didn't somebody write a song about that once?

'David!' I hear someone shout. 'Put him down *now*!'

I look blearily over David's shoulder to see Jessica hurrying towards us, rage writ large across her face. She reaches her brother, and proceeds to start landing punches to his kidneys, punctuating each one with another call to release me from his powerful grip. 'PUT. HIM. DOWN!'

'Ow! Ow! Jessica! Stop it!' David wails, releasing me from his grasp.

Aaah . . .

Sweet, sweet Californian air, how I have missed you so.

As I crouch gasping, Jessica continues to whack her brother as hard as she can. 'Why are you hurting him?! Why are you being such an asshole?!'

David looks jolly confused, and who can blame him. He's probably had weeks of hearing about what an awful dickhead I am, but now Jessica's opinions have quite clearly changed, and he's therefore getting a series of sharp rabbit punches in the stomach for his troubles.

'You said he was a bastard!' David protests. 'You said he'd hurt and humiliated you more than any other man!'

She said that? I didn't think I'd got under her skin *that* much.

Jessica stands away from her brother. 'Yes, I know. But . . . but we were horrible to each other, David. It wasn't just Adam.'

'See,' I say hoarsely to him. 'I told you.'

Jessica gives me a conciliatory look. 'We got thrown together into something neither of us were prepared for, and that just brought out the worst in us both. That's what happens when you're *scared*.'

Blimey. She's right.

That's exactly what it's all been about. The both of us scared out of our minds by the pressure of this marriage, and lashing out at one another because of it.

'But he's not a bad guy, David,' Jessica continues. 'In fact, all the petty bullshit aside, he's one of the best men I've ever met.'

'Really?' I say, finally getting enough breath back to stand up.

Jessica walks over to me. 'Yeah.' She takes my hand. 'Look, I don't know if we can still have anything together, but I just want to say sorry for the things I've done and said.'

'God no!' I protest. 'It's me who should be *sorry*, Jess. Not you!'

'Oh, for crying out loud,' David interjects. 'Maybe you should *both* be sorry? See how that works out for you?'

Jessica looks back from her brother. 'Works for me,' she says.

'Me too,' I reply.

Then I go massively light-headed, because of all that squeezing that happened only moments ago. 'Er. I think I might need a sit-down,' I report, fearing an approaching blackout.

Both Madisons – sorry, one Madison and one Holborne – help me over to the nearest bench and sit down either side of me as I gratefully collapse on to it.

'Just a few minutes while I catch my breath,' I tell them, head turned towards the sky.

A few moments of silence pass, before David breaks it.

'So, did her Eiffel Tower really look like a cock and balls?' he asks me thoughtfully.

'Yep.'

'She always was a horrible cook. Quite how she's going to be a nutritionist is beyond me.'

'Hey! Screw you, David!' Jessica complains, and reaches over me to once again punch her brother, this time on the shoulder.

'Ow! Jess!'

'She does that a lot, does she?' I ask him.

'Yeah. Her hands are really bony. I end up bruised for weeks,' he tells me, rubbing his shoulder and wincing a little.

'She's got quite the right hand on her,' I confide.

'Oh, I know. She gave me a black eye that lasted for a month when I was twelve.'

'You stole my favourite Barbie and melted her head with a magnifying glass,' Jessica says in a thin voice.

'Only because you punctured my football,' David retorts.

I close my eyes, and try my level best to ignore the two siblings as they continue to harangue each other. If nothing else, it's quite pleasant to listen to somebody else on the receiving end of Jessica's temper for once.

I didn't think I'd have anything in common with David over which we could bond, but I may have been mistaken.

The next couple of days are the most pleasant I've spent in Jessica's hometown. With her father still recuperating and unable to do much, Jessica decides to show me every nook and cranny of the place she grew up in. We visit the diner she waitressed in one summer, and the video store she worked in after getting fired from waitressing for being hopeless at it. She takes me to visit some of her childhood friends who still live in Carmel, and we even drop in on her old English teacher, who is actually interested in hearing about my job as a journalist.

We even spot Jessica's first car parked outside a chocolate-box sweet shop in the heart of the small town. It's a 1993 Toyota Camry which looks like it should have been scrapped in 1994. Jessica squeals in delight when she sees it, and rushes into the sweet shop to see if the new owner is in there. Which he is, and of course it's somebody Jessica knows already – the little brother of one of her best friends from school.

If you come from a small town where everybody knows each other, you'll recognise this phenomenon, and appreciate it. I was born and brought up in Greater London so am comprehensively freaked out by the whole thing.

After two days of intensive exploration with my wife, I feel steeped in Carmel's ambience, and in Jessica's past. It's amazing how much you can learn about a person just by visiting their childhood haunts, and listening to them talk enthusiastically about life growing up in a place as bucolic as this.

We wind up back on the crescent-shaped, cypress-lined beach in the evening. Jessica has loved it here all her life, and I'm pretty much enamoured with it completely after only two visits.

Her favourite time to visit the beach is just as the sun is going down . . . because the sunset is *breathtaking*, so our timing is absolutely perfect.

'Can we move here?' I say to her as I watch the deep-red sun sink lower, and bury my toes into the wet sand, feeling the gentle lapping waves of the Pacific Ocean cooling them as I do.

Jessica laughs. 'It is pretty special, isn't it? This is the view that will keep me coming back here until I die.'

I manage to break my gaze at the incredible sunset for a moment and look at Jess. It's probably the happiest I've ever seen her. Needless to say, she looks beautiful . . . and I'm scared all over again.

'You do terrify me, you know,' I tell her in a soft voice. 'And you confuse me. I don't know whether I want to spend the rest of my life with you, or run away screaming.'

She moves round to stand between me and the sinking sun, so now I have two stunning redheads in my field of vision.

'I know. I feel the same way,' she tells me. 'Some of the time I think we're completely incompatible. But then something happens . . . like Oli, or my dad . . . that makes me think you're the perfect man for me. It's very strange. It was always so simple in the past with other men. With you, it's anything but.'

'So, what do we do?'

Jessica smiles. 'My dad always used to tell me that things only stay scary when you let them.' She bunches her fingers into a fist and thrusts it melodramatically into the air. 'You've got to meet them head-on, and not run away with your tail between your legs.'

I chuckle. 'Sounds like good advice. But how do we meet this thing head-on? How the hell do you tackle something as terrifying as *marriage*? You can't hit it with anything.'

Jessica looks thoughtful for a second, before edging closer to me. 'I'm not sure. But you could maybe start by kissing me? See how things go from there?'

'That's an excellent idea, Mrs Holborne,' I say, putting my arms around her waist.

'Thank you, Mr Holborne,' Jessica replies.

As the sun sinks below the horizon, Jessica and I kiss in such a way that promises there will be many more to come in the future – if we can avoid ever eating KFC again.

With Jessica's mother staying in San Francisco to be with Charlie, the house is empty, so my wife and I get to indulge in some much-needed and long-overdue sex.

A lot of it.

Like, a *huge* amount of it.

Seriously, you have no idea how much sex.

. . . and you're not going to know either, because I've already made enough mistakes in this relationship, and I'm sure as hell not going to compound them by discussing what happens in our bedroom. I learned my lesson on that score from Sindy Driscoll, when I made the mistake of telling my university mates about the way she gave a blow job. This got back to her, and I never got a blow job from her again. Just verbal abuse in the canteen and the nickname 'Needledick' for several weeks thereafter. Thinking about it, that may have been one of the reasons why she left me for her physics lecturer.

. . . she lied, by the way. My penis is *magnificent*.

Anyway, it can safely be said that relations between Jessica and me have thawed *wonderfully* in the past twenty-four hours.

We are well and truly out of the woods now, and in the clear.

What a lovely thought to have as I lie dozing in the massive bed in Jessica's old bedroom. Everything is right with the world for once, and Adam Holborne is a man satisfied – at least temporarily – with his lot.

Nothing is wrong at this particular moment in my life.

. . . let's see how long it lasts, shall we?

Wait for it.

Wait for it . . .

'Oh my God, Adam!!'

There you go. Roughly thirty-six seconds. A new record.

'Wstfgl?' I say into the pillow.

'Adam! Wake up!'

'Why?'

'Because we're fucked, that's why!'

'That's what happened last night, baby.'

Jessica clonks me on the back of the head. 'Roll over, you idiot. You need to read this!'

I struggle to turn myself over, and am greeted by the sight of an iPad being waved dangerously close to my nose. 'What's the matter?'

'I searched for articles online about us,' Jessica begins, and sees the look on my face. 'Oh, don't pretend you haven't done it too.'

I do. I still have a Google alert set up.

'And what have you found?'

The iPad is virtually touching my nose now. 'Something really, *really* bad, Adam. Read!'

I sit up, rubbing my eyes, and take the iPad from Jessica's grasp.

Still groggy from sleep, I begin to read the web page she has open in Safari.

By the time I've finished it, I am *wide awake*, and having heart palpitations.

'We're fucked,' I say in a quiet voice.

Jessica throws her arms up. 'I know, right? What the hell are we going to do?'

'I don't know! We'll have to fly home. We've got to sort this out.' My eyes widen. 'What will Cassie be doing?'

'Murdering innocent bystanders? Taking hostages?'

'Probably both.'

'We can get flights going out this afternoon, if we start looking now,' Jessica says as she sits on the bed, chewing one fingernail nervously.

'What about your dad?'

She waves a hand at me. 'He'll be fine. He's already threatening to go out on the boat this week. Mom won't let him, but he's definitely in no danger now. We can go back to the UK.' She gives me a desperate look. 'We *need* to go back to the UK.'

'Agreed,' I say, throwing the covers off. 'I'll get dressed and have some breakfast, then we'll get cracking.'

What a horrific, but somehow entirely expected, turn of events.

Just when you thought the lives of Mr and Mrs Holborne had reached some kind of pleasant equilibrium, something like this happens – a bloody article on the web that pretty much destroys you.

This is the worst thing to be posted on the Internet since that video of a bloke French kissing his camel.

. . . or that porno movie starring Kim Kardashian, which is inexplicably *less sexy* than a man kissing a camel, for some reason.

ARTICLE IN *THE DAILY TORRENT* ONLINE NEWSPAPER

22 June

THE LIES THAT SOCIALITY TOLD: THE SHAM
MARRIAGE OF THE HOLBORNES!

By Sonny Duhal

It was meant to be the marriage of the moment. The wedding of the year. The dream couple from Sociality's burgeoning empire. Instead, the whole thing has been a lie – a bogus marriage designed to fool subscribers, the public and the media alike.

When Sociality founder Cassie McFlasterton announced the competition to find two of her subscribers to marry off into the perfect relationship, many were sceptical it would work –

this reporter included. The business entrepreneur was hanging her entire reputation on her patented 'love algorithms' to prove that two complete strangers could be put together and have a successful partnership over the long term. In my considered opinion, those algorithms have *failed*, and McFlasterton's reputation is in *tatters*.

At first, the relationship between Adam Holborne and Jessica Madison appeared to set off on the right foot. The wedding day went off without a hitch – other than a rather exuberant priest – and the honeymoon only suffered from a mechanical problem with a speedboat. But then I, and many others, started to notice a few cracks appearing in the facade.

There were reports of parties ending in acrimony, disastrous trips to California, even more disastrous events involving baked goods, and a tennis match that resulted in physical injury to both members of the fractured couple.

I myself attended a Q&A session that felt contrived and designed to put a sticking plaster over what was quite obviously a campaign not running on schedule. Even that event seemed to go awry, with Adam Holborne speaking out of turn about a ridiculous stunt involving public nudity, a one-man band and a tune made famous in the 1980s. Then there was the backstage discussion heard accidentally by us all, revealing how strained relations were between not just the couple, but their benefactor McFlasterton.

All of these rumours, reports and curious events forced me to do more digging, and from the evidence I've gathered, it's clear that Sociality has been comprehensively and blatantly *lying* to everyone about the success of their marriage project.

I have spoken to neighbours of the couple in their exclusive Kensington apartments, who have opened my eyes to the truth of what's been going on. 'We hear them arguing all of the time,' says Hugo Wentworth, 32. 'Shame. They seemed like the kind of young, thrusting couple I could really get behind.'

And Mr Wentworth is by no means alone in this opinion. Another neighbour, Lachlan Munroe, 27, agrees. 'Christ, they never stop. I don't even live on the floor below, and I know they're at each other's throats 24-7.'

'My art is being ruined,' complains Beedle, 45, an artist who lives below them, but is still affected by the Holbornes' constant rowing. 'They've ruined the vibe of our lovely building.

My work has become very dark and disturbing since they moved in.'

It's not just the people who live with the Holbornes who have seen the marriage degenerate over the past few months. I caught up with Sally Bleasdale, a long-time Sociality subscriber, who has been witness to more than one occasion when the Holbornes have shown their true colours. 'The cookery programme was awful,' says Bleasdale, adjusting her spectacles and twiddling a lock of her mousey brown hair.

She's obviously nervous about saying these things, but feels the truth must come out. 'He insulted her, then she *assaulted* him. There was sugar and cream everywhere. They certainly didn't act like a happy couple. More like two mortal enemies.' And the tennis match? How did that go, in Bleasdale's opinion? 'That was even worse. They *hated* each other. I came to see a lovely, friendly match between two people in love, and I got a war zone. She punched him in the face!'

And what does Sally think of Sociality now? 'I've cancelled my subscription,' she tells me angrily. 'I followed everything that happened with the Holbornes, from the lovely wedding onwards, and finding out how much I've been lied to has been very distressing.'

I did further digging into the Sociality campaign, and have discovered that over *a million pounds* has been pumped into it by McFlasterton, much of it raised through funding from business partners in the city. Quite what their reaction will be when the truth is exposed, I do not know, but it clearly won't be good for Sociality's long-term prospects.

This con job could spell the end of the online dating business – and for some, like Sally Bleasdale, that might be no bad thing. 'How can they possibly continue?' she says to me, shaking her head. 'It's been proved that those silly algorithms are a load of rubbish. I'm going back to Match.com. At least they're straightforward about the whole business.'

This whole travesty highlights the dangers of hanging your business around such a risky venture. Cassie McFlasterton has gambled everything on Adam and Jessica Holborne, and they've failed her on a spectacular level. Is there anything they can do to salvage the situation?

I have reached out to Sociality and Cassie McFlasterton for a comment, but have so far heard nothing from them.

JESS

Q. If it was your last day on earth, what would you do?
A. Spend it with the people I love.

25 June

'Exactly how drunk is she?' I ask Cassie's terrified personal assistant Jenny, who looks like she's already started to clear out her desk.

'I know she had a small bottle of vodka in her filing cabinet, but she could have more stashed in there somewhere,' Jenny tells us, wincing as something hard and heavy crashes into the wall. 'She wasn't too bad when the story was just on that funny little website, but then the *Daily Mail* picked it up . . .' Jenny's face goes ashen.

Adam gulps. 'Do you think we should leave her to it? Maybe come back later?'

I give him a look. 'Are you *kidding*? If we don't do something about this mess *right now*, we're never going to be able to turn it around. We need Cassie's help, and we're not going to get it by leaving her to smash her office to pieces.'

Adam goes as white as Jenny. 'I had a horrible feeling you were going to say that.'

I turn towards the office door, putting one hand on the handle. I pause there for a second, mentally preparing myself. What exactly do you say to someone whose livelihood you've played a large part in destroying?

Apologies. Calm, heartfelt apologies. That should do it.

I cautiously open the door and peek inside.

'Get out! Get the fuck out!' Cassie McFlasterton screams at me. Or rather her backside does, as that's all I can see of her, given that the owner of what was the country's fastest-growing dating site is currently ass-up, searching through the lowest drawer of a sleek black filing cabinet.

'Er, Cassie?' I venture, walking into the office.

'I said get the fuck out! I don't want to be disburbed!' I have a feeling she means 'disturbed', but I can see the empty vodka bottle on the desk, so assume that has something to do with her pronunciation.

'It's us, Cassie! Jessica and Adam. We thought we'd better come and see you.'

Cassie freezes. As does the air in the room.

Slowly she backs away from the filing cabinet, gets awkwardly to her feet and turns to face us.

Oh my, what a picture.

I know I don't look my best thanks to some heavy transatlantic jet lag, but by comparison with Cassie McFlasterton I look like I'm about to come third in the Miss Universe competition. Cassie's grey Chanel suit is a crumpled mess. Her usually coiffed blonde hair is wild and tangled. Her make-up, which must take hours to apply every morning, has been comprehensively ruined by a combination of cheap vodka and tears of rage. All in all, we're definitely not seeing the entrepreneur at her best this afternoon.

She points an accusatory finger at Adam and me.

'You!' she screeches. 'You!'

'Hello, Cassie,' I reply in a calm, level voice. 'We just thought we'd come round to say we're sorry, and see if there's anything we can do to help?'

'Help?! *Help?!*' she hollers, kicking the filing cabinet door shut with the kind of ferocity that I sincerely hope is not going to be aimed at me any time soon. 'You two have ruined my bloody life! You've fucked me beyond compreheesion!'

'Compreheesion?' Adam asks, confused. 'Do you mean "comprehension"?'

If there's one habit I'm going to have to break my husband of if this relationship is going to work out, it's his uncanny ability to say the wrong thing at precisely the wrong time.

'Oh, *fuck you*, Adam!' Cassie snarls at him – justifiably, in the circumstances. When you're faced with the two people who have put your life's work at the brink of collapse, having one of them correct your use of the English language isn't going to make things better.

'Hey! That's not very nice!' he protests.

'Not very nice?! *Not very nice?!*' Cassie storms towards Adam, who has the good sense to back away quickly. 'You know what's *not very nice*, Adam? When the people you've entrusted to keep your business afloat can't even be civil with each other for *two fucking minutes*! All you both had to do was *pretend*. Pretending's not hard, is it? Actors do it every day!' A look of sick realisation dawns on her face. '*Actors*. Why didn't I just hire *actors*?'

'That's exactly what I said,' Adam remarks with a sniff, folding his arms.

'Be quiet, Adam!' I snap at him. This is not the time for an *I told you so*.

'Look, we're so sorry this happened, Cassie,' I say to the distressed woman. 'We came here to see if there's anything we can do.'

Cassie looks like she's about to start raging at me, but then all of the anger seems to drain out of her in an instant and she deflates in front of me. 'Oh, what the hell do you think you can do, Jessica?' she asks, swaying slightly. 'It's quite clear you two can't stand each other, so this whole marriage is over and done with – along with my company.

You've both conclusively proved that Sociality doesn't work, and I'm haemorrhaging subscribers as we speak because of it.'

Okay. So this is difficult.

I give Adam a guilty look, which he returns with interest. He comes over and stands next to me, taking my hand in his.

'That's the thing, though, Cassie,' I say to her . . . very carefully. 'We couldn't stand each other, you're right. But some things have happened in the past couple of weeks that have shown us that we do have feelings for one another. *Strong* feelings.'

'Yeah,' Adam continues. 'So much so that we're not going to split up. We're going to see if we can make this marriage work.' Adam then squeezes my hand, and to prove that we're not telling Cassie lies, he kisses me. It's quite breathtaking.

As we look away from each other and back at Cassie McFlasterton, the dumb smiles are instantly wiped off our faces.

Oh God. She's going to attack.

'Jessica, I'm scared,' Adam whispers and squeezes my hand even harder.

'You . . .' Cassie gasps. 'You . . .' She seems unable to find more words. 'You . . .' The finger points at us again, this time shaking with unholy rage. 'You . . .'

'. . . two are my favourite couple?' Adam guesses.

'. . . look like you've both come a long way?' I hazard.

'. . . fucking pricks!' Cassie finishes.

'But we thought you'd be pleased!' Adam objects.

Cassie actually, properly claws at her own face. That one's right up there in the crime-thriller book of big clichés, right next to your blood running cold.

'*Pleased?* Why would I be *pleased?*' she moans. 'You spend months proving that you're completely unsuited for one another, arguing over every little bloody thing, and now you're telling me – when it's too late to be of any bloody use – that you actually have *feelings* for one another?

That you actually want to be together, when all you do is *argue*? What the hell do you call that?'

'A marriage?' Adam ventures.

I hold my hands out. 'Look, we're not saying everything is perfect. We know there are still issues to work on, but at least we've discovered that there really is something between us. Something *real*.' I gently walk towards Cassie, as a lion tamer might move towards one of his grumpier cats. I place one tentative hand on her shoulder. 'What we're saying, is that your algorithms *do* work. That Sociality *does* put the right people together . . . in a roundabout kind of way.'

Cassie points at Adam. 'But he filled his profile in while he was having a shit,' she reminds us. 'And you were drunk on prosecco, you told me.'

Both of which are very good points.

Adam steps forward. 'Ah . . . but there you go, you see. That shows you just how *good* the algorithms really are!'

It sounds pretty thin, but we'll go with it, as Cassie has stopped screaming, which can only be a good sign.

'Yes, that's right!' I agree. 'They really do work, Cassie. We're living proof!'

For the briefest of moments, a small, hopeful smile appears on Cassie's lips, but then it's gone again. 'It doesn't matter!' she spits. 'It's too late! That bloody online news rag put the story out, and now the nationals have picked up on it. I've had to turn my phone and laptop off because the email and text notifications were driving me mad!'

'There must be something we can do to turn this around,' Adam says, a thoughtful look crossing his face.

'Maybe we could go on TV or something?' I suggest. 'Tell everyone the truth?'

'Hah!' Cassie exclaims. 'Who's going to believe you? Everyone thinks the marriage is bullshit – mainly because up until five minutes ago, it bloody well *was*. That little shit Duhal has ruined any chance we have of recovering the situation. He's been on my back since this whole thing started.'

'Then we should go and talk to him,' I say, eyes narrowing.

'What?' Cassie looks dismayed. 'Why would I want to go anywhere near him? He's the cause of all our problems!'

'Then he's the perfect person to speak to,' I point out. 'If we can convince him that things have changed between me and Adam, then he might help us prove it to everyone else.'

Cassie groans. 'It'll never work.'

I look her square in the face. 'What other choice do we have?'

Cassie returns my gaze and nods disconsolately.

Adam blows his cheeks out. 'Fuck it, it's worth a shot. Where is his office?'

'Are you sure this is the right address?' I ask Cassie, looking at the building across the street from us with a very unsure look on my face.

'This is the contact address I have in my Rolodex,' she replies.

'He didn't pick his phone up,' Adam remarks. 'Maybe his address is wrong as well.'

'But the website is registered to here,' Cassie insists. 'I make a habit of finding out as much as I can about the press when they come calling.'

'So, what we're saying here,' Adam says, regarding the building with scepticism, 'is that *The Daily Torrent* newspaper – one of the most popular independent news sites on the Internet, by all accounts – is run out of a curry house in Clapham.'

'Yeah. It looks like it,' I agree.

The restaurant is tucked between a betting shop and a Polish green-grocer. It looks like any one of a thousand other Indian restaurants you can find on most British high streets, but has a rather unforgettable name to make it stand out.

'The Spicy Wind,' Adam observes. 'I'm not sure I like the sound of that.'

'Well, we're here now,' Cassie says. 'Let's just go and see if we can find Duhal.'

'Between the poppadoms and the mango chutney, you mean?'

'Come on,' I urge them both. 'We won't get to the bottom of this standing on the sidewalk.'

'Pavement, love,' Adam corrects. He's doing it again.

I give him a dark look, but say nothing more. We have a job to do.

The restaurant is empty, as you might expect for two fifteen on a weekday afternoon. The décor of the place is definitely what you'd call old school. You wouldn't think it would be possible to squeeze this many golden statues of Vishnu into such a small space, but the owners have achieved it magnificently.

The pleasant aroma of Indian cooking floats into my nostrils, reminding me of how bland the chicken-salad sandwich I ate an hour ago was. I hear Adam's stomach rumbling loudly, so he must feel the same way.

From the back of the restaurant, a small, smiling Indian gentleman appears, dressed in a smart suit. 'Good afternoon!' he says cheerily. 'Table for three, is it?'

'Um, we're not here for food actually,' I counter.

'Do you know Sonny Duhal?' Cassie interrupts in a cold tone. 'I want to see him.'

The cheery expression is replaced by one of mild terror. 'Oh no. What has he done now? We told him not to annoy the men at the council again! Is that what this is about? We are sorry! We do not think they are all racist! Sonash gets these funny ideas that we do not agree with. He can be such a—'

'We're not from the council!' I jump in, before the poor man gets any more worked up.

'No! We're from the company that Sonny Duhal has *ruined!*' Cassie cries. This makes the little Indian man even more scared. Diplomatic skills are not Cassie's strong suit, especially when there's still half a bottle of vodka sloshing around in her veins.

'So, this is where *The Daily Torrent* is run from then?' Adam says, giving one of the large golden Vishnu statues a curious look.

'We told him!' the little man cries. 'We told him he could not do it any more! But does he listen? Does he listen to his own father?'

'I don't know,' I reply, 'does he?'

'No! No he does not!'

A lady in a sari appears from the back of the room. 'What is going on, Anish? We can hear you from the kitchen!' She spots us and instantly drops into customer-service mode. 'Good afternoon. Was it a table for three you were wanting?'

'Ah, don't bother, Deepa,' Anish tells her in an exasperated voice. 'These people are here to see Sonny about something else he has done wrong.'

Deepa's face freezes into stone. 'What has he done this time?' she asks us.

'Ruined me!' Cassie wails melodramatically.

'Are you Sonny Duhal's parents?' I venture.

'To our eternal shame!' Anish exclaims.

'Oh, don't be so stupid, Anish,' Deepa chides. 'The boy is good at what he does, he's just overenthusiastic and gets himself into trouble.'

'And us! Gets us into trouble too!' Anish complains, shaking his head vigorously. 'Why could he just not work here, like I wanted him to? Who am I supposed to leave this business to when I am gone, eh?'

'Can we speak to him?' I say, trying to move things on a bit. There's still the little matter of saving everyone's reputation to think about, and we're not going to do that discussing the finer points of Sonny Duhal's career choice.

'I will go get him for you,' Deepa replies, and hurries off back towards the rear of the small restaurant.

'Are you sure I cannot tempt you with some food?' Anish says. 'A little something on the house?' He's obviously trying to butter us up so we don't try to sue his son for defamation. It's a tactic that shouldn't work, but then Adam is with me, and thinks largely with his stomach at the best of times.

'A few poppadoms wouldn't go amiss,' he says.

'Excellent!' Anish replies. 'I will also bring out a selection of bhajis and samosas for you to try.'

'And a chicken bhuna with pilau rice?' Adam ventures, pushing his luck.

'Absolutely!' Anish tells him.

My stomach rumbles, and I once again remember the limp chicken sandwich. 'Do you do lamb tikka?' I ask.

In the end, Anish has a full order of free food to go and cook. Cassie asks for a vindaloo. I don't know whether that's her rock-solid constitution talking, or the vodka.

I think half the reason Sonny's father is happy to ply us with free food is that it gives him an excuse to bugger off back into the kitchen and not talk to us any more.

'It's very nice in here,' Adam remarks, as we sit down at the round table Anish pointed us towards. 'Lovely and clean.'

'I don't care about how nice the restaurant is,' Cassie says, throwing cold water on Adam's enthusiasm. 'We're here to bury that little shit into the ground, not stuff our faces.'

'You ordered a curry as well,' Adam protests.

'We can do both,' I remark. 'And we're not here to bury anyone, Cassie. Just talk.'

Cassie picks up her fork. 'Says you. If he doesn't do what I want him to, I'll stab him in the thigh with this.'

It may have been a tactical error bringing her along.

The object of her anger appears with his mother from the rear of the restaurant a few minutes later. He looks decidedly unhappy. I can see Deepa leading him by one elbow, hurrying him along.

'Here is Sonny,' she announces, pushing him forward. 'He will be happy to help with whatever you need, *won't you*, Sonny?'

Sonny mumbles.

Deepa then launches into a short but effective tirade in Hindi, giving her son an evident tongue-lashing.

'Yes!' he says to us, much louder. 'I'll help you with whatever you need.'

Deepa smiles. 'Good. I will go to see how your food is coming along.'

Sonny's mother leaves us again, and he nervously sits himself down at our table – thankfully with Cassie and her fork the furthest away from his unprotected legs. 'I guess you've read the article then?' he asks in a wavering voice.

Luckily, my reflexes haven't been too badly affected by the jet lag, and I'm able to wrestle the cutlery from Cassie's hand before she gets the chance to do any serious damage with it.

By the time Anish has brought out what amounts to a small banquet, Cassie has calmed down, Sonny has stopped using his place mat as a protective shield, and Adam has happily munched his way through three whole poppadoms.

'So, you run an entire newspaper, on your own, from this restaurant?' I ask Sonny, still not quite believing it.

'Yes,' he says proudly. 'My cousin Bhupinder helps me from time to time, but other than that, it's mainly just me.'

'But you get hundreds of thousands of hits every day,' Adam says.

'I know,' Sonny beams. 'It's because I write good stories.'

'Ones full of lies,' Cassie remarks darkly.

'I didn't tell any lies, though, did I?' Sonny says defensively. 'Everyone I spoke to about you all said the same thing! *You* were the ones lying about the marriage. I had every right to publish that story!'

'Yes . . . yes you did,' I reply, trying to calm things down again. 'But it's done us all a lot of damage, Sonny. Especially when the nationals picked the story up. Our reputations are in the gutter. You've made us look really bad to a lot of important people.'

'That isn't my problem!' he objects. 'I did what any good journalist would do – I followed a good story where it led. Perhaps you should have all been more honest from the start, then none of this would have happened!'

'Yeah, okay, but you got your facts wrong,' Adam argues, before taking a mouthful of chicken bhuna. 'Blimey, this is fabulous, Mr Duhal,' he says to Anish, as the restaurant owner plonks down the last of our dishes.

'Thank you, Mr Holborne. It is a recipe we guard closely here at the Spicy Wind.'

Cassie clears her throat meaningfully and glares at my husband. 'What Adam is trying to say, is that you've told the world that they hate each other and don't want to be married any more, when the truth is the exact opposite.'

'What do you mean?' Sonny asks. 'Everyone I spoke to said you couldn't stand each other.'

'We couldn't,' I admit. 'But we've worked our differences out, and discovered that we do want to be together. The marriage is *not* a failure.'

'And neither is my million-pound campaign!' Cassie exclaims triumphantly, her face sweating a little thanks to the large mouthful of curry she's just consumed.

Sonny looks dubious. 'Well, you say that. But you've all lied about it before. Why should I believe that now is any different?'

I reach across the table and take Adam's hand in mine. 'You'll just have to trust us, Sonny,' I tell him. 'We're not saying we've suddenly developed the perfect relationship, but we do want to stay together and see how things go. That should be enough, shouldn't it?'

Sonny still looks dubious.

'Come on, mate,' Adam continues, 'haven't you ever been in a relationship that had loads of ups and downs? Arguments? Stuff like that? They're all part and parcel of being with someone, aren't they?'

Sonny looks astounded. 'Yes, they are. But I've never been punched in the face on a tennis court before! Or wrecked a sports car! Or smothered anyone in butter!'

Adam cocks his head to one side. 'Fair point,' he says, and sticks a forkful of rice into his mouth.

'Look, will you help us salvage this situation or not?' Cassie snaps, cutting through all the niceties and getting to the crux of the matter.

Sonny makes a face. He's not convinced. I'll have to come up with something more persuasive.

'Think of the *coverage*,' I point out. 'Think of how great the *story* will be. Two star-crossed lovers, who everyone thought hated each other . . . solving their differences and discovering that love really does conquer all.'

I see Adam's eyes go wide.

I've just said the 'L' word.

Should I have said the 'L' word?

Did I *mean* the 'L' word? Or was I just waxing lyrical to convince Sonny to help us?

Is that how I feel about my husband now? And if it is, does he feel the same way?

Even if we do get this immediate problem sorted out, there's still a lot of confusing emotions flying around that we have to resolve before this marriage is in any way stable.

Sonny doesn't need to know all of that, though. He just needs to believe that there's more to this story than two people being at each other's throats, and lying to the general public about it.

He looks out of the window behind my head, deep in thought. 'It would make a good twist,' he agrees.

'Yes it would!'

'And it would build on the exposure I've already had in the mainstream media. Get me noticed even more.'

'Exactly!'

Sonny appears to make his mind up. 'Okay. I'll help you.' He raises a finger. 'But if you're still lying, I will make sure you live to regret it.'

Anish, who has been hovering quietly a few feet away during all of this, steps forward and cuffs his son around the back of the head. 'Be polite, Sonash!'

'Ow! Dad!' Sonny complains, his superiority punctured somewhat.

It's a little difficult to play hardball when your father is within smacking distance.

'Well, it's great that you want to help us, Sonny,' Adam says. 'But what exactly are we going to do?'

This is a very good, if also very annoying, point. It's one thing getting the architect of our downfall onside; it's another getting him to come up with a plan to save our skins.

'You could do an interview online,' Cassie suggests. 'Lay the truth bare for everyone to hear.'

Sonny waves his hand. 'Wouldn't work. People wouldn't be convinced. It's just more words.'

We all lapse into thoughtful silence, taking the opportunity to eat a little more of the delicious curry Sonny's father has made. I don't know about anything else, but Adam and I will be coming back here again for a proper meal one day . . . if we ever get the chance.

'I have an idea,' Sonny eventually says, slowly looking between us. 'But I'm not sure you're going to like it.'

'Go on,' I encourage. 'Anything's better than nothing.'

Instead of immediately answering, he pulls his phone out of his pocket. 'Hang on,' he tells us, starting to look for something on the screen. 'Here we go,' he says with a smile after a minute or so, and deposits the phone on the table in front of him.

From it, something awful emanates. It sounds like a fully grown man having his testicles slowly twisted in a vice. Accompanying this is a light percussive beat.

'*Eee ooo eee ooo, ooo eee ooo eee ooo, ooo wee umm bum ba-waaaay . . .*'

I see Adam's face fall. 'Oh God, no.'

Cassie's eyes widen. 'Oh bloody hell.'

Some jungle drums kick in underneath the high-pitched wailing. Sonny sits back in his chair, a smirk on his face.

'Please God, *no*,' Adam repeats, dropping his curry-laden fork.

'I don't get it,' I say. 'What song is this?'

'*In the jungle, the mighty jungle, the lion sleeps tonight . . .*' sings the man with the painful testicles.

The penny drops.

I've never heard this version of the song before, but that is surely 'The Lion Sleeps Tonight'. I know it from *The Lion King* soundtrack, but this is a strange, more high-pitched version I'm not familiar with.

What I am most assuredly familiar with is the glib comment Adam made during our disastrous Q&A session back in May.

'You've got to be *kidding* me,' I exclaim in horror.

'It would be a grand gesture,' Cassie remarks.

'Actions speak louder than words,' Sonny adds.

'It'd get *loads* of coverage,' Cassie points out.

'And it'd do a really good job of convincing people you two actually mean what you say this time,' Sonny finishes, lacing his hands behind his neck.

I look at my husband. My terror is reflected in his own.

'Adam?'

'Yes, Jessica?'

'I think I want a divorce.'

'Do you? I want a bloody shotgun.'

And so, it comes to this.

A stunt so *apocalyptically stupid* it may scar me for the rest of my days.

Adam told everyone that night in Neon Joe's that the best way we could declare our love for one another was via the medium of a public kiss in the middle of Leicester Square, both of us naked as the day we were born.

It was a *joke*! A terrible, terrible joke – that has now returned to efficiently remove whatever self-respect we may have left.

I protested. Of course I did!

What person in their right mind would even consider such an act of utter stupidity?

But then Cassie made a face. A face of such pitiable misery that she should bottle it and sell it to the local goth community.

It could save the company, she said.

It could restore all of our reputations, she said.

God damn her!

And we know how good Cassie McFlasterton is at manipulating people into her way of thinking, don't we? And we also know how good she is at arranging large-scale public events at short notice, *don't we*?

Would you believe she had the name of a one-man band on her Rolodex?

Who in the *ever-living fuck* has the name of a one-man band on their Rolodex?

Kissing Adam in the middle of Leicester Square on a busy Saturday afternoon in the middle of summer, while we're serenaded by a man covered in musical instruments is one thing, but to do it completely *naked*?

That moves us from an embarrassing public episode into the realms of an arrestable offence.

I pointed this out to Cassie and Sonny over the remnants of my half-eaten curry.

'It'd be really quick,' Cassie countered. 'And if you want, we can get you a nice merkin.'

'A *what*?'

'A merkin, Jessica. You wear it over your downstairs parts. I know a woman who makes them. I've got her name in my Rolodex somewhere.'

'I don't know what you're worried about,' Adam said to me. 'You do yoga and have a body to be proud of. I look like someone's come along and let the air out.'

Okay, I am proud of how flat my belly is these days, and how good my core strength is, but that doesn't mean I want to demonstrate either by slapping a pubic wig over my hoo-hoo and potentially getting arrested for indecent exposure!

It was a stupid, stupid plan from start to finish. A horrible idea that would backfire on us massively.

So why – for the love of God – am I sat in the back of Anish Duhal's van, on a Saturday afternoon, in a back road just behind Leicester Square, wearing just a dressing gown, and wishing it was at least five degrees warmer outside?

Because I have taken complete leave of my senses, that's why.

'What are we doing?' Adam says quietly from beside me. 'What the *hell* are we doing?'

'I don't know, Adam. One minute we're kissing with a beautiful sunset behind us, the next we're sat in a slightly rusting Ford Transit, about to flash the whole of Leicester Square.'

'In many ways, this is probably all my fault,' he concedes.

I turn slowly to look at him. 'You don't fucking say?'

'Hey! At least you've got that merkin thing down there.'

'Oh yes! This won't be embarrassing for me *at all*. After all, it's not like the merkin is bright pink and has the Sociality logo stamped on to it or anything!'

Cassie McFlasterton will do anything for a bit of free advertising.

'But my willy will be out,' Adam complains bitterly.

'Oh well. Why not jump in the nearest time machine, pop back to the day of the Q&A and tell yourself not to be such a smart-ass?'

Adam looks distraught. 'My life is over.'

'*Our lives* are over, you mean,' I say, reminding him that we're in this together.

The driver's door opens and Sonny Duhal sticks his head in. 'Okay, so everything is pretty much ready to go, guys. The one-man-band bloke is setting up just by the William Shakespeare statue.'

A small groan of fear escapes my lips.

Sonny gives me a lopsided smile. 'Don't worry too much, Jess. Leicester Square is the kind of place where this kind of thing happens *all the time*. I'm sure you won't stand out . . . too much.'

Aah. I see. Sonny Duhal obviously believes that I'm a *total idiot*, who will believe anything I hear if it's said in a calming tone of voice.

The passenger door opens. It's Cassie. 'All set then?' she asks us cheerfully. This is the first time we've seen Cassie in a good mood in the three days we've been back from the USA. I hate her for it.

'I don't think I could ever be ready for something like this,' Adam remarks, putting his head in his hands.

'Oh, it'll be fine!' Cassie replies, waving a clenched fist. 'Just think of how much this will do to set things straight!'

I stare her down. 'Oh, in that case, perhaps you'd like to join us?'

Cassie looks momentarily scared to death. 'Can't, sweetheart. We've only got one merkin. Now come on! Out you both get. The sooner it's done, the sooner we can leave . . . and the sooner Sonny here can write up a lovely story about how you two are so much in love that you're prepared to makes arses out of yourselves in front of ten thousand tourists.'

'If I die of embarrassment,' I say to her, 'I'm coming back to haunt you.'

Cassie appears to weigh this up. 'Fair enough. Now come on, let's get to it!'

Sonny slides the van's side door open and Adam reluctantly crawls out.

If I had a penny for every time I've regretted filling out that stupid dating profile in the past few months, I'd have enough money to go and buy myself some proper clothes.

I follow Adam out of the van and look around. Already people are staring at us, and we've still got dressing gowns on!

Sonny takes off at a marching pace with Cassie right behind him. Adam and I are both wearing flip-flops, so it takes us a while longer to make our hesitant way through the crowds of people, out into the main square and towards the statue of Britain's most famous writer.

Oh sweet Jesus on a big white fluffy cloud, there are *millions* of people here.

There's only enough space in Leicester Square to hold a few *thousand* people, but somehow there are still millions of them here. All of them watching *me*.

The weather is relatively fine, and the temperature is in the very low twenties, so people are out in even more force than they might otherwise be on a Saturday afternoon in June.

There's a crowd already milling around the William Shakespeare statue, all curious as to why there is a man standing beside it with an entire orchestra glued to his body.

Cassie backtracks a bit and walks between the two of us. 'Now, don't worry. We're not going to be here long. We just need enough time to get a few photos—'

'Photos?!' Adam and I both cry in unison.

'Oh, don't worry, we'll blur things out in Photoshop.' She puts her arms around us both. 'We'll need some evidence that you've actually gone through with this for the story, won't we? Alex will be as quick as he possibly can be.'

I hate my life.

'No Derek taking photos, then?' Adam says, almost with a tinge of regret. I think he's grown to like the portly photographer over the past few months. Probably not least because he threw Cassie into a lake once.

'Er, no. Derek is otherwise engaged,' Cassie responds cryptically.

We reach the statue and we hurry through the ever-growing crowd of onlookers. Perhaps if we just stand around for a while, they'll get bored and move on.

Then I remember that we have a one-man band accompanying us, and that pleasant thought goes right out of the window. Who doesn't stand around in the sun and wait when there's the prospect of some live music to brighten your day?

We get closer to the man that will serenade us as we perform an act of public indecency, and my jaw drops.

'*Derek?*' Adam says in disbelief.

'Afternoon 'Olbornes,' Derek replies.

'You're the one-man band?' I ask, incredulous.

Derek sniffs. 'Everyone's got to have a hobby.'

Cassie looks around the square once and glances at her watch. 'Alright, let's get on with it. Sonny, go stand in the crowd and see what the reaction is. Derek, get into position. Adam, Jessica . . . stand in front of him and face each other.'

Oooh.

Déjà vu.

I am suddenly and sharply reminded of my wedding day.

Replace Derek and his drums with Julian and his cocaine, and we're standing in exactly the same positions, in front of roughly the same-sized crowd. It feels like these two events have become bookends to this entire bizarre period of my life.

'Okay then,' says Derek, picking up his banjo. 'Just make sure everything's alright . . .' He smacks his knees together to test the cymbals, then thrashes one leg out to the side to make sure the big bass drum on his back is working. Then he turns a small switch on the microphone pack he's got on his belt, and a whine of feedback erupts from the small Marshall speaker beside him. 'Okay. We're good to go.'

No we're not. We're really, *really* not.

Derek clears his throat. Sonny pulls out his Dictaphone and note-pad. Cassie crosses her fingers. Adam gulps nervously. I close my eyes and take a deep breath.

Then, I feel a warm hand take mine. I open my eyes, and Adam is looking at me with a broad smile on his face.

'What?' I ask him, wondering why he suddenly looks less like someone's about to shoot him.

'I've realised something,' he says. 'Had an epiphany, if you like.'

'What?'

'This is *worth it*,' he says, meaningfully. 'This stupid stunt is *completely* worth it.'

'Is it?'

'Yeah, Jess. It is. Because I get to show everyone something very important.'

'Your penis?'

'No! I get to show them—'

'Eee eee eee ooo, ooo eee eee ooo, ooo eee bim bee waaaaaay . . .'

Oh, for God's sake.

Derek cannot sing.

Not at all. Not even close.

He can't get the lyrics right either.

Derek doesn't attempt the high-pitched tone used by the Tight Fit lead singer – he just shouts at the top of his voice like a drunk football fan.

'Eee eee eee ooo, ooo eee eee ooo, ooo eee bim bee waaaaaay . . .'

BANG, BANG, CRASH!

You know what's worse than 'The Lion Sleeps Tonight'?

'The Lion Sleeps Tonight' with badly timed accompanying cymbals and bass drum. Add a banjo into the mix and we've entered some very dark musical territory.

Derek continues to scream at the top of his voice, playing a few random chords on the banjo as he does.

This might not be such a bad thing, though. If he keeps going like this he's going to frighten everyone away.

Oh, who am I kidding? There's nothing more likely to draw even more people to a crowd than a pot-bellied man murdering a song about a lazy fucking lion.

'In a jungle! In a jungle! Lions sleep tonight!' Derek sort of sings, still getting the lyrics completely wrong. *'In a jungle. It's a jungle. Lions sleep in shite!'*

BANG, BANG, CRASH,
AAAWWWOOOOOGGGAAAAAAAHHHH!

That last sound was from a big car horn strapped to the back of Derek's leg. I don't know what the lion will actually be doing tonight, but with this God-awful noise going on, it sure as hell won't be sleeping.

'Do it!' Cassie hisses, motioning with her arms.

Oh yes. The naked kiss.

I look round to see hundreds of eyes staring at me, along with nearly as many smartphone cameras.

Nope.

I can't do it.

No, no, no.

This is ridiculous.

I look at Adam and shake my head. 'I can't.'

'What I was trying to say,' Adam continues, having to raise his voice over Derek's caterwauling, 'is that I *want to do this*, because there's something I need to show these people . . . something I need to *prove* to these people. And to everyone we've lied to, for that matter.'

'What do you mean? What have you got to prove?'

Adam shuffles forward, dropping his dressing gown off his shoulders as he does so. 'That I love you, Jessica.' Gasps from the crowd – more for the penis than the declaration of love, I'd hazard. 'That I will stand here naked in front of a thousand people, and do it willingly, because I love the woman I married four months ago – and it's about time I told her that.'

Oh well, if *that's* the reason why we're doing this . . .

I quickly shrug off my dressing gown as well. A cool breeze plays across my bottom as I wrap my arms around my husband and hug him tightly.

'I love you too, Adam,' I tell him. 'I can't *believe it*, but I love you too.'

He smiles, then grimaces. 'We make a terrible couple, don't we? A really bad match.'

I look at Derek, glance over at Cassie shaking her hands triumphantly, see Sonny energetically writing in his notepad, and turn back to my husband. 'We're both dumb enough to stand butt naked in the middle of Leicester Square in front of thousands of people, Adam. I'd say we're the *perfect* match.'

With that said, I kiss my husband, because, after all, that's what I came here to do.

. . . and then *we run the fuck away*.

With Derek still slaughtering 'The Lion Sleeps Tonight' in the background, Adam and I throw our dressing gowns back on, as Cassie tries to make a hole in the pack of onlookers for us to escape through.

We then slap away as quickly as we can in our awkward flip-flops through the amazed crowd, towards the waiting van, and away from this insane situation once and for all.

And because we're married – and also, quite unbelievably, *in love* – we do it holding hands the entire time.

The End

NEWS HEADLINES

26 June

The Daily Mail

LEICESTER SQUARE LOVEBIRDS LET IT ALL HANG OUT

The Sun

WAR TURNS TO *PHWOAR* FOR SOCIALITY COUPLE!

The Guardian

PUBLIC NUDITY – A BEAUTIFUL OR DANGEROUS THING?

The Financial Times

DATING SITE SOCIALITY COULD BE SAVED BY LAST-MINUTE STUNT

The Daily Torrent

HOLBORNES PROVE THEIR LOVE BY LAYING THEMSELVES BARE

GamesReport.com

WHY NONE OF US NEEDED TO SEE ADAM HOLBORNE'S JOYSTICK

The Daily Star

I BLEW HIS TROMBONE! REALITY STAR CONFESSES TO NIGHT OF LOVE WITH LEICESTER SQUARE ONE-MAN-BAND MARVEL!

The Carmel-by-the-Sea Herald

LOCAL GIRL DRIVEN MAD IN LONDON – THE PERILS OF LIVING ABROAD

ACKNOWLEDGEMENTS

It's that time again to thank those who help me with this rather silly job of mine. Each and every one of these people can be proud that they have enabled a complete idiot like me to earn a living writing books full of bad language and bodily functions:

My wife, Gemma; my mother, Judy; my sister, Sharon; my agent, Jon; my editors, Emilie and Sophie; my friends (too many to name here, damn them) and last – but most certainly not least – my readers. All of this, when you get right down to it, is entirely your fault. I love you lots.

ABOUT THE AUTHOR

Photo © Gemma Waters

Nick Spalding is the bestselling author of nine novels, two novellas and two memoirs. Nick worked in media and marketing for most of his life before turning his energy to his genre-spanning humorous writing. He lives in the south of England with his wife.

Printed in Great Britain
by Amazon